GUARDIAN ASSASSINS

GUARDIAN ASSASSINS

THE COLLINS TWINS SERIES
BOOK 2

MICKEY HULL

Guardian Assassins

Published by BooxAI
ISBN: 978-965-578-593-7

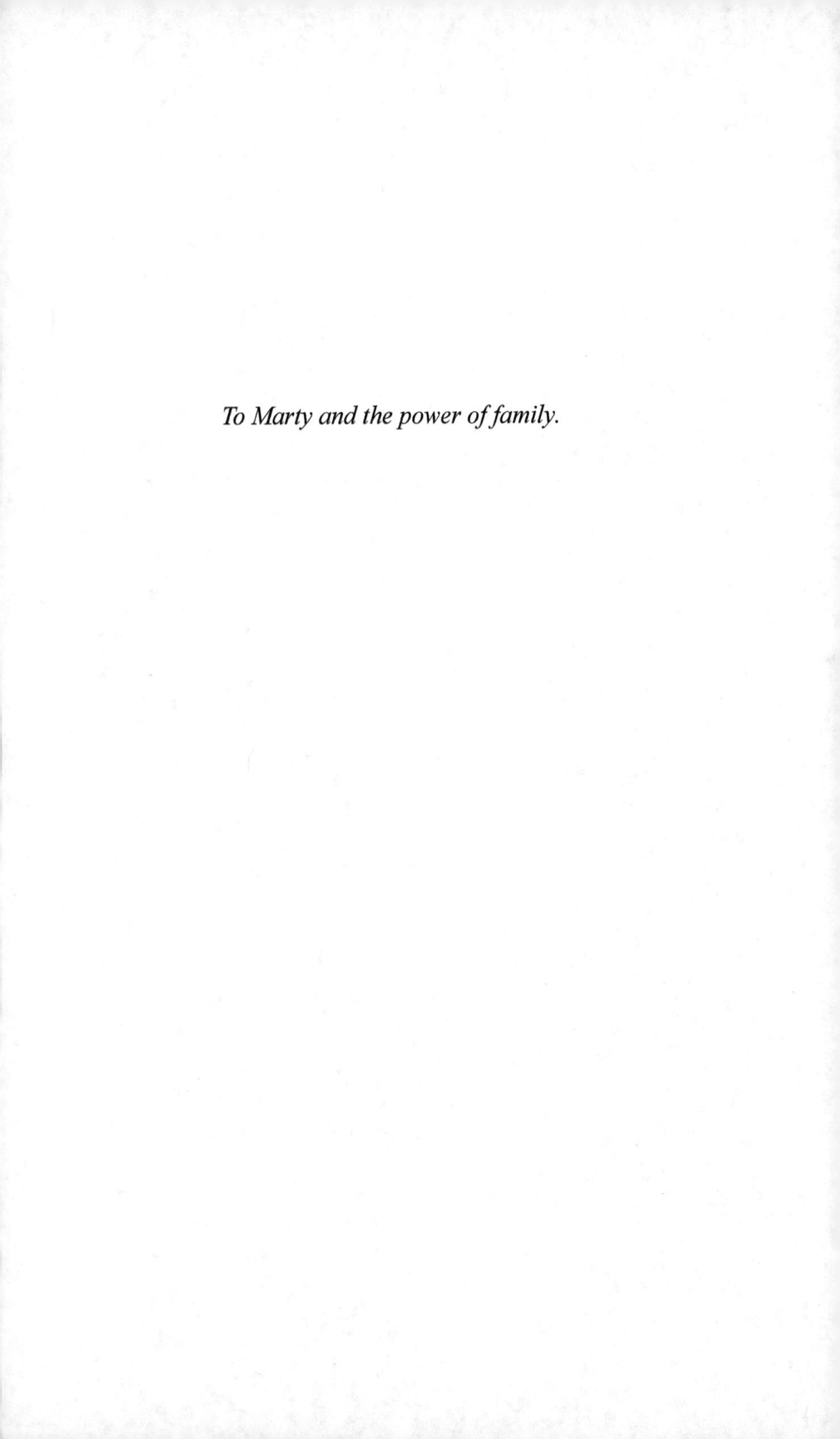

To Marty and the power of family.

CHAPTER ONE

Once the helicopter lifted off, Conjar immediately called Colonel Sullivan. 'Mission accomplished. The twins are on their way to Austin via Boston.'

The Colonel responded. 'How did they do on their first mission?'

Conjar simply responded. 'Impressive.'

The Colonel asked. 'Please elaborate and be specific. Why did you change the mission plan?'

Conjar paused. 'Iceman has an uncanny ability to read into a mission, develop a plan and execute his plan. Zeus has a calming impact on Iceman and facilitates communication within our team.'

'Continue and to reiterate, I want specifics.'

'All right, but I will go into more detail in my report and during my debriefing. Iceman gathered a tremendous amount of intel to build the mission plan in a most unorthodox fashion. As I said, he blew through all the analytical data and quickly zeroed in on the essence of the target. He mentally stowed the files I gave him and just got up, leaving in the morning two days before the mission. I asked Zeus, *what the hell is he doing?* Zeus just shrugged and told me to *let him be*. Iceman returned eight hours later. He clearly had been drinking and returned with a case of beer and two bags of tacos.'

The Colonel interrupted. 'He did what?'

'I know, but let me finish. I went to question him about his antics, but Zeus just shook his head at me. I gave Zeus the benefit of the doubt and waited. After Iceman cracked a beer and began to dig into a taco, he started by asking if either of us wanted a beer or taco. Zeus took both. I was confused about their behavior, so of course, I declined at first. After Iceman made quick work of his first taco and started on his second, he relayed his report. As it turns out, he went to some dive bar at 1000 hours, outside the Long Island Gold Coast, to be in the environment of workers who provided service to the super-wealthy, like the target. After a couple of rounds, he identified the workers that were the crew for the target's yacht. The workers had a couple of days off for the Fourth of July holiday and were to report on the fifth to ready the ship for departure. He got all the intel we needed by befriending these workers. I mean everything. He got these workers to take him to the Mexican restaurant where the landscapers frequented. They, too, had the day off for the Gatsby-like holiday party hosted by the target. The landscapers were set to return to work on the fifth of July to clean the grounds after the party. Together, the two sets of workers gave complete details about target's itinerary and security. The workers gave Iceman all this intel without realizing it. They were just drunk on their day off, telling stories about their daily lives. Iceman steered the conversation and the flow of drinks, but remembered the entire day with perfect recall. His method was unorthodox but utterly amazing.'

'I see. How did Iceman handle the computer extraction?'

Conjar took a cleansing breath and replied. 'Very efficiently and with a powerful dark force. I was amazed by his poise while he tormented the target. He acted with extreme prejudice. I watched him through the drone, sniper scope and listened with my earpiece. He was just so calm while being relentlessly brutal. In my report, I will detail the utterly amazing.'

'Which was?'

'There were two secret computers, not one as the mission had targeted. The true targeted computer was in a safe room not identified in our intel. The computer we identified was a fake, a ruse. Iceman figured out the scheme on the fly, in the moment. He had studied the blueprints of the target's yacht and discovered the room sizes did not match. A safe room was hidden, but incredibly, Iceman was able to destroy the target and unveil his secrets.'

'Remarkable.'

'Yes, wait until you read my report.'

'And how was Zeus?'

Conjar responded. 'Very professional. He has an amazing ability to manage the project. Very cerebral and calm. He did not hesitate to execute the termination aspect of his assignment, but he was a little disturbed by Iceman's inner demon. He was glad Iceman made him stay away from the interrogation. Iceman tortured the target prior to termination to retrieve the necessary intel and package.'

The Colonel and Conjar spoke a little more about the mission's details. The Colonel concluded the conversation. 'I look forward to your full report and reading your debrief. When are you set to arrive in Austin?'

'Jumping on our G450 now, call it three hours.'

'Have a safe trip, well done.'

CHAPTER TWO

At the end of the Napoleonic Wars and the War of 1812, a group of nine men formed the Elders. The Treaty of Ghent that ended the War of 1812 built the foundation for Great Britain and America to be powerful allies. The relationship has endured well-documented challenges. Nine of the greatest minds in business and academia from the United States and Great Britain came together at the end of Jefferson's presidency in 1809 and the peaceful resolution of the War of 1812 to form the Elders. The Elders believed the future of the two countries was forged in the past. America was built on a British foundation, and while independent, the two countries needed to be aligned to support each other to prosper in the coming century. The nine elders were comprised of four great minds from America and four great minds from Great Britain. The ninth member was Chief Elder, a position that was elected every ten years and alternated between countries. The founding Elders established the simple mission statement: *promote and protect British and American interests in the global theatre.*

The Elders are above all radar and government agencies. Conspiracy theories persist as to a secret organization within the global power structure working behind the scenes, but the reality is the Elders are simply just a rumor and a whisper as far as the world is concerned. The total assets of the Elders' Fund were $900 billion. The contributions of new members over two centuries, coupled with enormous investment returns, fuel an operation without a budget. The Elders' largest expense is research and development. Apple spends $16 billion on research and development annually; the Elders invest $90 billion.

The Elders utilize four divisions led by four group leaders to achieve their mission statement. Research and development (R&D), the first group: the primary function is the development of algorithms and codes to stay ahead of all government and clandestine intelligence agencies. The hacking and interpreting information through their software is paramount to the Elders' success. The Elders unite data through hacking. The NSA, Google, CIA and other international governments and private companies protect their information and rarely share the information. The Elders hack into their systems to create a complete global picture. Their software systems afford the Elders the ability to not only gather information deemed not accessible, but filter and interpret the overwhelming volume of data. America has agreed not to spy on their allies. The Elders have made no such promise. The relentless pursuit of information and the ability to interpret and respond to information is the driver for the Elders program. The second group, analytics and investments, interprets and acts on the information generated by R&D. Superior data access provides valuable insight for the investment team. Companies, institutions, technologies and commodities that clear the analytics department offer sound financial investments in the short and long term. The analytics team also gathers and interprets data for potential targets for the Black Ops team. The third team, Black Ops, operates in the field and is utilized when a threat is deemed too large, too sensitive, or too politically connected for national governments to address properly. The threat, after intense and exhaustive investigation, is voted on by the Elders to become a target. Once classified as a target, Black

Ops is tasked with elimination. The fourth team, recruitment and training, is considered the most valuable department to the Elders. The ability to find the greatest minds of each generation is a challenge. Recruiting the identified candidates is a very delicate process. How does one lure a teenager or sell a young adult to join an organization that does not exist and ensures the Elders remain ghosts?

The four group leaders report to Bill Zera, the director of the Elders program. Prior to being named director, Zera was a successful Black Ops agent. After Black Ops, he was sent to Princeton, where he received his master's in finance. He returned as a senior agent in analytics and investments. He was then promoted to group leader of R&D. He served three years of his ten-year term as director. Seated in his conference room, he had called Dr. Grace Monroe, Senior Agent Conjar and Jasper Cooper. He called the meeting to discuss the Collins twins and their first mission.

Zera welcomed the group and asked Dr. Monroe to begin. 'Grace, you know the history of the twins better than anyone in the room. Can you begin with a little background and your assessment?'

Dr. Grace Monroe was a Black Ops agent for ten years, and upon completion of her time as an agent, she was chosen to pursue academia. Prior to Black Ops, she graduated from Oxford, where she earned a master's in experimental psychology and took third in her class. After her tour as an agent, she attended Harvard University's Chan Department of Social and Behavior Sciences for her doctorate. She is charged with the fourth group, recruitment and training. She also monitors the Black Ops agents' mental health.

'Thanks, Bill. I identified the twins at 15 years of age. Seamus Collins, Zeus, was a brilliant student and physical specimen who dominated his peers in Ennis, Ireland. The decision to bring him to West Point was triggered by the death of his father when

Seamus was nine. I believed at that time, and continue to believe, that Colonel Thomas Sullivan was the perfect choice to be his recruiter and trainer. Seamus was desperate for a father figure and in need of being a part of something special. He graduated from West Point, having accomplished both.

'From the moment I read Jack Collins' initial reports, I was extremely committed and invested in his recruitment and training. In all areas of testing, he scored off the charts. Iceman is gifted athletically, mentally and has a fierce moral compass that matches our own. What has always separated Jack, Iceman, from other recruits is his extraordinary gift of perception. In several reports from his three years in Black Ops training and his time at West Point, he has been referred to as Sherlock or, in some cases, Hannibal. He is comfortable with violence when appropriate. As valuable as Sullivan was to Zeus, his role in Iceman's development was more important and impactful. Iceman can be a handful, a talented Mustang that Sullivan, with much assistance from Conjar, cultivated into an exceptional Black Ops agent.

'Both excelled at the highest level individually during their time with Sullivan at West Point. They continued to set new standards of excellence in their three years of Black Ops training with Senior Agent Conjar and Colonel Sullivan. What makes the twins so unique is the chemistry they share. They got the nickname twins on their first day at West Point as a joke. Roommates, both named Collins, one white, one black, but even early in their relationship, they acted like twins. They have complete trust in each other. Both are fiercely loyal to and protective of each other. As you know, the twins, like other Black Ops agents, were expected to train for four years at university before we read them in on the true purpose of their training. Iceman was too perceptive and began to question the true intent of the twins' training at West Point. We were forced to accelerate their timetable, have the twins graduate, and be briefed in three years. The success of the first mission, while extraordinary, did not surprise me.'

Zera nodded his understanding and moved the meeting forward. 'Conjar, I believe Grace has offered you a nice transition. Why don't you pick it up?'

Conjar was the twins' senior agent. The Black Ops teams operated with two agents and a senior agent to execute their missions. The agents trained with their senior agent for three years, then stayed with their senior agent for ten years to conduct assassinations. After ten years, if they survive, the agent is promoted to senior agent and assigned to a team. The senior agents graduate to statesmen after their tour with the team. Statesmen is a minimal-impact position that involves teaching, training and support to new and senior agents.

After clearing his throat, Conjar began. 'At first, I was skeptical of the twins. I had read all their reports from West Point and their summer military training; I was certain they were not as advertised. They beat up other cadets in Airborne School, boxing, or what have you. Great. Iceman was some genius basketball star and Zeus was a computer wizard and rugby monster. Lovely. To me, they were just a couple of overhyped, cocky kids that would get their asses kicked just like every other recruit in Black Ops training. They changed my mind in the first 48 hours. I knew they were different. They are big, fast, and smart, I mean crazy smart. They pick up everything so quickly it's alarming. The thing is, they are tough, and I don't just mean physically, which they are extremely, but also mentally tough. That's what surprised me, their toughness. I thought the superstars would be soft, but I was wrong. Grace touched on it. Individually they are exceptional, but together, holy shit is all I can say.'

Zera took in the reports and scanned the room. 'Duke, you do not seem to be in sync with Grace and Conjar. Do you have any concerns about their reports?'

All Black Ops senior agents are responsible for executing the mission plan provided by the architect. The architect, Jasper Cooper, a statesman, worked with the Black Ops' senior agents,

Conjar in this case, to design the assassination plan. Duke, his code name, was a play on his nickname Jazz, short for Jasper. Duke was a tribute to the famous jazz artist Duke Ellington. He was the bridge between analytics and operations, turning the theoretical from analytics to reality with input from senior agents. Physically not imposing, Duke was successful as an agent and senior agent due to his amazing tactical skills.

'I have no reason to question the reports. Grace and Conjar know the twins better than I do and I trust their judgement. The twins came through training with exceptional marks. My concerns rest in the mission, not training.'

Zera paused as he examined Duke. 'We have the mission briefing packets, but more information will be coming courtesy of the recovered computers. Initial reports are extremely encouraging; the recovered computers hold a wealth of Intel. As we agree for now, training was a success, so let us move on to Duke's concerns and discuss the mission. Conjar, please briefly give us your feedback from your mission.'

'Fredrick Byron IV was from an extensive line of bankers from an extraordinarily successful and influential family. His ancestors made their fortunes conspiring with the British to betray the colonies during the American Revolution. The family tradition continued through to his father, who made an obscene fortune due to the events of 9/11. IV, the target's identity during the first mission plan, also profited on the victims of terrorism. However, IV took his inhumane investment strategy one step further. He directly funded the attacks and banked the organizations that execute terrorism. He knew an attack, which he helped fund and bank, was coming, but he was untouchable, because of generations of relations built with the most powerful and the tens of millions he had contributed to Washington. Needless to say, he had friends in the highest places. There was another reason, a reason Iceman did not take well, and that was the reason the target was identified as Pervert for the revised mission. He kidnapped students from colleges, got them addicted to drugs and offered them as gifts to the elite, who are the handlers of the terrorists. His hobby was human sex trafficking.'

Conjar paused and took a sip of water before he continued. 'We ran a clean Op and the twins exceeded expectations. Duke and I built a good plan that had the twins undercover as waiters. They were expected to penetrate the target's party, poison him to fake a heart attack, and secure his computer on their retreat. I sensed during the briefing that Iceman held in silence some reservations about the plan, but he did not offer comment. Iceman, after questionable technique, secured better intelligence and brought it to my attention. We studied the intel, built a better plan and executed the revised plan. We changed the takedown location from his home to his mega yacht. During his interrogation of the target, a very dark, violent interrogation, Iceman believed the target was withholding information. Information that was not made available to us, nor known by the analytics team and extracted from the unknown computer. The second computer, along with the targeted computer, is with the hackers and we should have more information in the coming days, weeks and, in all probability, months. As Bill identified, the initial results of the forensic dig are extremely encouraging. My team terminated a known terrorist banker whose hobby was human trafficking. We are ahead of their network, because of the mission and the hackers are in the process of unearthing an onion of data on global terrorist threats. The previously unknown computer exposes a tressure of international networks.'

Duke deliberately elected to bypass the success of the mission and attacked the team instead. 'Questionable technique? He was drunk when he gathered intelligence and your team was fortunate his drunk plan worked. I have serious reservations about Iceman, and quite frankly, I have concerns about you too, Conjar. This was your first mission as a senior agent. Because of your inexperience, we spent extra time meticulously constructing the plan. You had no business or authority to deviate from the mission plan. Iceman shows up with a beer and taco party. Months of intel and planning are scrapped? Your team flew from the seat of your pants and got lucky. Iceman is a problem and not Superman. You have no control over him.'

Conjar was beyond insulted by Duke and desperately tried to control his rage. 'Before I was interrupted, I was going to address the exit strategy, but allow me to reply to Duke's comments first. You have no idea what you are talking about. Iceman used alcohol as a tool to gather new intel. Moving past that and addressing the mission, your conclusions are petty and insulting. The team built the plan. Iceman was the visionary, but the team built and executed the plan. To qualify the mission as a drunk taco party is an insult to Zeus. Zeus did an amazing job attacking the plan in search of weaknesses in our process. He directed the input from the team into a working model that built consensus. Any conclusions to the contrary are wrong. Returning to my point regarding exit strategy, Iceman's vision was simply significantly better than the original plan. In the original plan, the target was to die of an apparent heart attack, and in the confusion, the twins were to secure the computer. The missing computer would have been noticed, and within hours, contingency plans made to protect the target's operation would have been initiated. By attacking the yacht instead of the house, Iceman bought us time to maliciously interrogate the target and, through his unique abilities, secure the unknown second computer. Just as important, the team agreed to send the yacht out to international waters after killing the target and disposing of the bodies in the ocean. The yacht has still not been found. We disabled all tracking devices, yet here, the computers are being cracked by the hackers as we speak. Even when the yacht is found, the related parties to the target will assume he and his computers have made a run for it. They will wait for him to resurface to return to business as usual, buying us even more time to take additional action.'

Grace remained quiet. After reading the debriefing, she was stunned at the simple genius of the plan. Grace had studied years of field reports concerning the twins. She was not surprised at Zeus' value, if understated, role in the mission. She knew Duke's ego was wounded because his plan was scrapped. Duke took tremendous pride in being the architect of all missions, which meant to him being the smartest person in the room. The only attribute larger than Duke's talent in strategic planning was his ego. As soon as she read that Iceman had changed the plan, she knew Duke was going to be a problem. What concerned her more was Conjar's team working with Duke going forward. Duke was no longer the smartest guy in the room, that now belonged to Iceman.

Sensing Conjar's need to continue his retaliation against Duke, Zera forcefully took control of the meeting. 'Duke, you were out of line.'

Duke turned to Zera, ready for confrontation. He was well prepared to defend his position and his mission plan. He was furious that Iceman's cavalier attitude was celebrated and no one in the room saw Conjar's inability to control him as a fundamental problem. Duke stared at Zera for several seconds.

Zera remained calm, in control of himself and the meeting. A dynamic leader, exemplified by his undisputed ability to lead prideful warriors, he was always in command. He met Duke's stare and continued. 'Iceman is a force. Conjar, I read your report and I congratulate you on executing a better plan due to better intel. You operated with appropriate field, on-the-ground intel and authority. The results speak for themselves.'

Conjar, still furious, tried to accept Zera's praise, but still subtly attacked Duke. 'Thank you. The key component to the revised mission plan was training. The decision to move the arena from the mansion to the yacht was made, because we had trained for three years assaulting a similar yacht during Black Ops training. We were better prepared to assault the yacht rather than the mansion. It was most certainly not a whim; it was three years of training. Iceman may have challenged the plan, but he has never challenged an order. He has committed himself to all orders with fierce resolve. With Zeus, the twins have never failed in their execution of an order once agreed upon.'

Dr. Monroe was incredibly pleased with Conjar's response. She had several more thoughts regarding Duke's behavior after his silent, yet deafening, confrontation with Zera, but elected to share her concerns with Zera in private. She hoped Zera would bring the meeting to a halt. She knew any extension of the meeting would result in Conjar declaring Iceman's plan was better. He was better. Grace knew she would defend Conjar if required. She was hoping for a less confrontational method.

Zera did just that. He extended an olive branch to Duke to soothe his massive ego so the leadership team could move on. 'This meeting was very productive. Conjar, great Op, excellent job, but Duke does have a valid point. Iceman's independent streak has been identified in reports since he was introduced to the Elders. We need to monitor that concern during the celebration. Grace, you are scheduled to meet with the twins this week, please spend additional time with Iceman and let's meet again in the coming weeks.'

CHAPTER THREE

While Conjar was being debriefed in Austin, Iceman smirked as they walked toward Logan Airport security from the helicopter field. 'How are you feeling? And no bullshit, because you are walking funny.'

Zeus had banged his knee and slipped on the wet deck of Pervert's mega yacht during the assault. 'A little sore. You?'

'Same. I am not sure, but I hurt my shoulder somehow.'

Zeus evaluated his knee injury. 'You know, I banged my left knee exiting the water and that is sore, but my right knee hurts more. I think I must have tweaked it when I planted it on the wet surface and almost went down.'

'That's probably it. I saw you stumble and almost go down out of the corner of my eye. Not that I cared; the mission came first.' Iceman said half joking, but also profoundly serious.

Neither spoke of how they felt emotionally.

'Dude, you smell and I mean smell.' Iceman told Zeus.

'Trust me, you are no bag of roses.'

'I know.' Iceman replied as they walked past the departure board. 'When a horse can smell his own shit, you know you smell. Hang on, our flight is delayed two hours.'

Zeus smiled. 'Cougar time?'

'Fuck yes, but we are wearing dorky clothes and smell like ass. Give me a minute.' With those words, he hatched a plan and Zeus just shook his head, waited and laughed.

'So, here's the plan. After security, we go to Brooks Brothers, grab a new set of clothes, go to the latrine and take a trucker's shower. We will change and be ready for Cougar Town. Conjar said we had to blow some money to confirm our cover, so perfect.'

Zeus asked. 'What's a trucker shower?'

'Really, I thought you weren't from Mars.' Iceman smiled as he continued to tease Zeus about his lack of knowledge of slang, given his Irish heritage. 'Truck drivers use it on long hauls when the rest area doesn't have showers. You get down to, in your case, panties, grab paper towels, soap and water. It's like a dry shower we use in the field. The trucker shower is not perfect, but it is all we got.'

Zeus nodded and the twins cleared Logan's security and headed to Brooks Brothers. The twins bought proper clothes for travel, including a sports coat and carry-on bag. In the latrine, they trucked it up and Iceman used the time to examine the recovered bag from the mission. He opened the bag and counted $350,000. He removed $25,000 and put it in his carry-on bag. He exited the stall and handed Zeus $25,000.

'What's this?'

Iceman secured the mission bag with the remaining $300,000 and explained. 'From the mission, the safe on Pervert's yacht that housed the first computer had this cash in it. Conjar told us we could keep it. $25,000 is your travel money. I am going to find an airport locker and secure the other $300k.'

'Fuck me. $350k?'

'Roger that, courtesy of your and my favorite target, Pervert. I'll keep it in the locker away from the Elder's eyes. It will be our secret fund. You never know. When we travel back through Boston, I'll find a better storage method. One with two keys, so we each have access. We need to have a second life away from the Elders; again, you never know.'

* * *

Exiting the latrine after a brief view of themselves in the bathroom mirror and a quick inspection of each other met with approval, the twins exited to find a locker, followed by the airport bar.

They found the locker and Iceman handed Zeus the key. 'Here, you keep it. If anything happens, they'll suspect me. I trust you.'

'Thanks, Iceman. Let's find Cougar Town.'

Unable to secure a proper target, the twins skipped the first bar they saw. As they approached the second bar, Iceman paused.

Zeus asked. 'Got her?'

'Yep, she'll be alone with three empty bar stools around her. A little young for a cougar, but she is definitely traveling on an expense account or has bank. Let's go get those free drinks and snacks she so desperately wants to buy us.' Iceman eyed the target and walked over. 'Hello, are these seats taken?'

'Why aren't you lovely? One seat is taken, but please sit down.'

Iceman did not bother to ask who she was referring to as lovely, knowing it was Zeus. He just sat two seats down from the cougar and left the seat next to her open for her friend. Iceman eyed the empty beer in front of the empty bar stool and smiled. The friend's empty drink had lipstick; the cougar was not waiting on a guy. Perfect. When he sat down, the bartender approached and he ordered a roast beef sandwich with provolone, spicy mustard and held the vegetables.

The cougar sat at the corner of the bar with Zeus next to her. He asked Iceman. 'No turkey? You always get turkey.'

The mission took Iceman's taste away for turkey. He just needed to reboot. 'Seamus, I need a minute, a palate change.'

'How about a beer then?' Zeus asked. Zeus, after years together, knew Iceman well enough to know what *I need a minute* entailed. Iceman was in pain and a tremendous feeling of darkness lingered after the mission.

'No, I don't think so.' His thoughts were lost until she approached the group. Iceman was looking at the back bar mirror and caught the reflection from a distance of one cool chick. She had to be 5'11" with a long, athletic build. She was wearing a t-shirt from some beach, leggings, and a Boston Red Sox hat. Her auburn hair was tied into a ponytail that ran through the hole created by the adjustable half-meshed trucker-style hat. Iceman laughed to himself as he thought of the trucker shower, which was kind of ironic. *She wears a trucker hat and I smell like a trucker.* To his mild surprise and delight, she sat down next to him. She was cougar's friend.

She smiled at Iceman. 'Hello.'

What a great smile. A smile that almost broke Iceman out of his dark mood. As she smiled, a Guinness and Jameson appeared in front of him. He turned to Zeus, who smiled and raised his pint in the air, *cheers.* Iceman immediately drank the shot, followed by a long gulp from his pint.

The new girl looked at Iceman and then at the bartender. 'That looks yummy. I'll have what he is having, but hold the whiskey.'

She then turned to the cougar and asked, 'Who are your new friends?'

Katherine introduced herself to Iceman and Zeus. Colleen, the cougar, did the same.

Stunned, he witnessed Iceman quiet for the first time ever. Zeus quietly asked. 'How do you two know each other? Right, sorry, I am Seamus and that is Jack.'

Colleen responded, 'We are sisters and are taking a trip to London. I have a bit of business and my baby sister is my escort. The trip is my graduation gift to her. Seamus, I love your accent.'

Seamus responded. 'That's cool, you two taking a trip together. My accent is Irish.' He watched his lad oddly distant.

Colleen asked. 'Where are you off to?'

Seamus responded, 'Austin.'

Colleen nodded. 'What do you do?'

Jack was still silent, so Seamus responded. 'We are forensic auditors.'

Katherine, not a fool, asked. 'Doing what?'

Seamus answered. 'This and that, we review the financial stability and integrity of government contractors, that sort of thing. We work for a company called OWL.'

OWL was a legitimate private equity firm that the Elders controlled. The Black Ops agents used the cover of forensic auditors for OWL to justify their travel. The twins were trained to be effective forensic auditors to enhance their cover story.

Jack ordered another pint for himself, but as he waved his hand to attract the bartender's attention, Katherine noticed the tremendous bruising on his hands and thought, *forensic auditors, my ass,* but kept her observation to herself.

Colleen asked Seamus. 'Is your friend always this quiet?'

Seamus responded. 'No and very much no. You'll see.' He then mouthed without speaking to Colleen. *He likes her.* Colleen nodded and smiled.

Jack stood up from the bar stool. 'It was lovely to meet the two of you, but we better be off.'

Katherine looked surprised to see Jack's pint empty. She shook her head with disapproval. 'Don't be silly. We just met and haven't gotten the chance to get to know each other. Stay, you clearly have time for another pint; that one sure didn't last long. Are you sure you do not want to stay? Of course, you do. Sir, can you get him another Guinness, please?'

Jack began to say no, but Seamus jumped in, still in shock that his boy remained distant. 'Thank you.' He accepted Katherine's kind gesture and asked. 'Iceman, you're in, right?

Before he could answer, Katherine jumped in. 'Iceman, why did he call you Iceman?'

Again, Seamus had to come to Jack's rescue. 'He got the nickname Iceman back at university from a guy on the basketball team, because he is one cool ass whiteboy. The name didn't stick until we hung out with the football team after practice, and they agreed. We were hanging out after practice, waiting for the bus and Jack left to run back to our room when the bus arrived. A member of the football team confirmed to the group when Iceman left. *You guys were right; there goes one cool ass whiteboy.* We had a long last couple of days, but when he comes alive, you'll see.'

With that, Seamus drank his beer, watched and waited. He knew his boy fancied this girl; it was just a matter of time. Zeus thought the mission had hurt them both and made them vulnerable, but Iceman was hurting more. He went beyond dark to get those computers. The high he carried from the mission had worn off. He was lost in a fog and refused to expose himself. Seamus gave him a minute, but he knew his man was coming.

Colleen asked. 'So, you two went to college together and now work for OWL. Where did you go to college?'

While Seamus answered, 'West Point.' Colleen mouthed for only Seamus to see; *she likes him too.*

Seamus asked. 'What do you two do?'

Colleen answered. 'I am a consultant. Katie has a start date as a financial analyst in three months.'

Katie, the name her family called her, responded. 'An analyst for an investment banking firm in Boston.'

Jack mumbled. 'I like the name Katie; it fits you better.' He then shut back down but was warming up.

Seamus continued to make chit-chat with the sisters for a couple of minutes. The beer Katie ordered for Jack began to bring him back to the living world. Zeus felt the change. *Here he comes. The fog is lifting.*

Jack started in. 'I got a quick story.'

Seamus just smiled and drank from his pint. He thought, *my man is waking up* and waited for the show. Seamus knew he was Watson to Holmes, and the game was afoot. His boy was back and Jack was falling for the girl. He knew Jack's eyes. His charming eyes, his violent eyes, his bored eyes, but he had never seen his vulnerable eyes. He knew his lad feared falling for her.

Jack continued. 'So, my parents hosted a family party for no good reason and after dinner, they moved the living room furniture to the front yard to make room for dancing. I was maybe four at the time, sitting between my grandmother on my dad's side and my great-grandmother on my mommy's side. I was having a grand time watching all the fun. Singing, dancing, drinking, old stories being told too many times, you know, the usual family party. Suddenly, my sickly grandfather pops up and grabs my aunt to dance. Grandmother, shaking her head, said: *Would you look at yourself out there dancing up a storm and to think at home he can't fetch himself a glass of water.* The two old ladies to my left and right just shook their heads and laughed like little girls they once were.'

Just as Seamus' man was back in form, a man bumped into Katie. Iceman immediately jumped off his stool, and too aggressively, turned to the traveler and spoke. 'Excuse me, you fuck. You owe her an apology. Trust me, if I have to say it a second time, you won't hear it, because I will have already dropped you.'

Seamus knew the mission was not out of Iceman's system just yet. He typically would have confronted the traveler, but not in such a violent fashion.

'I am sorry.' The rude business traveler responded. He was clearly surprised and frightened.

Iceman shook his head.

'I am really sorry. Let me buy you a round.' The traveler quickly offered.

Iceman calmly replied. 'Apology accepted, but we don't need your round. I only asked for the apology, but thank you for the offer.' He then sat back down and finished his pint.

With that, the traveler was quickly off and had the good sense to find another bar.

Katie touched Jack's knee and smiled. 'Come back to us.'

Jack investigated her beautiful blue-green eyes and nodded.

Jack turned to Seamus. 'I don't know if you have heard this story before, but…'

Seamus interrupted. 'I am quite sure I have.'

Jack smiled and changed gears. 'As I was saying, *I could tell you blood curdling stories about him but, but my throat's gone dry.*'

Katie laughed before Jack could order another round. '*The Quiet Man.* Michaleen Flynn, I love it.'

Jack was impressed and incredibly surprised. 'I can't believe you got that.'

'Please. What self-respecting girl from Irish heritage in Boston wouldn't know it? We watched it every St. Patrick's Day as a kid.'

'Us too, best fight scene in movie history.' Jack, tilting his head with a smile on his face, commented. 'You have a great laugh.'

Katie smiled back. 'You have great eyes, especially when you smile. And that big voice and laugh, you have a voice made for radio.'

'I think you meant a face made for radio.'

'Shut up, Jack. You know I didn't mean it like that.'

Jack, uncomfortable with the intimate exchange, just dropped his head. 'I was just joking.'

Watching their exchange in utter amazement, Seamus whispered to Colleen. 'I have never seen him blush before.'

'You know I am from Boston, and I know you went to West Point. Where are you from?' Katie asked and again dropped her hand on Jack's knee.

'I am from Chicago and you went to Boston College.' Jack smirked as he took an innocent drink from his pint. He had a unique ability to read people, a carnival-like profiling skill he used as a party favorite.

'How did you know that?'

'An upper middle class, Irish Catholic girl from Boston could not have gone to Boston University. You had to go to BC. What's the matter? Couldn't get into an Ivy League school?' Jack offered a simplistic answer rather than scaring Katie with his intense observations that led to his conclusion.

Banging her pint on the bar, Katie stared Jack dead in the eye. 'As a matter of fact, I could have, but who would want to go to an Ivy League school? So, West Point, couldn't get into an Ivy League school?'

Upon hearing this, Seamus coughed up some of the beer he was drinking. While he was wiping his face, he said. 'Excuse me, I am sorry.'

Jack smiled and let off a little laugh. 'Same thing for me. No interest in being an Ivy League snob. I guess that's redundant.'

Seamus shook Colleen's right shoulder to get her to lean in. 'I can't believe your sister just said that. Jack could have gone anywhere if he hadn't gone to West Point. He hates Ivy League schools. This is unbelievable. Where did you go to school?'

Colleen tilted her head. 'Harvard.'

'Shit.'

'Just kidding, I went to BC also.'

The two laughed and not so subtly turned their attention back to the main attraction. Jack and Katie didn't notice, nor would they have cared. They were very much engaged with each other.

Jack, absorbed in Katie's eyes, asked. 'Volleyball or crew?'

'Crew, is it that obvious?'

'Yep. You walk like an athlete.'

Taken aback, Katie asked. 'You were checking me out?'

'Yep, using the bar back's mirror.'

She laughed. 'Are you sure you just work for OWL and are not some sort of secret agent spy guy?' Katie was also observant and harked back to Jack's beaten hands. She had three hockey players for older brother and knew the signs of a warrior's hands.

Jack shook off her mesmerizing laugh and recovered. 'Now that we have established you are into me, I can officially tell you my secrets, but then I would have to sleep with you.'

Laughing again, 'I thought the rule was you would have to kill me.'

'No, silly. That is only in the movies. Real spies, the super dark cover spies, must bed their confessors.' Letting the words linger to build sexual tension, Jack got up to use the men's room.

'Where are you going?'

Jack dropped his wallet, bent down to pick it up with his ass facing Katie and executed a perfect drop and pop. Popping back up, he looked over his shoulder and flirted. 'What's good for the goose is good for the gander. You get to check me out.'

'With that radio face, this is clearly your better side.' Katie shouted, laughing and taking a drink from her pint.

As Jack used his Sean Connery walk, he waved in acknowledgement while he stalked to the latrine. He heard the three he left at the bar roaring with laughter.

When Colleen thought Jack was out of range, she began to talk about Katie's new friend. She was quickly interrupted by Seamus.

'Wait one second, his hearing is ridiculous and I am sure he is using some reflective device to watch us.'

Colleen waited for Seamus' nod of approval, then started in. 'So, when is the date?'

'We haven't made plans for a date.' Katie smiled and quickly grabbed her pint and took another healthy swallow.

'Not a date. The wedding date. Little girl, I do believe you are in love.' Colleen declared, using a fake southern accent.

Seamus, feeling comfortable enough due to a little buzz and a connection with Colleen, jumped in and sang. 'You like him; you want to kiss him.'

Colleen and Seamus broke out laughing while Katie just drank her beer and turned away. She did make sure to turn back to look at them so she could glance past them for Jack's return trip. As she saw Jack walking back, she smirked and thought to herself, *that is some walk.*

As Jack jumped back on the bar stool and Katie gathered her composure, Jack asked. 'What did I miss?'

Colleen and Seamus again broke out laughing; Katie cut them off with a stare.

'Nothing. So, you played basketball, no football or baseball?' Katie asked to redirect the conversation.

Before Jack could answer, Colleen jumped in over Katie's stare and tried to hold back her laughter. 'That is some walk you got there, Jack. Katie sure noticed.'

Pretending to take the joke seriously, Jack responded. 'My James Bond walk? Here's the thing: Katie thought Seamus and I were spies, so I thought I would walk like one. Little known fact: Sean Connery was an unknown actor before Bond. Ian Fleming's books were so successful, largely due to President Kennedy's fondness for them, that the producer, Albert Broccoli, conducted open auditions. Taking a break from a long day of casting, the production team lit cigarettes and began complaining that no one was right for the part. Broccoli, while tuning them out, looked out his office window. He spotted this handsome man walking across the parking lot toward the audition, *like a Panther stalking his prey*. He declared without Connery reading, *I just found 007*. If the walk was good enough for 007, it is good enough for me. All three sports in high school, but just basketball in college.'

Seamus reintroduced himself to their conversation. 'Just basketball, please. Iceman was a star.'

Colleen rode Seamus' comment. 'Did you hear that, Katie? You are flirting with a star, and Seamus and I are but humble observers of this grand moment. I feel humble. How about you, Seamus?'

'Very humble indeed.'

Katie turned to her sister, but before she could speak, Jack responded. 'Zeus, knock it off.'

Katie jumped all over Jack's lead. 'Zeus? Really, Zeus? Colleen, you have been in the presence of a god. Jack, is Zeus treated differently, being a god and all?

'Most certainly. Regal treatment is below the aura which he commands. He is treated with pure divinity.'

Colleen smiled and stared right at Jack, then turned and looked Seamus up and down. 'I certainly can see why they call you Zeus. You earned it, baby.'

Jack turned to Katie. 'She sucks.'

'I know, right?! People don't like her very much. I have to hang out with her, because we are family.'

After a brief pause and a stare-down between team Katie and Jack against Colleen and Seamus, Colleen announced. 'From the powers of Mt. Olympus, I summon another round.'

Katie responded. 'Let it be said, let it be done.'

Colleen turned to Seamus as another round was served and asked. 'Football?'

Seamus shook his head. 'No, rugby.'

Colleen knocked her hand against her head. 'Right, Ireland.'

Colleen and Seamus began to talk about rugby and Ireland while Katie turned her attention back to Jack.

'So, what's in Austin?' Katie asked Jack.

'Work, some meetings and training. Nothing big.'

'Jack, guessing Irish Catholic from Chicago. What is your last name?'

'Collins.'

'An Irish spy named Collins? What are you related to Michael Collins or something? Are you working secretly with the IRA?'

Jack understood the Michael Collins reference to the Irish leader. 'Again, your intentions of bedding me are obvious as you continue to bring up espionage. Yes, I am related to Michael Collins, but I'm not a spy. We are going to a computer conference for training.' Jack responded using the cover assigned to them by Conjar, his handler.

'I see. You sure find any reason to bring sexual attraction into our conversation.'

'You just...'

Katie leaned over and gave Jack a long, slow, moist kiss right at the bar.

Taking a sip of her beer, she asked. 'You were saying?'

Jack took stock of what had just happened and asked. 'So, you like the Red Sox?'

'Yep, you just got to first base.'

The trance Jack and Katie shared was broken by Colleen, who began to clap. 'That's what I'm talking about; enough talk, more action.'

Jack nodded. 'Well, we really should be going. I mean, we need to catch that flight.'

Katie put on a fake pouty face. 'Kiss and run?'

'No, no. Nothing like that.'

Again, Seamus came to Jack's rescue. 'We have time for last call, but then we do have to catch that flight.'

As Seamus ordered the last round, Jack mumbled. 'One for the ditch.'

Katie asked. 'Did you say one for the ditch? Like you are going to ditch me?'

'No, no, no. Sorry. In my family, the last round was never the last round. So, when the last round came and went, and another round was ordered, it was called one for the ditch. The ditch being, in most cases, the last round.'

Smiling, Katie leaned over and kissed him on the cheek. 'Sweet boy.'

Jack smiled back and gently rubbed his cheek where she had kissed him. 'It's my secret; don't tell anyone.'

Moments of further laughter continued as they finished one for the ditch. Jack shocked Seamus when he asked for the check, not just their check, but the entire check. Iceman violated rule number one of Cougar Town. He paid for everyone in full. Jack left Cougar Town with what one had to assume was one great kiss.

With the bill settled, the four said their goodbyes. They all hugged and Jack started to walk off. Katie grabbed a stunned Jack and gave him the biggest, most beautiful kiss. The kiss lasted several seconds, but felt like hours to Jack.

Pulling away, Katie walked away with a hair flip and said, 'See you soon.'

Confused, Jack, with the vision of Katie's dancing ponytail, asked. 'Zeus, what the fuck is she talking about? We don't even know and…'

Zeus stopped him. 'I slipped her my and your number on a cocktail napkin.'

'Dude…' Iceman started and again was cut off by Zeus.

'You like her. It's all good, just let it go.'

Iceman dropped his head, nodded, then added. 'You are a good man, Charles Brown.'

They both laughed and pushed each other, laughed again, but their pain kicked in. The shove was not the best idea.

'You think she likes me?' Iceman asked.

'You know, you are a cool ass whiteboy, but you are a joke one has to get. If you get the joke, that is you. It is funny and awesome. If you don't get the joke, you are horribly offensive and arrogant. I get the joke and she gets the joke. Ice, I am sorry to inform you, she likes Jack and not Iceman.'

Iceman just nodded and used all his emotional strength to get on that plane. He wanted to turn back. *Who was that girl? What just happened? What the hell was Zeus thinking giving her information?* Checking himself, *just get on the plane.* He looked down at his boarding pass and noticed.

'Hey Zeus, we're in first class. Did you know that? Because I didn't know that!'

'I did.' He said simply.

Iceman wondered. 'You always fly first class?'

'I am sorry, what was the question?'

'Shit, rich kid be flying first class all the time while us lonely folk are just excited for the free pretzels.' Iceman entertained himself as he tried to use shit talk to fuel the walk to the plane and away from Katie.

'Nice try, but we flew first class to Key West on holiday. I looked you up, remember, computer genius. Your whole shanty Irish thing from the South Side of Chicago is bullocks. Your father is a very successful attorney. In fact, everyone in your family is financially successful. So, let's cut the rich kid shit out. I am tired, drunk and just want to get on the plane.'

'Roger that. Sorry, Zeus, won't happen again.'

The twins boarded the plane. Zeus found his seat and Iceman went to grab a pillow from the overhead. The flight attendant approached him. 'Can I help you?'

'No, just grabbing a pillow.' Iceman answered.

'Sir, those are for first-class passengers. Can I see your boarding pass so I can help you find your seat?'

Iceman, laughing, responded. 'Pretty sure I can find 3A and sit down next to my friend right here.'

'I am so sorry. What would you like for dinner and would you like something to drink before takeoff?'

Iceman held the joke he wanted to tell Zeus. Zeus looked like first class and he looked like Greyhound, but refrained out of respect to his promise.

'Can we get a beer and, if possible, I don't know the rules, but could I ask you to wait on the meal for an hour? We are tired, had a long business trip and want to grab a quick nap. Seamus, are you cool with that?'

'Sure.'

The flight attendant smiled and returned with the beers. 'We have a chicken with pasta or...'

Iceman cut her off. 'We don't care. Again, if you are kind enough to bring us food in an hour, that would be great. I am sorry if I am being rude.'

'No problem at all. You most certainly are not being rude and aren't you just lovely.'

With that, Iceman destroyed the beer and began to go to sleep in peace, because he had been called lovely rather than Zeus. As he continued to joke with himself, he was interrupted in thought. His mind drifted. *Motherfucker, I am in pain. Man, my back is on fire, my shoulder and hands hurt and I am sore. I like her; that Katie is intriguing and mesmerizing.* As he continued his thoughts on Katie, he fell asleep before takeoff.

The flight attendant presented horrible lasagnas that the twins ate greedily. Iceman opened the shade and wondered what the next mission would bring. Would he really see Katie again?

CHAPTER FOUR

They took the escalator to baggage claim at Austin-Bergstrom Airport. Iceman asked. 'What do we do now?'

'No clue, but we have ourselves, boy band cash in our pocket, a credit card and serious bank. You'll figure it out. I trust you.' Zeus responded.

As the twins rode down the escalator, they saw a driver holding a sign, *Conjar Consultant Group*. Ice and Zeus smiled at each other. Zeus went to speak but was second in the draw.

'You two must be Zeus and Iceman. I am Robert, and I will be your driver.'

Iceman responded. 'Thank you, very nice to meet you.'

Zeus whispered. 'Told you, always fine, my man.'

Robert had instructions to drive the twins directly to the Factory. Iceman had other ideas. 'Did you receive our proper destination?'

'Most certainly, I am to take you straight away to the Factory.'

'Your orders are dated. New orders issued. The Factory, after a quick stop at Stiles Switch, we are craving BBQ and beer.'

'I am sorry; my orders were explicit and they included no stops. They warned me of the serious trouble if I let you talk me into a pub visit. Iceman, they especially warned me about you. I am sorry, but no.'

'I respect that, but here's the thing: I am not talking you into anything, as there is nothing to discuss. Take us there, or we are leaving on our own.'

'I really can't.'

'Thank you in advance and don't worry, the powers that be will know it was my fault.' Iceman did not give the notion of skipping Stiles the slightest thought.

With nervous regret, Robert agreed. 'They did tell me you would do this, but I tried my best as ordered. They instructed me, when I failed to execute my first order, to make the stop on one condition: the visit is limited to two hours. The two-hour order is firm.'

Zeus answered before Iceman refused. 'The two-hour order is fair, we agree.'

Robert then offered. 'If you want BBQ, let me take you to La Barbeque. It's better and closer to the Factory, so you will have time for an extra beer.'

Iceman smiled. 'Robert, I like a man with a plan. I am nothing if not flexible.'

Zeus laughed. 'Yeah, sure, Iceman, that's exactly how I would describe you.'

Robert was right. The twins were instantly hooked on la Barbecue. They ate, enjoyed good company and conversation, and left promptly two hours later as ordered. The twins were on their way to the Factory to be debriefed, medically examined and introduced to advanced training.

CHAPTER FIVE

Robert drove the twins to Govalle, TX, an east-side neighborhood in Austin. He crossed the automated chain-linked fence and the twins saw from their windows a large rundown commercial warehouse building. After clearing the chain-linked fence and the large shipping and receiving yard, the group approached the massive, old, dilapidated warehouse. Robert paused for one of the shipping and receiving doors to open and guided the twins into the darkened warehouse. The shipping doors opened and they entered. When the outer doors closed, the lights illuminated the old warehouse. Robert waited again for a second set of doors to open. The second set of doors were modern, as were the second set of exterior walls. Robert navigated the car into the indoor parking garage to find his assigned parking spot. Crossing the second set of doors transformed the dilapidated warehouse into a modern office building. The Factory was a state-of-the-art facility hidden within the shell of the warehouse. The twins exited the vehicle with Robert, who escorted them to the elevator. They entered the elevator and the car operating panel offered three upper levels. To the twins' surprise, they descended and exited several basement levels below the garage. When the elevator stopped, the doors opened and the twins followed Robert.

'Hello and welcome. I'm Trinity, the facility manager for the Factory. I know who you are. Please follow me. Thank you, Robert. That will be all. Kindly take your post.'

Iceman looked to Zeus, who offered. 'Toto, I have a feeling we're not in Kansas anymore.'

'Roger that. It's kind of funny that we are being greeted by Trinity from the Matrix. She is a dead ringer, but we should have been greeted by Morpheus. A badass brother, like yourself, escorting me on a journey into Wonderland.'

Zeus did not care for the term brother. If Iceman were to use the term in reference to their twin-like relationship, he would have been fine. Having a black father from Atlanta and an Irish mother from Clare, Ireland, he was not pleased with the use of brother to describe him. Iceman knew it bothered him and used it on limited occasions to fuck with Zeus to relax his tension. If he was pissed at Iceman for calling him brother, Zeus would be distracted from his primary worry. Even though he knew what Iceman was doing after almost seven years together, it still worked, which pissed Zeus off even more. He sometimes wondered why they felt like twins.

'Would that make you Neo, the one?' Zeus asked Iceman, baiting him.

'I like to think so, but now I feel like Alice.'

'Now, you are Alice?'

'Mars boy, have you seen the Matrix?'

'Still Ireland and not Mars, yes, of course, your point?'

'I may be Neo, the chosen one. But right now, I am Alice from Wonderland chasing the white rabbit.'

Zeus laughed and remembered to himself; *brothers do talk shit. He got me again, fucker.*

Just as Iceman released Zeus from his worries, Trinity began. 'Take a seat.'

The twins followed her into an imposing conference room; they were offered no refreshments.

'Background first. The Factory was established in 1825 in New York City due to the opening of the Erie Canal and that is where it stayed until the events of September 11. International attention pushed the Elders to relocate to a more secluded setting. Getting lost in the crowd was no longer feasible in NYC, hence the outskirts of Austin. We have a sister location on the outskirts of London.'

Iceman joked. 'Are you sure it wasn't NYC's aggressive gun laws that forced the move? Hello, Texas.'

Trinity ignored Iceman. 'We were the first to find east Austin. Now we face the popularity and gentrification of the area and may have to relocate again. The outside of the building is a shell. The new infrastructure within the warehouse is more secure than the White House. Our entire artery of operations is located underground, similar to the presidential bunker, with the exception that ours is ten stories down, not five. The packet I am handing you details the security measures. We are nuclear secure.'

Zeus asked. 'The elevator reflected three floors above the garage. Are they active?'

'Yes, those floors house the gym, medical, and guest quarters, your quarters. The upper-level activity is conducted at street level in the front of the building. We need the appearance of activity, people coming and going, you get the idea. Enough about the facility, it is in your readings. Like all things Elders, we take it seriously.'

The twins nodded their consent as they glanced at their thick briefing packet detailing the Factory.

Iceman asked. 'What now?'

'As soon as we conclude, I will escort you on a tour of the upper level to your rooms, then escort you to medical. You will spend the rest of the day and tomorrow with medical, including Dr. Monroe. After the medical is finished with you, I will discuss your prepared schedule. We are concluded. Follow me.'

The twins did as instructed and followed Trinity back the way they came. 'The sunny floors are accessible with this elevator bank. A second elevator bank is located near the front of the building. The front elevators only access the sunny floors and do not provide service to the Dungeon.'

The twins were bright enough to piece together, the sunny floors were above ground and the Dungeon was used in lieu of the presidential bunker.

Zeus asked. 'You mentioned street traffic. How does that work?'

'As I described earlier, you use the front entrance to enter and exit the building for the sunny floors to create street traffic flow. Once you are secured in the building, the garage elevator is the only passage to and from the Dungeon. When you elect to leave the Factory, walk to an offsite public location to manage your transport, typically an Uber or, like Robert used to pick you up, a Factory car.'

Zeus nodded. 'Thank you.'

'The east side of the Dungeon is R&D and the west side is analytics and investments. The offices and conference rooms that surround the perimeter are safe rooms with gun safes and small armories. The office workstations in the center of the Factory are assigned an office or conference room in the event of a breach. Once secured, locked down, and a situation report assessed, a counter-assault is executed. Here we are, off to floor three, the residential level.

On the ride up, Iceman asked. 'Has there ever been a breach?'

'No, your rooms are to your right. When you visit medical, you will be injected with an identification chip that allows access to the sunny floors. After three days, your chip will be programmed to allow you access to the Dungeon. Until then, you require an escort. Off to your rooms and be quick about it. I'll wait here by the elevator.'

The twins found their small hotel-style room among the dozen or so other rooms with ease. Per Trinity's curt request, they were quick about it. They found Trinity holding the elevator, 'any difficulty finding your rooms?'

The twins shook their heads and went off to medical.

Trinity remained in the elevator as the twins exited and were greeted by a vision of warmth. Iceman smiled. 'You must be Flo.'

Trinity and Zeus looked at Iceman, confused. Zeus spoke first. 'What are you talking about?'

Before Iceman could respond, *Flo* responded. 'Nice one, Iceman, Florence Nightingale, I get it. Sorry to report, I am more Nurse Ratched from *One Flew Over the Cuckoo's Nest.*'

Iceman smiled. 'Ouch.'

Nurse Ratched smiled, and the twins turned their attention to their next introduction. 'Nice to meet the young, talented Iceman and Zeus; your reputation precedes you. I am Donna, not Flo, and I am charged with getting you back to fighting form. The tour is quite simple. You are on the medical floor. We have exam and treatment rooms as well as physical therapy as needed. Iceman, you are with me in exam room A, and Zeus, you are with the doctor in room B.'

Donna conducted Iceman's intake including the injection of the security chip, while the doctor performed a complete physical on Zeus. When completed, the twins traded rooms. After four hours, the twins were escorted to massage therapy to work out the impact of the mission.

Trinity was waiting with the elevator open when the twins exited the massage room. 'I'll escort you back to the third floor. I took the liberty of securing sandwiches for you. As it is late, you will eat in your room tonight. I will pick you up tomorrow morning for breakfast at 0530 hours. You will meet Dr. Monroe after breakfast.'

Trinity abruptly turned and left the twins. Iceman went to talk with Zeus, who cut him off. 'Save it, Iceman. I'm hungry and tired. I will listen to your crazy thoughts in the morning. Get some sleep.'

* * *

The twins exited their rooms at 0525 hours and Zeus commented. 'I'm surprised Trinity is not here to check our toothbrushes.'

Iceman was in no mood for jokes. He was locked in on absorbing the mothership and her crew. 'She's probably holding the elevator for us.'

Sure enough, when they turned the corner, they found Trinity holding the elevator. 'Good morning.'

Iceman was silent and Zeus responded for the twins. 'Good morning. Are you joining us for breakfast?'

'No, I already ate. I trust the attire left in your room is suitable.'

As they descended to the second floor and the cafeteria, Zeus again spoke for the twins. 'Yes, dress, casual, business casual and exercise gear, all present, accountable and suitable. Thank you.'

While Trinity ignored his pleasantries, Zeus could feel Iceman zeroing in on Trinity. Her rude behavior was about to eclipse Iceman's tolerance level. 'After breakfast, you meet with Dr. Monroe.' Trinity reminded the twins.

'You already said that last night.' Iceman coldly responded.

Zeus knew to be concerned.

'I am simply...'

Iceman was rounding into form; he was going to take control of their relationship with Trinity. 'I wouldn't celebrate being simple.'

Zeus understood Iceman was toying with her now. He also knew Trinity was not the type accustomed to being challenged and her world was about to change. He understood Iceman was quicksand when he zeroed in on a target that he felt had disrespected him. The more you fight it, the quicker you sink. A target that gave him no respect earned an attacking style of communication from Ice. The problem for the target was Iceman could be brutal with even a whisper of disrespect. He used his powers of observation and a blistering mind to punish his prey. Zeus silently felt sorry for Trinity.

'Excuse me. You need to understand...'

Before Trinity could finish her statement, Zeus was silently pleading with her to stop. *You need to understand? Ouch. Girl, you are about to find out how much you need to understand stings. Hang on, is the use of girl the equivalent of brother? Am I being hypocritical? Never mind that; next question: am I going to run interference to slow Iceman or...*

'Unlike you, I speak for myself.' Iceman was calling Trinity a puppet. 'You will not tell me what I need to understand. That was rude. In my experience, only the eclectically simple, there's the word again, remember simple from earlier? I was standing here and you were standing there. It was just a couple of seconds ago. Forgive me if I am moving beyond the speed of simple, driving a thought that blows too fast through simple town. Allow me to regain my manners and thank you for your efforts. We will not need you to speak again. After breakfast at the kiddie table, kindly escort us to Dr. Monroe in silence.'

Zeus shook his head as he witnessed Trinity's emotional response. *She's fucked.*

'Iceman, I was told about your problem.'

Zeus thought: *impossible. Now she tipped Iceman off to an enemy.* Iceman got Zeus hooked on movies when they had down-time and he remembered his *Gladiator. People should know when they are conquered.*

'Which one? Which problem? I have so many.' Iceman patiently responded as he waited to pounce.

Zeus ran the tab. *A soft verbal jab, like in boxing, followed by another jab, maybe a left hook, then depending on when he is done with her, his nose breaking straight right missile. Iceman holds the West Point boxing record for most broken noses delivered. The physical punishment delivered in boxing was no match to his verbal assaults.*

'Always the smartest guy in the room.' Trinity smugly answered.

Fight over. Fuck her, she's a grown woman. She should have known better. Here it comes. Zeus readied himself.

Given our gender-sensitive, race-sensitive, height-sensitive, weight-sensitive, confused about gender and race-sensitive society, I do not believe your use of guy is appropriate. Please forgive me. I will clarify the simple. Your use of guy; does that eliminate you from the conversation? Or is it you are indirectly asking me if you are the idiot in the room as I am the smartest? If you are confused, refer to the old card player adage: *if you can't spot the idiot in the room, it's you.'*

Strong left hook, but he is holding back. Zeus thought.

'I don't need to take this from you.'

'Yet here you stand. Fascinating. Could it be that you have no idea what it takes to be Black Ops? Why do you feel superior to Black Ops agents when you push a pencil? Would you care to relive the torment of your latest paper cut? I am guessing you are overcompensating and are either jealous of or intimidated by Black Ops agents.'

'You have…'

'Shut up, you child. While you speak only to ensure your lips still function, your eyes betray you. You gape at us, which means you hold in awe for the simple. There is that word again: simple. Fuck me. I am a thesaurus carrying motherfucker. You gape at those in Black Ops.'

'What?'

Iceman knew he had hit a nerve with her, *what,* response. She was trying to buy time to catch up with the verbal assault. 'You heard me. You asked *what* to buy your simple brain time to recover. While you were busy gaping at us, you mentioned being informed of my problem. Someone you value must not hold us in much regard. Given you gape at those in Black Ops, I am guessing that is the source. You never met us, so this Black Ops person must have quite the influence over you. Who could it be? Who could it be? Few in Black Ops operate from here.'

Zeus knew Iceman already had the source. He was just waiting for Trinity to offer him visual confirmation with the slightest tell.

'I am going to report this disgraceful exchange.'

Iceman smiled, *got you.* 'To whom? Could it be the person that issued you a code name even though you hide in cubicles and offices?'

'Excuse me?'

'You're excused. As I said earlier, we are eating our breakfast, but given our recent exchange. I am now advising you that we have elected to find our way to Dr. Monroe without you. Before you go, kindly do me a favor: when you see Duke later today or tonight, hmm, tonight, give him our best.' Iceman turned and went to eat breakfast.

Zeus just nodded uncomfortably at Trinity, turned and followed Iceman. Trinity exited the cafeteria in search of Duke.

* * *

Zeus made a tray of food and joined Iceman at the table. 'That went well. A nice, pleasant conversation to start our first full day.'

'Thank you, I thought so. You know how much I value pleasantries and minions who fancy themselves as kings. I was genuinely concerned with her feelings.'

'That came through nicely. How fucked are we, now that you just verbally undressed Trinity?'

'Zero. She is paper, she is nothing, but she holds the key to the mystery.'

'What mystery is that?'

'We graduated from the Colonel with the completion of our first mission, right?'

'Right.'

'Who is his replacement?' Iceman asked, finally letting Zeus into the plan.

'Conjar, he is our team leader.'

'He is Pinocchio. A good guy, but Pinocchio. Who is Geppetto?'

Zeus was beginning to see the picture when he asked. 'You think there is someone holding his strings?'

'Don't get me wrong, Conjar is our boss and I respect him. We are lucky to have him. The Colonel was always there for us behind the scenes. Do I think someone is going to replace him? I attacked Duke just now, right?'

'Right.'

'Who is going to handle the problem I just created? In the past, the Colonel would have gotten involved. Will Conjar be the guy or someone else?'

'You exposed what? Who is the player around here? It's obviously Zera.'

'For sure, but he won't soil his hands with this bullshit. I drew back the curtain. Let's watch the play unfold.'

'Who do you think it is?'

'I don't know, but I will be watching.'

'Bullshit, you know.'

Iceman believed one of two players had Zera's ear. The twins were only agents and the director of the Elders did not have time to be directly involved in their careers. If it was Duke, that would be a huge suck. Iceman did not care for Duke after meeting him to discuss their first mission. His exchange, if one could call it an exchange, with Trinity exposed Duke's position on the twins. Iceman was certain the twins were not going to eat any of his shit. In Iceman's eyes, there was one other player that he believed was their Oz. Their guardian angel that operated behind the curtain now that the Colonel was gone.

'Hurry up and finish your breakfast. I want to be early for our appointment with Dr. Monroe.'

CHAPTER SIX

'Where's the fire?' Zeus asked as he chased Iceman out of the cafeteria.

'I want to catch Dr. Monroe before Simple tattles.'

'Simple, you mean Trinity?'

'Like I said, Simple.' Iceman was building his list grounded in Irish diplomacy. *The art of telling someone to go to hell so they will look forward to the trip.* He was coming for Duke and was determined to strike first with overwhelming force. Charm was his weapon of choice for this mission, but he held it in reserve until the time was right. While he had never met Dr. Monroe, he knew the Colonel reported to her. He knew she had a vested interest in the twins. The Colonel did not walk alone with the Elders. Dr. Monroe was the wind in his sails. Although not as high on the food chain, she reported to the Elders the same as Zera. Duke did not; he reported to Zera. Iceman was on a mission to find a powerful ally. His thoughts drifted. *I hope she does not need to be recruited; she just needs confirmation. With Zeus, my brother by another mother, I got and trust him. Conjar, a rock-steady senior agent, I can run with. The Colonel in the background is always in my corner. I need Dr. Monroe. With her things would be all right. Then Katie, wait, Katie? Get your head focused, you fucking idiot.*

Iceman found Dr. Monroe's office and neglected to knock. He walked smoothly in with a bit of a Charlie Chaplin stumble and a confused face. 'Hello, I think I might be lost. It's my first official day and all. I am looking for Dr Monroe. Any help with that?'

Dr. Monroe internally took a deep breath. *Here comes the hurricane.* Even though she was prepared for Iceman, had studied him since he was a teenager and was the driving force behind his development, he caught her. Where was Trinity? Trinity's status, while unsettling, was extremely rewarding to Dr. Monroe. She took pride in the moment. Iceman had just confirmed that which she already knew, he was different. The recurring theme of all the reports detailed his impact in person. The reports documented that as much as you prepare for Iceman, you are not ready.

Dr. Monroe dug in and started their first meeting. She wanted to ask where Trinity was and how the twins arrived at her front door, but thought better of it. She didn't want to give Iceman the satisfaction. 'Hello, and you must be Seamus and Jack. What a pleasure.' She deliberately used their given first names. 'Gentlemen, please take a seat. Can I get you something to drink?'

'Sure, Iceman and I would like a Budweiser.'

My motherfucking man. God should have retired when he created this genetic freak. My guy recognized the game. Let's play. Iceman held his prideful grin as he took a seat.

'Zeus, I'm sorry. I can offer water, coffee, or tea.'

Zeus smiled as he sat down. 'Just kidding, thank you for the offer. We are good.'

Dr. Monroe took a mental step back. *Zeus has grown up. The reports detailed his importance to the twins, but this stand is certainly a strong evolution in his development. The twins have grown as a force together. Ready? I better be. The twins are not just about handling Iceman. The reports were accurate. The quiet, reserved Seamus had evolved into the mighty Zeus. A brilliant mind with a kind soul, captured in a 6'3, 235 lbs. frame with freakish athletic skills, Zeus scored off the charts in all areas of training, matched and exceeded in some areas only by Iceman.*

'As you know, I am Dr. Grace Monroe. I am the group leader for recruitment and training. In addition, I provide mental health support for Black Ops. I just wanted to meet the two of you today to say hello. I feel close to you already, given that I have been monitoring you both since the age of 15.'

Zeus spoke for the twins. 'The pleasure is ours.'

Dr. Monroe nodded in appreciation. 'I believe you are aware that I work very closely with Colonel Sullivan.'

Zeus spoke again. 'Yes, we are.'

'I have all these reports over the years, but obviously, meeting and working with you will better help me understand and assist you. I was hoping we could just talk about your journey to date in a casual conversation.'

Again, Zeus spoke for the twins. 'Sounds good.'

Dr. Monroe was amazed at Iceman's intense inspection and dissection skills. When Zeus spoke and she turned her attention to him, Iceman made a quick inventory of her and her environment. When her eyes returned to the twins, his eyes were on her. To even the most skilled professional, his examination would have been missed. He would have appeared to be casually engaging in conversation.

'How did the two of you meet? Tell me all about it.'

Iceman smiled and Zeus laughed and responded. 'I guess we are a bit like a married couple; we have been together now for over six years. As you know, we met on our first day at West Point. We were roommates and assigned to the only company that experienced the same intense first-year training demanded of cadets prior to 2012. We have the Colonel to thank for that.'

Dr. Monroe knew Zeus was referring to the training philosophy used at West Point. Prior to 2012, Beast Barracks was used to place fearsome demands on first-year cadets. After 2012, the elimination of Beast Barracks and other intense demands brought an easier road. 'Did the special training upset either of you?'

Zeus again responded. 'At first, we felt it was unfair, but looking back, they never should have changed it. Our company was much better off for having endured Beast Barracks and the demanding first year.'

Dr. Monroe turned her attention to Iceman. 'Jack, what do you think?'

'I agree with Zeus.' Iceman responded, noting Dr. Monroe's use of his proper name.

'How was your first year?'

Zeus answered. 'Good. We got along from the jump. I played rugby and did well in school. Ice killed it in hoops and, while he hated school, did well also.'

'You took 24 credit hours, played sports, and had all the military requirements; was that too much?'

Zeus responded again for the twins. 'No. Some of the classes were a waste of time, but no, it was fine.'

'So, everything was just cruising along, no problems, no concerns?' 'Not really, if there was anything, the Colonel was always there for us. There really is no point in going year by year. It was all pretty much the same thing. During the school year, we went to class and played ball. In the summer, we took specialized classes and knocked out several military schools. Airborne, Air Assault, Pathfinders, that kind of stuff.'

'Jack, how did you feel about your three years at West Point?'

'I agree with Zeus.'

'What would you have changed about your experience?'

Zeus answered. 'I don't think we needed the summer classroom work. That was a waste of time. We only got, like, two weeks off a year, that was a suck. The school year is the school year and the army specialized schools were critical. Going to Airborne school made sense, but taking military counter-terrorism and military countermeasures was a waste of time. We should have gotten more leave. We did like graduating early. Iceman missed his senior basketball season, which was a big necessary loss, but after three years, it was time to move on.'

Grace knew the importance of Jack's senior year in basketball. After three years, he had established himself enough to garner national recognition and the attention of NBA scouts. A fourth year of basketball would have jeopardized Iceman's desire and ability to be an agent. 'Jack, do you agree? Anything else you would change?'

'No, I agree with Zeus.'

Dr. Monroe was keenly aware that Iceman was not actively engaging in her efforts to open the lines of communication. Her intent in meeting with the twins was to lay a foundation to build on their individual sessions. She wanted to use the twins' strong relationship as a catalyst for her now active involvement in their development. She was specifically instructed by Zera to develop a better understanding of the twins, especially Iceman. She was surprised by how easily the twins dismissed their time at West Point. Zeus was national player of the year in rugby all three years at West Point. Iceman was a nationally ranked basketball player with NBA talent. They graduated at the top of their class in cadet scores. The cadet score tallied their scores in academics, military and athletics to build a composite cadet score. To listen to them describe their time as nothing more than grabbing ice cream impressed Grace.

'We will come back and talk a little more about your experiences at West Point later in the week. Let's move the conversation to your three years of Black Ops training. Talk to me about meeting your senior agent, Conjar.'

Zeus, as expected, spoke for the twins again. 'Rough, in the beginning, training was tough. In fairness, Conjar has always been fair and respectful. Well, not initially, but after we earned his respect, he has been great.'

'What was your favorite section of Black Ops training?'

Zeus continued to respond for the twins. 'Strangely, you people trivialized the three weeks of SEAL Hell Week. It was a mighty suck, but what a feeling after completion. We conquered three weeks rather than five days and endured hell for three years. To be clear, we had 63 days of Hell Week, not five. No offense intended.'

Grace had read the after-action reports on the twins' performance during hell week. Zeus was correct. The ruthless training experienced by SEALS during their hell week was expanded to three weeks for the twins and repeated in each of their three years of basic Black Ops training. Dr. Monroe, knowing it was futile, asked. 'How about you, Jack?'

'I agree with Zeus.'

Dr. Monroe continued her efforts to draw Iceman into the conversation. She felt comfortable with the repour established with Zeus as she wrapped up their first meeting. In a final effort, she reached for a subject she felt Iceman could not help but celebrate.

'Iceman.' She changed names in an effort to change the result. 'Back to West Point, tell me how you managed to successfully run a bootlegging operation?'

After countless reports and conversations, Dr. Monroe and Colonel Sullivan agreed that despite his many accomplishments in basketball, the classroom, training and the first mission, bootlegging was Iceman's pride and joy. The series of systems he incorporated, including the waiters in the mess hall, provided an elaborate scheme to bootleg alcohol and tailgating parties for the core of cadets was masterful. Alcohol and parties were forbidden to cadets in their first three years at West Point, but that did not stop Iceman from running an extremely profitable bootlegging operation that avoided senior cadets and officers' police efforts and lined the mess hall waiters' and twins' pockets.

Iceman's eyes betrayed him slightly. His eyes showed a smile that celebrated his pride in the secret bootlegging operation. 'I have no idea what you are talking about.'

Dr. Monroe accepted the response with a small laugh, but was even more determined to crack Iceman's defensive shield that prevented her access to his thoughts and feelings. As she was set to dismiss the twins, with the expectation of turning them over to Trinity, she received a text from Zera. *Escort the twins back to medical for physical therapy, then report to my office.*

* * *

After Dr. Monroe escorted the twins to medical and physical therapy, she returned to the Dungeon to meet with Zera.

She started. 'Hello Bill, what can I do for you? Is there a problem?'

Zera smiled. 'Grace, I believe you have some idea why I called you to my office.'

Grace had already deduced that Trinity's failure to escort the twins to her meeting was an indicator of a problem. 'I am guessing this has something to do with the twins' behavior.'

'Good guess.'

'I figured.'

'How was your meeting with them?'

'Enlightening.' Grace paused to quickly gather her thoughts and continued. 'Although identified in the reports, Zeus spoke for the twins with such force that I was taken a bit by surprise. I feel comfortable with the connection Zeus and I shared in our first meeting. He impressed me.'

'And Iceman?' Zera asked, getting to the elephant in the room.

'Iceman's behavior, I suppose can best be described as he startled me. I was impressed with his ability to put me on guard and make me feel uncomfortable. I am assuming something happened with Trinity prior to our meeting. I want to reserve my report on Iceman until I hear from you what happened.'

'That's fine.' Zera began. 'He verbally assaulted Trinity, who is deservedly upset. She expectedly ran to Duke to unload her anger with Iceman.'

Grace nodded. 'Duke came to you and used Iceman's treatment of Trinity as another example of Iceman's behavior problem. He's a loose cannon, not controllable; all the points Duke made in our meeting.'

'Correct.'

Grace paused and reflected on her meeting and Zera's report. 'What did he do exactly?'

Zera reported Iceman's behavior in accurate detail.

Grace's response took Zera by surprise. 'That's great. That's just great. Bravo.'

'Grace, forgive me if I fail to share the need to celebrate Iceman's behavior.'

'Bill, we can't have it both ways.'

'You most certainly need to explain yourself. Grace, you know how much I value you, but this. This is something that I am having difficulty understanding. I see Duke's anger as appropriate. Convince me otherwise.'

'Bill, again, we can't have it both ways. Iceman infiltrated our facility and Zeus helped him. He probed and observed. He dissected us and found Trinity. Through Trinity, he found Duke and me and our underlying assessments of the twins. Iceman's behavior, and the twins' behavior, is quite brilliant.'

'Grace…'

'Sorry, let me explain. We identified, trained and witnessed exceptional agents in the twins. When they deploy their talents, we should not be upset. Take a step back and look at what the twins have done. They walked into our domain with a stroll and we are reacting to them. Through the interrogation of Trinity, they know more about us than we know about them. We are reacting. We are on the defensive. Our Factory is scrambling, reacting, while they are just watching us, studying us. Iceman is laughing at us. We handed him all he needed with our reaction.'

Zera smiled for a moment, took a sip of water and returned to character. 'Let me understand you, they infiltrated our organization?'

'Yes.'

'Duke is not going to like this one bit.'

'No, he will not. However…'

'Grace, I already listened to you about Duke's ego; it is a problem, but he is brilliant.'

'Agreed.'

'Iceman needs to understand…'

'Bill, if I may. As an organization, if we are going to continue to believe *Iceman needs to* fill in the blanks, we are making a mistake. Iceman needs to understand, accept, do what we say and blindly accept orders; we have a problem. We need to believe and respect Iceman, then he will be our greatest asset. Does he have to respect Duke's genius? Absolutely. Does, or better said, will Duke respect Iceman? Will he listen to Iceman? It will be a tough lesson for Duke, but, as I told Tom when he was preparing to work with Iceman, he is a load. You can fight him, or you can accept him. I know where I stand.'

'You are prepared to placate Iceman.'

'No, not at all. If we do not listen to him, that is our problem, a problem we do not want. Imagine this: what if he turned against us? He believes, why give him a reason not to? Believe in him; he will give more than we could ever ask. As he likes to say, *I'll make you famous.*'

'He's worth it?'

'He is, but that is not the question that needs to be asked.'

'What is the question?'

'I am profoundly serious; Iceman must feel respected. If we do not respect and believe in him, we will pay a mighty price. What he demands is more than reasonable. He has earned it and is worth it. Take a moment to think about it, then ask yourself: do you want him as a friend or an enemy?'

'Enemy?'

'Yes, he has made it clear. He will work against us and continue to wreak enough chaos to ensure he is respected. Why are we even considering placing restrictions on him? He did not operate outside of any orders issued. In his first mission, he asked to be heard. Conjar made the decision to amend the mission. His demand to be heard and respected dates from my initial reports when we recruited him. I can confirm Conjar's report that he follows orders with tremendous commitment. His intense commitment to the mission has never been challenged, and candidly, no other agent can match his drive. He knows that he has much to offer in analytics and mission planning, and he is right. We must use his genius and not fight it. Iceman challenging Duke in a professional approach will only serve to improve the mission.'

'Grace, I am inclined to agree with you. The issue is how do we introduce Iceman into the arena of planning and architecting a mission?'

'Bill, we must go one step further. How do we build trust in our hierarchy when he changes the Op in the heat of the moment? Iceman has already proven a unique ability to absorb and dissect data in milliseconds in the heat of battle. Finding that second computer puts him in legendary status after just one mission. Bill, we need to accept that the twins are unique. Put Iceman into analytics, and Duke will have no choice but to accept his genius. Place Zeus with the hackers and watch their reception. We must set them free.'

'I agree. We need to amend their training program and build an operating theatre that supports and believes in them. What do you suggest?'

'I have strong thoughts and have already designed a special program for the twins. We have focused on Iceman, but it is the twins that have created the need to build a model that maximizes their unique abilities. While I believe Conjar is doing an excellent job, he needs support. Conjar, being young to the senior agent position, needs help, if for no other reason than to build confidence from the Factory and the Elders.'

'I like that. What are you thinking?'

'I must talk to Tom and get him involved in the twins' mission statement. Let me reach out to him and I'll get back to you. The Colonel knows the twins and they have tremendous respect for him. My hope is that this innovative approach could be duplicated if we find another team like the twins and Conjar.'

'Do you think that is likely?'

'No. They are a once-in-a-generation phenomenon. However, as they set a new standard, we can learn from the twins. They have raised the bar and our organization has a unique opportunity to build a better mouse trap.'

'I have tremendous respect for Colonel Sullivan's contributions and I am initially supportive of bringing him into the fold. How much time do you need and what do you suggest we do with the twins in the meantime?'

'If Tom is open to my idea, then I should have a plan ready for your approval by the end of business. I recommend giving the twins this afternoon and evening off. If you elect to endorse my plan with Tom, then we can meet with the twins and begin the new deal tomorrow morning.'

'End of business? We are 24/7, can you be more specific?' Zera was a stickler for detail. He never accepted general deadlines.

'1900 hours.'

'Agreed.'

CHAPTER SEVEN

After Dr. Monroe exited Zera's office, she headed to medical to brief the twins. She entered the physical therapy treatment ward expecting to find the twins struggling to keep up with the demanding therapists. Instead, she found the two of them fighting. After three years of Black Ops training, the twins continued to become proficient in the various martial arts disciplines, such as Brazilian Jiu Jitsu, Marine Corp hand to hand, Krav Magna, to achieve Bruce Lee's ultimate philosophy, total freedom. The twins used all the lessons they received to develop, with years of training, their own fighting style.

'I see physical therapy went well.' Grace shook her head as her eyes moved from the twins and settled on the head therapist. 'Donna, what is going on here? What am I watching?'

Donna was Nurse Ratched when administering physical therapy, and responded. 'They did all I asked of them and somehow managed to retain enough energy to play fight with each other. They look like kid brothers tussling over the last chicken wing.'

Grace smiled. 'And I am the frustrated mother dealing with their brotherly love. If this is play fighting, I am not sure I want to watch them fight each other without restriction.'

Iceman exited the gladiator arena and, after careful examination of Dr. Monroe, offered a charming, almost alarming smile. 'Hello Grace. What's the plan, Stan?'

Grace smiled to herself. She identified the change in Iceman's tone. He went from distant, disinterested, cold to playfully engaging. Grace was certain Iceman knew she had sided with him in her meeting with Zera. He had put events in motion. She was a little uncertain how to respond to the morning's phenomenon. She decided to trust herself and her instincts. 'Zeus, if you are looking for a sparring partner that offers you a challenge, just say the word.'

Zeus smiled and thought to himself, *Iceman got to her. We are good to go. That clever bastard, here we go.* 'Trust me, Iceman is more than enough, but thank you for the offer.'

Grace pushed Iceman's button when she responded. 'Zeus, I am here for you as needed.'

Iceman watched the exchange and elected to continue to engage with Dr. Monroe in an innocent tone. He had taken an instant liking to her and felt a need to trust her. A tremendously sexy older woman, she reminded him of Faye Dunaway in the remake of *Thomas Crown Affair* starring Pierce Brosnan. Iceman adored Brosnan for his Irish dedication to his wife and daughter in their battle with cancer as young women. A young and stunningly sexy Dunaway was more than a match for Steve McQueen in the original *Thomas Crown Affair.* Her limited role in the remake hit a keynote with Iceman. If he ever felt the need to allow freedom to express his darkness, Grace was a person he believed he could trust. Colonel Sullivan was aces in Iceman's eyes, but there was something… something magical about Grace. The name said it all. Grace, who lived the name, a special lady who dripped grace.

Iceman elected to take a chance and believe in Grace. 'Let it be said, let it be done. Zeus is special. You couldn't have better invested your lovely talents in this near-perfect subject. I, myself, will continue to muggle along and live in the mighty shadow of Zeus.'

Grace accepted Iceman's retort and those eyes, those hypnotic eyes of his. His eyes cried for her. Behind those welcoming blue eyes, that miraculously added a tint of grey when he was violent, was a cry of darkness and adventure. She had believed in Iceman for years, but those devil eyes brought her beyond any level of commitment she had ever experienced. So dark, so welcoming, very safe yet disturbing and dangerous. Danger not directed at her. The danger was alluring to his journey. He was not them. He prided himself on not being them. The common. Hitching her wagon to Iceman's journey was a complete resignation of choice. Grace had to decide in that moment to be completely committed to the twins or walk away. Iceman would never tolerate anything less than full commitment. He would hunt those that betrayed the twins. He opened the door to Grace. Her invitation to Iceman's soul came with a price. In or out? You had better be sure, because *if you are sure, you are sure*, as Iceman liked to say.

'Excuse me, correct me if I am wrong.' Iceman continued. 'Aren't you lovely to be so kind to escort us to PT and then confirm our wellness with a follow-up visit? Don't I feel the fortunate one? Aren't you so kind? How can we repay such kindness?'

Grace understood the ultimatum that was buried in Iceman's comments. 'Your successful training and first mission are thanks enough.'

Iceman smirked while Zeus observed. 'Dr. Monroe, that was yesterday. Where are you directing us now?'

Grace paused as she was taken again by Iceman's glance. 'We are in the process...'

'We? Are we speaking French? Who is we?'

Grace regretted the slip; the, *we,* was a mistake. 'Iceman, enough. I can only offer reciprocity; you must give me that which I am prepared to give to you. If you allow me to support the twins' vision, then you must take a chance on me. I will not play games with you.'

'Agreed.'

Dr. Monroe was taken aback by the simple, powerful response. 'Agreed?'

'Yes. All in.'

Grace took a moment to assess Iceman. She was rewarded with cold, warm eyes. Eyes that revealed the coldness of an assassin committed to excellence, with the warmth of a man open to her help. She had diagnosed and reported Iceman with bipolar disorder tendencies. A condition that allowed tremendous highs with sustained surges of energy that generated near superhuman results. The cost of his greatness was punishing dark moments of depression and frustration littered with crippling self-doubt. Iceman accepted his condition and celebrated it. He considered the mutant high worthy of an avenging rage that inflicted internal pain without remorse. Pain administered with such violent intent gave him joy and a sense of freedom.

Iceman studied Dr. Monroe in silence, waiting patiently. He offered an engaging story to offer Dr. Monroe a final invitation to join the twins in their journey. His thoughts ran to flirtation to further connect with Dr. Monroe and were derailed by Zeus.

'Money.' Iceman lured Zeus into the moment. 'Remember that time?'

Zeus shook his head with a look that begged Iceman to *kindly shut up. We have done enough damage, don't push it.*

Grace watched the exchange and refused the better judgment of silence. 'Iceman, I am interested in knowing all your grand moments. I have to offer, with regret and retained curiosity, a willingness to hear you out at a later date. For now, we focus on the training mission and the team.'

Iceman took the response with calm joy and *he we go*. 'Here is the thing. I'll be brief: those who are anointed king are not always worthy of wearing the crown.'

Grace understood the backdoor comment was directed at Duke. 'Iceman, I've heard it said before. *Heavy is the head that wears the crown.*'

Iceman's eyes went dark. Grey clouded the blue. 'The quote is actually, *uneasy is the head that wears a crown.'* Zeus just shook his head during Iceman's response, *more trivial knowledge, let it go.* 'I have no interest in debating Shakespeare nor do I intend to justify Duke's arrogance. If you elect to ignore my insight, that is your decision. I said anointed, not earned nor deserved. I didn't stutter, and that English accent of his, coupled with his proper journey through the best of schools since birth, built an elitist fuck. Got me?'

'I do.'

'What are you prepared to do?'

'Well done, Iceman. A Sean Connery quote from *The Untouchables.*'

'Nice catch on the quote, but you did not answer the question.' Iceman withheld being impressed with Grace's recognition of the quote.

'I am in and will be a champion to the mighty twins with one condition. You show Duke proper respect. He has earned it.'

Iceman dropped his head, took a pause as his mind rapidly processed. He looked to his shoes for answers. He raised his head to meet Grace's steely eyes and responded. 'I understand Duke's legendary ability to design an Op, but here's the thing…'

'He will listen and respect the two of you on the condition we offer Duke the same decency.'

'Roger that.'

'I will accept and believe in your commitment; let's flip the page. I have work to do and will be ready to meet with you tomorrow at 0700, having had. We will meet and discuss your new mission statement.'

Grace looked at Zeus and waited. He calmly responded. 'See you tomorrow after having had breakfast. What do we do now?'

Grace turned her attention to Iceman, who offered a nod of acceptance. 'Now that we have made a mighty commitment to each other, you have the afternoon and evening off. Go to your rooms, shower and change. I will escort you out of the building and explain how you are to return.'

Zeus nodded and asked. 'What time are we expected back?'

Grace took a moment and decided to take a chance. 'Like I said, *a mighty commitment to each other.*'

'Roger that.'

'Iceman, I very much look forward to working together, but be advised: don't take my respect offered to you as a sign of weakness. I offer you my trust with the expectation of greatness. It would be a mistake to be clever with me.' Grace settled the conversation with a wicked stare, took a moment, and, in a flash, turned her demeanor into kind and confident. 'Let's be great together.'

Iceman mumbled loud enough for Grace to hear. 'Not like you won't know where we are.'

Grace heard, as did Zeus. 'Excuse me?'

'What?'

'Iceman, what did you just say? *Where are we*? I didn't catch the whole statement.'

'Nothing. It was nothing much, really. Let's move on.'

'Iceman, I…'

'Ma'am.' Iceman quickly responded to avoid answering a direct question. Ice loathed direct questions; he answered them honestly. 'I was clear, let's move on.'

'A commitment requires trust.' Grace was not satisfied and needed to address the open issue head-on.

'Like injecting us with a chip? Always tracking us? That kind of trust?'

Grace paused; she knew the chip that gave the twins access to the building would be a problem when they left. She quickly dismissed, offering the standard response. 'Iceman, I could tell you it's nothing more than a formality, but you would quickly dismiss that. The two of you are extremely dangerous men, men we trained to be agents of death and hence our responsibility. The chip is also for your protection. We can find you if you are in mortal danger.'

Iceman took a moment to cage his rage. 'You can track us, always.'

'Yes, but that is for your protection.' Grace regretted the words as they left her mouth.

Iceman leaned back in his chair. Zeus turned to Iceman and waited. Iceman rewarded him with a look Zeus had only seen once before. On their first day at West Point, Iceman looked at Zeus with the same awe-inspiring look that demanded mutual trust with the certainty of greatness. Iceman was engaged. Not gentle, not polite, the chip injection was a problem. 'Dr. Monroe, Grace, a hell of a thing, trust. We accept the chip with the expectation of complete honesty from the Elders.'

'Absolutely.' Grace responded with a tremendous sense of relief.

Zeus gave himself a moment to reflect; *what was Iceman up to?*

'But here is the thing. It is a tricky thing; you just made us a promise.'

At that moment, Zeus knew. He just knew. The Elders had not earned Iceman's trust, but Grace had.

CHAPTER EIGHT

After Grace escorted the twins from the Factory, she returned to her office and called Colonel Sullivan.

Tom answered after the third ring. 'Hello Grace, what did the twins do?'

'Hi Tom, they assaulted the Factory to create chaos and danced with a feeling of control and freedom at our response. Iceman quickly identified Duke's tragic flaw and zeroed in.'

'Duke, predictably, was angry with the change in the mission plan. At our meetings with Duke, Iceman was not a fan of Duke's arrogance and his British accent does not help.'

'Yes, but Iceman attacked before he even met with Duke. He cracked Trinity and went on the offensive.'

Tom laughed. 'I know it is a problem, but what a great problem to have. The twins assaulted the Factory. How good do you have to be to accomplish that?'

'That's what I said to Zera, but now we need a plan. Our original plan for the twins clearly requires upgrades. We need to adjust our thought process and operating procedures to maximize the twins' talents.'

'Grace, you need to quickly construct a plan that immediately stops the twins' assault on the Factory and channels their talents back to the Elders' core mission.'

'Exactly, that's exactly what we need to do.'

'Grace, I cannot help but notice your excessive use of the plural pronoun. What do you want from me?'

'Tom, we need you to accept an early promotion to statesmen.'

Colonel Sullivan was marked a candidate to join the Elders after multiple tours as a Delta operative in Iraq and Afghanistan. He suffered spinal injuries that removed him from being a field operative. Dr. Monroe found him and identified him as a perfect fit for her team. A graduate of West Point, the Elders steered the Pentagon to send Sullivan to Duke to earn an M.S. in Quantitative Financial Economics (MQFE) and a master's in Economic Sociology. Colonel Sullivan operated in a remote basement office housed at the United States Military Academy at West Point. Tom kept a one-man office charged with leading Manpower and System Resources for the US Army. While his staff was based in Washington under the careful eye of Lt. Col. Black, Sullivan preferred to raise his daughter in the sanctity of West Point. His beautiful and lovely wife Laura felt West Point was a better place than Washington D.C., to raise their only child, Molly, age nine at the time of assignment. While the world believed Colonel Sullivan had chosen West Point as the perfect place to raise a child, the true reason behind the decision was the ability to operate without drawing attention to his clandestine work as head of US recruitment for the Elders.

Colonel Sullivan was credited with the successful recruitment and development of potentially the greatest Black Ops team in Elders' history. Greatness comes with a price, and when the twins flashed frustration, Colonel Sullivan calmed the waters.

The twins liked to joke that, given his looks and cool demeanor, Sullivan reminded them of Roger Moore's James Bond. Grace knew she needed Sullivan to be the bridge between the Factory and the twins. The Colonel was needed to support Conjar and appease the Duke. With the Colonel, Grace had a plan that she could bring to Zera.

'Grace, I have no interest in babysitting the twins.'

'Tom, you do. The term, in fairness, is a mentor, not a babysitter. You love the twins and being a part of their journey. We both know it is special. Tom, your only daughter is off to college. You can be part of something special. Your body is betraying you; the injuries you suffered as a young man have matured. You need to become a statesman and use your wisdom to help the cause. Continue to mentor the twins; it is time.'

Statesmen are deployed in less stressful and dangerous work. Statesmen are required to maintain fitness and attend continued training once a year, called rust proofing. Serving the Elders is a lifetime commitment, and after 20 years of deadly missions, becoming a statesman was a fitting reward.

'Am I afforded the same privileges as other statesmen?'

'Yes, Tom, what do you want?'

'If I were to leave my post at West Point as you suggest, I could cash in my pension and choose my own duty station. Correct?'

'In a compromised way, yes. I am going to ask the Elders to support my plan to incorporate you into the twins' Ops team. I am going to recommend they release your $10 million statesmen award early. In exchange for the exception I am offering, you will not only retire from your position, but also relocate to Austin to better support the twins.'

'Grace, you are throwing a lot at me. When do you want my answer?'

'Tom, I already have it. I wasn't asking. I was hoping. Hoping you accept this assigned mission with the same enthusiasm I am investing in the twins.'

'Austin? As I do not have a choice, I accept and make your hopes come true. I am excited to work with the twins and Conjar. I very much look forward to working with them in Austin and Barbados.'

The Elders purchased an island 45 miles northwest of Barbados as their base. The Island, as it is called, was originally a naval base used to protect merchant ships from pirates that roamed the Caribbean. With the extinction of pirates, the base was abandoned and forgotten. The Elders silently purchased the Island from Great Britain and used the Island for training and meetings. The Colonel was no fool. He parlayed his relationship with the twins into a home in Austin, a second home in Barbados and $10 million. His daughter, Molly, and wife, Laura, were certainly going to enjoy the second half of the Colonel's secret time with the Elders.

'Well done, Tom. Yes, I will request you have a second home in Barbados. Are you sure we are good with this?'

'Absolutely. Between you and I… I hate living at West Point; I did it for my bride. I much prefer Austin and Barbados and I know I would miss the twins. You have put me in a position to succeed. Thank you.'

'Tom, it is very much my pleasure. Let me get to work on Zera and then the Elders. I'll be in touch.'

* * *

While Grace was constructing her plan, the twins settled in at Tamale House.

Iceman ordered the twins ten tamales and a pitcher of Herradura Anejo margaritas to start. 'Zeus, check this shit out.' Iceman read the Tamale House's website page. 'They are just like the family we worked for in Vegas. The Lindo Michoacan restaurant. You loved the family, their history, and we did learn the shit out of street Spanish.'

Zeus reflected on their unique stop at Lindo Michoacan as part of their Black Ops basic training. The time served in the kitchen was the finishing touches to their fluency in Spanish. 'The training was perfect, and the family with their story is cool, but that kitchen was hot as hell. I could have done without doing the dishes. You loved it there. I hated the job as prep cook and dish-washer, but the family was amazing.'

'I did love it. The Vasquez family got started here in 1958, old school like the Vegas family, and back in the day served the community that was African American and Mexican American, yeah right, Mexican American, illegal.'

'Undocumented, but moving on.'

'To sum it up, the neighborhood has changed, but they haven't. Their grandkids run this place. That's cool as fuck. A real American dream.'

Iceman and Zeus made quick work of the tamales and a pitcher of margaritas in silence. The waitress returned and Iceman ordered. 'Give us four dishes that you recommend and a bucket of Negro Modella.' After he smiled at the waitress, he turned his attention back to Zeus. 'Tootsie, we need to slow our roll. Down-shift to the bucket of beers and destroy some seriously tasty food.'

'We have the night; we could head over to 6th Street and make a memory.' Zeus offered.

'6th Street is a nice opportunity to introduce ourselves to tourists and some serious University of Texas talent. 6th Street and the female Longhorns offer some beautiful babies, but we need to stay in our lane.'

'Because of Katie.'

'What? No, not at all. What the fuck are you talking about? Hear me, please. Dr. Monroe stepped up for us; we owe her. Duke is waiting for us to get fucked up, hook up with a couple of smokin honeys, and walk in cocky as motherfuckers with the stink of booze and sex. The kind of smell a shower is powerless against.'

'What's wrong with that?'

'Fuck off, you know exactly what I am saying. We're getting up at 0330; go for a run like your mother is chasing us with a rolling pin and work out.'

'She would do serious damage if she ever caught us.'

'I am fairly certain she would, but I train so I never need to find out.'

'As you would say, *roger that.*' Zeus smiled and paused. 'But you have to admit Katie ran through your head when I mentioned 6th Street.'

'Who's Katie?'

* * *

Dr. Monroe knocked on Zera's door at 0730 hours. She did not wait for him to offer to *enter*. She just walked straight in and announced. 'I have a video I must show you.'

'Knock, knock, enter? Good morning? Sound familiar? It's called civil decency.'

'Yeah, yeah. Watch this.'

'What am I looking at?' Zera asked, still distracted by the sudden interruption.

'The twins' morning.'

'Grace, the video shows 0330. I am not interested in their drunken escapade. Duke is driving me nuts and this is the last thing I need to watch. Hold on, I thought you were on their side, I thought...' Zera paused to watch the beginning of the video. 'Did they leave the complex at 0330 to go for a run?'

'Yes, and using the tracking device we injected, we marked them at five miles at a five-minute mile pace. Those big boys were moving. I will fast forward to their return to work out in the gym.'

'They throw some serious weight in an angry fashion.' Zera observed.

'You thought that was medieval; watch the next clip.'

'What am I watching?'

'Give it a minute.'

'Holy cow, is this their version of sparring? It's like watching a death match.'

'Agreed, I am going to fast forward.' Grace smiled as she found the end of the twins' sparring session.

Zera asked. 'Are they giggling? What are they doing now? Yoga?'

'Yes, they consider sparring play fighting and Conjar told them yoga was important, so they signed on. They have no interest in yoga but follow Conjar's order.'

'My, very subtle Grace; *follow Conjar's order.* Clever.'

'Yeah, yeah. Give it another minute.'

'Why?'

'Another minute, please.' Grace was fast-forwarding the tape in the interest of time.

Zera understood why Grace demanded his attention. 'Is that their average breakfast?' After studying the twins' tray, he continued. 'Is that how they look, the way they do? What is Iceman 6'5" 225 and Zeus 6'3" 235?'

'Yes, but wait.'

'Are they going back for seconds?'

'Yes. The video gets worse. They go back to the yoga room after breakfast to stretch and meditate.'

'Please shut off the video. I get it; let's move on to your plan.'

'Watch.'

'Are they going for a swim?'

'Yes, three miles, then they jog two miles at a six-minute pace to cool down. I was scheduled to meet them at 0700. Iceman wrote me a lovely note that pushed our meeting back. *We have previous engagements. Return some emails. We are training.*'

'They are sending us a clear message. They are certainly unique.'

'Yes, but Bill, their message is clear: *we are in, you better be too.* They laid down the gauntlet.'

'Give me the plan.'

Grace did.

CHAPTER NINE

After clearing customs, the twins took the escalator to baggage claim at Shannon Airport even though they had no bags. Iceman asked. 'What do we do now?'

Dr. Monroe offered the twins no explanation for their trip to Ireland. The Factory needed two weeks to prepare to execute their new plan for the twins, so the decision was made to give them a controlled leave. Even the best thought out plans have an unforeseen wrinkle.

'Do we have to go through this again? You'll figure it out. You always do.' Zeus responded.

As the twins rode down the escalator at Shannon Airport, they spotted the sign, *Conjar Consultant Group*. Ice and Zeus laughed.

'Zeus and Iceman, I am James, and I will escort you directly to Mrs. Boyle.'

Zeus asked. 'Can we skip to the chase?'

'Of course, I am taking you straight away to Mrs. Boyle's.' James expressed confidence in his response.

Iceman exhaled. 'I don't care if your name is James, Pete, or Repeat; we are going to Durty Nelly's.'

'I am sorry, sir. My orders were explicit and they included no stops. They warned me of the serious trouble…'

Iceman, bored, interrupted. 'That's lovely, but here's the thing. I am duty bound to pay tribute to the 17th-century castle guards and their patron bar. We are visiting Durty Nelly's. Skip the canned material and drive us.'

'I really can't.' James' confidence began to falter in his response.

Zeus had now grown tired of the needless banter. Iceman was going to escort Zeus to Durty Nelly's, enough said. 'Right, two hours and you're serious; move on.'

The twins enjoyed the warmth and charm of the 400-year-old pub. They toured the castle next to the pub and caught local musicians playing in the snug. They ate, enjoyed good company and conversation.

Iceman stood to leave to meet up with James when Zeus ordered another round. Iceman asked him. 'What are you doing? You made the promise that we would be back by now.'

'We have time.' When the drinks arrived, Zeus informed Iceman. 'I reached out to Katie.'

'You did what?'

'You heard me. She is just across the way. A hop, skip and jump across the British Channel, and a 90-minute flight. She will meet us when she is done with her sister next week.'

'Lad, not cool.'

'Iceman, it was incredibly cool of me. Knock it off and let me get busy doing my job being your friend. Trust me, it is hard work.'

Iceman took a sip that extended to a gulp, resulting in the termination of his beer. He motioned to the bartender, ordered another round of Guinness, and added a Jameson to the order. Katie's unexpected visit was serious business. 'Zeus, if you were going to drop this bomb on me, you should have negotiated more time at the pub.'

'I did, now lock it up; you know you are excited.'

'You think she likes me? Did she say yes?'

'Of course, just stop whatever is going through that monkey brain. I have never seen you be this type of bitch before. You are making me uncomfortable.'

The twins exited and were on their way to be greeted by Ellen Boyle.

CHAPTER TEN

Mrs. Boyle was a statesman. After successful tours as an agent and senior agent, she purchased a bed & breakfast complete with an equestrian center. The farm was in the town of Tulla, thirteen miles from Ennis, Ireland. Seamus was raised no more than 25 minutes down the road. Ten acres with mature trees surrounding the perimeter ensured a very secluded setting. The main house was approached via a long gravel driveway behind an electric gate that surrounded the property. Motion sensor lights were hidden in the trees and pressure plates were buried throughout the grounds. The lights and plates were set to avoid small animal movement. The equestrian center included a sand arena, five-box stable block and tack room, a feed shed and a pen for younger or smaller animals. Mrs. Boyle added a second barn equipped with a full gym and rehab facility and two guest cottages. Mrs. Boyle was born in County Clare and grew up with a love of horses. Her father was a well-respected horse trainer in local circles. She elected to operate a safehouse for the Elders in her position as statesman. The stable and B&B provided perfect cover for the transient agents and senior agents.

'Well, aren't you two as lovely as advertised?! Come in, but wipe your feet.' Mrs. Boyle greeted the twins.

As he began to take off his shoes, Zeus put his hand on the wall to stabilize himself after drinking. Iceman just laughed to himself. Mrs. Boyle reminded him of his godmother, a strong, tough lady who raised five kids as a widow on the South Side of Chicago. She amazingly earned a doctorate in education and was a high school principal as a single mother. She ran her household with an iron fist, inspired by her fiery red hair with a temper to match. Jack was crazy about her; she was an idol to him. He thought to himself, *here it comes*.

Mrs. Boyle looked at Zeus and stated gently but firmly. 'Would you look at himself now, putting his filthy hands on my clean walls.'

Zeus, embarrassed, apologized while Iceman just giggled internally and thought Zeus lucky, *if that were my godmother, she would have been much harsher. This was one strong lady.*

Colonel Sullivan entered the front room and added. 'Mrs. Boyle, you are correct, as always. The twins are lovely and filthy hands have no business on clean walls.'

The twins looked at each other. Iceman processed the Colonel's appearance, while Zeus greeted the Colonel. 'Good to see you, sir.'

'Surprised to see me?' Sullivan asked with delight, having surprised the twins.

Iceman smiled. 'I thought we were done with you; do we have to recycle through first grade again?'

'Typically, my journey is complete with agents after their basic training and first mission are completed. The Elders felt our unique connection warranted an extension of our time together. I believe your juvenile humor and behavior at the Factory warranted my invitation to further guide you two on your journey.'

Iceman smelled an ulterior motive. 'In what capacity?'

'I am not in your chain of command, just a vested resource for you and the Elders.' Sullivan explained.

'Checking up on me? Are you my babysitter?'

'I wouldn't say babysitter, Iceman. Consider me your guardian angel.'

Zeus entered the conversation to calm Iceman. 'That's great news. We both have tremendous respect for you. Right, Iceman?'

Iceman paused and tried to dismiss the insult he felt for having been assigned a babysitter. He clearly understood the Elders wanted the Colonel around, to parlay the respect he held for the Colonel, to control him. He relented because he did value the Colonel in his life and understood this was Grace at work. *Well played, Grace.* 'Right, this is great news.'

The Colonel nodded. 'Mrs. Boyle, please hold our late lunch; we have business to discuss. Gentlemen, follow me.' As they sat around the dining room table, the Colonel continued. 'I will meet with each of you individually, starting with Iceman. Zeus, while I am with Iceman, enjoy a conversation with Mrs. Boyle and I will be with you shortly.'

The Colonel and Iceman adjourned to the reading room. This brief conversation served to reintroduce the Colonel into Iceman's life.

The Colonel started straight away. 'Iceman, tell me about the mission.'

Iceman did in vivid detail. The brutal interrogation process that included cutting off the target's pinkie finger with a cigar cutter coupled with searing the wound with a torch lighter highlighted the mission brief.

Sullivan thanked him for the report and asked. 'Did it feel good to assassinate that loathsome target?'

'No.'

'Are you having feelings of guilt?'

'No.'

The Colonel was relieved to hear that Iceman had no feelings of joy or despair. After the mission had the chance to be processed, the last trait the Colonel wanted to observe was pleasure or undue remorse in his trainees. He was not interested in murders but, on balance, could not employ missionaries. 'Allow me to try a different approach. Now that the event has had a chance to settle in, how do you feel and be specific? Remember, it's me you are talking to. You are safe.'

Iceman paused. 'I feel like a coal miner who just finished his shift. It was a dirty job that somebody had to do and I am proud I did it well. The guy goes to the mine for his family; I went to work for families. I guess I also feel similar to a win in basketball. I never understood why guys celebrated after a victory. We did our job, that's all. We were there to win; our job was to win. Losing drove me crazy, but when we won, I simply shrugged. Pervert, that is what we named the target, was evil and needed to go down. When you factor the young girls into his behavior, an easy job becomes an afterthought. He needed to die. I did my job. What really annoyed me, though, was his arrogance. His security was a joke because he felt he was untouchable and above society. He never thought someone like me would dare knock on his door. He was wrong.'

'You believed his security was a joke?' The Colonel did not share Iceman's assessment of the four former Spetsnaz soldiers. He was pleased with the outcome, but the twins were met by a highly professional foe. The mission was deadly, most certainly not a joke, and to walk away with only minor injuries was fortunate and a testimony to their talent and training.

'Yes.'

Absorbing the simple response with a simple nod, Sullivan continued. 'How was Zeus?'

'He was great. During the planning stage, he helped the team work better together, and during the Op, he was the first man to fight. He did not hesitate. When the Op was over, he took time to process, but he has made peace with it.'

'Thank you, Iceman. Tell me about this drinking bender as an information gathering tool.' As it was decided the Colonel would become a statesman whose only mission was to monitor and continue to mentor the twins, he had to address the concern. The twins were emerging as their most talented operatives who only truly trusted the Colonel. They respected their senior agent, Conjar, but did not have the same level of faith as they had in Sullivan. He raised them at West Point and was clearly a mentor to the twins. Iceman was extremely guarded with his trust, except for Zeus. The Colonel was the Elders' best hope to monitor Iceman. He showed signs of trusting Dr Monroe. The Colonel could help facilitate that relationship.

Iceman shrugged. 'Generally speaking, society ignores people who feel they are somehow superior. The guy that brings your food, cuts your yard, drives, or cleans your boat and on and on is just ignored. I never understood that phenomenon. I was a land-scaper. My great-grandparents were of the class that is dismissed by what is considered the upper class. My great-grandparents worked hard, were good people and raised a great family. They made a better life for the next generation. How does it get better than that? What is hilarious to me is that the upper class is so arrogant and ignorant that they talk freely as if the lower class are not in the room. The upper class is somehow oblivious to their existence. A bright, observant person is cutting your yard or cleaning your boat with eyes and ears. The laborer typically only talks to other laborers for some reason. Maybe the class system, maybe fear? I don't know. A couple of drinks and a couple of laughs bring people together. In my neighborhood, we call the corner pub the poor man's country club. Your team uses all this spy shit. I just bought a couple of rounds at a couple of pubs and I get all the intel I need. I am out a few bucks. How much does your intel cost? I get to meet nice people and enjoy the day. The analysts sit in pods smaller than prison cells and chase shadows. I am good with my way.'

'If it is all the same to you, we will not be adapting your intelligence gathering strategy at a macro level. We will tolerate and accept your approach on an individual basis.'

Iceman smiled. 'In that case, where do I turn in my expense report?'

'I said tolerate and accept. I never said fund.'

The two shook hands with a smile. 'Thank you, Iceman. Wait here a minute.' The Colonel walked back to the dining room. 'Zeus, join Iceman, I will be right out.' He waited for Zeus to exit the room, then turned to Mrs. Boyle. 'How's Zeus?'

She responded, 'A lovely young man. He is in a good place. He has processed the mission and has accepted his role as an assassin. He believes in what he is doing.'

Sullivan had no further questions. 'Thank you.' He opened the door to the reading room and ordered. 'Iceman, come in here and visit with Mrs. Boyle. Zeus, stay where you are. I am coming to join you.'

The Colonel asked Zeus to summarize the operation. Zeus gave the same details as Iceman. When asked how he was feeling, Zeus answered, 'Good. The knee is fine.'

'So, I have been informed. What I am asking is, how are YOU feeling?'

Zeus dropped his head and thought for a moment. 'Obviously, we were trained to kill people and that was my first time, so I had to process it a little, but we ran a clean Op and that makes me feel good.'

'How was Iceman?'

Zeus' body and eye language immediately changed. He appeared as if he were mission-ready again. Iceman's demeanor on the mission clearly impacted him. 'I really don't know how to explain it. He was scarily settling, if that makes sense. I knew he was good, but he was amazing when the Op went from training to live. He just saw the mission and calmly executed it with dark intentions. The only way I can describe it is, I'm glad I'm on his team.'

'Thank you, Zeus. Iceman, come back in here; I just need a moment with Mrs. Boyle.'

The Colonel waited for Iceman to exit and closed the door. 'How is Iceman?'

'Charming and the reports are correct, very perceptive.'

'Yes, I know that, but how is he?'

'I haven't a clue. He is very guarded. My clever charms were powerless against him, but I had fun speaking with him.'

Sullivan stood to switch rooms and turned to Mrs. Boyle. 'We are ready to eat. If you would be so kind to excuse us, I have something to discuss with the twins.'

Mrs. Boyle smiled. 'Of course.'

After closing the door, the Colonel began. 'Conjar provided you with your legal documents. The envelope I am handing you is your alter ego. You will find a second passport, driver's license, debit card, and American Express card. In addition to all the same documents you received earlier, here are your first set of false identities. Conjar already gave you the codes to your safe deposit box in Manhattan. You will find codes for a safety deposit box here in Clare. The box here, as well as the box in Manhattan, contains three additional sets of false identities. I deposited $200k in cash in your Clare security deposit box as an additional performance and commitment bonus. We believe in you. You two will share the box. We add an identity and cash bonus to a box prior to and after each mission. As your missions take you around the world, the new safety deposit boxes will be opened with new sets of IDs and cash in each new city prior to the mission. The boxes in the field are for emergency use only. You will accumulate boxes in various cities. If problems arise, you have emergency access around the world. These boxes are never to be touched unless you have no other option.'

He waited for the information to settle in and for the twins' curiosity to be satisfied as they looked through their envelopes. Once the twins' attention returned, he continued. 'You will also find your Swiss bank account documents in your birth name. You have and will continue to receive compensation of $125,00 a year from your start date deposited into a civilian Chase checking account. Your declared salary is paid by OWL. To anyone looking, you are legitimate young forensic accountants making $125k per year employed by OWL. The remaining of your earnings, typically $500k a year, are off the books and deposited in your Swiss bank account. We have your declared salaries and we manage them for you. All your finances, including bills, taxes, retirement accounts, investments and any financial questions raised, are handled by us. I encourage you to regularly withdraw cash from your checking account to pay for your day-to-day activity. If you come across cash in the line of duty, ensure you do not stop making cash withdrawals from your account. Going a month without withdrawing cash is suspicious. When you are working as an alias, obviously, do not use your personal account during a mission. We do not want a paper trail of you in the target cities. We do all this so you can focus on your training and mission. If the mission is compromised, you are prepared to run and regroup in Austin once the danger has passed. To review, $125k in declared income, income that you use to live and keep a paper trail of your everyday life expenses. You will continue to accrue security boxes around the globe to be used in the event of an emergency. All other compensation is deposited in your Swiss account and is not to be touched without approval. We want to ensure your use of proceeds does not draw unwanted attention. I will maintain regular contact with you, and I trust you will contact me if the need arises. I am here for you; you are not alone. Understood?'

Iceman recognized that the comment was directed at him. 'Yes, I get it. Thank you.' He also appreciated that Conjar had allowed them to keep the funds from their first mission, the $350k, their secret. If possible, Ice's opinion of Conjar grew as he reflected. *There are good guys and nice guys and the two are often confused. Nice guys, pleasant and popular, fake; Iceman had no patience for. Good guys, guys who stood a post, were hard to find. Guys you could believe in, guys you went to war with.*

The Colonel nodded. 'Let's eat.'

After they enjoyed Mrs. Boyle's lunch, the twins stood to say goodbye to the Colonel.

'Gentlemen.' The Colonel started. 'I am excited to be a part of your journey. It is an honor.'

'Colonel, before you leave, any update about the human trafficking operation?' Iceman asked with a steely demeanor.

The Colonel knew the eliminated target's side business of human trafficking was a critical concern to Iceman. The Elders knew of five locations that kidnapped college students, got them hooked on drugs, and gave them as gifts to the target's most valued clients. The Elders identified the Arizona-based operation using missing person reports from several colleges in the area. Students from Arizona St., other Arizona schools and surrounding schools, including New Mexico, Utah, Nevada and southern California, go missing. They fall off the grid from their parents and families for various reasons. Because the operation preys on multiple campuses, no one school raised concern. The Elders zeroed in on the operation because the profiles of the missing students did not match a runaway. As part of the mission plan, Iceman secured a guarantee that the human trafficking operation would be terminated with prejudice. 'Iceman, we are still working through the two computers. Once we have all the data, we will take appropriate action. Don't worry. We share your sense of importance and urgency.'

Iceman nodded. 'So, in the next month or so?'

'As soon as possible. We will send a team or more as needed. We need to secure the extent of the operation; we cannot strike prematurely and miss potential targets. You understand what I am saying. The hackers will find what we need and Duke will design a plan.'

Satisfied, Iceman shook the Colonel's hand and said goodbye.

* * *

'Okay, boys, allow me to explain the rules.' Mrs. Boyle continued. 'I am your handler; you are in my keep. You will always use proper language and be proper gentlemen. You are free to enjoy yourselves for the next two weeks. You will eat right, attend to your injuries, and maintain physical conditioning. At 0900 sharp, you will report for breakfast and 2100 for supper. You have had quite a journey and you smell.' A full day of travel took a toll. The twins had to agree with Mrs. Boyle. 'I imagined you would like to enjoy a pint after a good shower as I rang your transportation. He will be here in 30 minutes, but he is bringing you back by 1800 hours tonight because it has been a long day.'

Mrs. Boyle paused to allow the twins to digest her orders. 'Boys don't test me.'

'Yes, ma'am.' The twins responded in unison.

The twins slowly walked up to the third floor, finding their rooms and a closet full of casual wardrobes. They showered and dressed.

When they were presentable, the twins walked down the staircase and Zeus asked Iceman. 'Pretty cool to see the Colonel again. Nice to have him back in our lives.'

Iceman responded. 'I guess.'

'You're just pissed off, because you think he is our babysitter.'

Iceman nodded his head. 'You mean my babysitter. And it's not just that.'

'Don't be like that. He's good people and you know you like him. He sure likes you.'

'Yeah, you're right. Let's go have some fun.' Was all Iceman could think of saying. He didn't want to upset Zeus with what he knew to be true. How Duke handled Pervert's human trafficking was a key indicator of the true nature of the Factory and the Elders. Iceman recognized the intelligence value of the trafficking centers. The flow of human traffic led to destinations that instantly became targets of interest. Iceman was confident that the Elders were aware of most, if not all, of the recipients, but the network would produce important intelligence. Iceman was concerned about the price the Elders were willing to pay for that valuable intelligence. Was using human trafficking as an intelligence gathering device acceptable to the Elders? If the answer was yes, the Elders had better prepare themselves for Iceman's reaction.

So, the twins said thank you to Mrs. Boyle, jumped in their ride and headed for town.

'Hey, James! Zeus, look, it's James.'

'Hey James.' Zeus acknowledged as he googled to find a pub. He showed Iceman the picture on his phone and went to speak but was interrupted by James.

'No, don't even waste your breath. I have deliberate instructions from Mrs. Boyle as to your destination. We go to Connors. I have to live in this town and there is no chance I am going to disobey her instructions. I'll be seeing you boys at 5:45 sharp, so you are in time for supper.'

Zeus responded. 'Thank you.'

Connors was everything a proper Irish pub was meant to be. A warm atmosphere with music and laughter set the environment for an enjoyable escape from the day's worries. In between the pints of Guinness and a shot of Jameson, Zeus asked Iceman. 'What about the men that took those girls? What do you think?'

Iceman wanted to avoid the topic with Zeus. He just stared darkly; he was not satisfied with Pervert's death. He wanted vengeance at his hand for the human traffickers. 'Let's just enjoy our pint.' But the devil was certainly exposed. Zeus knew Iceman was dark on the subject and turned back to his pint. He knew the subject was closed only for now. The twins were certainly not finished with the human traffickers.

Zeus decided to change the subject. 'What do you think of the safe house? Pretty cool cover, don't you think?'

'Yeah, and I really like Mrs. Boyle. A cool, sharp lady.'

'I'm not sure how old she is, but I wouldn't dare mess with her.' Zeus added, grateful for the slight improvement in Iceman's mood.

Iceman sat his empty beer down and motioned for another round. 'No chance I would fuck with her. She had to be one hell of an agent. I am pretty sure she could still kick our asses.'

'Absolutely.' Zeus took a drink from his Guinness and continued. 'Weird about the Colonel, you sure you're cool with it?' Zeus tried to play devil's advocate to ensure Iceman was comfortable with the Colonel's reintroduction.

'Next play.'

'Do you want to grab a snack?' Zeus asked, again changing the subject.

'Always.'

CHAPTER ELEVEN

The twins ate their potato soup and brown bread, chased with rounds of Guinness, were picked up and prepared for an early supper as instructed. They walked slowly into the house, tired from the long day of travel and the time change. They entered the living room only to find Iceman's parents and Zeus' mom waiting to greet them. Mrs. Boyle had sent the twins to the pub to set up the surprise. Unknown to the twins, Colonel Sullivan, with the help of Mrs. Boyle, with Dr. Monroe's consent, set up the reunion to remind the twins of why they joined the Elders. Sullivan knew the twins had little contact with their families during West Point and their secret Black Ops training. He set the stage for a corporate reward courtesy of OWL as a thank you for the family's patience and understanding. Sullivan knew how much the twins' foundation was built by their family. Sullivan acted as OWL's ambassador and smoothed out the confusion and concern shared by the parents about their sons. The reality behind the Colonel's actions was to reintroduce family into the twins' lives, to remind them why they fought, why they sacrificed. Both had strong connections to their families, especially Zeus with his mother. The curtain was being pulled back, because the twins needed the stability of family brought to their lives. The Colonel wanted to prevent them from feeling so isolated, so unappreciated, so used.

'Seamus, my beautiful boy, I missed you so much. Why are you walking funny?' Seamus' mam asked while giving him a hug.

'Rugby, but I am fine. Please, mam, nothing to worry about.'

Jack's hello was a bit different. While he kissed his mother on the cheek, he turned to his father and gave a tremendously strong handshake to let him know boys grow into men. With his beaten hands, courtesy of Pervert's face, the aggressive handshake exchanged with his father sent pain through Jack's body. He ignored the pain. Jack adored his father but sent the message, *I am the bad ass in the room*. His father, a marine, and while not an active marine, was always a marine. Make no mistake, his father was brilliant and while getting his hand crushed, he looked at Jack's face. He knew. When his father was informed of the cover story, he knew his son was never going to accept being a forensic accountant. He looked into his son's eyes and knew. Jack did not carry the eyes of a forensic accountant.

Jack's father asked. 'How are things at OWL? Haven't heard from you much.'

Jack looked and recognized that his father knew the twin's cover was bullshit. He simply said. 'Fine.'

'How's the back? Did surgery go well?'

Jack did not respond; he could not lie to his dad. The cover story for Jack's early departure from West Point and basketball was back surgery. Instead, he directed his attention to his mother and as charming as she was, there was a very tough lady that hid within. They just made eye contact. She looked at him and nodded. She also knew. They did not know the extent of the action required in the twins' position at OWL, but they certainly knew violence was included by the look of Jack. They were not surprised. They knew their son and tried to hide their worry.

They did their best to raise a peaceful and gentle man who would do something special. He just could not find peace, but they still held confidence that their violent and clever boy was going to do something special. They just wished and worried that he would take care of himself. He was just so fearless, they both thought to themselves.

The absurd then happened. His cousin Kelly walked in from the kitchen, and it was on. Kelly and Jack were remarkably close growing up together on the South Side of Chicago. Kelly's mother was Jack's godmother and they lived on the same street as Jack's family. They were the same age, shared the same birthday, and Jack was her protector and biggest fan. 'Well, isn't it Captain Famous? Why aren't I the fortunate one? I get to see Captain Famous in person and not just on ESPN. Just look at Mr. Madison Square Garden in all his glory. Sir, I humbly request just a moment of your most valuable time to say hello.'

When Kelly heard about the trip, she demanded an invitation.

Jack interrupted the sarcastic hello before Kelly got on a roll. While he ran from the South Side, the South Side of Chicago found him. 'So, how have you been?'

Kelly exploded. 'You must be joking. After six almost seven years, you ask how am I doing? Seven years. Seven. Count them seven. Well, I will tell you how I am doing. I went to junior college and then transferred to Loyola University of Chicago. I completed my degree in nursing and worked in the emergency room at Loyola Medical Center. I am in graduate school and will finish in the spring.' Before Iceman could congratulate her, she punched him in his sore shoulder and finished. 'I missed you. Jerk'

Mrs. Boyle interrupted. 'My nephew Danny runs a transport company. The boys met one of his drivers tonight, his younger brother James. Tomorrow, James or Danny will take you on a tour of the Ring of Kerry. You will return, clean up; supper is served promptly at 9:00. Tonight, we will eat at 7:30, because we have jet-lag travelers.'

The group nodded their understanding and returned to pleasant conversation until dinner was served. Dinner was nice but quiet because, as Ms. Boyle noticed, the group was tired. After dinner, Mary returned home, and the rest turned in for the night.

The next morning, the group began to get their sea legs. After a hearty breakfast, the group climbed into the van and toured the Ring of Kerry. As part of the tour, they drove past Jack's great-grandmother's birth home. They stopped for soup and brown bread at a local pub and pushed through the ring. Around 4:00, Jack asked the group if they could cut the tour short and head to a pub. The van agreed.

'I read about a nice pub down the road a bit and I was wondering...'

'Jack, we go to my cousin's bar, Connors. You are visiting, but I have to live in this town. We go to Connors.' After Danny's declaration, the visitors just nodded.

Seamus responded. 'We got the same message from James last night. My apologies and we didn't mean to offend.'

'None taken.'

Seamus and Jack informed the van that the twins were already familiar with the pub. The van pulled up, the crew climbed out and marched in. Pints, glasses of wine, and laughs followed. New friends were made with the assistance of Patrick, the owner, who was not in the previous evening. Patrick greeted the group as old friends and his warn charm triggered lively conversation.

Patrick turned to Jack and Seamus. 'Apologies for missing you last night. From the kind words of Mrs. Boyle, my brother, cousins and the patrons last night, I feel as if I know you well.'

He served the group not just drinks, but stories with each round. A marvelous storyteller, the group and Patrick bonded instantly. Promptly at 8:00, the van loaded up to return to the inn.

Mrs. Boyle continued to be an amazing handler as she held fast to her rules. They ate promptly at 9:00 and shared more laughter. While the tour was enjoyable, dinner was the show. Almost lost in the festive mood, Zeus saw his friend was still frequently lost in thought. He knew Iceman's crazy brain was racing to process his two worlds colliding. Seamus, Jack, and the group were beyond tired and all turned in again immediately after supper.

CHAPTER TWELVE

Jack, who never slept in, was the last to arrive for breakfast. He was just waking up, still tired, but he started to feel himself again. As he descended the stairs, he took a morning inventory of himself. His hands were still a little sore from the beating he administered on Pervert. The scabs on his back from the assault by Pervert's sex slave's spiked sex toy were healing, but still itched. He shook his head in disgust, regretfully remembering the sex slave safe room that housed the second computer. Shoulder still sore for some reason, maybe when he threw the crippled Pervert, who he had kneecapped, over his shoulder in search for the hidden computer. He was feeling better, but a new pain greeted him at the bottom of the stairs. The new pain was in his ass, care of his darling cousin Kelly.

'Good morning, Iceman. I really like your new friend.' Kelly was grinning from ear to ear.

After he mumbled shit, Jack looked up to see everyone looking back at him. 'Hi, Katie.'

Katie got up, walked over to Jack, kissed him on the cheek and whispered. 'I am so sorry, I didn't know.'

Jack looked at her confused. He obviously recognized the uniqueness of their situation, but he was happy to see her. 'This is great. I'm excited to see you, just a little surprised. I thought you were coming next week. I mean, it's great to see you, but what happened?'

'My sister's meetings in London got cut short, so work called her back to Boston. I decided to come early and surprise you.' Katie responded and Jack just smiled.

Kelly loved every minute of Jack's embarrassment. 'Iceman, is it?'

Mary smiled at her son and jumped in the fun. 'Yes Kelly, Jack is so cool, he is Iceman. My little boy, they call Zeus.'

Kelly eyeballed Seamus. 'I can see that, but Iceman? Get real. I remember this dork when he lost his two front teeth.'

Mrs. Boyle brought the room to her attention. 'I have plenty of room for all of you.'

Mary interrupted. 'Apologies, I would like to offer William and Nora to stay with me. I have plenty of room and I am just down the way, not too far. I would love the company.'

Nora answered for both Jack's parents. 'That would be lovely, thank you.'

Mary continued, 'At the risk of being forward Nora, I had the privilege of meeting your relations when Jack, or should I say Iceman, came to visit me. I am happy to pay them a visit once again.' Jack accompanied Seamus on one of his homecomings during their college years. Jack had made plans to visit his extended family that lived in Clare, and Seamus and Mary had joined him.

Nora smiled. 'We would like that very much. If it is not too much trouble?'

'None at all. I look forward to it. I had a lot of fun when we visited. What an amazing family.'

'With that settled, Jack's parents will stay with Seamus' mother, Mary.' Mrs. Boyle adjusted the group's agenda and continued. 'The two girls will stay on the second floor with me and the boys will stay in their rooms on the third floor. We meet for breakfast every morning. After breakfast, the adults will take Mary's car and have an adventure, while the kids will ride with Danny and make their own memories.' With the agenda set, they loaded up after breakfast, climbed into their assigned vehicles and were off.

Mrs. Boyle's itinerary was provided to Danny:

Day 1: Breakfast, Galway (oysters are a must), Connors, dinner with the parents.

Day 2: Breakfast, Aran Island, Connors, dinner with parents.

Day 3: Open.

Day 4: Guest departure.

Kelly was her typical prying self. As they left for Galway, Kelly was determined to get to the bottom of this mystery woman in Jack's life. She thought to herself, *what kind of girl gets picked up at an airport and decides to travel to Ireland to meet up with a guy? She seems cool, smart, and attractive; why the desperate move?* She paused and collected her thoughts. *Who am I to judge? I jumped at the first chance I could have an adventure and see Jack. I haven't seen him in forever and I jumped at it.* Kelly was very protective of Jack and continued to size up his love interest. *In fairness, maybe she was interested in seizing a unique risk-return experience. If that's the case, she picked the right guy.*

'Katie, where are you from?' Kelly started her interrogation of Katie.

'Boston.' Katie responded.

'College?' Kelly pursued.

'Boston College.'

'Family?' Kelly was relentless.

Jack turned to Zeus and mumbled. 'This is going to be a long ride.'

'An older sister and three older brothers. All played hockey at Boston College, including my sister.'

'You?' She would not stop.

Katie was experienced in this attacking style, having grown up like Jack and Kelly in a large Irish Catholic family, and more than held her ground. 'Crew.' Katie calmly responded.

Jack finally intervened. 'Kelly, enough.'

Kelly nodded. 'Not a problem, we have plenty of time to get to know each other.'

* * *

They wrapped up the tour earlier than scheduled to make extra time for their visit to Connors. Connors allowed Kelly to wash the dusty trail of touring from her lips and jumped into stories about Jack.

'Jack was not fond of going to class and could usually pull off a *Faris Bueller* and get away with it, but after his final basketball season was over, he got busted. After the season, he was done with school. He stopped caring and was ready to get out of dodge. He missed too many classes, recklessly broke his master system to miss classes undetected, and was awarded JUG. *Justice Under God* was the name used for detention in his Jesuit high school. The dean, who was also the track coach, needed a high jumper. The dean walked into the JUG room, pulled Jack, and directed him to the track. Even though he had never high jumped before, Jack was immediately the best on the team. The Dean declared, *Jack, you are our new high jumper.* So, here's the thing: I waited around to celebrate his long overdue misfortune. I saw Jack was initially bummed about track. I could see it all over his face. Then he looked up and for some reason, Jackie walked off the track with a smile. Keep in mind, I waited to celebrate that he finally got caught, then I was even more excited to hear that the dean made him run track. I couldn't wait and then I saw that fucking smile of his. You know what I mean? More of a mix between smile and smirk; it annoys the shit out of me. So, I say to him, *what the fuck?* Right? Like, how happy is he, the arrogant prick? He just nodded, holding that stupid expression, which did I mention I fucking hate, and said; *my poor attendance just became absurd attendance.* I go, *what the hell are you talking about?* He hit me back with, *the dean just gave me a free pass to miss class and all I have to do to work off JUGs is high jump, which I am being forced to do anyway. An hour on the track versus a couple classes, what do you think? I am off for lunch, off the next period and I used to have a class last period. I will show up only for tests in my first and last-period classes. I can show up late and leave early. What can he do? The school year ends on the same day as track, so I'll never have to work off all the JUGs.* Can you believe that shit? Only fuckin' Jackie. He went on to set records in class absences and still got great grades.'

The table laughed while Zeus just shook his head, knowing exactly what she was talking about.

Kelly continued. 'Wait, the story is not finished.'

Jack interrupted. 'How could it be? It was so short.'

'Shut up, Jackie.' Kelly continued. 'During lunch and afternoon periods, which he felt were optional, he rotated family houses that had nobody home because both parents worked, or he would charm his way with a stay-at-home mom and grill for himself, drink beer, and watch movies. Jackie is always soooo very clever. Such the clever one that he is.'

Again, the table erupted. Jack just shrugged and smiled at Katie. 'True story, but Kelly left out a piece. The dean figured out my scam after a couple of weeks. He was pissed and frustrated because he knew he was trapped. As punishment, he added me to the 400-meter and 100-meter relays. The 400 is a brutal event and I was forced to cut out the beer at lunch.'

Kelly added. 'You are right, I had forgotten about that. This prick won the Chicago Catholic League in the 400; he placed high in the high jump and carried his team to place in the relay.'

Jack smirked and celebrated. 'The dean was so excited the team won the Catholic League; he forgave my small indiscretions in classroom attendance and cleaned up my attendance record to show no missed classes.'

Kelly sat down her pint, shook her head and commented with resignation. 'Can you see why I hate this guy?'

Katie gave Jack a kiss and Kelly jumped in. After she set down the Guinness that she had quickly drank after she expressed her frustration and ordered. 'Please don't encourage him.'

Jack gave Kelly the finger and a 100-watt charming smile.

'Jackie, please, the powers of your smile have long lost their effect on me. Save them for Katie.' With that, Kelly gave Jack the finger and her own devilish smile.

The group loudly headed back to Mrs. Boyle's, who greeted the clan at the door. 'You are late, and the adults are waiting, but I need to ask first, did you have an enjoyable time? Wash up quickly as supper is ready.'

Dinner was lovely and Mrs. Boyle quickly caught up with the festive mood. Kelly offered the idea of playing cards after dinner. Jack suggested the group play Gin.

Seamus immediately rejected Jack's offer. 'No chance, you were banned at school from playing gin, spades and poker.'

Katie asked. 'Why was he banned from card games?'

Seamus was about to respond when Kelly cut him off. 'He always wins. A funny story about that...'

She was cut off by the table's collective, 'No.'

'Fine, I will tell you later. That's fine, no problem.' Kelly then offered. 'Bullshit. Let's play bullshit.'

Jack nodded his approval.

Kelly explained. 'Bullshit is a card game where the whole deck is dealt. When it is your turn, you can say what is in your hand, or you can bluff. The player can offer, say two 3's and anyone can call bullshit. If everyone at the table is quiet, then the player gets rid of any two cards and throws them in the community pile. The first player left with no cards is the winner. The fun starts when bullshit is called. If the player was bullshitting and gets called on it, they have to pick up the whole community of cards. If you weren't bullshitting, the player who called bullshit has to pick up the community pile.'

Everyone agreed that bullshit was the game of choice. William, being a brilliant attorney, was a hell of a bullshit player. His years of depositions and cross-examinations bred a keen eye for deceit.

On the first night, Jack won almost every hand and those he did not win, his father did. Jack read the player's micro expressions and factored his cards against the cards used when bullshit was called. The game became a battle when father and son clashed their male egos and the rest of the table became spectators to this Alpha dog struggle.

The second night of cards was quite different. After dinner, Jack's mom, Nora, directed. 'You boys sit down and get the game ready, and we'll do the dishes.'

William, Jack and Seamus looked at each other. They all knew something was up. There was no chance the ladies would let them off dish detail without something being afoot.

William mumbled. 'Boys, we are in for an interesting night.'

In the kitchen, Nora laid out the plan. 'We are going to cheat.'

Kelly exclaimed. 'I love it.'

Mary and Nora hushed. 'Shh.'

From the other room, William asked the ladies. 'Is everything alright?'

Nora responded. 'Everything is fine dear, just finishing up. Kelly was starting a new story, is all.'

To frustrate Kelly and her wonderful temper, William responded. 'Your, *shh,* is always an appropriate response to her storytelling.'

Kelly was going to respond when a look by Mrs. Boyle froze her. Mrs. Boyle then turned to Nora. 'I know I speak for all of us when I ask, how do we knock them off their mighty pedestal?'

As the group of ladies huddled up, Nora explained. 'There are more of us than them. We will have two of us sit out a hand. We will start with me and you, Ellen. Pretend to have some stuff to do around the house and peek at their cards. If you see one of them trying to BS, scratch your head. We will rotate, taking a break to not draw suspicion. Do not stare at the floaters. Just sneak a look out of the corner of your eye. Also, when playing, use a bathroom break or drink refill to peek at their cards. When you return, if you see a BS, do not call it. Shift your cards from your right hand to your left to signal to the other ladies. They will be the ones to call BS to deflect attention. If we win the first three games, we will play the fourth game clean to avoid suspicion. Okay? Got it?'

Mary smiled. 'I knew there was a reason I liked you.' Everyone nodded and to the group's delight, she continued and firmly stated with focused eyes. 'Let's get those arrogant boys.'

The game started and Mrs. Boyle was an expert at subterfuge. When Katie won the first game, the ladies were off to a fine start. The movement from the table to fetch a glass of water or respond to a quick text carried the next two games, with Kelly and Nora winning. After the third game, William rose from the table and asked the boys to help him with the dessert in the kitchen.

Once away from the celebration in the other room, and in the safety of the kitchen, William started to speak.

Zeus smiled and cut him off. 'We all know they are cheating.'

Jack asked. 'Right, they couldn't be more obvious. How do you want to call them on it?'

His father just looked at him and shook his head. 'Son, you may be the dumbest son of a bitch I have ever met. You have lost your mind. I need to school you two children in the ways of women. Do you honestly believe calling them out on cheating is a clever idea? The only way they could beat us is by cheating. Do you want them to continue to play, or if they don't play, do you think they will be pleasant? Do you suggest we call them on cheating and go back to winning? Or we decide to cheat better than them, win and rain on their parade? Listen to them. They are floating on air. Do you want to knock them back to earth? Beating them in cards is the worst idea I have ever heard. Play the game, enjoy the laughter and we will not have to face the icy blood flowing through five angry women. Mama is not happy, nobody is happy. Grab the dessert and grow up.'

The ladies went on to win and with every passing win the celebrations grew louder. Towards the end of the night, Nora subtly mouthed to her husband, *thank you*. He smiled back and blew her a kiss and mouthed back, *I love you.*

Sitting next to William, Katie caught the secret love message and smiled. She glanced at Jack, who was busy getting an earful from Kelly. Katie's mind drifted. *Who is this guy I just met? Why am I here and how did I get here?* Before focusing back on the game, she realized she more than fancied him, whoever he really was.

CHAPTER THIRTEEN

Mrs. Boyle asked the parents on the last day before departure. 'Maybe take a day of rest? Your time might be better served with some tea and the chance for the three of you to get to know each other better.'

Mary immediately replied. 'We are all set for the day. We made plans to visit William's family today, thank you.'

Nora immediately gave Jack and Seamus a kiss on the cheek. 'We are off, you kids have fun.'

The mood of the visit changed. With the adults away on their day trips, the kids began to build a tight union. After touring minor sights on the west coast of Ireland, Jack looked at Seamus. Before Jack could speak, Katie accepted Jack's unspoken offer. 'Connors for a late lunch sounds perfect.'

As the four walked into the pub with a warm reception, they took their seats and were served their usual order. Before Jack could lift his Jameson to his lips, while the Guinness was still settling, Kelly asked Katie out of nowhere, 'Brad Pitt or George Clooney?'

The game was called *Would You Rather?* And it fueled sex in the air. As expected, the sexual tension between Jack and Katie was obvious. What came as a surprise was the spark between Kelly and Seamus.

Katie immediately responded, 'George, Seamus, Eva Mendez, or Selma Hayek?'

Confused, Seamus asked. 'Who? What?' They all laughed and the question was turned to Jack, who chose Eva. He then asked Seamus. 'Rachael or Monica?' a reference to the show *Friends*.

'What are we playing? Better actor?' Seamus asked the table.

Kelly smiled above her pint. 'Not if you are doing it right. If you are doing it right, you don't have to fake it.'

Seamus caught the sexual reference and smiled as he stared at Kelly. 'Rachel, you naughty girl.'

Jack teased his guy. 'See, he is not from Mars, just from Ireland.'

The game roared on and others in the pub started to jump in, and now it was community, would *you rather?* Everyone yelled out their own choice and debates ensued.

'Paul Newman or Robert Redford?'

'Angelina Jolie or Kunis?'

'Old school, Marilyn Monroe or Jane Russell?'

'Back at you, Steve McQueen, or Sean Connery?

'Older current gentlemen, Denzel Washington or Robert Downey Jr.?'

After a few too many drinks and a few comments regarding, *would you rather,* that were beyond good taste, the four said their goodbyes. It was supper time.

After dinner and a brief game of cards, the four went to their rooms. Twenty minutes later, just as Jack was falling asleep,

Katie crawled into his bed. The girls decided to pay the guys a visit. As Katie slid into Jack's bed, Kelly was doing the same with Seamus. Any doubt Jack had about being with Katie was gone after a magical sexual encounter. As Katie spooned, 'Jack?' she asked. 'How many days of leave do you have left?'

'I have a little over a week.'

'Let's go to London.' Katie offered. She immediately felt him tense. 'Jack, it is OK, just relax.'

'I'll talk to Zeus about it.' Jack replied.

'Jack, they can travel with us, but I want you to myself.' Katie whispered.

'I'm sorry about the fooling around. I was just surprised.' If Jack had been completely forthcoming, he would have explained that the reason their intercourse was on the brief side was, because he was nervous.

Katie smiled. 'My sweet boy, it was perfect.'

'All the same, with your permission, I would like to try again.'

'Already? Yes, please.' The second encounter did not disappoint.

Katie, out of breath, told Jack. 'Wake me in the morning for round three.'

Jack just nodded and fell asleep. Throughout the night, he continued to reach over to Katie's side of the bed just to ensure she was still there.

First thing the next morning, Jack approached Mrs. Boyle to secure approval to travel with the girls to London. Mrs. Boyle approved the plan and promised to inform the Colonel. Shortly after securing approval, joined by the adults, they all enjoyed their final breakfast of the trip. After breakfast, everyone said goodbye to Mary. While Jack's parents said goodbye to Mrs. Boyle, Mary called Seamus over.

'Your father would be so proud of the man who stands before me.' She started to cry.

'Mam, I am fine.'

'Seamus, my beautiful baby boy, let me finish. I don't know what you and Jack are up to, but you just take care of yourself and him.'

'Yes, mam.'

With that, they hugged and she walked away. As she walked away, she turned over her shoulder with a knowing smile. 'Kelly is a lovely girl.'

Jack's parents said their goodbyes and William pulled him to the side. 'Whatever it is you are doing, and I will not be foolish enough to ask, but if you choose some form of special forces, dark Ops, your secret is obviously safe with me. You will remember that little boy who challenged all bullies. You have always been a deliberate man and we tried to calm the demon inside of you. The demon goes back beyond your great-grandfather and his cousin Michael when they brought troubles to England that brought freedom to Ireland. A relentless commitment to a noble-cause flows in your blood. We succeeded in helping you hide the devil you keep that you control well. You are a good man. Keep your values, but make no mistake, unleash the devil without remorse when duty calls.'

With that, they shook hands with mutual respect and not an Alpha male standoff. Jack hugged his mother, who gently stroked his cheek. In a blink, her eyes changed from soft and maternal to steel. The common observation of Jack's family was that his father was tough and his mother was sweet. Jack loved the way his mother used charm to mask the relentless resolve that hid behind her beautiful blue eyes. Jack learned to use his own striking blue eyes and charm as weapons from his mother.

'Jack, please be safe.'

'Always.'

Nora dismissed his typical cavalier response. 'I'm serious, Jack.' She stared at him briefly with laser eyes. Her eyes recast in a blink back to warm and caring. 'Katie is a special girl. Be kind.'

'I will, Mam. Thanks.'

While Jack gave his mom his final hug, William took the opportunity to chat with Katie. 'A very pleasure to meet you and get to know you. You met an incredibly special man in my son.'

'Thank you and I agree, Jack is special.' Katie smiled and gave William a goodbye hug.

William stepped back from the hug and laughed. 'He's a handful. I wish you luck.'

'Will I need it?'

'Not my business to answer that, but I think you might be just fine.'

After the goodbyes, Jack turned to the remaining three and asked. 'We have a couple of hours to kill before our flight. Head to Connors so the girls can say goodbye?' The group nodded.

They walked through the door and were greeted by Patrick. 'Would you rather Scarlet Johansson or Jessica Alba?'

The twins answered at the same time, but the vote was split. Jack took Scarlett and Seamus chose Alba. Naturally, the debate started on the walk to the table. Kelly told the boys to stop; the game was over.

Katie thanked Patrick for the round. 'Always poking the bear, Patrick.'

'That's me. I see the bags and Danny standing at his post, ready to drive to the airport, I am guessing. Heading home already?'

Kelly was the first to answer. 'No, off to London, just popping in to say see you soon.'

Patrick caught the message. 'This is not goodbye then; you will be coming back for a visit. A pleasant phrase of Mrs. Boyle's. You could do no better than her. Grand lady.'

Seamus agreed. 'The finest.'

'She's a widow, you know. Her husband, bless his soul, was from London.'

Iceman looked at Zeus. They both shared a curiosity about Mr. Boyle. After 20 years, an agent can choose other positions within the organization. *Did Mrs. Boyle marry another agent?* 'Did you know him well?' Zeus asked.

'No, when Mrs. Boyle moved to town and bought the bed and breakfast, he had already passed. As a matter of fact, he had just recently passed away. It was a training accident of some sort, as I recall. He was a proper soldier, a graduate of Sandhurst and some important unit of some sort, as the rumors tell it. Well, thanks for popping in to say goodbye. Let me fetch you another round. These drinks are on me. You have all been so kind and what loving parents you have.'

Katie thanked Patrick as Iceman stared at Zeus. Zeus nodded. They both knew Mr. and Mrs. Boyle were both agents.

CHAPTER FOURTEEN

With London calling, the twins booked first-class tickets on Air France and suites at the Savoy. As Jack pointed out to Seamus, we have all this money and a fancy trip with two great girls was as good an investment as any. Before checking into the Savoy, the four popped into the Grenadier for a couple of pints and a snack. While ordering a round, the group agreed to meet for lunch each day during the trip, but otherwise go their own way. After a little liquid courage, the twins dipped into the cash recovered from Pervert and gave each girl $2,500 to go shopping as the twins headed off to Saville Row. The twins had clothes from Mrs. Boyle, but upgrades were needed for fancy dining. They all agreed to meet at the Savoy upon completion of their shopping excursion.

The twins picked up a few additions to their casual clothes, including better shoes for the day and two suits with all the accessories for the night. They shopped in Saville Row and spent a small fortune. The salesman named Graham joked at the tailoring needs of the twins.

'Mr. Jack, you certainly have some of the longest arms we have come across and Mr. Seamus, your shoulders offer us a fine challenge.'

Jack informed Graham with regret. 'We just flew in and have a need for at least one of the suits in the next two hours. We can pick up the other suit tomorrow.'

'We will manage without any problem.' Graham responded in a pleasant tone.

Seamus shook Graham's hand. 'Thank you.'

Giving the girls extra time, the twins walked over to the pub. On the way, they passed a luggage store and walked in. They were stunned by the prices. The twins were struggling to accept their newfound bank balances, but listened to the salesman and made the required purchases. The twins agreed they would be back to training soon enough and in no need of money; the expense of a proper wardrobe was justified as they needed limited adult attire. They rationalized, *might as well buy the best.'*

As they sat at the bar eating fish and chips, Zeus asked Iceman. 'How are you going to figure this all out?'

Iceman knew Zeus was referring to the situation with the girls. Their connection and intimate relationship were clearly going to extend beyond London. Their mission with Conjar posed a mighty challenge. 'No clue.'

Zeus started to get nervous. 'We start training in a week and then we are off the grid for a year.'

'Zeus, what the fuck? You don't think I know that.' Iceman snapped.

'Sorry, I just like Kelly. Shit, I never asked you if you were cool with me being with your cousin.'

Iceman just looked at Zeus.

'Right.' Zeus continued. 'I am just going to enjoy the trip. You'll think of something you always do.'

Upon arrival at the Savoy, the twins were immediately shown to their suites and discovered their recently purchased attire and luggage delivered. All the stores on Saville Row had agreed to deliver to the Savoy, but the twins were still surprised at the noble service. The girls had already checked in, but were not in their suites.

Zeus walked over to Iceman's suite. 'Pretty impressive suite and the service is sick. This must be how the other half lives.'

Iceman laughed to himself and responded. 'I guess we are the other half now. The problem is, how long will we enjoy it.' He was clearly reminding Zeus that the fairy tale may not have a happily ever after with their short life expectancy.

The elevator chimed, the girls exited, headed to the twins and their suites. After a quick wave to the girls, Zeus turned to Iceman. 'See you at lunch.'

Jack considered carrying Katie through the threshold, but quickly dismissed it. Once they entered the suite, Jack was greeted with a tremendous welcome. After an adult conversation between the sheets, a shower and dolled up in his James Bond suit, as he called it, Jack was ready for dinner. Katie walked out from the bedroom into the living room to find Jack waiting. Jack was taken back. Katie looked stunning in her cocktail dress. They walked through the lobby and the handsome couple turned heads. They enjoyed their first meal together in an establishment without a television. The night was pure magic.

They returned to the room and made love. After their second act, Katie spooned Jack and whispered. 'I love you.'

Jack did not tense. 'I love you more.' With a pause, Jack's real life, the life a week away, invaded the dream. Jack went to sit up, but Katie held him down.

Jack settled down, went to speak about the challenges without going into detail, but Katie spoke first.

'I understand there are going to be challenges, and while I do not understand your job, I have seen your body. You are not an accountant. You tell me what you can and I will just trust you. We will find a way to be together. We are young and time is on our side. We will be great.'

Jack laid there baffled. He was not comfortable requiring reassuring words. He never let a girl invade his emotions. His flight instinct could not engage. Katie was too amazing. He nodded, took her spoon arm and pulled her closer. His mind went into hyperdrive. Sleep was not coming; his sole focus was on the search for solutions. He thought back to Katie's words: *time is on our side*. His only thought was *maybe not*.

* * *

Katie and Jack woke up early and decided to head to a local diner to grab an early breakfast, return to the hotel to shower and make their plan for the day.

As they walked to the diner, Jack offered. 'I would like to visit Churchill's bunker today if that is cool with you.'

'Sounds good.'

'There will be a line because it's Saturday, is that a problem?'

'No, not at all. We can spend time planning the rest of the day and the next couple of days.'

'Sounds good.'

They arrived at the diner after a short walk and parked themselves in a booth facing each other. They looked at the menu and ordered quickly.

'I'll have a double order of pancakes, two orders of bacon, home potatoes well done, two English muffins, a large milk and a large apple juice. Thanks.'

Katie shook her head at his continued absurd food orders. 'I'll have a half a grapefruit, oatmeal, a small orange juice and coffee, black. Thank you.'

After the waitress left, the two sat in awkward silence. Katie was concerned that this might happen. She was worried Jack regretted saying, *I love you more.* The words seemed so natural when she said, *I love you.* She hadn't planned to tell Jack. As soon as the words left her mouth, she wanted to catch them in flight and bring them back. She was surprised and delighted by Jack's response, but was concerned that he would regret saying it. She feared he would shut down and run away from her. She knew his job was a problem. Maybe their relationship was a short fairy tale, because reality had hit Jack. He did not sleep well and the other side of the bed felt cold. She was concerned the rest of the trip was going to be uncomfortable and distant, ending with Jack just vanishing. She sat and looked around the restaurant to appear occupied. The silence grew to be deafening. She decided, *fuck it, let's get it over with. I am not going to walk on eggshells.*

'*I love you, pumpkin.*'

'No fucking way.'

Before Jack continued, horror ran through Katie's stomach. She felt sick. Her fear was realized. *Jack shut her out and she pushed too fast. He was emotionally gone, what was I thinking and-*

'*I love you, honey bunny.* I was thinking the same thing. That's too funny. I totally feel like we are sitting on the set of *Pulp Fiction.* Hilarious. I love that movie. Definitely top five in my book. Unreal. *All right, everybody be cool this is a robbery!* Jack continued the dialogue.

'*Any of you fucking pricks move and I'll execute every mother-fucking last one of you.*'

They were a little too excited and their dialogue too loud that they drew the attention of the other diners. Jack smiled. 'We better keep our voices down.'

Katie was beyond relieved. 'I love that movie too.'

The food came and they continued to quote their favorite lines from the movie.

After breakfast, they decided to pop back to the room with a plan, not to make one.

As they walked into their suite, Jack tested Katie again. *I'm gonna take a piss.*' He quoted John Travolta's character, Vincent Vega, as he walked into the washroom.

Katie did not miss a beat and with her best Uma Thurman voice, she offered her line: '*That's a little bit more information than I needed, but go right ahead.*' She undressed and laid on the unmade bed and waited for Jack to return. She stayed with Pulp Fiction. '*Do you love me?*'

Jack snatched the lead and switched actors to Bruce Willis. '*Very, very much.*'

'*Butch, will you give me oral pleasure?*'

After Jack fulfilled the request, they showered together, got dressed again and headed to Churchill's Bunker. As they walked, Katie reached out to hold Jack's hand. He instinctively pulled back.

Katie, shocked, asked. 'What the fuck?'

'What?'

'I was trying to hold your hand.'

Jack looked at her, surprised and confused. 'Sorry and reached his hand out.'

'What did you think I was doing?'

'Don't know.' He wiggled his fingers and adjusted his grip.

Katie looked at him in wonder. 'Have you ever held hands before?'

Jack paused and thought. 'Last time was with my field trip buddy in second grade.'

'Ok? That's a little odd. You're good at it and we'll do this quite often.'

'Pretty sure it's because it is a perfect fit.'

'My sweet boy.'

'Don't tell anyone, it's my secret.'

'Jack, can I ask you a question?'

'You just did.'

'Funny. Have you ever had a girlfriend?'

'One, in college.'

'You ever been on a date?'

'With her, yes.'

'Not in high school? '

'No, and that is enough. I was with girls in high school. Let's move on.'

'Almost, what did you do? How did it work?'

'I don't know. I'd go to a party and a girl would come up to me and start talking. If she eventually annoyed me, which was almost every time, I would just walk away. If she didn't, I talked to her, met up at other parties and picked up where we left off. Eventually, she would annoy me and then I ignored her.'

'Annoying, like want more? Maybe she wanted to talk to you on the phone, text her back, or go on a date?'

'Yeah, that.'

'How long until they became annoying?'

'A couple of weeks.'

'Am I going to crack the couple of weeks barrier? Am I pretty special to you?'

'And then some.'

'One last question. Have you ever told a girl you love her?'

Jack stopped and stared at her. He was done with the conversation. 'No.'

'Cool. Do you want to know about me?'

'No.'

'Why not?'

'Whoever he is, he's not me.'

'Well, aren't you impressed with yourself?'

'As Kevin Costner said as Crash Davis in Bull Durham: *I'm not interested in a woman who is interested in that boy.*'

Katie paused; she was speechless for a moment and thought, *who is this guy? Who does he think he is?* She reconciled her feelings. 'You're probably right.' Jack looked at her with that smile. Kelly hated and Katie loved. 'No, you are right. Damn you, you suck.'

Jack expanded that smile into a knowing smile. Katie was briefly lightheaded when she investigated Jack's sparkly, big, electric blue eyes. He looked right through her while at the same time inviting her in.

Jack looked away and true to form, broke the intimate moment. 'Hey, let's pop into this pub. Look, they have potato soup and chicken wings.'

'Jack, it's 11 in the morning. We just ate breakfast a couple hours ago.'

'Exactly, Guinness and potato soup, mother's milk.'

'You're such a romantic.'

Jack and Katie left the pub and arrived at Churchill's bunker. While they toured, Seamus and Kelly were walking to the Tower of London. They slept in because Kelly loved London; this adventure was her first trip anywhere and she kept Seamus on the move late into the night.

'I really needed that grease.' Kelly and Seamus had just finished a big breakfast on their way to the Tower of London.

'The food was good.'

'For sure, but I ate too much.' Kelly moaned.

Seamus smiled. 'I don't think so. You burned a lot of calories last night and well into the morning. That last club was crazy.'

'Right? That DJ had the club jumpin'.'

'Pretty sure alcohol was a bigger factor than the DJ.'

Kelly laughed and agreed. 'You are probably right. Also, after midnight, you get a new wave of energy from the late-night crowd. The industry crowd joins the fun and they are the pros. The restaurant bartenders and waitstaff get tuned up at their bar after work for free. They hit like a hurricane. We just jumped the wave and had a great ride. I should know, I was in the industry to help pay for college.'

'That's a clever way to put it. We certainly rode the wave.'

Kelly rubbed her hamstrings. 'I'm sore.'

'I am a little sore too. I used muscles I didn't know existed.'

'That and we danced for over four hours.'

'True.'

'I am sore, but not hungover.'

Seamus had the same thought. 'Hard to drink and dance. Besides, we sweat it all out.'

Kelly offered her devilish grin. 'We didn't just sweat on the dancefloor.'

Seamus blushed and changed the subject as he spotted a corner market. 'Let's pop in here and grab a couple of big waters. I'm dehydrated.'

As they exited the market and continued to the Tower of London, Kelly started up again. 'What do you want to do tonight?'

'Anything but a club and dancing.'

'Why? Wait, I almost forgot; you didn't want to go last night, but I thought we had fun?'

'I don't know. I just wasn't up for it.'

Kelly disagreed. 'That's not it. You said you didn't like to dance, but you had a fun time.'

'I did.'

'Then I don't get it.'

Seamus dropped his head. 'That was my first time.'

'The first time what?'

In abrupt embarrassment, Seamus responded. 'I have never danced before.'

Kelly exploded in laughter. Seamus felt uncomfortable and humiliated at Kelly's response. He started to shut down.

'Honey, you got nothing to worry about. You can boogie.'

'Really?'

'Trust me. You can go.'

'Thanks.'

'In fact, I have an idea.' Kelly was talking more to herself than to Seamus.

'No, you don't.'

'Yes, I do. I am going to break Katie's rule and we are going to have a playdate with Jack. The four of us are going dancing.'

'He won't dance.'

'He will.' Kelly's devilish smile was back. Her grin was even more evil than before. 'I see the way he looks at her. If Katie wants to dance, Jack will dance.'

'You are excited to torment him.'

Kelly looked at Seamus like he had ten heads. 'You bet your ass I am excited. I have been waiting for this opportunity for years.'

Seamus went to speak, but Kelly cut him off. 'We are meeting at Twin Anchors at 4:00, right?'

'Yes, the pub at 4:00, then we split for dinner.'

'Perfect.'

Seamus went to respond, but was cut off again. 'I am really excited about tonight.' Kelly paused briefly. 'I am also excited about our time together this afternoon.'

'Yeah, OK.'

'If I were to try to get Jack to go dancing, he would tell me to piss off. I'll have to recruit and coach Katie, but that might not be enough. I'll have to breakout Jack's kryptonite to help Katie.'

'Jack doesn't have Kryptonite.'

'Sure, he does.'

'What is it?'

Kelly laughed. 'Like I am going to tell you. You'll tell him.'

'No, I won't.'

'If I tell you, he will absolutely find out. You won't even know what is happening. He is going to pull you aside today to follow up on us. He will want to see if I am pulled together and ready to be with you. He loves me like crazy and he'll want to make sure I am for real. He'll soften you up, all the while, he will be reading you. You'll feel comfortable and he'll notice something is up. He will subtly tighten the vice and you'll crack. I'm not saying that is exactly what is going to happen, but something like that. Once he picks up a scent that we are up to something, he will be relentless. You'll give it up without knowing it. The less you know, the better. The same with Katie. You know how he is.'

'I get it.'

'Ok, let's enjoy the Tower of London. Wait.'

'What?'

'Give me a second.'

Seamus felt a wave of panic run through him. *Give me a second?* One of Jack's favorite expressions was, *give me a minute.* The planning, the profiling. Seamus thought for a moment, *am I falling for the girl version of Jack?*

'We have a problem.'

'We?'

'Shut up, you are already in. Time. We have too much time. I can't release the kryptonite at 4:00. It will wear off. We need to fill between 4:00 and 10:00. I can release the kryptonite no earlier than 9:00, any sooner and he'll know.'

'You are being paranoid.'

'Am I? Am I really?'

'Yes.'

Kelly ignored him and returned to thinking aloud. 'I have to get Katie onboard first, but I cannot draw any suspicion. I have to wait as long as possible to bring her into the sting. We meet them at 4:00 as scheduled, but we have to break up the time. They have to go back to their hotel room, but we need a reason for them to return and not follow Katie's schedule. A break in the routine will set off every alarm bell in Jack's head.'

My God, I have fallen for the girl Jack. Wait, that is stupid. She is just excited. Right, that makes sense. She is smart and has spent a lot of time around Jack. She kind of looks like Jack. Similar blue eyes, similar light brown hair. Iceman has a shade of red in his; Kelly has blonde. They are cousins, of course they look similar. You are being ridiculous. Besides, she is not tall. He tried to return to the conversation, but failed. *She is not Jack; she is just trying to use what she knows to get him. Yes, smart and experienced, that's all it is. She is not Jack; definitely not Jack. One Jack in my life is plenty.*

Kelly began to repeat herself. 'Six hours to kill and all I have is Katie. She has to have as little time as possible with the knowledge, but I am stuck on breaking their dinner plans. Seamus, I thought I had him, but I don't think so.'

Seamus had tuned her out. He continued to struggle with Kelly not being the girl version of Jack. 'I'm sorry, what?'

'Shit, I am stuck; it was a clever idea, but it won't work. We'll just meet them at 4:00 and keep the schedule.'

'That's great news.' Seamus celebrated his release from concerns about Kelly being another Jack. Jack would never dismiss the mission, ever.

'Excuse me, that was rude.'

'Sorry, that came out wrong. You are stuck.'

'Was that supposed to be an improvement? Yes, I just said I was fucking stuck.'

Seamus spoke without a filter; it was his turn to think out loud. 'You are doing it wrong.'

'More criticism? Nice.'

'No, not at all. You are looking to yourself for answers, right?'

'Right. What's your point?'

'You don't have the answers.'

'Yes, Seamus, I am aware of that. You celebrating it is not helpful and you are making me feel shitty.'

'But you do have the answers; you are just asking the wrong questions.' Seamus paused and let the thought hang in the air. 'You need to ask, what would Jack do?'

'What would Jack do? I like it. We need to think like Jack to catch Jack.'

'We?'

'We covered that. You're in.'

'Right.'

They arrived and held hands as they walked through the Tower of London. Kelly smiled and pulled Seamus closer. She gave him a gentle embrace and kiss, then slipped her lips to Seamus' ear. 'Let's gut the bastard.'

They both laughed and Seamus asked her. 'Can we be here together in the moment and enjoy the Tower of London? After that, we will allow enough time to construct our plan.'

'I like it.'

Kelly and Seamus walked through the attraction and paused to briefly listen in on a couple of tours. As they exited, Seamus asked. 'Do we need to come back tomorrow?'

'Yep, I didn't pay attention to a thing, but I have a plan. You were right; I got lost in Jack's monkey brain and it worked.'

Seamus laughed. 'Me too. Let's compare notes.'

'After a 20-minute walk, they took a seat on a bench overlooking the Thames River and reviewed their plan.

'Ok.' Kelly started. 'We agree that we have to stick together, not let Jack separate us and pick us apart.'

'Agreed, and it is important to note that we have two targets; we have nothing without Katie. This is fun.'

'Focus. We will use 4-6:00 time to recruit Katie. We enjoy the usual day summary and laughs over drinks. I'll ask Katie to join me in the little girl's room at 5:30. I'll ensure she understands the script to meet up at 8:00 and have her ready for her alone time with him. After I flip her, we return to finish the last round, business as usual.

'What is she going to do for two hours?'

'Her job is easy; she just has to sleep with him.'

A naïve and embarrassed Zeus responded. 'Right, the obvious answer is the best choice.'

'You have to stand strong while I am in the bathroom with Katie.'

'I know what to do; I got it.'

'What are you going to do?' Kelly asked, excited with anticipation.

'Before he starts his examination, I'll ask how he feels about Katie.'

'Perfect, that will shut him right up. He never talks about feelings; you two will drink in silence.'

They left the bench and started to Twin Anchors when Kelly ran more thoughts past Seamus. 'The difficulty is changing the plan for the night at the last moment. Over the last round, Katie will have to convince Jack that she is doing him a favor. We need them back at Twin Anchors by 8:00 for pub food and laughs.'

'He'll buy it, because he likes routine and familiarity.'

'Correct, but she has to go one step further. She won't like it, but she will have to be a little needy. *Jack, the pub does sound like fun, but tomorrow has to be about us* kind of thing. After she sets the bait, she demands tomorrow's plan has only her in mind.'

'Exactly. Jack will think Katie is manipulating him to get her way and not suspect us.'

'When everything goes to plan, I will release the kryptonite at 9:00; then we have to hang on.'

Seamus was visibly shaken. 'Wait, hang on? You didn't mention a hang-on. You said dancing. What's this hang-on business?'

'Have you ever seen Jack released into the wild? Have you ever seen him go native, seen his war feathers?'

'I think so.'

'You haven't. If you have experienced him off the chain, there would be no, *I think so*. Brother, trust me, you would know. You would have answered, *yes, and what a ride.*'

Seamus elected to ignore the use of brother and replied. 'Shit, I already had quite the ride when he was apparently chained.'

'Yep. No backing out.'

'No backing out.'

They walked into Twin Anchors at 4:05 and found Jack and Katie sitting at a table. Kelly whispered to Seamus. 'He already had a whiskey and is almost done with his beer. Good start.'

Seamus approached the table and sat. 'Sorry, we're late; how long have you two been here?'

Katie looked at Jack's pint and shrugged. 'Five minutes.'

They ordered another round, talked about their day and the previous night's adventures.

'Seriously, Seamus, you were getting your groove on?' Jack was surprised and impressed.

'Yep, apparently I was good.'

Kelly set down her pint. 'You bet your ass he was good.'

Katie responded. 'Sounds like fun. I love to dance. Jack, do you like to dance?'

'Nope.'

'How embarrassing.'

Jack smiled. 'Nice Susan Sarandon line to Kevin Costner in *Bull Durham. God, I love this song.* He added a follow-up *Bull Durham* quote.

Kelly looked at Seamus with a face conveying how well things were going. 'Pretty amazing how you two are already finishing each other's thoughts.'

The beers caught up with Katie at 5:25 and she got up from the table. 'I am going to the ladies' room. Kelly, do you want to come?'

Kelly looked at Zeus again and mouthed, *perfect.* 'Yeah, sure.'

As the girls washed their hands and looked over themselves in the mirror, Kelly sold her plan to Katie.

Katie paused for a moment. 'I do want to protect my time with Jack, but the chance to go dancing is impossible to resist. I am all in. I love it.'

They exited and returned to the table. Katie started. 'This is so much fun. I love this trip and I love catching up with you guys.'

'Yeah, me too.' Jack nodded. 'One for the ditch?'

Kelly enthusiastically replied. 'Absolutely, throw in a whiskey with the beer.'

The drinks came and they all took their whiskey. 'Jack, this is fun. I have an idea. Why don't we pass on a fancy dinner tonight and just eat here?'

'Really? Katie, you made it pretty clear about our nights.' Jack was a bit suspicious of Katie's idea.

'I know, but this is fun and you really like this sort of thing.' Katie responded, setting the hook.

'What's the catch?' Jack guardedly asked.

'No catch. We can just make tomorrow extra special. Try something new.' Katie knew she had Jack's attention.

'Such as?'

'I thought, after dinner tomorrow, we could try the champagne bar; there is live jazz.' Katie knew she had hooked Jack, but could she reel him in?

'The penny drops. Do I look like a champagne and jazz kind of a guy?' Jack knew the deal was fair, but needed to add a level of drama to increase his level of acceptance. 'Alright, I am cool with that, a fair trade.'

'Thanks, Jack. There is a dance floor.' Katie offered, asking a little too much of Jack to reel her catch into the boat.

Kelly was extremely impressed. Katie had floated, dancing into the air. 'That sounds romantic.'

Seamus picked up Kelly's lead. 'Let us know how it is. Now that I am a dancer, I would be down with that another night.'

Jack shook his head at the group. 'Let's start with listening and not dancing to the music.'

* * *

The group left Twin Anchors and returned to their suites. Katie used the time wisely and shared a passionate engagement with Jack. After they had showered and dressed, they left the hotel and headed to Twin Anchors around 8:00. Kelly and Seamus arrived at 7:45 to ensure a proper table was set for their sting. Katie brought Jack right on time. The group ordered dinner and was promptly served. The girls looked at each other with disgust as they watched the boys consume their absurdly large dinner. After dinner, Jack went to order another round of beers. Kelly checked her watch to ensure it was time and looked subtly at Seamus and Katie, ready to speak, when Katie took control and launched the mission with the magic words. 'Let's have a round of Jager bombs with the beers.'

The waiter was confused with the order. 'Jager bombs?'

Kelly explained. 'Yes. In a cocktail glass, mix one shot of chilled Jägermeister with three parts Red Bull.'

The waiter nodded. 'Okay, you got it, coming right up.'

Jack looked at Katie, puzzled. 'Jager bomb? Where did that come from?'

Kelly had told Katie when they discussed the plan the importance of Jager Bombs. 'I thought we could change it up and have some fun.'

Jack, still baffled, drank his Jager bomb. Kelly looked over her glass at Zeus to convey, *hang on, here we go.* Iceman's enormous energy reserve was enhanced and sparked with the flow of heavy caffeine courtesy of Red Bull.

Kelly jumped in and fed the momentum of the moment. 'Let's play, *would you rather?'*

Katie immediately endorsed Kelly's idea. 'Absolutely.'

Seamus was confused, but he followed the girl's lead. What Seamus didn't know was Kelly let Katie in on Jack's kryptonite. Caffeine from the Red Bull and primal sexual urges from, *would you rather,* took Jack to another place.

Kelly started. 'J. Lo. or Beyonce?' The night was on.

Kelly knew they couldn't individually keep up with Jack, so they took turns taking him to the bar to talk to him privately over another bomb. They each had rehearsed their individual conversations with Jack.

Katie: *we are really going to enjoy tomorrow night.*

Seamus: *tell me about tomorrow night. If it doesn't suck, I think I will take Kelly.*

Kelly: *I really like Katie. She is perfect for you.*

When the group hit their pinnacle and Kelly knew Jack was primed, she looked over at Seamus, who promptly asked for the check. Katie was ready. 'I have an idea…'

Jack cut in. 'Where do you want to go dancing?' He looked across the table at Kelly and Seamus. 'Back to the club you two went to last night?'

The three conspirators were stunned. Jack just smiled.

Katie was first. 'Really, are you serious?'

'Yep.'

Seamus followed. 'How?'

'I knew something was up when Katie played the part of needy girlfriend. Kelly, when you made eye contact with Katie after she ordered the Jager bombs. Get me tuned up, fueled up with sex in the air courtesy of, *would you rather*, the subtle dancing comments, you two went dancing last night; there is more, but do I really need to explain? Elementary.'

Katie anxiously asked. 'So, you will go? You played along to get ready, right?'

'Right.'

Kelly asked. 'You're not mad?'

'No, flattered.' With that, Jack got up and walked to the bar. He ordered two Jager bombs for himself and turned to the table, raised his glasses and drank both.

Kelly turned to the table. 'We are in trouble. He's not mad or flattered. He is excited to make us pay.'

They arrived at the club. Jack paid the cover and headed straight for the bar.

Seamus took a deep breath and muttered. 'We are in big trouble.'

Kelly answered. 'He's off the leash. Let's go. This is going to be a night for future stories.'

As they approached Jack at the bar, Katie asked the two of them. 'Have either of you ever seen him dance?'

Both Kelly and Seamus shook their heads.

Katie continued. 'Maybe he can't dance?' They all just looked at each other. 'Right, he probably can dance.'

Jack walked with his James Bond stalk, grabbed Katie and hurried her to the dance floor. He yelled. 'Let's light this fuse.'

Kelly dropped her head and turned to Seamus. 'We're fucked, he is on fire. Let's go, baby. As Ernie Banks said, *let's play two.* Last night was just the warmup. Here comes the real hurricane.'

'Who's Earnie Banks?'

'A famous Chicago baseball player. Never mind that, grab your dancing shoes and thirst. We will be hungover tomorrow, but tonight we ride.'

'I can't believe he got us.' Zeus commented with wonder.

'Maybe… the night is still young.' Kelly responded suspiciously.

'Maybe? What is that supposed to mean?'

'Shut up and dance.'

Jack looked deadly serious into Katie's eyes and switched character lines. 'Mrs. Mia Wallace, *now I wanna dance. I wanna win. I want that trophy, so dance good.'*

'Mr. Vincent Vega, I do believe that is my line.' She joined Jack in the Jack Rabbit's twist dance scene.

Kelly slapped Seamus on the shoulder. 'Would you look at those two straight out of Pulp Fiction? Fucking Jack looks like John Travolta and she looks like Uma Thurman.'

Seamus agreed. 'They can dance, I mean really dance. I guess all questions about Jack's dance talent have been answered.'

'Yes, Seamus, I can see that. Come on, let's get our game on.' Kelly was fiercely competitive and no one brought it out more than Jack. She was determined not to be shown up on the dancefloor. Granted, he was pretty badass at other things, but the dancefloor was hers. She summoned the powers of Zeus to show Jack up on the dancefloor.

They danced, danced and danced some more. They switched partners, only took breaks to hit the bar and use the restroom.

Jack was a relentless force of energy; he refused to pity the other three.

As they walked out of the club, still laughing and full of sweat, Jack thanked the group. 'Your efforts were worth it. That was great. Nice effort trying to get me.'

Kelly spoke up. 'You think so?'

'Yep.'

'You're just too good.'

'Apparently.'

'Too smart for us.'

Jack paused, knowing Kelly was up to something, but he wasn't sure what. 'Where are you going with this?' Jack, Seamus and Katie were confused and concerned that Kelly was angry. This was not part of the plan.

'Seamus told me he loved me today.'

Jack was speechless.

Before he could recover Katie piled on. 'That's nice, Kelly, but Jack told me he loved me more when I told him I loved him.'

Seamus was stunned, but Kelly's and Katie's laughter broke him out of it. He looked at a wounded Jack and just cracked up.

Jack's face was emotionless as he approached Kelly. He gave her a hug and whispered. 'I am so proud of you.'

'I got you.'

'You did.'

Katie asked. 'How did you do it?'

'I took Seamus' advice and put myself into that crazy brain. Trust me, it wasn't pleasant. I knew love was his kryptonite, not caffeine and sex, but I had to hide it.'

Seamus interrupted. 'You used Katie and me.'

'Absolutely. Misdirection, right, Jack? You thought Katie was playing you to go to the champagne bar. You thought caffeine was the big play. You thought dancing was an effort to get you. You had it all figured out.'

'I underestimated you.'

'You sure did.'

'Enjoy it, it won't happen again.' Jack laughed and hugged his cousin again.

'No control over love, right Jack? Don't you hate it? Doesn't that warm, fuzzy feeling just eat at you?' Kelly stayed in character, but the others were laughing.

'Well played.'

* * *

The next morning, Jack's voice woke Katie. He was speaking with room service, wheeled in and set up breakfast at the edge of the bed.

'With how much you eat, I'm surprised they got it all on one cart.' Katie's joke was interrupted by a knock at the door. *Here is the rest of your order, sir.*

'Just leave the cart in the hall. I'll grab it.' Jack walked in carrying two additional dishes. 'You were saying?'

'Amazing. What do you want to do today before we drink champagne?'

* * *

As Jack and Katie ate, Kelly and Zeus laid in bed.

'You know, I never said I love you.'

Kelly rolled over and laid her head on his chest. 'I know, but it was good for the operation. Besides, you don't have to say it, I know.'

'Kelly, I love you.'

'Goose, you big stud. Take me to bed or lose me forever.'

'Who's Goose?'

'It's from Top Gun, the movie? Never mind, just make love to me.'

* * *

The next day, Katie and Jack just walked, stopped at sights and talked. Jack kept waiting for Katie to be not so great. The opposite happened. The more she talked, the more he was amazed by her. They met Seamus and Kelly at the pub for lunch and a recap of the morning's events. After lunch, the group split up and were off again.

As Katie and Jack walked toward Knotting Hill, Katie slipped her hand into Jack's and they just kept talking. Katie's wonder washed over Jack. He never felt so special and he didn't even know this feeling existed. He played in Madison Square Garden and achieved much in his short life, but this was different, strange. They took a pause from their walk, stopped for a pint and Jack just stared at her with glossy, confused eyes. They headed back to the room, celebrated each other's company in bed, showered, got fancy and headed to a late dinner. Jack's feeling of euphoria carried him to enjoy jazz, champagne and dancing.

* * *

The trip continued with the same vigor until the time came to say goodbye. They rode to the airport in silent resignation. The boys boxed all the purchases they had made in London and shipped them to Seamus' mam. They packed the clothes they had brought from Ireland. The group exited the cab and did not have time to stop at the airport bar. The girls' flight was a couple of hours ahead of the guys. The twins escorted the girls to security and said goodbye.

Katie hugged, kissed Jack and whispered. 'Everything is going to work out.'

Jack's eyes turned so very cold to the point of making Katie uncomfortable and he deliberately responded. 'I know.' He was lost in thought, worried about their future, when he responded. He realized he had scared Katie and returned to the moment. 'Sorry, let me try again.' He repeated the response. 'I know.' The second response came with the softest, bluest eyes and a warm smile.

Seamus told Kelly. 'This will work.'

Kelly kissed him. 'Of course it will. We got this.'

After the girls boarded, the twins headed off to their gate and Jack asked Seamus. 'Do you want to get hammered? We have 90 minutes.'

'Yes.'

The girls flew to Boston together and Katie waited with Kelly for her connecting flight to Chicago. After exiting the aircraft, Kelly asked if she could buy Katie a drink. After the drinks were delivered, Kelly started. 'Now is when I must warn you about Jack. I really like you and love you two together, so let me apologize in advance for being too forward. I have seen too many girls think they are in a relationship with Jack, but what they fail to realize is he is closed for business. He has never let anyone in. He has been amazing to me, his parents, family and friends, but he has never let anyone in. He can make you feel so warm without giving up his emotions. You think he is emotionally connected, but he is not. He loves me and I have tried to crack his shell, but it is impossible. I cannot begin to describe this trip to you. Finding love for the first time, meeting you and watching Jack. He loves Seamus and would do anything for him, including dying for him. I don't know their job exactly, but he would die for him. That's who Jack is and that did not surprise me. Here is the thing: you broke in. Seamus broke in. I finally broke in. We are the first people other than himself that he trusts. He is never vulnerable, but he is with you. He will go dark at times and when that happens, just give him space. He will come back to you. You have no idea how great a guy you have. He can be a lot of work at times, but he is worth it.'

'I heard that about him.'

'His mother?'

'Father.' Katie answered and they both laughed.

'Wait until you meet my mom, his godmother. Jack can do nothing wrong in her eyes. It's so annoying. He is nuts about you. Right now, before he reports back, he is solving how you two will work given his work challenges.'

Katie interrupted. 'I think it started last night. He didn't move and there was an energy coming from him.'

Kelly continued and nodded. 'Make no mistake, he will go dark until he has you two figured out. I guarantee you he is obsessing right now over your relationship. When he calls, and he will, it will be magic.'

'Thank you.'

'I'm not finished. Whatever you do, do not disrespect him. Love is his kryptonite, but disrespect is his tsunami.'

* * *

The twins waited for their flight in silence over the first round and then Seamus ordered a second. Seamus waited for the second round to be served and offered. 'Let's celebrate the past week and the future ahead of us rather than focusing on the goodbye.'

Jack was gone and Iceman was back. 'Roger that.'

Zeus and Iceman destroyed the second round and Iceman joked. 'Kind of nice not to need a cougar to buy our drinks and turkey sandwich.' They laughed and while the laughs continued, Zeus saw that far-off look in Iceman's eyes. He was problem-solving while managing to stay in the moment.'

On the flight, the party continued. Danny was there to pick them up when they landed.

'Hi Danny, how have you been?' Iceman asked as they loaded the truck.

As they pulled away, Iceman stated firmly. 'Connors.'

Danny replied. 'No, I have instructions to take you back to the Inn.'

Iceman coldly whispered. 'Connors and I won't say it again.'

Danny looked back at the two monsters sitting in the back. They stared through him. 'Ok, Connors, it is.'

Iceman responded. 'Thank you. Pick us up at 8:30 so we make dinner at 9.'

The bar erupted when the twins walked in, and the fun was on.

Patrick cried out. 'Would you rather Megan Fox or Margot Robbie?'

Jack answered Robbie and Seamus chose Fox. The debate swept through the bar.

Patrick served the usual. 'Good to have you back. Where are the girls?'

'Back to America.' Seamus responded.

'How about you two, staying for a while?'

Seamus answered. 'No, we head back tomorrow.'

'Thanks for stopping in. Hope you come back soon.'

'You can count on it.' Jack shook Pat's hand to seal the commitment.

* * *

The boys returned to the Inn and were greeted by Mrs. Boyle, who was prepared to scold the twins for the stop at Connors until she saw their faces. She saw broken hearts. 'Go upstairs, put your clothes away, ensure you are proper for dinner by 2100. Whatever you are feeling ends. Do not bring that emotion to my dinner table.'

The twins nodded and did as they were told.

After becoming proper, the twins approached the dinner table. They saw Conjar. 'Come, sit down.' The twins did as instructed and Conjar continued. 'I understand we have an issue.' He was referring to Katie and Kelly. 'Will this issue be a problem or a distraction?'

In unison, the twins responded. 'No.'

Conjar stared at them both. 'You disobeyed an order. You stopped at the pub when you were instructed to report to the Inn.'

Iceman was not in the mood. 'Conjar, with all due respect, we do not take orders from Danny. We followed our standing order and reported for dinner. We are at our post and will stand tall at 0530.'

Conjar saw the resolve in the twins and felt the rage in Iceman. He thought back to the profiles done on Iceman. He will be our most fierce warrior and the twins our finest team, but they require a measure of consideration. The first mission proved the report accurate. Iceman will have no trouble with wartime. The report continued that he would have trouble with peace time. Conjar decided the twins were simply transitioning back to warriors. 'Let's eat. We fly out tomorrow at 0900.'

Zeus asked. 'Back to Austin?'

'Yes. Now, get back to our world, moment over.'

CHAPTER FIFTEEN

The twins and Conjar exited the Elders Gulfstream G500. The flight from Shannon to JFK was quiet, with the twins preferring to eat, drink their beer, watch movies and sleep. They wanted to delay their return to the Elders. JFK was Conjar's final destination. He was set for a much-deserved extended leave.

As Conjar escorted the twins to the main terminal and their American Airlines flight to Austin, he pulled the twins to the side. 'Are you two ready to play nice?'

Zeus answered for the twins. 'Yes, we get it and understand. You and the Colonel have been clear, we accept and agree.'

'Iceman?'

'Yes, we were heard and that is appreciated. We are good soldiers.'

'Alright then, safe travels and continued success in your training.'

* * *

When they landed in Austin and exited the airport, they were again greeted by Robert. Robert drove the twins straight to the Factory. Because they made the promise to Conjar and the Colonel to play nice, the twins passed on their usual demand to stop at a pub.

As they exited the elevator to the Dungeon, Zeus turned to Iceman. Before Zeus could speak, Iceman held up his hand. 'I got it.'

The twins got the message and transitioned to greeting Trinity.

'Gentlemen, welcome back. Nice to see you again.'

Iceman held his smirk; *she is so full of shit. Duke hasn't changed his tune; he is just playing the long con. Two can play that game.* 'Nice to be seen. What's the game plan?'

'Your medical exam identified areas of concern. Zeus, you are scheduled for arthroscopic surgery on your left knee and Iceman, you are being scoped on your right shoulder. Tomorrow at 0630, I will drive you to Dell Seton Medical Center at the University of Texas. The procedure requires general anesthesia, so you cannot eat after 1900.'

Zeus asked. 'Got it. How long will our hospital visit last?'

'The surgery should take around two hours, but given the damage, it may last longer. Your recovery due to anesthesia should run for another two hours. You should be discharged around 1400.'

Iceman nodded. 'Sounds good. What's on the docket for the rest of today?'

'I'll show you to your rooms and you are free to go out and get something to eat. You are expected back no later than 1900. Relax and grab some sleep, but I remind you, no food after 1900.'

Iceman gave Trinity his mighty smile. 'Alright, sounds like a plan. Do you want to join us? If not, can we bring you anything back? We are grabbing either Mexican or BBQ, any preference?'

Trinity was taken aback by Iceman's engaging smile and kind offer. 'Thank you, but no. I am all set for dinner.'

Iceman replied. 'Not a problem, anything for a teammate, right? We can find our rooms without a problem, and I assure you, we will be back by 1900.'

'Thank you, Iceman. If there is nothing else, I will see you in the morning.'

Zeus, surprised, looked at Iceman, who feigned confusion and responded. 'What? Told you I was good to go. Let's go eat.'

* * *

As the twins made their way to exit the Factory, they waved at the two agents who staffed the front desk. A fair number of the Factory's staff were Ronin agents. Agents and senior agents were identified as Ronins if they lost a team member. Named in tribute to the feudal Japanese samurai who traveled to offer his service, Elders' Ronins searched for a team. Those stationed at the Factory may have lost their ability to be in the field, but were extremely valuable to the Elders, especially in analytics. The Ronin agents at the Factory rotated shifts through front desk security and Duke's staff to assist him in his duties as the architect. They gathered the intel from the nerd heard in analytics and investments and did deep dives for Duke to develop the Black Ops mission plans. Their boot on the ground experience, coupled with their advanced education, made the Ronin agents a critical resource for Duke. After passing the front desk, the twins approached the Closet. The Closet was a 10'x10' bulletproof glass space with two doors. One door allowed entry and exit into the Factory and a second door allowed entry and exit to the street. The closet was similar to dramatically enhanced airport security with a biometric scanner. Duke's Ronins rotated six-hour shifts in front desk security followed by six hours of analytics with 12 hours off, six days a week.

After exiting the Factory, the twins walked one looping mile to ensure they were not being followed before securing an Uber to take them to their destination. They followed the same routine on the return trip.

After following security protocols, the twins settled in at Tamale House. Iceman ordered a pitcher of their favorite margaritas and chorizo sausage nachos to start.

After their order was served and the twins were alone, Zeus asked. 'What are your thoughts about Trinity? She was much cooler to us the second time around. She was obviously also briefed to change her tune.'

'It was all bullshit, an act. There wasn't a sincere bone in her body. Duke briefed her to play a different character, but her role and mission are the same. Pretend to be respectful, but at the same time, stuff a file with all of our shortcomings. She is nothing more than a mole.'

'What are we, by that I mean you, going to do about it?'

'Flip her.'

'Flip her?'

'Yes, flip her to our side. She is brainwashed by Duke. He manipulates and uses her to get what he wants, which includes the bedroom. She is doing her best to play her role, and she is fairly good at it, but I see right through her. She is an easy read. At her core, she is a good person. She is gullible to the cause and the greatness of Duke. She is lonely and insecure; Duke uses her fundamental decency to manipulate her. Duke is a fuck stain.'

'You really don't like him.'

'Zeus, that is a tremendous understatement. I hate him with an evil passion. I know the type. He enjoys using his power and status to bully people. You know how much I hate bullies, especially when directed at women or girls. I'll give him credit; he is exceptionally good at it. He has Zera fooled, but I see right through that piece of fuck.'

'What about Dr Monroe?'

'What about her?'

'What do you think she thinks of Duke?'

'She gets it, not as much as she should, but she gets it. She is in a tough spot because he is good at his job, plus the Elders and Zera think highly of him.'

'So, what are you going to do to flip Trinity?'

'You mean, what are we going to do to flip her? We are going to be sincere. We are going to be honest. We are going to be beyond amazing to her. In short, we are going to be ourselves. Once she spends time with us, she will become a believer. Once she is a believer and comes over to our side, Duke will go ballistic. Taking on Duke will be like a balancing scale. On one side of the scale, you have Duke, who has a 50 lbs. weight, tipping the scale in his favor. We walk in after training and our first mission, and we have 10 lbs. on our side. There is no 40 lbs. weight we can drop to balance the scale. We just have to add one, two, five-pound weights through little victories to our side of the scale. Witnessing us being our badass selves just accumulates to our side of the scale in small increments. The scale won't move in the beginning. Six pounds added after an especially good day, followed by two pounds; the continued application of pressure our greatness produces will, in time, balance the scale and eventually tip it in our favor. We will never show our hand to our objective to expose Duke. We will just continue to be a relentless force. He is most certainly in my crosshairs, but we cannot rush. This is a long play, not a short one. Got me?'

'I do.'

Iceman waived the waiter over. 'We'll take two of your steak specials and one of the seafood combination platters. Might as well throw in a bucket of Modelo Negro and more chips and salsa while we wait. Thanks.'

Iceman again waited for the waiter to move away before he addressed Zeus. 'About our mission, while I have you away from the Factory, I want to talk to you about something. After we are done with our surgery, we will be split up for our advanced training at the Factory. I will be placed in analytics and investments and you will be assigned to research and development.'

'Makes sense, given our backgrounds. Together, we will make a damn good forensic audit team.'

'Agreed. Here is what I want from you; I want you to identify the best hacker, the best of the bunch.'

'Alright. For what?'

'Recruitment. Just as we are recruiting Trinity to team Collins and just as we are recruiting Grace. W…'

'You are recruiting Trinity and you recruited Grace?'

'You were there when we recruited Grace. Now shut up and listen. You never know when we will need a hacker that is better than even you. Consider the recruitment of the hacker as an insurance policy or an umbrella for a rainy day.'

'Is this one of those plans you answer with *just trust me, I'll explain later* to all my questions.'

'Yes, moving on, our food is on the way.'

* * *

The next morning, the twins were greeted pleasantly by Trinity, who drove them to the hospital. After the procedure, which ran for almost three hours, because the damage was more than expected, the twins exited the hospital at 1500 hours. Iceman's body did not react well to anesthesia. He spent the first two hours of recovery vomiting. As they exited, they were surprised to see Trinity parked curbside, ready to chauffeur the twins back to the Factory.

Zeus smiled. 'Hello, we were expecting Robert?'

Iceman added. 'What a nice surprise.'

Trinity responded. 'Anything for a teammate, right?'

Iceman laughed. 'You are stealing my material, but yes, correct.'

Trinity asked. 'How are you two feeling?'

Zeus answered. 'Fine, no problems.'

Trinity grabbed Zeus' crutches as he prepared to enter the front seat and asked. 'How long are you on sticks?'

'They're all yours. The brace is enough; I'll never use those again.' Zeus responded, dismissing just how invasive his procedure was.

Iceman jumped into the back of Trinity's Grand Cherokee; he gave up the shotgun because he wanted to give Zeus more space to stretch his leg. After closing the backdoor, he removed his sling, threw it with Zeus' crutches, then turned his attention to Trinity. 'We really appreciate you picking us up and all, but here is the thing: we…'

'I know, I know. You somehow always convince your drivers to make an unauthorized stop at a pub.'

Iceman shrugged. 'Unauthorized is a strong word. I think amended is the proper word.'

'Iceman, save your breath. I was already told to take you where you wanted to go on the condition you stay for only two hours.'

Zeus nodded. 'Thank you.'

Iceman wanted to ask who had authorized the stop but promised to play nice. He turned to his charm instead. 'First, you were authorized to take us for three hours, but instructed to try for two.'

'That's true.'

'So, three it is. As you blew us off yesterday, will you kindly join us today?'

'I don't think so.'

'I believe you said you would join us next time when you shot us down yesterday. Right now is the next time.'

'Hang on, Iceman, I don't think I said that.' Trinity answered truthfully.

'Zeus?'

'Pretty sure you did.'

'Besides, you cannot leave us alone. We could have a medical emergency.' Trinity simply shook her head in defeat. Iceman clapped his hands together. 'Great, then it is settled. Mexican or BBQ?'

'What did you two have yesterday?'

Iceman thought *like you don't know.* 'That wasn't the question and it doesn't matter to us. You pick.'

'Anything?'

'Yes, between the two choices.' Iceman smiled as he delivered Trinity with her options.

'You are nothing if not flexible, Iceman.' Trinity teased.

'It's been said. I am guessing Mexican.'

'You guessed correctly.'

The Grand Cherokee parked and the three entered Tamale House. The same waiter from yesterday, Tony, approached the same table and asked. 'A pitcher of margaritas and chorizo nachos to start?'

Iceman laughed. 'How did you know? Three glasses, please.'

Trinity spoke up. 'None for me, I am driving.'

'No, you're not, don't be silly. Robert and another guy can pick us up and drive your car back or drop you off or whatever. You're in. It'll be fun. You do have fun, right?'

'Yes, Iceman, I know how to have fun.'

'Great, then it is settled. You are in good hands; Zeus and I excel at fun.'

As they casually sat around the tall boy's table, Trinity was hypnotized by the twins' machine gun banter. Iceman had a way of telling stories that made her feel like she had lived the experience. He caught her with a joke twice in mid-sip that caused her to spray a little of her drink out of her mouth. He made her ability to be funny somehow funnier. He casually primed her stories and framed them in such a way that humor was produced. She laughed so hard during the three hours that her sides hurt. She found Iceman's self-deprecating humor refreshing. He was always the star of the story, but some twist of fate always made him the brunt of the joke. She easily felt the genuine love the twins shared for each other; it was magical. Simply put, she felt comfortable and enjoyed their company. She felt safe being herself in the company of the twins.

As Iceman worked his magic, he used his humor to mask his careful study of the Trinity. After 20 minutes of scrutiny, he decided he just liked her. She was a good person. Fuck Duck, he was never Duke. Halfway through lunch, Iceman decided to be Trinity's self-appointed protector. She was now a part of the twins' tribe. The days of her being used were ending. Iceman vowed the twins would eventually set Trinity free.

CHAPTER SIXTEEN

The twins spent their first three weeks of advanced training at the Factory performing forensic audits on previous Elders' examinations of targeted businesses for investment. Unknown to the twins at the time of their audit, the targeted businesses were rejected due to revelations found during the examination. The test for the twins was to examine the business, find misconduct and document any concerns in their report. During this period, the twins attacked their physical therapy and recovered from their surgeries well ahead of schedule. The twins also spent considerable time with Dr. Monroe during those first three weeks.

At the conclusion of their first phase of Factory training, Zera asked Dr. Monroe and Lori Segal, the director of analysis and investments, to join him in his office. Duke heard of the meeting and requested to be included, but Zera denied his request. Duke's responsibilities did not extend into Segal's and Dr. Monroe's areas of expertise. Duke's request was viewed by Zera as his own fact-finding crusade to fuel his concerns about the twins. The unique and unwarranted request raised warning flags for Zera and Dr. Monroe. Duke was threatening his own credibility to effectively evaluate the twins. Zera was disappointed with the request and made his feelings known to Duke.

'Good morning, ladies.'

Dr. Monroe and Segal acknowledged the greeting and Segal spoke first. 'How can I be helpful today? I have not had a chance to complete my report on the twins but expect to have it ready in two days' time.'

Zera waved his hand. 'That's fine, Lori. And the same goes for you, Grace. I will be traveling for the next two weeks and wanted a chance to hear about the twins' progress before I go. I will read the reports when you have them ready, but I am satisfied for now with just talking through their status. Are the two of you prepared to speak about the twins?'

Lori again spoke first. 'I am more than prepared and happy to get started.' Zera and Monroe smiled and nodded, so Lori began: 'My report is very straightforward. They are exceptional. With very little guidance, the twins attacked their first project. They split the demands of the project and worked incredibly well together. They are amazingly hardworking and efficient. Zeus used his computer expertise to gather all the data, no matter how hidden and deliver it to Iceman in a usable presentation. Just as fast as Zeus gathered the data, Iceman interpreted the data and made requests for more. Iceman steered Zeus' ensuing data dives, instructing him where to look for, as he calls it, the dead *bodies.'*

Zera lightly chuckled. 'Iceman can be colorful.'

'Most certainly. The twins took one week to deliver their report. The original fully functional team took two weeks.'

'Impressive.'

'Very. Even more impressive when you consider they unearthed more financial concerns than the original report.'

'I see, half the time and a more detailed report.' Zera paused and thought for a moment. 'How did you react to their first report?'

'I challenged them with the second file. A complex business that did well to bury hidden liabilities and overvalued assets.'

'And?'

'Again, please keep in mind we had to replace our first team on the project with our absolute best team due to the complexities. The twins turned in the report in two weeks. Our total time commitment between the two original forensic teams was six weeks. The twins again found everything and additional issues that were not identified. The second audit will be the focus of my full report.'

'Ok, I think I have heard enough. Let's graduate the twins to stage II of their training at the Factory, unless you have any questions or concerns, Grace.'

'I do have a couple of questions. How were they with the other members of your department?'

'They did not have much interaction. They worked alone and did not ask any questions. Just worked hard to execute their projects. I will say they were exceedingly popular. When they pulled their heads up for air, they lit up the department; they made quite the impact.'

'Second question, how were they at taking orders and instructions?'

'Not an issue. They listened attentively to the project summary including expectations. They went about the work and turned in the reports as identified above. When we challenged their findings, the twins were gracious and replied with respect. I often experience defensive behavior from new teams. Black Ops agents typically dismiss the importance of forensic accounting in their training, but the twins understood the need and value of their work. They enjoyed being challenged. They used it to show off a little. They know they are good, but do not have an ounce of arrogance. They are an enjoyable pair to have on assignment.'

'That is settled. Grace, what do you have for us?' Zera asked. He needed to keep the meeting on schedule. He had a full day scheduled.

'Before we transition to my report, I have something to offer the two of you.' Grace had promised Iceman to deliver his message and request. 'Iceman believes this place is like a morgue. He was thinking of kicking off a Friday happy hour. He believes the twins and a couple of guests from your team have earned the reward.'

Bill nodded. 'I assume you are in favor of this, given you have raised the issue.'

Grace answered. 'I am. I like the idea of a team-building exercise between diverse groups. Lori, what do you think?'

'I like the idea.'

Bill turned his attention with a deliberate look directed at Grace. 'Have you run this past Duke?'

'I have not.' Before Bill could respond, Grace turned to Lori. 'Thank you for your report, Lori. I have a better understanding of the twins. Well done.'

Lori understood. Grace gently told her to leave. 'Bill, if there is nothing else?'

Zera took the cue as well. 'No, nothing. Well done. I'll follow up with you when I return from my trip and had the chance to study your report. Well done.'

Dr. Monroe waited for Lori to exit before she started. 'I hope you understand. As you know, Iceman is a unique case and…'

Zera held up his hand in a motion to convince Grace to stop. 'I more than understand. Our conversations about the twins should most certainly stay between just the two of us. Before we get started on the twins, I must ask you about Duke. What is your takeaway from him asking, almost demanding, to be included in our meeting today?'

'Disappointing, extremely disappointing. His desire to be included was a clear power play to regain the twins' narrative. He feels pressured because of the twins' outstanding performance during their time at the Factory. He has paid no mind to your words about working with and respecting the twins. Their ever-growing popularity is a source of further frustration to Duke. Every person that has encountered the twins reports nothing but good things.'

'I regret having to agree with you. What is it about the twins that drives him to be so irrational? He is the most rational man I have ever known.'

'Control. Bill, Duke has always been in control. He is in control of himself, the mission plans, the people around him, and especially, the people that work below his pay grade. He expects to be in total control. The twins, especially Iceman, are not going to be controlled. The twins will be under control in their actions, but not controlled or dominated by another person. Tom works with them well, because he listens to the twins and incorporates their brilliant thoughts into his decisions. The twins do not demand control; they follow orders. They just want a voice that will be respected.'

'Yes, Grace, you are onto something. Duke is a terrible listener. He can, at times, bully his message through. His mission plans are usually so good that, in hindsight, I may have perceived his bullying as passion. I am going to pay close attention to Duke's behavior.'

'I do have something to add. It is the type of thing that reveals just how cunning the twins are. They play goofballs at times, but make no mistake, they are calculated operatives.'

'Continue.'

'After their surgery, the twins took Trinity out to lunch. She became smitten with the twins, especially Iceman.'

'How does that impact Duke? The obvious answer would be that Trinity is just another fool, falling under the twins' mystic spell.'

'Bill, Duke's relationship goes deeper than that. Duke was the object of Trinity's infatuation. He used and controlled Trinity, including relations.'

'Sexual?'

'Yes. During Iceman's assault on Trinity during their first hours here, he identified the relationship. The relationship went unnoticed until I read Duke's report about the twins, which included his interview with Trinity. I studied his report, paid close attention to the tone and discovered a controlling intimacy. The romance has probably ended, but Iceman was correct.'

'Now, Iceman is using Trinity and Duke is upset?'

'No, to the contrary, Iceman genuinely believes in Trinity. He, through kind words and gentle whispers of support, has built Trinity's confidence level. She is no longer completely subservient to Duke. She is respectful, but no longer blindly defers to Duke. She stands her ground. I am certain Duke is even more furious at Iceman given the Trinity turn of events.'

'I hadn't realized Duke was so manipulative. An egomaniac, certainly, but this kind of behavior is very disappointing. How did we miss it?'

'That's not the question we need to be asking ourselves.'

'What question should we be asking?'

'How did Iceman see in hours that we had missed for years?'

'I see your point. How do you think we should proceed?'

'Give it time to play out. Iceman was a shock to Duke's system. Give Duke time to digest. Iceman is clearly managing the arrangement. Let's give Duke a chance to play catch up.'

'Agreed. Let's return to the subject of the twins.'

'Before I begin, I must disclose some conversations with Iceman must remain confidential, just between he and I. Iceman was the first agent to ask me if his conversations were reported to others. I explained my responsibility to share my reports with a very select group. He nodded that he understood, then completely shut down. We eventually compromised, and I was forced to accept, *off the record,* conversations. By making that small concession, Iceman opened up. If he used the exception, but I felt compelled to report it, I agreed to inform him ahead of time. He approved and understood. Additionally, he identified you to have full access and disclosure without restriction or permission.'

'I am obviously not a fan of this special *off the record* business, but I have full confidence in you. I appreciate and value being included by Iceman in full reporting. I trust your judgment, Grace, and I know you will put the good of the Elders first.'

'I understand.'

'How often has he used the exception?'

'He hasn't. He takes comfort in just having it there. He understands, as he likes to put it, *no one is bigger than the tribe.'*

Zera smiled. 'I like that.'

'Iceman lives it.'

'Just another aspect: Duke is blind due to his tunnel vision towards Iceman. I approve Iceman's idea of a happy hour and will handle Duke.'

The two were silent for a moment as they paused to reflect. Grace broke the silence. 'Let me begin with Zeus. I am happy to report that he and I have built a nice rapport. He is open and engaging. He is comfortable in his deadly role with the Elders. He relayed that he was a bit shaken after their first mission and admitted to having some nightmares. The nightmares ended after his first night in Ireland and have not returned. He confided that he enjoyed our weekly sessions and requested video sessions as needed when he was away from the Factory. He is in a good place and we are in a good place.'

'Good to hear. You have said it in past meetings, and you are correct. Much attention gets paid to Iceman, but the twins are truly a two-man team. Speaking of Iceman.'

'Yes, he will take a bit longer. As you know, I met with him, as required, twice a week. He requested two double sessions, because our sessions were running over. I was surprised after I made the exception by just how open he was. He holds nothing back and is blessed with a keen sense of self. I was pleased and stunned at his openness regarding sensitive subjects. I openly introduced my observations regarding his bipolar tendencies. After I explained the symptoms of the condition, he quickly agreed and wanted to learn more about the subject. In addition to our sessions, Iceman has conducted significant research to learn all he could about bipolar. While he did not know of any mental health conditions, let alone bipolar, he explained he knew he had the symptoms starting at age 12. To his amazing credit, he worked independently on solutions. He acknowledged having amazing highs that allow him to perform with super energy for prolonged periods of time. His highs fuel his greatness and he views them as his superpower. He is just learning to adjust to the cosmic end of the high. The euphoria he feels can push him to take on dangerous risks, because he feels invincible. He openly discusses his depressed periods, calling them crippling. He does not refer to the period as depressed, but to it as *going dark*. Initially, I thought the expression was a romantic term he used as a defense mechanism. I challenged him on it, and he, and I quote, replied: *Imagine waking up in the middle of a pitch-black tunnel. Look back, or the past and all you see is dark. Then, look forward to the future to see the same darkness. Continue to imagine that you don't know which way is back and which way is forward. Does that sound romantic?'*

'Wow.'

'Yes. He manages the darkness through great achievement. Running from the darkness motivates and pushes him. He is quite literally afraid of the dark. He is overwhelmingly motivated by fear of failure.'

'Amazing work, Grace.'

'Thank you, but I must add that he is also afraid of euphoria. He was never afraid of the cosmic highs before Zeus. He knew the cosmic highs were an incredible ride, but dangerous. The only person that paid the price for his reckless behavior during his supernova was him and it was worth it. With Zeus in his life now, there is someone else to get hurt. He adjusted at West Point, specifically listening to Zeus' valuable insight and guidance. In their roles as Black Ops agents, he carries the burden that hurt now translates to possible death. We talk about what an amazing team we have in the twins, but that love, and mutual respect, transcends special.'

'I should say so. I am beyond relieved and feel safe with my confidence in the twins. As I said above, when I cited you, Zeus is just as much a part of the twins as Iceman.'

'As Iceman fancies to say. *Roger that.*'

CHAPTER SEVENTEEN

Iceman made the command decision to add Fogo de Chão to the twins' restaurant rotation. Fogo de Chão, located in downtown Austin, offered a change of scenery. The Brazilian steakhouse prepared and presented a limitless amount of food to build an enjoyable churrasco experience. The quality of the meals was only surpassed by the value created by the twins' amazing food consumption. The market table brought a bottomless reserve of the highest quality meat, chicken and pork. For an additional charge, the twins added two seafood dishes to share. Once the meats were seared, the gauchos made their way around to continuously serve the patrons. The set price of $59.95 was steep. The twins followed Iceman's order and rejected the Feijoada Bar loaded with side dishes to include aged cheese, exotic vegetables and a full salad bar for a $14.95 upsell that wasted calories much needed for more meat. The price, given the amount of food the twins consumed, made their Thursday night visits a bargain.

As the twins were shown their table for their inaugural visit, Iceman reminded Zeus. 'Remember, no bread, no carbs, no wasted calories. That's where they get you. We are here to destroy and enjoy the endless river of meat.'

'Ice, I got it each and every time you have drilled the message into me. I got it.'

The first gaucho brought a skewer of filet mignon, the second brought beef ancho (ribeye) and the third lombo (pork). The twins made quick work of their first serving and were greeted with a second serving that consisted of medalhões com bacon (bacon-wrapped chicken and steak), cordeiro (beef ribs) and linguiça (spicy pork sausage).

After their fourth serving, which included the seafood dishes, the twins took a breath and Iceman commented. 'I knew the hackers and research had mad skills, but the data generated by the team's manipulation of that crazy software is absurd.'

Zeus finished his bite of the filet and added. 'I know my shit, but yeah, they're damn good. I am working hard to close the gap. What amazes me is the depth of the analysts' knowledge of their terrain. All that data could be overwhelming, but analysts' ability to work through the blizzard of data to find the core issues is impressive. The software the Elders run to dissect the data is beyond amazing.'

'Agreed.' Iceman elected to remain silent about his skill level. The analysts were incredibly good, Iceman was better. 'Are you set for tomorrow's late happy hour? Who are you inviting?'

'I have two from the dork squad ready to go. You?'

'Just bring one. I've got Trinity plus a decent enough chick from analytics; did you ask the supreme hacker?' Iceman had asked Zeus to identify the most talented hacker.

'I did, but she declined.'

'That's good. We should probably herd her from the group and keep our blossoming relationship private.'

Zeus paused, allowed the gauchos to fill their plates and asked. 'Iceman, she didn't seem interested. She doesn't engage with the others; she is private. Is there a plan B?'

'No, she is perfect. The fact that she is private is all the better. I'll land her.'

After several more servings and beers to wash down their feast, Zeus paid and the twins headed for the exit. As the twins approached the exit, the team of gauchos applauded and exclaimed. 'Bravo, bravo, bravo.'

Iceman turned to face the applause and gave a slight bow. 'See you next Thursday.'

CHAPTER EIGHTEEN

Friday at 1540, Zeus and Iceman arrived at Tamale House and were greeted by their usual server, Tony. 'Hello, gentlemen, welcome back. Is there a change in plans?'

'Hi, Tony. Zeus shook his hand. 'Same plan and the girls will be joining us shortly. They wanted to freshen up after work.'

'Fine, very good. I set up your usual spot and added a table as requested. I will bring you the usual while you wait for the ladies.'

Iceman thanked Tony as he took his spot next to the window.

Tony arrived with a pitcher of Herradura Anejo margaritas on the rocks with chips and salsa. Iceman asked Tony. 'Please hold off on the chorizo nachos for 10 minutes so the girls can enjoy a taste. After they are situated, can you bring us an order of queso compuesto with extra chips, wait 25 minutes and bring a tamale plate and taco plate for the table to share? After 30 minutes, bring us two orders of enchiladas. Bring a sample of everything, beef, chicken, whatever for the tamale, taco and enchilada orders. Thanks.'

'Sir, you do not have table space for such a large order. Maybe I submit one of the orders every 15 minutes or so?'

'I like that, thanks Tony.'

'My pleasure.' Tony nodded and headed for the kitchen.

After pouring the margaritas, Zeus commented. 'That Tony is a really cool guy.'

'Good people.'

After the twins enjoyed their first round of margaritas and chips, the nachos arrived. Shortly thereafter, the ladies arrived just as planned. The ladies took their seats and introductions were made. Another pitcher of margaritas arrived with more chips and salsa, with the addition of spicy guacamole.

Iceman was impressed with the ladies' appearance. They each took the time to change out of their work clothes and dress for a Friday night of fun. What struck Iceman the most was Trinity. She looked good. She wore a short sleeveless floral sundress with boots and a cowgirl hat. Having only seen Trinity in stuffy office attire with her hair pulled back, Iceman was delightfully impressed with the transformation. The sleeveless dress displayed her tanned, toned arms and the short dress provided a clear view of her amazing legs. Trinity was a looker. Who knew?

As Zeus poured, Patti crinkled her nose. 'I'm not much of a margarita drinker. I think I will stick to beer.' Iceman gave her a look over the rim of his glass, which made Patti feel uncomfortable. She asked him. 'What?'

Iceman smiled, and Patti's face relaxed. 'Nothing, it's nothing. Don't worry, there will be plenty of time for beer. Zeus and I have a firm policy of only two margaritas for guests.' What Iceman did not explain was the margarita's recipe. Two shots of tequila, one shot of Cointreau and one shot of freshly squeezed lime juice. The delightful recipe masks the power of the margarita. The cold drink was so smooth, with a lemonade-like taste, that it went down too easy. Two margaritas at Tamale House and the effects were immediate.

Trinity asked. 'How *many* are the twins afforded in this policy of yours?'

Iceman responded. 'Mind your Ps and Qs.'

Zeus shook his head and warned the group. 'Here it comes, worthless knowledge.'

Iceman ignored Zeus. 'Ps and Qs? Anyone? *Bueller? Bueller?* No? Alright then, in Ireland, sometime in the 1600s, the barkeep ran tabs on a chalk board behind the bar. The patron's name was column one, pints was column two, and quarts column three. The reason and application of my fabulous lesson is Trinity. Busy-bodies, nosy people and gossips would glance at the board with judgment. *So, that's how many he has had, my, my.* The innocent patron, some would identify as a victim, would declare, *mind yourself, mind your Ps and Qs,* pints and quarts. *I'll worry about myself just fine, thank you very much and concern yourself with your own affairs.*'

The table laughed and Iceman continued. 'Alright, drinks are served. Tony just cleared the nachos and brought queso compuesto. We got our first laugh out of the way; time for proper introductions. A little life summary if you please.'

Iceman turned his attention across the tallboy table and smiled at Patti. 'You're up.'

'Hello, I'm Patricia, everyone calls me Patti. I am from Massena, Iowa, about an hour outside of Des Moines. I attended Iowa St. for undergraduate and graduate school, Masters of Science in Computer Science with a focus on AI. I had a double major in college. I am fluent in Spanish. I was accepted and enrolled into the Foundation for a Better Tomorrow scholarship program, which I later found out was run by the Elders. I joined OWL after graduation and worked in the New York office in research. I joined the Factory five years later and I have been here ever since.'

Iceman nodded and asked. 'Nice, thank you. So, what makes you so special that you were identified and targeted?'

'Nothing much, really. I worked the farm and was really good at school.'

'Are you sure that's it? There's more spill it.' Zeus challenged Patti for more details.

'Alright, my dad got really sick and I ran the farm for four years while my older brother studied agriculture at Iowa St. He came back to run the farm while I was away at school. My dad is feeling much better but is still weak. My brother runs the farm full time.'

Iceman raised his glass. 'That sounds more like it. Very impressive. Do you have a special someone in your life?'

'Yes, a serious boyfriend. We will be engaged soon.'

Trinity asked. 'Who chose to wait on the engagement?'

'I did.'

'How do you explain your job to him and your family?' Zeus asked, thinking about his own relationship with Kelly.

'I use our cover story. I was and continue to be paid by OWL. They just think I relocated.' Pati answered.

Iceman passed the queso compuesto, encouraging the ladies to eat. They needed food in their bellies to help manage their margarita intake and the tamales were coming soon. 'Zeus, you're up.'

'I am from Ireland, was recruited into the program and I like to play rugby.'

Iceman nodded. 'Thanks, Zeus.'

The girls were passive in their response to Zeus' brief bio. A couple may have mumbled, 'Yeah, thanks, Zeus.' and simply drank their margaritas.

Trinity followed. 'Yes, thanks, Zeus.'

As Iceman studied the group the tamale plates were delivered. Iceman's radar was up. *There was no chance the girls would ever accept Zeus' weak response. They had to have something planned, they were up to something. He knew their leader was Trinity, the assistant to the architect and the person who knew the most of the guests at the table. She was up to something.*

Trinity noticed Iceman's stare in her direction, casually smiled and looked away. 'You're up.'

'Hello, I am Fawn.' She paused to take a sip of her margarita for courage. 'I am from a small town you have never heard of outside of Albuquerque, New Mexico. My heritage is a mix, half white, half Native American.'

Iceman interrupted. 'What tribe?'

'Apache.'

'*Your enemy,* nice.'

Fawn was surprised by Iceman's knowledge of Native American culture. 'That's right, one translation of Apache is *your enemy.*' After a momentary pause to regather herself, Fawn continued. 'I am a rodeo girl. My father is a ranch wrangler and my mother is a trail guide. I grew up a part of a large horse farm and ranch. I am proud to be an NHSFR World Champion Cowgirl.'

Zeus asked. 'NHSFR?'

'National High School Finals Rodeo, it is the *World's Largest Rodeo.*' Fawn offered with immense pride.

Trinity spoke for the table. 'Holy shit, how cool is that?'

'Yeah, it's a pretty big deal. I also majored in history and English; my Master's degree is in Latin American Studies.'

Zeus set down his margarita to respond, 'I should say: that is a pretty big deal.'

Trinity, who had now taken over the lead, turned to Iceman. 'You're up, Cowboy.'

'Funny. Hello, I am Iceman. I am from the South Side of Chicago. I met Zeus in college and we were roommates.'

The three ladies again made subtle eye contact with each other. Iceman knew the twins were coming under the microscope; the girls were about to launch their plan. He thought to himself, *good luck with that. Bring it, you little girls.*

Trinity started. 'Where were you two roommates?'

Iceman stared at Trinity. 'We are not going there.'

Patti spoke up, to Iceman's surprise. 'Jack Collins, we all know you went to West Point with Zeus. You were a big basketball star and Seamus was a superstar rugby player. What we don't know is why you two are called the twins.'

Zeus and Iceman made eye contact, and Zeus spoke first. 'You are already read in on us.'

Iceman added. 'You ask questions to which you already have answers. Trinity is clearly read in and you all have access to data. You are a professional researcher and analyst, for fuck sake. Stop being clever, it doesn't suit you.'

Patti refused to back down. 'Yeah, yeah, we know all about you. The question still stands: *why are you two called twins?*'

Iceman finished his margarita, poured himself another, smiled at Patti and answered. 'Fair enough, you are correct. We got the nickname on our first day at West Point, as a joke. Both named Collins, but with vastly unusual backgrounds, obviously, including race, twins was funny and it stuck. The interesting thing about the nickname is, while funny on the surface, it became accurate in short order. We are closer than twin brothers could ever be.'

The ladies were taken aback by the candor and power of Iceman's response. They had a plan all laid out to get to know the twins better. They wanted to be in the know and hold the answer to the secret of just who the mighty twins were. They expected to be the talk of their cubicle colony. Iceman left them speechless.

All except Trinity, who was determined to dig further. 'Why do you two get such special treatment?'

Iceman gave Trinity a very dark stare and quietly responded. 'You have no idea what you are talking about. Leave it alone.'

Trinity was forced to suppress the series of questions she had prepared for the twins. *Why does Iceman get to wear jeans to the office? Why were the twins awarded special leave to Ireland? Why do they get to do whatever they want? Why are they in control?*

After the intense exchange between Iceman and Trinity, *the get-to-know-you* game was over before Trinity's turn. Zeus broke the tension using his unique ability to keep a group together. 'Now, I know you three don't look this good for happy hour. Any big plans for the night?'

Patti and Fawn felt relief and Patti answered. 'We are having a girl's night out. We are catching up with a few other girls from analytics and assaulting 6th Ave.'

Iceman paid particular attention to Trinity's reaction. *She wasn't invited.*

The table's mood continued to lighten with the arrival of a bucket of Modelo Negro and enchiladas. The group came together over great food, atmosphere and lively conversation.

The experiences the group shared with each other built a trust and comfort level between themselves.

As the group said their goodbyes after the very happy hour, Iceman made eye contact with Zeus, who understood. 'Zeus, why don't you jump this ride with Pattie and Fawn? Trinity and I will pay the check and catch up with you later.'

Zeus nodded his consent and escorted the girls to the Uber, while Iceman turned his attention to Trinity. 'You and me kid. Let's grab a seat at the bar and make a plan.'

'A plan for what?'

'Us, silly. You got plans for the next couple of hours?'

'Well...'

'That's shitty water. You have plans now.'

'I do?'

'Yeah, you got me. I really haven't been to the Red River District. Want to show me around?'

Trinity paused, uncertain, asking herself, *why is Iceman making an effort with me? What is he up to? What does he want from me? What...*

'Get out of your head, we are going to have some serious fun. Simple. Knock it off, enjoy your beer while we make a plan.'

They finished their beer and took an Uber to Red River. Red River was the base camp for *keeping Austin weird*. Home to great live music, the historical area boasts a true Austin experience at its finest. Trinity and Iceman bounced around the hot spots, enjoying the music and each other's company.

'When I first met you, I thought you were a real jerk.'

'I was, but calling me a real jerk is putting it lightly.' Iceman smirked and continued. 'I was a dick, but in all fairness, you made it awfully easy, trying to be all hardcore and shit.'

'I was just doing my job. I do it very well, thank you very much.'

'Fuck off, don't tell me for a second you treated us like the other new Black Ops agents. I am not going to relive Duke's bullshit. We've moved past that, clean slate. Cool?'

'Very, so which Iceman are you? The guy from our first meeting or the guy sitting with me now?'

'Let's revisit the concept of a clean slate.'

'Right, sorry.'

'It's cool, I am an acquired taste. Having said that, I don't waste my time. I only invest it in worthy people. Time is my most valued resource. Why waste it?'

'Can I ask you a question?'

'You just did… sure.'

'Why me?'

'I like you.'

'That's it? Just that simple? You don't feel sorry for me?'

'For what? Not having plans tonight? I didn't either.'

'Thanks.' Trinity responded, slightly embarrassed. She wanted to give Iceman a better response, but was lost for words.

'I am here just to be here. I am not looking to hook up and I am not working an angle. I am just here having some fun. I am safe, you'll see.'

Trinity, feeling a bit confident, asked. 'Want another beer?'

'Yep.'

Trinity excused herself to use the ladies' room. Iceman walked to the bar to grab the beers and waited for Trinity to return to ask. 'Quick question: what happened in Black Ops?'

Trinity choked on her beer; Iceman had waited for that moment to ask his question. 'Excuse me?'

Iceman silently waited for Trinity to continue.

'How did you know?'

'Dad in the military?' Iceman asked, keeping Trinity off guard.

'Yes, a retired admiral. How did you know about my dad?'

'It's what I do. Your real name is not Trinity; it is your code name. You had to have some affiliation to Black Ops to have a code name.'

'I was in Black Ops.'

'It didn't go well. You have a bitterness towards Black Ops, but at the same time, an envious manner about you.'

'During training, I hurt my back during a night jump. My back required surgery, and as I was not far enough along in Black Ops training, I was rotated out. I was sent to graduate school and groomed to be the perfect assistant to the architect.'

'I can see that, but why the bitterness? People get hurt, it happens, and now you have a cool job. You are pretty much a Ronin.'

'Yeah, I know. Thanks for the comment about being a Ronin. I have never thought about it like that.'

Iceman broke the conversation for the moment and enjoyed the music with his thoughts focused on Trinity.

They enjoyed their silence as the band finished their set. When the band took their break, Trinity set down her beer, leaned in towards Iceman and confided in him. 'Nobody knows this and I can't believe I am telling you this: it wasn't just medical; I healed up just fine and was ready to cycle back in when I got shot down.'

Iceman cracked several peanut shells while he waited for Trinity to continue. He gave Trinity a handful of peanuts and asked. 'Trinity, what is your name?'

'Alicia.'

'Nice to meet you, Alicia. I am Iceman.'

'Fuck you, Jack. Jerk.'

'Dick, remember. Want to tell me the rest of your Black Ops story?'

'Why not?! I am pretty sure I was bounced because of my dad. First, let me start by saying, he doesn't know anything about the Elders. He was never a fan of me training in special Ops and when I had back surgery he was done. He started asking questions about my training and he struck a nerve. The easiest way to shut him up was to rotate me out of Black Ops and herd me into OWL and a support position. I know I would have made a great Black Ops agent.'

'I totally agree, but here is the thing: while I don't know exactly what you do, you are doing bad ass shit.'

'I am a glorified office manager.'

Iceman knew Trinity did more than order staples for the office, but he elected to shelve the discussion for another day. Telling Iceman her story, Trinity felt a release.

'Your turn.'

Trinity was still lost in thought. 'I'm sorry?'

'Trinity, I asked you a delicate question. You were wonderfully open; it is only fair for you to ask me something. I am not going to leave you hanging from an emotional cliff like that.'

'Thanks, that's really cool. I was serious when I asked you earlier: why do you and Zeus get special treatment?'

'We don't get special treatment. We follow the same training program as everyone else. We just do it faster and better. We have earned the respect that is given to us.'

Trinity had more questions. She found Iceman fascinating, but didn't want to overstep the invitation. She wanted future invitations, but didn't want to ruin their fun by asking too many questions. They continued their exploration of the Red River with vibrant success. As the night wore on, Trinity became concerned with the time.

'This has been a great time. Thank you, Iceman.'

'Yeah, for sure, I'll be right back. Taking a piss and grabbing us another beer.'

'Wait…'

'Shut up. Don't even think about calling it a night. The night is young and we are having too much fun. Give it one more hour, just 60 tiny little minutes.'

'Alright.' Trinity smiled to herself as Iceman left. She was having a great time, but was worried that Iceman was done with her. She was elated that he was having as much fun as she was. While she waited for Iceman, she decided to address the elephant in the room.

Iceman returned and handed Trinity her beer. 'Girlfriend, you are turning some serious heads. You are a hottie.'

'Stop it.' Trinity playfully pushed Iceman on the shoulder.

'Whatever, just call 'em like I see 'em.'

'Kind of on that subject, I want to talk to you about something. It's kind of embarrassing.'

'Friends don't judge, no need to feel embarrassed.'

Trinity was taken aback by Iceman's response. She felt so safe being with him. 'I want to explain me and Duke.'

'You don't need to.'

'I want to. This was before Duke was the architect. He was a senior agent visiting the Factory for four weeks. We went out a couple of times and I slept with him. He was just so cool. Well, while his Black Ops status was cool, he wasn't. After, he talked about it, like bragged. Made me feel like another notch on his belt.'

'That sucks. Your story about Black Ops sucks, your encounter with Duke sucks. Your time with the Elders has not been ideal.'

'Tell me about it.'

'Look, I can only speak for me and offer my insight if you are interested.'

'I am.'

'I can't argue with your frustrations, but there is plenty more to you than you give yourself credit. I gotta believe your talents and experience will carry you to a higher calling in time. You are just too good. People as wonderful as you cannot be held down. Only you can hold yourself back. You'll find your path to greatness.'

Trinity nodded and surprised herself by accepting Iceman's words. 'Thank you, Iceman. That means a lot.'

'No problem. Let me understand something: you were an assistant to the architect before Duke?'

'Yeah, why?'

'No reason.' As they returned their attention to the music and fun, Iceman couldn't help reflecting on Trinity's role with the Elders. If she was the assistant to the previous architect while Duke was a senior agent, how much of Duke's success was truly his? How much credit should go to the previous architect? How much should go to Trinity? If possible, Iceman's rage towards Duke grew. Remembering Little Bill, Gene Hackman's character from the movie *Unforgiven*, speaking of the Duke of Death, *Duck, I say.*

CHAPTER NINETEEN

'Last night was a good time.' Zeus commented as the twins waited for Atalanta to join them for Sunday brunch.

'Yep.' Iceman was more interested in his beer than Zeus.

'I asked you a couple of times about your Friday night with Trinity, but you really didn't say much. Normally, I would appreciate your silence, but not this time. What gives?'

Iceman followed his Saturday routine when in Austin. He ate breakfast, exercised, and visited Dirty Bill's. Whenever possible, Iceman fueled his need for isolation. He required and enjoyed blocks of time alone to recharge. While at the Factory, he blocked 1300-1800 to visit the dive bar, catch a ball game, read for entertainment, enjoy several beers and sit in solitude. He carried his iPad loaded with his favorite adventure authors. Ted Bell, Vince Flynn, Brad Thor, James Patterson, David Baldacci, Ian Fleming and his favorite, Jack Higgins. Iceman called his solitude time, his mini vacation and invited F. Scott Fitzgerald, Earnest Hemmingway, and James Joyce for a change of era and scenery. After his mini vacation, he met Zeus for dinner.

'Nothing, not much to tell.'

Zeus, not satisfied, was forced to hold his frustrations when he spotted Atalanta entering Café Blue. 'Here she comes. We are not finished with this.'

Atalanta took a moment to take in the environment, took a deep breath, and approached the twins. Atalanta was a very private and reserved person. She enjoyed the warmth and comfort of her computer and her two cats, Bob and Patrick. The cats named after her favorite TV show as a kid, *Sponge Bob Square Pants*, were plenty of company for her. As she drew close to the table, she suffered a mild panic attack. *How did I get here? Why did I agree to meet them? What was I thinking?*

As she approached the table, Zeus made the introduction. 'Hey, Atalanta, glad you made it. This fellow here is Iceman.'

'Hi, Atalanta, good to meet you. Zeus is a huge fan of yours.'

'Thank you, nice to meet you too.'

Zeus guided Atalanta to her seat. 'Do you want a Bloody Mary or a mimosa?'

'I am not much of a drinker.' Atalanta responded with her anxiety set on high.

Zeus joked to ease her tension. 'Trust me, if you are going to spend a couple of hours with Iceman, you will join us.'

Atalanta looked over at Iceman, who nodded. 'It's true.' Iceman made eye contact with the waitress. 'We'll take three spicy Bloodies…' He looked over at Atalanta. 'Is spicy alright?'

'Sure, spicy would be fine.'

'Great. Three of those, a Budweiser and a pint glass, please? Also, after the drinks, please bring us a dozen oysters and three empty tumblers.'

The waitress was confused by Iceman's elaborate order. 'Empty tumblers?'

'Yeah, like you serve orange juice in.'

The waitress smiled, she understood. 'Maybe I'll add an extra shot of Absolute Peppar to those empty tumblers. You are fun and to think I almost called in sick today.'

'Make it four tumblers, we can sneak you a little hair of the dog.'

Once the waitress left, Atalanta turned her confused attention back to Iceman, only to be met with another riddle. Iceman filled half of his pint glass with his Bloody Mary, followed by his Budweiser. While she was impressed that he hadn't spilled, she had to ask. 'What do you have going on over there?'

'What? This? Where I am from, my neighbors to the north in Wisconsin make a Redeye. This is my version of it.'

'So, an Ice-eye.'

'I like that, thanks Atalanta. I am going to use that.'

Before the group could settle into conversation, the waitress returned. 'Here you go. I'll be back in a jiffy to join the fun.'

Zeus knew the plan and watched Atalanta ask: 'What are you creating now?'

'Just like the Ice-eye, I am a man with a plan.' Iceman dropped an oyster into each of the tumblers partially filled with the spicy vodka, followed by a little horseradish, hot sauce, Bloody Mary, with a squeeze of lemon. Stirred and served.

Just as he presented his creation, the waitress returned. 'Oyster shooters, just what the doctor ordered.'

Atalanta studied her tumbler, while the three held theirs in the air waiting for her. 'You seriously expect me to drink that?'

'No not at all.' Atalanta was temporarily relieved with Iceman's response. 'I expect you to enjoy it. Don't you trust me?'

Atalanta looked at Zeus for support. 'I have enjoyed these with Iceman everywhere oysters are served, from Key West to Ireland.'

Not satisfied, Atalanta turned her attention to the waitress. A fellow female might bail her out. 'Hurry up, I could get in trouble for this.'

Am I really doing this? Atalanta raised her shooter. Her first shooter was met with a slight gag on the way down, but she muscled through in one motion as ordered. Once the shooter hit the back of her throat, she was rewarded with a heat sensation, a pleasant burn that shot through her nostrils. She reached for a napkin to tap her eyes and wipe her runny nose. 'I have no idea why, but those are tasty.'

The group laughed and the waitress ordered as she left. 'I am coming back for seconds. Hold the next round for me.'

'Roger that.'

The table extended their laughter with fun stories about their past. The last of the oysters were enjoyed as shooters with the waitress' full participation. They agreed to eat family style with the entrées delivered to the table to share, one at a time.

Iceman explained to Atalanta. 'You are not exactly what I expected.'

'What did Zeus say about me?'

'Nothing.' Zeus explained. 'Iceman fancies himself quite the profiler. I thought you presented a nice challenge.'

'What were you expecting?' Atalanta asked, caught up in the frenzy of being the center of attention. The oyster shooters and the carnival atmosphere of the table certainly broke Atalanta out of her shell. 'Are you disappointed that I am not, *The Girl with the Dragon Tattoo?*'

Iceman laughed and admitted. 'I was expecting a little more goth. Happy to be mistaken. Blond hair and blue eyed midwestern Barbie very much works for you.'

'I see you have narrowed it down the Midwest.' Atalanta observed playing along.

'But you have no accent, which is a clue. I can take out Wisconsin, Chicago, Indiana, and upper Michigan. You are not a farmer girl, so I am stuck between Columbus, OH and Ann Arbor, MI.'

Atalanta's eyes betrayed her. Iceman was just fishing, and she took the bait. 'Columbus, home of the Buckeyes. Your dad was a computer professor at the Ohio State University. You went there as well.'

'Zeus, you told him.'

'I did not, I couldn't have, I didn't know that.'

'What makes you so unique is, your master's degree did not bring you to the Elder's doorstep.' Iceman observed while he intensely studied Atalanta's micro expressions. 'You were lured by the hackers. You beat their challenge, didn't you?'

'I did.' Atalanta confirmed with great satisfaction.

'As we close this chapter of our day, your handle suits you. You gave yourself the dark web identity. Atalanta, Greek goddess, equal in weight, known for her speed. Faster and better than men in the male-dominated world of hackers.'

'Impressive.' Atalanta replied with genuine admiration for Iceman.

Zeus saw his opening. 'Impressive enough to take this show on the road for a couple more hours?'

Iceman intervened. 'Yes, Zeus, I do believe I have enjoyed the company of you and Atalanta enough to invest a couple more hours of my time.'

Atalanta laughed and thought for a moment. She was prepared to excuse herself but a voice in her head gripped her. *I am having fun. I look and feel good. I cannot believe the twins are so welcoming, I feel safe with them.* 'Iceman, I think Zeus was talking to me.'

Iceman scanned the table with a look of confusion. 'You? Why would he be asking you? Of course, you are in. I already took the liberty of ordering an Uber. Finish up, I'll take care of the check.'

Atalanta asked. 'How did you order an Uber without a destination?'

Zeus asked. 'Where do you want to go?'

'I may sound cliché, but I have never really experienced 6th Ave. I have visited a few times but have never experienced it. Does that make sense? Do I sound pathetic?'

Iceman turned his screen around to show their destination. He had already ordered an Uber to take them to 6th Ave.

Atalanta felt embarrassed until Zeus spoke up. 'We haven't experienced 6th Ave either. We were hoping you would say yes.'

CHAPTER TWENTY

Phase II of advanced training at the Factory consisted of studying the intense operating procedures that scrubbed the targets. Iceman continued to report to Lori Segal to investigate the life cycle of previous missions. Lori's group was responsible for monitoring the global landscape to identify potential targets for investigation. The group was divided into regional teams that patrolled their portion of the globe. At risk targets were submitted to Lori through the regional team leaders. If the group believed the target warranted further investigation, a request to open a target file was submitted to Bill Zera. If Zera green lit the target file, Lori's dedicated regional team went to work with the assistance of the hackers. Once the report was completed, the Elders made the determination if termination was warranted. If the file met the criteria for termination, the target was routed to Duke, then to Black Ops. If the target did not warrant termination, the file was slowly leaked, hidden in plain sight, for the various government agencies to pick up the investigation. The Elders provided subtle breadcrumbs to manipulate the government agencies to pursue non-lethal targets through traditional methods of investigation. CIA, MI6, and other government agencies believed the targets were brought to justice due to their relentless investigations, never knowing the Elders built the path to justice. Iceman studied the process of a target being identified straight through to target assignment. After careful study and examination, Iceman was surprised by the number of targets not assigned to termination. The Elders were very selective in designating a target to Black Ops and termination. He enjoyed working closely with Segal and found her to be extremely bright, resourceful, and creative. Several of the target packets Iceman reviewed; documented the clever investigative skills on the part of Segal and her team. The answers were never obvious nor easy to identify. The targets were resourceful and building a file that met the Elders' rigorous requirements for assessment was a daunting task. Lori and her team amazed Iceman with their relentless diligence and resolve to uncover the layers of deceit built by the targets. All files analyzed uncovered wrongdoing; that was not the problem. Building a file that sanctioned termination was the challenge.

While Iceman worked with Segal and her team, Zeus worked with Mark Comer. Comer was the head of resource and development. R&D were responsible for the software and technology that kept the Elders several years ahead of the private, public, and government markets. Using his near unlimited budget, he ensured the Elders were a generation ahead in technology. As part of his duties as chief of R&D, he was responsible for the hackers. Like his predecessor, Comer found little value in a hands-on approach with the hackers. The hackers were a unique subculture within the unique subculture of R&D. The hackers were free to tackle their projects with total freedom provided deadlines were met. The hackers came and went at all hours. Their only commonality was their greatness. Individually, each hacker was among the finest in the world. Together with the Elders technology, the hackers worked with unparalleled genius. Comer was a college prodigy. He was unique because he excelled in the dark universe as well as the light. He graduated from Georgia Tech at 19 and had his PhD by 25, thus conquering the light universe. He was a brilliant manipulator of the dark side of the internet and other intelligent gathering methods. The hackers worked in small private offices that were transformed by their occupants. Each office was decorated very differently. The only universal thread was that a genius was the master and commander of the small fiefdom. While he did see Atalanta daily, Zeus rarely worked with her. She was absorbed in a project that was in the final phases of identifying a termination. The target had proven quite the challenge for the Factory, but Atalanta was more than capable of finding the data requested by the analysts.

While Iceman focused on the analytics invested in completing the dossier, Zeus studied the hackers diving into data mining. The process started with analysts working on a project to the extent of their abilities. When a team hit a roadblock that required more information to continue their investigation, the requests were routed to the hackers. The hackers returned the file to the analysts who continued the dig. When the analysts hit another roadblock, the file was again routed to the hackers. The production cycle continued until Lori was satisfied with the work product. Lori knew her brilliant audience would settle for nothing less than a complete discovery. Once she was satisfied, she submitted the file to Zera for approval. Despite Segal's best efforts, virtually all files submitted to Zera were returned with his notes for further examination requests. Even with all the effort and approval of Zera and Segal, the Elders typically returned the files with more demands for information. For a file to reach final assignment to either a government agency or termination status, great minds had exhausted all resources.

During the second week of phase II training, Iceman reported for the second of his weekly session with Grace. Iceman's confidence and trust in Dr. Monroe had grown to the point that he looked forward to their sessions. As he entered her office, Iceman was taken back by Sullivan's presence. 'Hello Colonel, I am a little early. Do the two of you need more time? I can come back later.'

Grace pointed to Iceman's chair, directing him to take a seat, and replied. 'Iceman, I asked Tom to join us today.'

'Everything alright?' Iceman was concerned the session was going to become a lecture. He knew the reason for the Colonel's invitation.

Grace responded. 'I asked the Colonel to join us, because you are at a crossroads in your current phase of training and I thought, rather than have multiple conversations, we might simplify things and meet together.' Grace paused and waited for Iceman's guarded consent before continuing. 'I unexpectedly received your evaluation from Lori Segal. Typically, I do not get a report until the last week of training.'

'Ok, so what's the problem?'

'No problem, her report detailed your outstanding performance. She was dutifully impressed with your analytical skills and the speed at which you consume and digest information. She documented with praise your ability to work with her team, and your willingness to accept direction. You completed the four-week course in 10 days. She identified you as a tireless worker who arrived early, stayed late, and worked independently of structured hours including weekends.'

'Thank you.' Iceman held further comments until the penny dropped.

'Well done.' The Colonel added.

Iceman made direct eye contact with the two of them and remained silent. Grace took a breath and explained the reason for the Colonel's presence. 'Before we continue, I would like to emphasize your extraordinary work during the first 10 days, but I must ask what happened yesterday and this morning?'

'I don't follow.'

'Lori explained to me that she completed her report on Tuesday. She called me this morning, because you did not report to her yesterday or today. She assigned you additional case files to examine but you have not been present. What is going on?' Grace asked with concern.

'Nothing. I completed my assignment, and I got interested in other case files. The files she assigned me were just more of the same. The additional files were a waste of time, so I studied and completed a different file, the one I chose. I just got started on a second file. I am done with Phase II training, so I see no point in returning to that cubicle of hers.'

Grace paused and looked to the Colonel for confirmation. 'Iceman, you don't get to select your own projects.'

'Why?'

Dr. Monroe and the Colonel spent the previous hour discussing the situation. They knew Iceman liked to drift on his own especially when he became locked into or obsessed with a project. The Colonel had reported the behavior throughout his time at West Point. He took this question. 'Iceman, you know why, don't play dumb.' Iceman sat silently. 'We have a carefully designed training program.'

'When I run extra miles, do you stop me? When I train harder, do you slow me down? When I learn more languages that are assigned, do you restrict me?'

Grace answered. 'No, we do not.'

'Look, this is silly and pointless. I did the work, and I did it well. After spending time with Lori, I understand her department. The additional files she assigned me were a waste of time. She didn't know what to do with me, so she handed me busy work. I am not a fan of having my time wasted. Either give me leave when I finish early or stay out of my way when I make better use of my time.'

The Colonel asked. 'What have you been working on for the last two days?'

'I studied the complete file and work history of team Conjar's last target, Pervert. I knew how that story ended, so I wanted to better understand the beginning and middle.'

Grace asked. 'How is that going?'

'I finished.'

'And?'

'I was impressed. I knew a lot of thought and research went into the decision to terminate, but I was still surprised by studying the file. I suppose the thing that struck me the most was that analysts never stopped; they were relentless. Even when the decision to terminate was obvious, Lori's team did not stop. What occurred to me is that they are seekers of truth. They are not satisfied until every piece of information is discovered and documented. Knowing the end, I benefitted by studying Pervert's case file. If they had stopped once they satisfied the termination requirements, Lori's team would have never discovered human trafficking. That really hit home with me.'

The Colonel accepted Iceman's response. 'I see your point, but you need to get approval for your adventures and keep, in this case, Lori informed.'

Iceman again remained silent.

Grace took a shot at explaining. She was incredibly careful not to use, *you need to understand.* If she used that phrase, although appropriate, she would have lost Iceman. 'Can you empathize with what we are trying to do?'

'I do. I am the ugly duckling, different from the ducks that puddle through here.'

'Iceman, it's not like that. We…'

'Grace, it is exactly like that. The issue is that of total control that reeks through this place like a disease. In the field and in all other aspects of training, we are challenged and asked to perform incredible things within a structure. We have freedom within that structure to operate and grow. Here, this is more of a petty office or government bureaucracy that I find grotesque. The teams are amazing, despite the culture, not because of it, it's bullshit.' Iceman elected to end his observations without identifying Duke as the cause of the damaged culture.

Grace grew frustrated not at Iceman, but because he was right. She knew his point was valid, she also knew the unspoken cause, but still she felt restricted to act, which was exactly Iceman's point. Why should she feel restricted? Why should Iceman be censored for doing independent study that went beyond their training program?

Iceman continued. 'Look, I am not looking to jam Lori up, and I certainly do not want to cause trouble for the two of you but, and you both knew a but was coming. I'm not doing it. I owe no apologies.'

The Colonel responded. 'I hear your point, but (he smiled at his own use of *but*) where were you the last two days?'

Iceman smiled. 'I got up, worked out, ate and went to work.'

'Where?'

'My room.'

The Colonel knew Iceman would not lie to him. Withhold? Yes. 'Iceman, I asked you a direct question.'

'Dirty Bill's. I read the complete file in my room in the morning. When I was finished, I headed over to Dirty Bill's to process and to get the hell out of here.'

Grace recognized the thread. 'What time?'

'Yesterday, like 1430.'

Grace nodded but the Colonel asked. 'And today?'

'1000.'

Grace was taken back. 'You were there this morning? Before our meeting?'

'Yep. Early this morning, I reviewed the files again to answer a couple of questions I raised for myself and headed over to the pub to reflect. I was here on time.'

The Colonel struggled to find a response. 'You understand the position that puts us in.'

'No, I don't. I am operating on my own time. I did the work and now I am operating independently. Listen, during the last mission, when I went to the dive bar and built the whole mission plan based on that visit, it worked. Dickheads will always find a reason to criticize, I am not interested in them. Winston Churchill operated just fine in his own way. When you work every waking hour, seven days a week, the concept of time is irrelevant. What is 1700 hours and quitting time, the appropriate drinking hours for most people, is irrelevant to me. I have no quitting time. A dive bar is just an escape, a minor detour to the absurdity of this place. I don't operate naturally in this theatre. Let me be me. I am more than enough.'

Iceman paused to assess his audience. They were not convinced. 'I'll make our meetings twice a week and I will submit a report on my latest project.'

Grace was encouraged, she asked. 'What is your latest project?'

'I just started and need more time.'

'What or who is the subject?'

'Colonel, I am not ready to answer that, I am not far enough along.'

Grace replied. 'Sorry Iceman, if you want our support, check that, in order for us to support you, we need to be included.'

Iceman paused and considered Grace's request. His initial reaction was to dismiss the request, but after thought he reminded himself of the promise he made to both the Colonel and Grace of total respect. 'Alright, you are right that is fair. The subject file I am studying is COVID-19.'

Grace was again confused by Iceman. 'COVID-19 was never a subject that required Black Ops.'

'True, but if I am correct, it should have been.'

CHAPTER TWENTY-ONE

Iceman departed the Factory after his meeting with the Colonel and Dr. Monroe and headed directly to Dirty Bill's. After processing his appointment with them, he returned his focus to the COVID-19 report. He did not remove any materials from the Factory, with his near eidetic memory, there was no need. Earlier that morning, before his first visit to open Dirty Bill's, he poured through hundreds of pages of the report and supporting data. After countless hours of dissecting the report, he came up empty. The report was thorough and accurate, a job well done. Despite his reluctant acceptance of the report, Iceman felt something was amiss. Until he was satisfied, Iceman recognized, and had prepared the Colonel and Dr. Monroe, of his potential to become obsessive, near manic over the file. He checked his watch, and realized it was time to go and meet Zeus for their Thursday dinner at Fogo de Chão. Although he had no interest in food and wanted to blow off Zeus to continue his work on the file; he knew he could not.

After a short Uber ride, Iceman entered the restaurant to find Zeus already seated at the usual table.

'Am I late? Glad to see you started without me.' Iceman asked and noticed Zeus half eaten platter of food.

'No, you're good. How long did you think I would last watching all this beautiful meat pass me by?'

'True that.' Iceman's head was on a swivel looking for the waitress. He found her, made eye contact, and she came to the table. 'Could I get a shot of Jameson and a Budweiser, please?'

'Sure. While I walk to the bar, would you like me to steer any particular gaucho your way?'

'Nice use of the work steer, very clever. I will start with the drinks and move on to food later, thanks.'

The waitress left with a smile to secure Iceman's drink order. Zeus was immediately concerned. 'No food? Just drinks?'

'I'll eat.'

'What did you have for lunch?'

'What?'

'You heard me.'

Iceman paused to accept his drink order. Rather than answer Zeus' question after the waitress left, he elected to drink his whiskey and take a healthy pull from his beer. His delay tactics were not effective.

Zeus asked again. 'Lunch?'

'Nothing.'

'What did you eat yesterday?'

'Breakfast with you.'

'That's what I thought. I figured you were *in your laboratory* when I was paid a visit from the Colonel this afternoon.'

'Was he cool?'

'Yeah. He's always cool; sometimes you forget that. He was just worried about you. We both recognize when you start to disappear. So, what's going on? What's got your panties in a bunch?'

'Nothing. I'm all good. Just a little curious about something. No worries.'

Zeus nodded and got the steak-wielding gaucho's attention. 'A double serving for both of us.' He switched his attention to the chicken gaucho and repeated his instructions. Turning back to Iceman after they were served, he demanded. 'We are not finished with this conversation, merely placing it on pause for you to eat.'

Iceman ignored Zeus, but paid close attention to the waitress. 'Another Bud, please.'

Zeus remained stoic and Iceman acknowledged him. 'Fine, fine, fine.' He attacked his plate to appease Zeus, but the meat that normally melts in his mouth tasted like metal. Clearing his plate of food was a chore, like chewing on aluminum foil. He had zero taste for food, but suffered through the massive serving to shut Zeus up. His beer arrived just in time to save him from his last bite of razor blades. He drank half his beer in one motion and exhaled. 'Tasty. Are you satisfied?'

'No.' As he answered Iceman, Zeus summoned more food much to Iceman's dismay. 'The Colonel told me you blew off the last couple of days to go drink at a dive bar.'

'That's not true. What did you say?'

'Nothing. You know me.'

'Cool.'

Zeus continued. 'He stayed at it and just wanted to make sure you were good to go. I told him, you are fine and just being you.'

'I thought you didn't say anything?'

'Shut up.'

'Roger that.'

'So, what gives? What's up?' Zeus asked with mild concern.

'Nothing. Like I told you over the weekend, I finished my level II training and had nothing to do, so I worked independently. I dove into our last mission file by the way.'

'No shit, talk to me.'

'Lori, who is cool as fuck, tried to give me some piles of bullshit files to keep me busy. I was having none of that.'

'Of course, I told the Colonel that when he mentioned you being missing.'

'We really need to get on the same page about this said nothing concept. Anyway, our mission file was bad ass. Before reading the entire file, I felt more than justified erasing Pervert, but the file went beyond anything I expected. All the files I reviewed, to be fair, were exceptional. One of the last items to be identified in Pervert's file was his human trafficking disease.'

'No shit?'

'No, they just kept going at it until every buried body was unearthed.'

'Good to know. Is that what took you away from the land of the living? Doesn't sound like it would.'

'No, it wasn't like that. After I finished with the Pervert file, I stumbled onto the COVID file.'

'Interesting.'

'I thought so.'

'Eat another platter of food, I'll join you in another beer, then tell me what's going on with the COVID file.' Zeus offered, using his interest in Iceman's work to parlay him to eat more food. If talking about the file was not enough to get him to eat, hopefully Budweiser would.

Iceman followed Zeus' instructions, and if possible, the meat tasted worse. Iceman suffered through another, what he knew to be a delicious platter, with the generous assistance from Budweiser. 'I call it the COVID file, but all the scientific names for every mutation are identified. Unless a need for specifics arises, I'm just calling it the COVID file, like Mulder in *The X-Files.*'

'I like it, but why not call it the C-Files?' Zeus responded without any understanding of the X-Files reference.

'Because I didn't think of it.' Iceman returned his attention to a new platter of food before he continued. 'The virus was created in a laboratory and that lab was the Wuhan Institute of Virology. The virus leaked from the WIV lab via infected scientists and hit the wet market and the rest is history. Okay, here is where it begins to get interesting. The C-Files do a nice job summing up the events. After all the dust settled, a British and Norwegian scientist wrote *of retro engineering in China*. They were largely ignored probably, because they supported much of what Trump claimed.'

'I thought that was dismissed by WHO as a conspiracy theory?'

It was 27 out of 27 votes. The World Health Organization is so full of shit, but then more information surfaced. Information the Elders knew well before the retro *engineering in China report,* all documented in the C-Files. Chinese scientists were hospital-ized in November 2019, months before the virus infected Wuhan. Also, the Chinese scientists who wanted to share their information have disappeared or have not been made available.'

'Shit. What about Pfizer and some British company owned by the company that created this mess?'

'Total bullshit. The British company, GSK and Pfizer had nothing to do with it. GSK and Pfizer did enter into a joint venture in 2018, but it had nothing to do with this. Several foreign companies invest or operate within WIV labs using shell companies to avoid the rigorous safety standards required by their host country, but that had nothing to do with the C-Files. The C-Files document that the specific WIV lab that was behind all this was a secret military operation. COVID was developed to be a military weapon. WIV is part of the Chinese Academy of Sciences, which is controlled by?'

'The Chinese government.'

'The State Council of the Chinese government, you got it.'

'Why did the world accept WHO's explanation and why the change of tune?'

'The world doesn't want to piss China off. China is the playground bully. China denied access, told tales, and pulled all kinds of misdirection and bullshit to sell that shit. In March of 2021, the Director General of the WHO called for further studies after offering a lame report because of difficulty accessing raw data. Look, there is a shit ton of information in the C-Files if you want to study it all. I read the Executive Summary that was 57 pages and did a fuck ton of spot investigation on the areas I questioned. At the end of the day, do you doubt the Elders ability to generate an accurate report?'

'No, not at all.'

'Right. China built a secret lab to build a secret weapon and it blew up in their face.'

'Got it.'

'But that's not the interesting part.'

'Really? Do tell, old wise one.'

'Let's get out of here and hit The Liberty and I will tell you more.'

* * *

The Liberty was Iceman's public dive bar. Unwilling to share his special place, The Liberty served as protection for his sanctuary, Dirty Bill's. If Iceman had not committed to Dirty Bill's, in his practice of monogamous relationships with dive bars, he would have ceded to the alluring treasures of The Liberty. A proper dive bar with the value added alure of a tasty food truck in the rear makes for great temptations. Bringing a proper chaperone on his visits to The Liberty ensured his faithfulness to Dirty Bill's.

After the twins were settled, the first round was consumed with a second being prepared; Iceman spoke. 'The thing about the Chinese is that they knew and withheld the dangers of the virus.'

'How so?'

'I mentioned the doctors that contracted the virus in November 2019 and the disappearing act of scientists that wanted to come forward, add on Chinese scientists created Coronavirus in the Wuhan lab and Chinese Communist Party fucked up. Get this, some nutty professor Shi Zhengli, dubbed *China Batwoman,* wrote in a 2015 paper that Coronaviruses, from an ant-eating mammal called pangolins, and not bats, pose the most dangerous threat to humans. The intensive lab work on Coronavirus started with that discovery to construct a WMD. After the CCP knew they were in deep shit, they tried for over a year after the virus was leaked to reverse engineer it to make it look like it came from nature via bats. Rather than notify the world after the virus was released, Chinese authorities silenced health care workers in Wuhan and jailed those who spoke out. In March of 2020, the Chinese Government issued a directive that instructed researchers to have all studies scrubbed by their agency before being published. China consistently blocked WHO investigators from entering. Since January 2021, the WHO and scientists from the US, Great Britain and Australia have tried to gather data and research from the Wuhan region, but their efforts were blocked or highly restricted. Requested information was severely delayed, scrubbed, and typically not provided. As recently as June 2022, the WHO tried to investigate the region to support their report that the virus was created in nature and not in a lab, but they were blocked again. Blocked, even though the WHO were supporting the very piece of bullshit propaganda China was selling. Biden is pushing for another round of investigations and being told to pound sand. There is a crap ton more, but you get the idea.'

'Shit, that is crazy fucked up.'

'That's just the beginning. China was celebrated for the zero COVID policy. While most of the world has worked with an Open policy, trying to live a normal life with restrictions, accepting the virus and maintaining economic stability. China has maintained a firm, militant Closed policy. China taunted their policy and medical procedures as an example for the world and the world somehow accepted their bullshit. Check this out, the US reported death rates of 825,000 and China's? 4,636.'

'Come on?'

'I am serious but that's not the worst of it. Let us focus on the death rate for a second. For those numbers to be true, 825,000 vs 4,636, the US would be 800 times higher than China because of the difference in population size. The same China where all this shit began somehow has virtually no deaths? As I said before, most of the West and WHO had accepted these statistics. Because I like you, here is one more: reported vs true. The US underreported the death toll by an estimated 7% maybe as high as 20%. Real estimates, not China's work of fiction, have China to be underreported by 17,000%. The number my Irish friend is not 4,636 try 1.7 million. Alright, one more but this is it. Of the

4,636 reported deaths, 97% were in Wuhan and all occurred in Q1 2020.'

'This is beyond crazy, it's scary. What the fuck is the WHO and governments thinking buying this bullshit?'

'I lied, one more but then I have important appointments to attend to. Their vaccines Sinovac and Sinopharm that they touted as their panacea, in fact totally blows. Their vaccine is 51% effective vs 95% for Pfizer. New C-Files variants and I will be specific on this one, Omicron, cracked China hard in early 2022. Tens of millions were quarantined in addition to the tens of millions quarantined in 2020 and 2021. 45 cities in the first half of 2022, including Shanghai, with a population of 22 million, and Changchun, with 9 million, were locked down in April 2022. That was after cities such as Xi'an, with 13 million, were put on strict lockdown in Q4 2021. Mass amounts of people have starved to death in addition to the C-Files related deaths. The Pfizer vaccine works well, but not perfectly, against Omicron. China's practice of quackery, peddling Sinovac and Sinopharm, was basically worthless against Omicron. China might as well have taken Pez candy to combat Omicron.'

'Why did they hide the results? Why didn't they switch to Pfizer?'

'Remember our CCP history lessons? The CCP was the answer to all your worries, much like the bar in the TV show *Cheers*. All their internet feeds, crap news and world narrative, have painted them as the greatest thing since sliced bread. Why would they need to change when everything was groovy?'

'What about all the lives? There is no way...' Zeus caught himself. 'They don't value human life, the CCP doesn't give a shit about deaths.'

'Right, but what they do worry about is the economy and their place as the rightful supreme world power. China built the virus as another powerful weapon to unleash on Americans in their terrorist war. When it backfired on them, they didn't want to be the only ones to suffer. If they were going to suffer a massive economic hit, they needed the world to suffer as well. They knew the economic impact of the virus and they didn't want to lose ground to the rest of the world, especially Uncle Sam.'

'A very CCP move.'

'Yep. In 2020, China reported economic growth of 2.3% and the US reported a loss of 3.4%. China was crushed in Q1 and Q2 2020, no way did they recover. Their statistics are a myth. The shipping logistic nightmare, zero-COVID policy, whole city lockdowns and mass quarantines hit them hard. External indicators support China being in a hurt locker. The Hang Seng Index was down 35% against the S&P and Shanghai's CSI was off 18%.'

'You have been busy.' Zeus noted.

'Alright, stop twisting my arm. If Omicron was not the knockout punch, XBB.15 might be. Just when China, after three years of Closed policy moved to Open in Q1 2023, they were blasted with the Omicron variant XBB.15. China might as well be starting from scratch. The US is certainly feeling the string of XBB.15, largely due to acceptance of the virus. The US has become complacent with COVID and has not maintained diligence with scheduled booster shots. XBB.15 is a speed bump for the US, for China it is a brick wall or a cliff. I'm telling you it is a total shit show.'

'Let me play catch up here, but before I do…'

'Not just yet.' Iceman interrupted. 'At the end of 2022, the WHO finally demanded COVID statistics from China. The rest of the world reports, why not China? China responded in historic fashion and scaled back their reporting. The world started to wake up in early 2023, requiring specific testing for Chinese visitors to their country.'

Growing frustrated with Iceman's interruptions, Zeus tried again. 'Got it, as I was saying...'

'One more and I will hand you the mic. Even without the COVID tsunami, China's economy would be in a hurt locker. China is experiencing a massive credit bubble as the property sector's woes have emerged within the financial sector. China is coming down from historic growth in the real estate market. The Chinese credit bubble, similar to the US in 2018, is of biblical proportions.'

'Enough, my brain is fried. Let me talk for a minute.'

Iceman held up his hand and waited for the next round of beers to be served. 'I know you got a little more in the tank. I'll be brief. Remember when China implemented the One-Child Policy?'

'Yeah, starting in 1979 until 2015 families could only have one child.'

'Right, now the chickens have come home to roost. China is faced with an aging population problem. Even with the one-child policy, China's shrinking economy has left the younger generation without quality jobs. The CCP pushed their version of the American dream of working 12 hours a day, punishing yourself with your studies and the world will be your oyster. The great jobs, such as in technology, are gone with the shrinking economy and the subsequent reduction in workforce. The unemployment rate for people in their twenties is reported at 27%. The real number, when factoring in the kids who have walked away and choose to live off their parents is 45%. The young people of China are pushing back. They are pissed.'

Zeus silently nodded his consent and continued his thoughts. 'I know you are miles down this journey already and just letting me in on it now. I know you; you are like a dog with a bone. You are on to something. How far gone are you?'

'Pretty far, but not close, if that makes sense. I have a theory, a good hypothesis, but I have miles to travel before it warrants opening a file for the Elders. Those Elders' files are bat shit crazy good no pun intended. I have no interest or ability to build one of those files, but I can raise interesting questions substantiated with enough intel to support opening a file. If I am right, that is.'

'There is that one small detail.'

'Roger that. But the way I figured it, when I started this treasure hunt, I had a little over two weeks to kill, so I might as well keep myself entertained. I am not far enough along in my research but, having said that, nothing I have come across has caused me to lose interest.'

Zeus nodded his understanding. 'I figured that was when you got me looped into this thing. What I don't get is why you are so interested. I mean, I must admit it is interesting, but what you are describing is yesterday. A big suck, but it happened, and the world is over it.'

'You sure about that?'

'How do you mean?'

Iceman slowed down his presentation to allow Zeus to catch up. 'Back up for a second. We both agree, based on our studies, that building a viral agent as an economic attack using a WMD is in concert with CCP philosophy, right?'

'Agreed.'

'Fucking up that project, having it leak with poor safeguards, is also very realistic.'

'Agreed.'

'Keeping it a secret to save face and not be the only economic victim of the fuck up fits.'

'Agreed.'

'Why would they stop? That's not very CCP.'

CHAPTER TWENTY-TWO

Iceman had Zeus cancel Friday happy hours with their group of coworkers at the Factory so that he could focus on his working hypothesis. On Friday morning, he woke at 0445, brushed his teeth, chased it with mouthwash and headed down to his cubicle. Iceman had read in his journeys that Winston Churchill started his day with a shot of whiskey. He called it his mouthwash. Iceman figured: if it was good enough for Churchill, it was good enough for him. Iceman also factored that the coming days were going to be a marathon and not a sprint, so he would need to severely limit his whiskey consumption. From 0500 to 0800, Iceman sat in his cubicle cell, devouring information from the Elders' secured server in pursuit of answers to questions that plagued him regarding the C-Files. His intensive research was disrupted at 0800 when the office began to fill up. He took his work back to his room and worked on the Elders' server for two more hours. He packed up his secure computer promptly at 1000 hours and departed for Dirty Bill's. Iceman arrived at the dive bar to find the door locked as he expected. He gently knocked on the door to gain entry.

'Good morning, Jack.'

'What's up, Tim? Thanks for letting me in early.' Jack smiled as he shook Tim's hand. Dirty Bill's was not yet open, but Tim always arrived early to check inventory and accept deliveries from his vendors.

'Staying with just beer, Jack? No little guy, right?'

Iceman knew Tim was referring to a shot of Jameson as *little guy*. 'No, I am cool with the beer, but thanks for checking. I believe there are times when you have more sense than I.'

'I understand. You need to keep your pace to write your book. How's that going anyway? You sure have been focused on that sucker.'

Tim had asked Iceman what he was so focused on when he sat alone at the bar on his previous visit. Iceman explained to Tim that he took a leave of absence from his forensic accounting job to give writing a shot. 'You know how it is, some good moments and some not so good moments.' Tim served Iceman his Budweiser. 'Thanks, all in all it is frustrating, but coming along.' Iceman smiled after his first taste of his beer. The C-Files were a bit frustrating, but hopefully coming along.

'Are you good for now? I am headed to the back for a bit. If you need another beer while I am gone, just serve yourself.'

'Sounds good, I know where to find it.'

'And I know where to find you, right on that stool hammering away.'

As Tim headed to the back, Iceman opened his personal computer. While he did not have access to the Elders' servers, he did have secured access to his private network. Every assignment, note taken, report prepared, all his work from his time at West Point through his time with the Elders was at his figure tips. In addition, with the wealth of knowledge available on the internet, Iceman kept himself more than busy during his daily pilgrimage to Dirty Bill's. Iceman was zeroed in on his studies in

The History of Military Art, which he took at West Point and the twins' work with Dr. Liu in *Asian Studies.* Dr. Liu's primary focus was the Chinese Communist Party. As the bar began to fill at 1530 with construction and trade workers getting off work, and later, as the office workers paid a visit, Iceman was able to block out the distractions. At 1800 hours, he closed his laptop and joined the after-work crowd for a bit of a laugh. At 2000 hours, he left for the Factory with a stop to secure an extra-large pepperoni and sausage pizza, a 12-pack of beer and a bottle of Jameson.

Upon returning to the Factory, he headed directly to his room, dropped off his laptop, ate a quick slice of pizza with a beer chaser and returned to his Dungeon cell to work on the Elders' server. The Dungeon was nearly vacant, much like his morning session and he was able to work in peace. From his cell he attacked the endless resources of the Elders until 2330. He logged off, departed for his room for a few more slices, a few more beers and streamed *Magnum PI* reruns. Pizza and *Magnum* took him back to his high school summers. After working his summer job in landscaping and construction, Jack ate a quick meal and headed to one of the South Side of Chicago play-grounds to engage in intense pick-up basketball games. The games were waged until 2200 hours when the lights were shut off for the night. If the last game was close and money was at stake, the games would not end until 2217. Cutting the power did not darken the court for 17 minutes, time enough to reconcile all bets. Jack had a standing order with the local pizzeria to have it delivered promptly at 2230. He left the money with a tip under the front doormat of his family home. Jack was cash-rich from his hoops gambling. Both he and the delivery guy benefitted from the transaction. Every weekday night, he ate his pizza with orange pop, while watching *Magnum.* As *Magnum* was his dad's favorite show growing up, he occasionally snuck down to avoid the watchful eye of Jack's mom to join him. His dad's secret slice of pizza, forfeited by Jack, was more than worth watching his dad enjoy a cold beer, relatively hot pizza and *Magnum PI*. Jack sat in his room at the Factory, enjoying the pizza, beer and his dad's favorite show, but it did not compare to his orange pop, Chicago pizza and the promise of his dad's potential bedroom prison break. The memories sparked the realization that he missed his dad and should give him a call over the weekend. It had been too long. He, of course, was too focused on the C-Files to follow through on his sentiments.

He took his pizza box with two remaining slices and placed it on his mini fridge. He finished his beer, shot it into the trash and brushed his teeth. He enjoyed his mouthwash, only his second whiskey of the day and headed to bed.

The morning came again at 0445 for Iceman. He ate the two remaining slices of pizza, brushed his teeth, enjoyed his mouth-wash and repeated the day until his Sunday dinner with Zeus.

Before joining Zeus for dinner, Iceman took a moment to step back, reflect on his work and give thought to the report he owed Dr. Monroe. Iceman's standing Tuesday afternoon meeting was coming up, and although he hated to be babysat, he had agreed to submit a progress report. Shaking off his dismay, he asked Shirley, Dirty Bill's weekend bartender, for a pen and a couple of cocktail napkins. He wrote his report on the cocktail napkin, examined it and nodded with satisfaction as he folded the napkin and filed the report in his rear jeans pocket. The report read:

C-Files: Report I

WHAT IS MISSING IN THE ELDERS' REPORT? NOTHING, REPORT LOOKS GOOD.

REPORT LOOKS GOOD, BUT IS THAT ALL?

CHINA KNEW THEIR WMD WAS LOOSE AND HID IT FROM THE WORLD.

CHINA TRAILING THE WORLD IN CONTAINMENT; WWCD?

CHAPTER TWENTY-THREE

Apart from Sunday's dinner with Zeus, Iceman remained locked into his C-Files routine. At dinner, Zeus tried to pry more information from Iceman regarding his progress. Iceman kept his work close to the vest and used the time with Zeus to relax. He did tell Zeus to ask Trinity and Atalanta to join the twins at Tamale House after work on Tuesday. He explained to Zeus that the meeting would answer his questions as he was recruiting the three of them to help him in his investigation. While not satisfied, Zeus accepted Iceman's invitation to learn more on Tuesday night.

Iceman left Dirty Bill's and arrived on time to find the Colonel and Grace waiting for his Tuesday meeting. Both were extremely interested in hearing what Iceman had to say.

'Hello, Iceman, take a seat.'

Iceman nodded to Grace, shook the Colonel's hand, and took his seat. 'Couldn't get enough of me, Colonel?'

'Typically, less Iceman is more, but I will admit, you have captured my attention with your latest adventure.'

Grace interjected. 'I am very interested to hear of your progress, but I must ask, how are you feeling?'

'Good.'

'Eating?'

'Some.'

'Sleeping?'

'Enough.'

Grace was getting frustrated with Iceman's one-word answers. He did not look well. 'Please, we are...'

'I am fine, let's move on. I have your report.' Iceman stood and dug into his jeans pocket, removing the folded cocktail napkin. He opened the napkin, smoothed out the wrinkles and slid the report across Grace's desk. 'Here you go, it's all there.'

The Colonel walked over and read over Grace's shoulder.

C-FILES: REPORT I

WHAT IS MISSING IN THE ELDERS' REPORT? NOTHING, REPORT LOOKS GOOD.

REPORT LOOKS GOOD, BUT IS THAT ALL?

CHINA KNEW THEIR WMD WAS LOOSE AND HID IT FROM THE WORLD.

CHINA TRAILING THE WORLD IN CONTAINMENT; WWCD?

'What is this?' Grace asked, trying to make sense of Iceman's intentions.

'Everything you need to know is right there.'

The Colonel was more interested than angry with Iceman when he asked. 'A couple of words on a folded-up cocktail napkin?'

'I believe it was Herb Kelleher, the founder of Southwest Airlines, who said *all great plans should fit on a cocktail napkin*. He sat at a table, sketched out a couple of flight routes within Texas and that was the start of the airline. Same thing here.'

Sullivan shook his head and thought *always something with this guy*. 'Alright, I'll bite on this progress report. While I do not know the Southwest Airlines specific reference, I imagine Kelleher gave an awfully good verbal presentation to accompany his cocktail napkin.'

'He did.'

Grace followed up on Iceman's response. 'Will we be receiving your brilliant verbal presentation?'

'If you like, but it's simple and the napkin says it all. After our last meeting did the two of you read the 54-page executive summary of the C-Files?'

The Colonel looked at Grace and then back to Iceman. 'The C-Files?'

'Yeah, that's what we are calling them now. Rather than all the scientific names and references, just simplified to C-Files, like the X-Files.'

Grace continued the questioning, 'Who is we?'

'Me and Zeus. Naming the project the C-Files was his idea.' Iceman did not want, nor did he feel the need to mention Trinity and Atalanta just yet. He knew enough to keep that bit of information to himself until absolutely necessary. Zeus was tricky enough, because he was assigned projects. Trinity and Atalanta had full-time jobs and Duke would go ballistic about Trinity.

Grace responded. 'Zeus has his training schedule firmly in place.'

'And what a wonderful program it is. We were just shooting the shit about all this over dinner. He was asking what I was working on, that's all.' Iceman's response was technically true. He had yet to pull Zeus in, which was a couple of hours away from dinner.

The Colonel directed Iceman to continue and he complied. 'If you read the summary, you know most of what the napkin reports already. The Chinese had a program in place to build a deadly virus with the intent of releasing it in the US. They screwed the pooch, unleashed it on themselves, and rather than take the hit, they hid it from the world.' Iceman went into more detail about the C-Files, covering most of the information he had shared with Zeus. After 20 minutes of summarizing his position on the C-Files, he waited for a response.

Grace placed her right hand to the side of her face and looked out the window as she processed Iceman's report. 'Let's break this down one point at a time. First: WHAT IS MISSING IN THE ELDERS' REPORT? NOTHING, REPORT LOOKS GOOD. You agree with the Elders report and concur with the conclusions.'

'Yes.'

'Fine. REPORT LOOKS GOOD, BUT IS THAT ALL? You question whether the Chinese have stopped. Are they actively spreading the virus?'

'Correct.'

'Got it. You base your hypothesis on the fact that CHINA KNEW THEIR WMD WAS LOOSE AND HID IT FROM THE WORLD.'

'Yes, that and because they are getting their brains beat in. CCP is drastically behind the world and getting crushed. If they kept the virus a secret, didn't tell the world, lied about everything from the origin to death statistics, why would they stop?'

Grace sat silent, nodding her head as she processed Iceman's responses. Explain this last bullet point to me. CHINA

TRAILING THE WORLD IN CONTAINMENT; WWCD? What is WWCD?'

'What would China do?'

The Colonel responded. 'Iceman, WWCD?'

'They sure as shit wouldn't stop. Take a step back, it's 2015 and this *Batwoman* discovers an anteater of sorts carries a virus much deadlier than bats. Wuhan sets busy building it, screws it up and it is released in China, and then, the world. Let me ask you, in the five years the virus was being developed, you don't think the CCP had a military deployment plan?'

The Colonel agreed. 'I am certain they would.'

'The CCP has the disease and variants, mutations of the disease and their biggest nightmare continues to be a reality. The CCP did everything in their power not to lose face and economic ground on the world stage. They have already proven a willingness to wreak havoc on the world, so their failures and struggles are shared globally, correct?'

'Yes.'

'Why would they stop? They wouldn't. Whatever the deployment plan was, they are implementing it now.'

The Colonel and Grace looked at each other impressed and Dr. Monroe asked. 'So, what is the deployment plan?'

'Come on, give me a break. I thought my cocktail napkin was a bad ass start. You will need to stay tuned. More is to come, but the guiding question remains, WWCD?'

* * *

Early that evening, Zeus was joined by Trinity and Atalanta at Tamale House. While the three sat at their usual table and waited for Iceman, the ladies decided to have fun at Zeus' expense.

Trinity sat down her margarita and asked Atalanta. 'What have you heard about Iceman?'

'You mean, why hasn't anyone seen Iceman?'

'Yes. He is a mere rumor, a whisper, a shadow that lurks within the Dungeon.'

Atalanta was dipping her chip in salsa and waited to finish before she responded. 'I heard that he is like Bruce Wayne.'

Trinity smiled. It was clear Atalanta was in on the gag and jokingly asked. 'Batman's Bruce Wayne? How so?'

'You know the Batman movie where Bruce Wayne is all old and beat up?'

'Not sure.'

Atalanta continued. 'Sure, you do, the one with Catwoman.'

Zeus answered. *'The Dark Knight Rise*s.' The ladies had successfully lured him in.

Trinity laughed. 'Yeah, I remember now. Bruce Wayne is locked up on the top floor, hobbling around, eating chicken broth and struggling through being a broken down, tired, former superhero.'

Atalanta joined Trinity in laughter. 'Yep, yep, that's the one. A friend of a friend told me that a friend of hers actually served Iceman chicken broth for dinner two nights ago.'

'No way!'

'Way. Apparently, he didn't look good. The soup server didn't know if Iceman was having trouble recovering from his surgery, or what was up, but it wasn't good. That she was sure of.'

Trinity poured the rest of the pitcher of margaritas into the ladies' glasses, bypassing Zeus and offering. 'That's not what I heard. I heard...'

'What did you hear?' Iceman arrived without notice and joined the group. 'Sorry, I am late.'

Zeus responded. 'You have no idea how sorry you should be.'

Iceman looked at Zeus with confusion and asked. 'What's up? What did I miss? What did you hear?'

The girls laughed and drank their margaritas, while Zeus answered. 'Don't ask.'

Trinity turned to Iceman and answered his question. 'I heard that you were like the guy in the iron mask.'

Iceman waved the server over, ordered another pitcher of margaritas and a Negro Modelo for himself. 'You mean the *Man in the Iron Mask* as described by Voltaire?'

'Yeah, that guy. You, Iceman, were sentenced to the tower that is your room for unauthorized absences from training.'

The girls giggled harder. 'You know, Trinity, he does look pale. He most certainly has not seen daylight. I do believe you are correct. Iceman is the *Man in the Iron Mask*.'

Trinity added. 'Why thank you Atalanta, but I must declare you to be correct. While he is pasty, he has also lost significant weight. Weight loss courtesy of a chicken broth diet. Iceman was squirreled in his room much like Bruce Wayne.'

'Trinity, if I am correct and Iceman was Bruce Wayne, does that make Zeus, Alfred, the butler?'

Over the roar of the girl's laughter, Iceman asked Zeus. 'Were these two idiots here before you arrived? They got an early start on the margaritas.'

'How did you guess?'

Iceman decided to take control of the table and instructed. 'Ladies, amateur night at *The Comedy Store* is over. Well done, you were both beyond hilarious.'

While wiping tears of laughter from her eyes, Trinity asked. 'What have you been up to?'

Iceman took a slug from his beer and answered. 'That's why I invited you here, to tell you what is going on.' Iceman broke into his routine, the same shared with Zeus, the Colonel and Dr. Monroe. The girls stopped him on a few occasions to ask questions, but the presentation went smoothly.

Atalanta, her face like the rest of the table, wore a stern look when she asked. 'I have to admit, it does make a lot of sense. What do you need from us?'

Iceman smiled. 'Glad you asked. I am at the point of chasing down facts to support my hypothesis. I need your help. Zeus, you will be the link between analytics and hackers.' Iceman stopped to eat the last of the chips and turned his attention to Zeus. 'You won't be missed, so you can devote 100% of your time to chasing down and digesting information. Atalanta, if Zeus gets backed up or stuck, you will handle the deep dives for information. Trinity, you will do the same, but in analytics.'

Trinity was confused. 'I am not an analyst.'

'Nice try. I read the files and your fingerprints are all over the Black Ops files.'

Trinity responded. 'Alright. So, are we are authorized to work on this?'

'Pretty much.'

Zeus interrupted. 'He means no.'

'It's just a little work on the side during the week, no big deal. Dr. Monroe and the Colonel know all about the C-Files. We good to go?' The three attendees nodded and Iceman continued. 'What we will do is meet Friday, Saturday and Sunday night at 1800 hours to discuss. Prior to our meeting, we will power through all our C-Files assignments. By next week, we should have enough clarity to bring this to Grace and Sullivan to get the official okee dokee for you two to officially work on the C-Files full-time. We just need to be focused on WWCD?'

Atalanta stopped picking at her food to comment. 'I like the name C-Files, like the X-Files, right?'

'Exactly. The name was Zeus' idea.' Iceman answered.

Trinity gave Iceman a mischievous grin. 'But of course, it was.'

CHAPTER TWENTY-FOUR

C-FILES: REPORT II

AFTER THE KOREAN WAR: TERRORISM/AMERICAN REVOLUTION, NATIVE AMERICANS, IRA.

WWI – ZIMMERMAN TELEGRAPH

WWII MOST AGAINST NAZI, BUT MX STILL TRADED WITH GERMANY AND AMERICA WAS FORCED TO ACCEPT

MEXICAN AMERICAN WAR

MEXICO IS THE GREATEST THREAT TO U.S. THE UNDERBELLY.

DID THE LACK OF BORDER SECURITY FACTOR IN THE SPREAD OF THE VIRUS?

WHO BENEFITS? THIS IS WHERE I NEED MORE MANPOWER.

Two days later Iceman delivered his second report to Grace and Sullivan as promised. After reviewing Iceman's report, Dr. Monroe commented. 'Thank you for another report. I appreciate the care in which you folded the cocktail napkin. Why don't we get started on the verbal explanation?'

Iceman nodded and began. 'During the course of our training dating back to our days at West Point, Zeus and I have spent a considerable amount of time dedicated to the Chinese Communist Party. The CCP rose to power in 1949 and tried to follow the blueprint of the US and the Soviet Union during the Cold War. After the Korean War, China realized that it could not compete in the Cold War model. China could not enter an arms race and win. China elected to follow the examples of the American Revolution, Native Americans, and the IRA. Mao Tse-tung sided with Stalin who considered the IRA leader, Michael Collins to be the founder of modern guerrilla warfare. The only way for a lesser opponent to conquer a superior foe was through modern guerrilla warfare.'

The Colonel responded. 'Yes, we have been schooled as well. We both accept that China has adopted a doctrine of modern guerrilla warfare against the United States. Everything from media manipulation, election tampering and theft of proprietary information, both from the government and private sector. Trade imbalance, debt holding and economic attacks through theft, rather than development, just begin the list of guerilla warfare tactics. We accept your first bullet point as fact, we do not need you to elaborate further.'

'We can then accept that China has done an exceptional job learning from the success of others, which leads me to the second bullet point: the *Zimmerman Telegraph* is an important document on world history that is overlooked. In 1917, the secret German diplomatic communication was intercepted by the British and served as a rallying cry for the United States to enter WWI. The communication proposed a military alliance between Germany and Mexico. Keep in mind the *Mexican-American War* and the *Spanish-American War*, which gave the US control of its hemisphere, had not long past the date of the memorandum. The

Germans, rightfully, saw Mexico as America's greatest threat. With the two oceans and Canada, America's underbelly has always been Mexico. In WWII, Hitler saw the same opportunity, but Mexico despised fascism, so nothing much came of it. Mexico did however declare neutrality and were a large trading partner with the Third Reich.'

Again, the Colonel responded. 'I see where you are going with this. China has adopted a policy of a death by a thousand cuts and is using Mexico as a part of their plan.'

Iceman nodded and added. 'Correct.'

Dr. Monroe directed. 'Understood, please continue.'

'China built a weapon in concert with their guerrilla fighting style in the form of the C-Files. We agree that if they built the weapon, they had to have a plan to deploy it. I wondered if the lack of border security between the United States and Mexico might be a weakness the Chinese would expose. If a wet market and some guy in the state of Washington, as was reported in the first US case, did all this damage, what would thousands or tens of thousands of infected illegal immigrants do? Second, what if China never stopped the invasion? We established the damage the virus has and continues to inflict on China domestically. We also established that they wanted, at a minimum, to balance the impact of the virus on the world and especially the United States. I believe the CCP continues to implement their guerrilla war doctrine by sending infected illegal immigrants across the border.'

Grace responded. 'Undocumented, not illegal.'

'Correct, that's my mistake.' Iceman was genuinely regretful about his choice of words.

Accepting Iceman's apology, Grace asked. 'How?'

'That I am not certain. I have a working theory, but I need more manpower to track down the source.'

The Colonel asked. 'That's the point of your last bullet point: *Who benefits?* You have established China, but am I correct that the beginning of your search for the source is who benefits on the Mexican side?'

'Yes, and who could execute guerrilla warfare? No chance that it is the government. The US and Mexico may have their differences, but they need each other.'

'Agreed.' The Colonel paused and then asked. 'Returning to your point about needing more manpower, are Grace and I to pretend not to know of you already involving Zeus?'

'No, I thought that was a given.'

Grace asked. 'And Trinity and Atalanta? Are we to ignore them as well?'

Iceman smiled. He figured they knew about Trinity and Atalanta. He gave them his prepared response. 'They really haven't been involved much. I would like them full time to explore my theory. I believe we will build a strong enough case to warrant an official investigation.'

Grace turned to the Colonel, who nodded his consent. 'We will have to bring this to Zera for approval. Lori and Comer should not be an issue.'

'Duke will be.' Iceman interrupted.

'Yes, yes, he will. But we will bring it to Zera straight away.'

'Thank you, Grace.'

The Colonel stood to signal that the meeting was adjourned. 'Thank you for your tireless work on this, well done. Now, if you will kindly leave the room, Grace and I would like to talk about you behind your back.'

After Iceman thanked them and left Grace's office, the Colonel asked Grace. 'What do you think?'

'He certainly is on to something.'

'Do you think he is further along in his investigation than he is leading on?'

'Absolutely.' Grace did not hesitate with her answer and continued her confident response. 'He knows and feels confident. He would not make his hypothesis public if he wasn't certain. He wouldn't want to be wrong in public. He doesn't need the team to investigate to get answers, he needs the team to build a file. Iceman knows his cocktail napkins will not work on Zera. He has no interest in the tedious work required to build files.'

'I see your point and I have to agree.' The Colonel responded.

'What I find fascinating is Atalanta and Trinity.'

'How so?' The Colonel asked.

'He has expanded his trust tree.'

Sullivan immediately understood and agreed with Grace's observation. 'Yes, I see your point. Me, you, Conjar and of course Zeus. He appears to have added two to his tribe, as he likes to say.'

'What is amusing is his recruitment strategy. I had identified his motivation behind the happy hour with the troops. He was winning over the Factory, so that when asked, the twins would have overwhelming support from the ground troops.'

'In the event of a challenge by Duke.'

Grace elaborated on her observations. 'Yes, but what I did not see was the second layer of his plan. The assessment and recruitment of Atalanta and Trinity. I am certain he targeted them and used the happy hour concept to camouflage his true intent. Lost in the parade of smiley happy hour customers was Iceman's deliberate intention to add to his team. He quickly targeted Trinity and Atalanta.'

'Very clever. Now, when he leaves, he will have both advocates and spies.'

'Spies is a strong word, but certainly agents.'

The two laughed and the Colonel commented. 'I would not have expected any less from Iceman. He is entertaining if nothing else. What are your thoughts about Duke in all this?'

'Quite candidly, I am done massaging Duke's ego. Iceman has certainly exposed Duke's true character, and I, for one, will not apologize for Iceman any longer. He has done exceptional work and Duke will just have to accept Iceman. I have no concerns about actively supporting this or any other future plans championed by the twins that I believe in. They have done everything asked of them and are working very well in the Elders' structure and training plan. Would you care to join me in the meeting with Zera?'

'I would, very much so.'

CHAPTER TWENTY-FIVE

Iceman returned to his post, anchoring the end of Dirty Bill's bar, while Zera approved the deployment of Atalanta and Trinity to officially join his research team. Iceman was not yet aware of the official approval, but it made little difference to him. He was going to use Zeus, Atalanta and Trinity either way. As he finished his last beer of the evening, he stared down at his next cocktail napkin. He nodded his head approvingly at his napkin, but also recognized he had much work to do before his Friday night meeting with the C-Files team.

C-FILES: REPORT III - FOLLOW THE MONEY

AM I WRITING THE PELICAN BRIEF?

HOW COULD THE CARTELS BE INVOLVED?

WHERE DID INCOME OR PRODUCT CONTROL SPIKE? MAQUILLADORAS

DID *LEGAL BUSINESSES* EMERGE WITH CHINESE FUNDING OR SUPPORT?

REMEMBER YOUR GODFATHER, *JUST WHEN I THOUGHT I WAS OUT…THEY PULL ME BACK IN.*

Iceman learned his lesson from their last meeting at the Tamale House. He elected to be the first to arrive at The Liberty to prevent being ambushed by margarita-filled Atalanta and Trinity. He nursed his beer as he studied the notes stowed in his monkey brain. The notes he dissected countless times were not in preparation for this evening's meeting. No, he was well past his preparations for tonight. His intense thought process was already working on the final conclusion to his hypothesis. Iceman remained several steps ahead of the others to guide the investigation. He was almost satisfied with the results when the C-Files team entered the dive bar.

'You three come together?' Iceman asked.

Trinity answered. 'As a matter of fact, we did. We took an Uber over together; Atalanta and I left our cars at the Factory. Obviously, we will be drinking tonight and working on our day off tomorrow, so we will pick up our cars after work.'

Not seeing a waitress, Iceman got up and headed to the bar to fetch the team a round. When he returned, he took his seat and commented. 'Makes sense. How's everybody doing?'

Atalanta answered. 'We are doing fine. How are you? If possible, you look even worse than the last time we saw you.'

Iceman studied the table and noticed that even Zeus had a look of concern. Iceman was surprised by Zeus' reaction. Zeus had seen Iceman lost in his laboratory before. Why should he be concerned? 'I am fine, always fine. We are really zeroing in on our C-Files conclusion. Let's worry more about that and less about me.'

He retrieved his report from his back pocket and set it on the small pub table. The team took a moment to read the cocktail napkin. Trinity was the first to speak. 'I am certain that your first entry has something quite clever behind *AM I WRITING THE PELICAN BRIEF?* Please explain.'

Iceman laughed. 'About that, that was a sanity check. *The Pelican Brief,* you know, the book by John Grisham that was made into a movie with Denzel Washington and Julia Roberts?'

Atalanta responded. 'We know the movie.'

'Even you, Zeus?'

'Yes, Iceman. Again, I'm from Ireland, not Mars.' Zeus responded not knowing the movie.

'Right, you are. Julia Roberts writes a conspiracy theory about the assassination of two Supreme Court Justices stemming from the protection of the natural habitat of these pelicans. The theory centers around drilling rights and a pending case before the Supreme Court.'

Trinity interrupted. 'We know the story, but how does it apply to you?'

'I will tell you. My theory at first pass sounds a lot like *The Pelican Brief,* and like *The Pelican Brief,* the more you peel back the onion, the more valid it becomes. We are entering the phase of our investigation when the curtain is pulled back.'

The three members of the C-Files team nodded to each other and gave their approval for Iceman to continue. Iceman delivered his vision with only drink orders and restroom breaks as interruptions. 'As I told you before, I quickly eliminated the Mexican government as a partner in the CCP's deployment strategy. *HOW COULD THE CARTELS BE INVOLVED?* I turned my attention to the drug cartels and eliminated them as well. The high-profile nature of the cartels, as well as their business philosophy and level of sophistication, made them too much of a risk for the CCP to trust with their plans.'

Trinity spoke for the group when she accepted Iceman's premise. 'I can see that. You make a valid point. Moving on to your third bullet point, *WHERE DID INCOME OR PRODUCT CONTROL SPIKE? MAQUILLADORAS.* What is a maquiladora?'

'Before I answer that, I want to take a step back. We have been chasing WWCD? The next question before us is, *Cui bono?*'

Zeus answered. 'Latin, for *who benefits?*'

'Correct. We already know who benefits on one side of the ledger, the CCP. What about the other side, the Mexican side?'

Trinity asked. 'That is where the maquiladoras come in?'

'Exactly. The maquiladora industry started 60 years ago under the National Border Development Program, but really didn't take off until the North American Free Trade Agreement in 1994. Maquiladoras are basically a duty-free or assembly factory that imports raw materials and exports finished products. Here is the thing, maquiladoras are exempt from import and export taxes. Cheap labor, call it $10 a day per employee, fast assembly and delivery times with no taxes make maquiladoras attractive.'

'Alright, so how does this fit into the C-Files?'

'To answer that, we need to better understand the maquiladora industry and all 3,000 businesses that employ 1.0 million Mexicans.'

'That is our next project?' Trinity asked.

'Roger that, which leads me to my last bullet point, *REMEMBER YOUR GODFATHER, JUST WHEN I THOUGHT I WAS OUT... THEY PULL ME BACK IN.*'

Atalanta was the only one who understood the reference. 'From Godfather III, Michael Corleone expresses his frustration about the struggle to make the family totally legitimate.'

Ice nodded and set down his beer. 'Exactly. What better way for a cartel to venture into legitimate business than the maquiladora industry? We assume all 3,000 of the maquiladoras are legitimate. What if they are not? The maquiladoras are nothing more than shell companies mostly owned by American corporations, an easy way to funnel legitimate income for the cartels.'

Zeus agreed. 'I see your point. What are we looking for?'

Iceman answered. 'We are targeting two things. First, we are looking for high minority Mexican ownership. The maquiladora corporations must be foreign-owned, but can have minority Mexican ownership. Like minority-owned businesses in the U.S. Companies that want to bid on contracts dedicated to minority businesses, bring in minorities at a 10-25% ownership stake and can still claim minority ownership. Mexican ownership of the maquiladora is the legitimate corporate front.'

Trinity asked. 'Got it. If you have identified the cartels as using a legitimate corporate front via minority Mexican ownership, are you implying the majority foreign-owned part of the business is illegitimate?'

'Yep, which brings me to our second target. As I said before, most of the ownership will be a shell company backed by obvious legitimate businesses. Most of the legitimate foreign companies that benefit from the maquiladoras will be easily identified. Some of the businesses will have several shell companies. Those are the businesses we want to examine.'

Zeus asked. 'You think those are fronts for the cartels?'

'No, I do not. Most of the companies that have several shell companies will be legitimate and, with a little investigation, will prove true.'

Zeus continued with his inquiry. 'But the others? The companies that do not prove true, how will we know the difference?'

'Good question. What we are hunting for is Russian nesting dolls.'

Atalanta replied. 'Matryoshka dolls, a set of wooden dolls that stack one on top of the other in decreasing size.'

'Very good. Our shell companies will be similar. We find one shell or doll only to lift it to find another, then another, then another. The cryptic shell companies will be our target. Each doll masks several income streams from divergent sources.'

Zeus interjected. 'The cartels or some other business can run money through the shell companies with the maquiladoras as the legitimate front.'

'Exactly, but here's the thing: we are talking about a very sophisticated business model. The person behind all this must be an unbelievably bad ass operator. The current cartel bosses are not going to be involved in this. They are focused on bloodshed and territory. We are looking for Michael Corleone.'

* * *

On Sunday night, the C-Files team took a breath from their nonstop research into the maquiladoras. They met for the third consecutive night at The Liberty to step back from the grind to recharge and refresh. The team has been inseparable since Iceman's meeting with Sullivan and Monroe on Thursday. The team used the late evening meetings as an action review to assess their status and chart their course for the next day. The late dinner meetings were also a chance to relax and enjoy a well-deserved break. As much as they promised themselves to dedicate some of their time at The Liberty to take a break from the C-Files, they were seldom successful.

After enjoying their first round in relative silence, using the ice-cold beer to decompress, Trinity was the first to introduce the C-Files into the conversation. 'Iceman, I cannot believe how good you look.'

The table looked at Iceman, then at each other, when Zeus laughed. 'Trinity, what in the hell are you talking about? He looks like shit!'

'No, he doesn't. I look like shit and I have only been doing this for a handful of days. He has kept this pace up for several weeks.

I'd be dead. Iceman looks damn good for a dead person, wouldn't you agree?'

'I see your point. I hadn't thought of it in those terms. Iceman, seriously, how can you possibly keep this up?' Atalanta asked with genuine concern.

'I'm fine, always fine.' Iceman responded with his typical canned material. The group did have reason for concern: not only had Iceman kept up his breakneck pace, a pace that was pushing the team's limits, but he had increased his own efforts and intensity. The team had done such an amazing job gathering and analyzing data that Iceman was flooded with information. He was the only member of the team that could truly decipher mission critical data from background noise. His attack on the data was at a manic high. Iceman was in a dangerous emotional zone. Obsessed was too soft a term to describe his current state of mind. He was eating and sleeping less than the already dangerous pace he had set for himself. He had not shaved for days, nor had he had his hair cut in several weeks. With his hair and eyes wild, loss of weight, pasty complexion and incomplete beard, he had the look of a crazy professor caricature. 'We made incredible progress. Excellent job you guys. I knew you were good, but this shit right here, the avalanche of good shit, is absolutely amazing. Well done, thanks. Let's talk about where we go from here.'

Zeus interrupted. 'Hang on a second there, Tex, just pump your breaks. I have known you for a long time and have seen you when you get like this, let's just calm down a second.'

'And do what?'

Zeus dropped his head in frustration and responded. 'Jack, enough. We are going to have a couple of beers, eat and enjoy each other's company. We are going to relax, just talk to each other and eat.'

'About what? What do you want to talk about?'

Zeus was caught off guard, he meekly replied. 'Stuff, things, you know like normal people.'

Iceman, overstimulated and overtired, giggled. 'You're silly. Like I was saying, great job, but now we are ready to move onto our next step.'

'Wait a second, you mean to tell me you already got through all the information we provided?' Trinity asked guardedly.

'Yep.'

Still not convinced Trinity asked a second time. 'Just so I understand: you got through all the data, you are satisfied with the data, you were able to extract the appropriate supporting data and have assembled all of this in a working file?'

'Yeah, that's what I just said.'

The ladies looked at each other and then to Zeus for help. Zeus took a sip of his beer to buy him a moment to decide how best to approach his friend. 'Ice, you may not see it, but you are in a bad place and that is fine, it is your choice. Here's the thing, we are gassed and need a break. That is not your choice.'

Iceman took a drink from his beer and studied the group. 'That's totally fair.'

Zeus was a bit surprised, but more relieved by Ice's response. 'Great, let's overeat, over drink and over laugh. We have earned it.'

Iceman grabbed his beer, stood from the table and continued to agree with Zeus. 'You are right. When you are right, you are right. Count me in, just give me a minute. I am going to go sit at the bar while you guys get started without me.'

Trinity went to protest, concerned for Iceman, but Zeus cut her off. 'Let him be. He's alright. I'll give him his minute and then fetch him. Let's wait on ordering the food and give him a little time. I don't want to eat while he is gone, I want to eat with him. We will enjoy our beers and relax. Don't worry about him.'

Atalanta wasn't sold. 'Are you sure?'

'I am. Him going to the bar is like us relaxing and enjoying our time together. His monkey brain is racing and he just wants to settle it before he joins us. He is decompressing.'

'If you say so.' Atalanta responded not convinced.

'He sees the finish line is close. He sees we are close to zeroing in on his target and he is pushing hard. Well, he always pushes hard, but you know what I mean. Keep in mind, he and I only have this week to finish. We ship out on Saturday.'

Atalanta and Trinity accepted Zeus' explanation allowing the table to relax while Iceman was away. Ice sat at the bar surrounded by cocktail napkins. As he wrote and reviewed his blizzard of notes and sketches that formed different drafts, he got up and walked to the men's room. He used the facilities and walked to the sink to splash several handfuls of cold water on his face. He dried his face, looked into the mirror and whispered at the zombie before him *you are a handsome devil.*

Iceman returned to his barstool, finished his beer, ordered another, balled up his surrounding napkins filled with drafts and successfully shot one napkin after another into the waste basket eight feet to his left. His beer and a fresh cocktail napkin arrived. He removed the beer, drank half and eyed the blank cocktail napkin in front of him with a smile. The napkin was not blank for long.

After he finished the second half of his beer, he folded his completed cocktail napkin into his back pocket and headed back to the table having already ordered another round for the team. He decided to add a shot of whiskey to the order. *If they want to have some fun, I'm ready.*

The waitress approached the table ahead of Iceman. Zeus saw the tray included whiskey and knew his friend was on fire. His cosmic high had shifted his attention from work to fun. Zeus knew the girls were not ready for him. 'We better order that food you wanted and a lot of it in a hurry. Be careful what you ask for.'

Trinity asked. 'Why?'

'Because you might get it. You wanted fun, here it comes and in a big way.'

Trinity responded with a bit of fear as she saw Iceman approach. 'We just wanted to relax.'

'That's not what he heard.'

Iceman, thanked the waitress after she delivered the order, sat down and announced to the table. 'Who missed me the most?'

Atalanta absorbed Iceman's energy and answered. 'We all missed you the most.'

Iceman responded. 'Did you really or are you just saying that?'

Caught up in the wave, Trinity laughed and answered. 'We really missed you. I counted the minutes.'

'Alright then, a toast.' Iceman raised his whiskey to the team. 'To relaxation, very overrated.'

The spark of fun instantly caught fire and the team burned through servings of food, drinks and laughter. Iceman led the assault on all three areas. Much to the team's relief, Iceman attacked the servings of food with the same enthusiasm as drink and laughter. As the night wore on, closing time approached and Zeus' concern returned. He knew Iceman would be ready to go first thing in the morning. The girls were already captured by Iceman's energy. Like the power of the sun, he created a gravitational pull. To make matters worse, Iceman had an uncanny ability to have an encyclopedic knowledge of which bars closed late and which bars opened early. Iceman could not only keep this pace for the evening and function in the morning. He could sustain the routine for the remaining week. The girls were doomed. Zeus knew he had to apply the brakes to this train before it became a runaway. Zeus had the experience of managing the storm to prevent his teammates from becoming victims of hurricane Iceman. Zeus had to act. He ordered another round of beers without whiskey and set his course to save the team from Iceman.

'Iceman.' Zeus called for his roaring friend's attention. 'What were you up to over at the bar?'

'What are you talking about? I have been sitting right here.'

Zeus shook his head as he tried to keep Iceman's attention. 'No, I meant earlier, when you left us to head to the bar.'

Iceman looked at Zeus, momentarily distracted from the fun and replied. 'Nothing, just cleaning up a couple of thoughts.'

The beers arrived and Zeus raised his bottle. 'I noticed you slipped a napkin in your back pocket. I sure would like to see it.'

Iceman ignored his beer and responded. 'Of course, got it right here.' He reached into the back of his button fly 501 blues and began to lift the napkin. Iceman was about halfway, then paused. Zeus took a breath knowing Iceman had caught on to his tactic. Iceman stared at Zeus with a look to convey he was on to him. He turned his head to the ground in search of answers. *Should I remove the napkin, play Zeus' game and turn my attention to the mission, or should I return the napkin to my pocket and continue with all the fun? Decisions... decisions.* After a moment, Iceman turned to his beer for more guidance. With some regret, he removed the napkin, silently congratulated Zeus for his successful subterfuge and handed it over. Zeus promptly unfolded the napkin, smoothed it out and found a clean spot on the table to display it for the team to study.

* * *

C-FILES: REPORT IV

FERNANDO AND EVE CHAVEZ EDUCATED AT MICHIGAN, ALL APPEARANCES OF LEGITIMACY.

SUCCESSFUL MAQUILLADORA BUSINESSES DUE TO TRUMP PLACING $250 BILLION OF TARRIFFS ON CHINESE IMPORTS.

DRUG MONEY PROVIDED THE SEED MONEY, MONEY LAUNDERING, HUMAN TRAFFICKING AND CHINESE INVESTMENT FUEL THE 'LEGITIMATE' BUSINESSES?

LEGIT BUSINESS, WHILE SUCCESSFUL ALSO PROVIDE VEHICLE FOR SEVERAL ILLEGAL ACTIVITIES?

STILL CONNECTED TO THE GULF CARTEL?

DO THE CHAVEZ TWINS ANSWER, WWCD?

CHAPTER TWENTY-SIX

Iceman arrived early for his Tuesday appointment with Dr. Monroe. As he sat outside her office, he figured Colonel Sullivan was meeting with her in preparation for the visit. The Colonel had become a fixture in these meetings during the C-Files investigation. While he very much liked and respected the Colonel, his involvement in Ice's meetings with Grace ended with the C-Files. If Iceman were to continue to accept regular meetings with Dr. Monroe, the Colonel could not be included. Iceman's work with Dr. Monroe had to remain private. He was sure Grace would agree. The Colonel's involvement in the C-Files made sense, so Iceman accepted his presence for the time being.

Dr. Monroe's door opened, and Iceman was invited in. After pleasantries, Iceman removed his cocktail napkin and handed it to the Colonel.

'Thank you, Iceman.' The Colonel began. 'I must say, the use of the cocktail napkin has grown on me. For the purposes of these meetings, might you consider writing out two? So we each have our own copy!'

Iceman gave Sullivan a blank stare and ignored his request. 'Any questions?'

The Colonel opened his notebook, copied Iceman's notes and handed the napkin to Dr. Monroe. After a quick study, Grace smiled and answered. 'Yes, Iceman, your notes came as quite the surprise.'

The Colonel added. 'Out of left field. Please help us with this report. Let's start at the beginning. FERNANDO AND EVE CHAVEZ EDUCATED AT MICHIGAN, ALL APPEARANCES OF LEGITIMACY. Who in the world are Fernando and Eve Chavez?'

Iceman casually responded as if the answer was obvious. 'As you know, we did a deep dive into the maquiladoras.'

The Colonel interrupted. 'All 3,000 of them?'

'Correct. Without going into all the details of our search criteria, we worked to identify those maquiladoras with a unique ownership structure, Russian dolls.'

The Colonel asked. 'Layers and layers of shell companies?'

'Right again. Doing a deep dive, we identified 73 parent companies that had questionable ownership structures and owned multiple maquiladoras. After intense scrubbing of the 73, I identified Fernando and Eve Chavez. They are minority owners of several maquiladoras, primarily located on the Gulf Coast. Fernando and Eve are twins from a small town outside Tamaulipas. The North American Free Trade Agreement, NAFTA had a significant impact on Chavez's journey. As the border and relations opened up after the signing in 1994, the Chavez twins were able to attend the University of Michigan. Fernando took a double major in mechanical and system engineering and went on to earn his MBA at Michigan. Eve was a political science major and earned her law degree also at Michigan. They were groomed to run large-scale maquiladora operations.'

Dr. Monroe was concerned the briefing was going too fast when she asked. 'How detailed will the C-Files be on the subject of the twins?'

'Very. Having said that, while the files will be extremely thorough, our mission was not to seek approval for Black Ops termination. We do not have the time nor expertise to build that file. We will not have enough bank account information nor other concrete evidence to endorse Black Ops. We are building a case that the identified maquiladoras and subsequent parent companies warrant a next-level investigation with a primary focus on the Chavez twins. Does that make sense?'

Dr. Grace responded. 'Yes, you answered my question. Please continue.'

'The Chavez twins returned to Mexico in 2010 and purchased a small maquiladora, an operation that started as a direct result of NAFTA. They learned the business, grew their business and became successful. Once they established themselves as successful operators, they bought other small maquiladoras and engaged in opening new startup maquiladoras. Business was good, exceptionally good which leads me to bullet point two: SUCCESSFUL MAQUILLADORAS BUSINESSES DUE TO TRUMP PLACING $250 BILLION OF TARIFFS ON CHINESE IMPORTS. The tariff and tax policies levied against China during the Trump administration were an enormous catalyst for the maquiladora industry. None benefitted more than the Chavez twins.'

The Colonel and Grace exchanged a look of consent and Sullivan asked. 'We are with you so far and look forward to reading the completed file for more details. Can you explain bullet three?'

'Sure, but the rest of the bullet points can be summarized together.'

DRUG MONEY PROVIDED THE SEED MONEY, MONEY LAUNDERING, HUMAN TRAFFICKING AND CHINESE INVESTMENT FUEL THE 'LEGITIMATE' BUSINESSES?

LEGIT BUSINESS, WHILE SUCCESSFUL ALSO PROVIDE VEHICLE FOR SEVERAL ILLEGAL ACTIVITIES?

STILL CONNECTED TO THE GULF CARTEL?

In studying the Chavez business platform several questions emerged. The ownership structure is extremely complex dating back to their first maquiladora. Starting with the initial purchase, moving through their rapid growth, the source of capital was questionable as were their earning streams. The Chavez operation was a little too good and a little too profitable. The operation has never had a setback, it has always outperformed the market. The question we posed from Cartel involvement, specifically the Gulf Cartel, because of their location and Chinese involvement, was, *are the Chavez's entities legitimate?* We think not. We believe, or I believe, a drug cartel was the source for the seed money and continues to be involved in the Chavez empire. If the Gulf Cartel is still involved, then that opens the door to human trafficking and money laundering. We know for certain that the Chavez twins owe much of their success to Chinese businesses, so there is a close tie there. The final bullet point summarizes our efforts to date. DO THE CHAVEZ TWINS ANSWER, WWCD?'

'A very compelling case.' The Colonel took another moment to gather his thoughts before he continued. 'Very compelling. You have certainly put your training as a forensic auditor to good use. Are you prepared to submit your final report?'

'We are not. We have been working on one more thread that we believe to be very promising. When you say report, please understand that the report will be an outline with supporting documentation. Again, we are not preparing a document to be presented to the Elders.'

The Colonel replied. 'We understand. You have little interest in drafting extensive reports and sitting through countless meetings to prepare a proper report. What you have brought us is enough to warrant further investigation on an official level.'

'That's great, but wait until you see Napkin V.'

CHAPTER TWENTY-SEVEN

'Are we really finished? Is it over?' Trinity asked almost pleadingly.

Iceman twirled his cocktail napkin as he watched the waitress clear the team's plates. He turned to her and ordered. 'We'll take another round please and kindly add a bit of whiskey to our order. We have a toast to make.'

The Liberty was busy for a Wednesday night and Trinity was desperate to make this visit the last C-Files meeting. A last supper of sorts, Trinity waited on the shot of whiskey with the hope that the toast would put this mission to rest. She was tired, worn down and mentally fatigued. She needed her routine back. She wanted her life back. She was proud of their work, but Iceman's pace was too much for her to handle another day. Finally, the waitress arrived and Iceman raised his hand and the team followed.

'What a team, what a team. To the last napkin, who wants to see it?'

Trinity responded. 'I don't give a shit. If I never see another cocktail napkin again, it will be too soon. I am only going to bars that have cardboard coasters. Just tell me it's over.'

'The C-Files are being turned in tomorrow.' The table clinked their glasses in exhausted joy and Iceman continued after the drink. 'That's the good news, the great news…' he stopped mid-sentence to take a drink from his beer and allow the tension to build. 'The great news is, I am recommending you two to be the project leaders. Hooray.'

Trinity and Atalanta looked at each other in disbelief and Atalanta exclaimed. 'You did what? I want nothing to do with people.'

Iceman dismissed her. 'You'll be great.'

Trinity added to her dismay. 'You're not serious.'

'I am. Now let's move on to more important business. What are we doing tomorrow and Friday night to celebrate?'

Neither Atalanta nor Trinity was finished with Iceman's proclamation that they should be project leaders. Both went to debate the point, but Iceman ignored their concerns. 'Move on, the two of you, just move on. You will be great, knock it off. Now, about the next two days, I say Red River followed by 6th Ave the next night. I know it is a bit of a cliché, but we had fun at those two places.'

Trinity and Atalanta were not happy and turned to Zeus for support. He immediately dismissed their concerns. 'Don't look at me, I happen to agree with Iceman. You two will be great. No one knows the project better than you and no one is as talented as the two of you. I'd wish you luck, but you don't need it.'

Trinity and Atalanta look at each other with resignation. Trinity raised her beer bottle and weakly declared. 'To Red River and 6th Ave and, watch out, because here we come.'

Iceman never reached into his back pocket to show the group the final cocktail napkin. The team was done with the project.

* * *

The next morning, Iceman walked into Dr. Monroe's office and handed each a cocktail napkin. 'Here you go, I brought you each one.'

The Colonel laughed as he accepted the napkin. 'Why?! You shouldn't have.'

'My pleasure.'

Grace's smile faded as she read her napkin.

C-FILE: REPORT V - GOT IT, GOT THOSE FUCKERS

JUAN GARCIA ABREGO (GA): CALI CARTEL GA MADE $10 BILLION A YEAR. $53 MILLION WAS CONFISCATED IN MONEY LAUNDERING. SMUGGLER 300 METRIC, TONS OF COCAINE AND WHERE IS THE MONEY?

GA, SEVERAL MISTRESSES, COUNTLESS CHILDREN – FAVORITE – HE INSISTED ON CONJUGAL VISITS WHILE IN PRISON.

RIVAL CARTEL TOOK HIM OUT FOR $500K BRIBE TO FJP COMMANDER FROM SINOLA AND SOON-TO-BE LOS ZETAS

LOS ZETAS AND GULF CARTEL WENT TO WAR LEAVING GHOST TOWNS AND A FRACTIONED GULF CARTEL.

After reading her napkin, Grace was again confused, but strangely confident in Iceman's presentation.

'I got the hang of this, so why don't you just start?'

Iceman began. 'I know this is a bit odd, but just hear me out. Juan Garcia Abrego, or GA, was the main man in the Mexican drug trade in the 80's and early 90's. He revolutionized the Mexican drug trade. He turned the Mexican trafficking operation from smugglers into suppliers. The guy was a genius. He renegotiated the terms with the Columbian Cali cartel from $1500 per kilo to 50% of every shipment as payment. He was able to do this, because he was a logistical wizard. GA shipped not only drugs, but huge sums of money as well. He used American Express employees, he used Immigration and Naturalization (INS) buses courtesy of NAFTA for transport of money and drugs, he paid off everyone. His conservative estimated net wealth was $15 billion. Sure, the government got some of it, but not all of it, not by a long shot. Guess what? He is still alive at 77 years old. Granted, he is in prison, but check this out: GA, SEVERAL MISTRESSES, COUNTLESS CHILDREN – FAVORITE – HE INSISTED ON CONJUGAL VISITS WHILE IN PRISON. He loved his mistresses, but only supported a select few. As part of his terms of surrender, he insisted on conjugal visits from his favorite. Since then, he has been able to slightly expand his invitation pool.'

'You have made your case that he was quite the operator, but how does that...'

'Quite the operator? No, no, no, this guy was the Napoleon of drug logistics. The government was satisfied with his arrest and just stopped trying to trace all his money and the methods by which he distributed it. His level of logistical genius has never been duplicated. After his arrest, RIVAL CARTEL TOOK HIM OUT FOR $500K BRIBE TO FJP COMMANDER FROM SINOLA AND SOON TO BE LOS ZETAS, THE LOS ZETAS AND GULF CARTEL WENT TO WAR LEAVING GHOSTS TOWNS AND A FRACTIONED GULF CARTEL.'

Dr. Monroe was still confident in Iceman, but also still confused. 'I am not there yet. Please clear this up for me.'

'Remember the quote from Godfather III: *Just when I was out... they pull me back in.* He is operating legitimate business through the fractioned Gulf Cartel. Why haven't the Los Zetas just taken over the wounded Gulf Cartel? Because of GA, that's why. He is not just an old former drug lord, sentenced to life imprisonment. Everybody, including the U.S. and Mexican governments, has forgotten about him, yet I am telling you his empire still lives.'

'Maybe I can see your point about GA, but that still doesn't explain the CCP in all of this. There is no link.'

'Fernando and Eve Chavez are Garcia's children, born to Maria Chavez in 1983. Holy shit, right?'

The Colonel was lost in amazement. 'Are you telling me, the Chavez twins, the successful maquiladora executives, are GA's lost children?'

'Yep, and their operations, through a series of shell companies, were funded and designed by GA's dynasty. Maria Chavez, the twins' mother, was an early favorite of GA. He set Maria and her family up on a nice small farming estate outside of Tamaulipas. What is Tamaulipas known for other than maquiladoras? Try the home of the Gulf Cartel.'

'Wow!' was all Grace could manage to say. 'Listen, I have clear threads that are easy to follow. I want to emphasize that we are not there yet. Duke will pick this apart if the C-Files are not presented as anything more than a solid thread. I really cannot emphasize that enough. The C-Files require and warrant a complete investigation. The brilliant smuggling routes developed by GA backed by the perceived stable of legitimate maquiladora businesses is the exact cover the CCP would reach out to.'

The Colonel responded. 'You certainly have our support to kick this up to Black Ops investigation.'

Iceman was not finished. 'One last thing, then I must go. I have the team waiting for me to be released into the wild and attack Red River. We may have stumbled on a Chavez shell corporation that may have opened a new maquiladora in Tijuana during the Trump administration. The maquiladora is in the business of purchasing and shipping empty freight containers to China. Due to COVID, the new business is in a growing industry; however, a lot of cash could leave Mexico and be laundered in China in those containers. The US only inspects 4% of incoming freight containers, they represent, and Congress passed a requirement of near 100%, but that is bullshit. How many containers do you think are inspected before departure from Tijuana?'

'China launders the money, employs the services of the Chavez's maquiladoras in exchange for the Chavez twins using their ties to their father and the Gulf Cartel to smuggle undocumented, infected immigrants into the U.S.'

'Roger that.'

CHAPTER TWENTY-EIGHT

After completing their training at the Factory and celebrating the completion of the C-Files, the twins were greeted by Conjar as they exited JFK. 'Ready for advanced Black Ops training?'

Iceman smiled. 'I don't know, life in a cubicle was great. Fuck yes, we are ready. I never thought I would be so excited for you to kick our asses. Are we headed straight to the Barn to kick off training?'

The Barn, the basic training center for the Elders, was very familiar to the twins. Located in Sullivan, NY. The Barn was 300 acres dedicated to building the foundation of the agents of death. Conjar used the two-hour ride from JFK to the Barn to brief the twins on their training schedule.

'You will follow the same training program that you executed during your three years of Black Ops basic training. You are now entering advanced training. Every year of your 10-year commitment to the Elders as an agent will be dedicated to building a better agent. Some phases will be cut short and some expanded, but the same program remains in place.'

Zeus smiled. 'Are you going to welcome us to advance training the same way you did basic training?'

Conjar laughed as he remembered meeting the twins for the first time almost four years ago. He was especially vicious to the twins sparking Iceman's temper. Iceman attacked Conjar and Zeus quickly joined the fight. Conjar administered quite the beating, but to their credit the twins kept coming. During their first meeting, the twins' fire and resolve immediately surprised and impressed Conjar. While he would wait years to tell the twins, he knew that first day he was working with unique warriors. 'No Zeus, I don't think I will pick a fight with the two of you today. We have graduated from that training technique.'

The three team members all smiled, knowing Conjar would have more than his hands full with one of the twins let alone both. They arrived at the Barn and Conjar took immediate control. 'Gear up and be ready to go in 10 minutes.'

The twins entered the same house used during their basic training. The house was one of four located on the large property. The other training homes were vacant, typically another team or two would be present. Each team bunked together and had a house to themselves. Team Conjar had the Barn to themselves. The twins dropped their gear in their assigned rooms and hustled up to meet Conjar.

Conjar ordered the twins to join him on a five-mile run.

During their run, the twins passed familiar sites. They stared at the big barn used for storage, passed the barn used for physical training, weight training, sparring and yoga. 400 yards later they fired with their fingers at the barn that housed the armory and indoor gun range. As the group looped back, they passed the commercial and apartment buildings used for staging insertions then came the outdoor gun range. The five-mile run ended at the 400-yard-long lake used to swim laps.

'You guys know the drill. Meet me back at the house after your three-mile swim.'

The twins reported to the house after the swim to find a freshly showered Conjar seated at the kitchen table. 'Same drill as before. Iceman, it's almost dinner time, so you are up. Zeus, I assume you have not learned your way around a kitchen. You got lunch and protein shake duty. I got breakfast. Grab a shower and we will eat. The husband-and-wife statesmen that run this place loaded us up. After chow, we will talk about this phase of training.'

Iceman got to work after his shower. After surveying groceries, he made baked lemon chicken, pasta with garlic bread and a salad.

'You two know the drill. We train from 0600 until dinner at 1800 hours. After you shower and eat dinner, you have a couple hours of homework to do. We will train here for six weeks. Your homework is to continue your studies in Mandarin and Asian Studies. Well done in Spanish and Arabic. The next two years are dedicated to building on your first year in Mandarin.'

Zeus nodded. 'Got it.'

Conjar continued. 'On land, we will continue to use the Heckler and Koch 45 Combat Tactical handgun with silencer and the HK MP7 assault rifle, with silencer as our weapons of choice. No sense of changing. Same with sniper training, we stay with Mawhinney's M40 sniper rifle. At sea we use the lake to refine your skills with the MK 25.'

The twins became experts with the LAR V Draeger Rebreather, designated MK 25. The MK 25 underwater breathing gear was pure oxygen that recycled air to prevent expelled air bubbles. The MK 25 was chosen for the twins, because of its small size and front worn configuration, suitable for shallow water over shorter distances. The front worn configuration provided better cover for stealth operations.

'Get your five-mile run and three-mile swim in before breakfast, then we go to work. The only amendment to training is the addition of a couple of elite specialized trainers. You have outgrown my ability to assist you in your fighting styles. You will be working with Woods on your fighting styles. I worked with him in my ninth year as an agent. You are working with him early in your advanced training, because of your exceptional performance and Woods' age. He only has five good years left. Don't tell him I said that, so we decided to push your timetable to face him in his prime. He arrives tomorrow and will be here for the full six weeks. Our second specialist you are already familiar with, you good pal Fingers.'

Zeus asked. 'Why the name Woods?'

Before Conjar could reply, Iceman interjected. 'Because he moves and attacks like a tiger. Good one, Tiger Woods.'

Conjar and Zeus laughed at Iceman's correct response. Zeus simply offered. 'Of course, you got it.'

Fingers was the twins' *Las Vegas* trainer. He schooled the twins in the art of working a casino at table games by taking advantage of the other players' weaknesses. The card games were the vehicle used to train the twins to detect micro expressions in their opponents. Equally important, the games challenged the twins to mask and manipulate their own facial expressions. The greatest skill he installed in the twins was the ability to read people and the skill to recognize the smallest tells. Similar to the training secret service agents received, Fingers drilled the ability to detect micro expressions. When the twins played Fingers in cards, he relentlessly detected the twins' micro expressions and eliminated all traces that could potentially betray them. He also taught the twins the art of pickpocketing, breaking and entering, and stealing cars.

Iceman was not pleased. 'Hang on a second. If he is coming here does that mean we won't be working with him in Vegas?'

'That's exactly what it means.'

'That's bullshit.'

Conjar nodded. 'Yes, yes, it is, Iceman. Fingers will invest his six weeks with you refining your skills with the addition of safe cracking and beating a lie detector. Iceman, I imagine this will be elementary for you given you live in the grey area of truth and lies.'

Iceman smiled. 'If ever a man was misunderstood.'

* * *

The twins believed their martial arts skills were exceptional. Woods set them straight. The twins achieved and were working to perfect their final discipline, Marine Corp martial arts training. The Corp incorporated many fighting styles including Muay Thai. Muay Thai or Thai boxing, was a stand-up technique that implemented striking and clinching techniques. The discipline was also referred to as the *art of eight limbs,* because it combined the use of fists, elbows, knees and shins. Also included in the training was Brazilian Jiu-Jitsu (BJJ), which focused on ground fighting and submission. The grabbling and striking style had its origins in feudal Japan. The samurai warrior could wind up bereft of his sword and needed a weapon-less method of defense. The twins were also experts in Krav Maga, the Israeli military fighting technique. The twins worked to achieve Bruce Lee's ultimate fighting style of total freedom. Lee believed in incorporating all fighting disciplines to develop one's own fighting style to achieve total freedom. Iceman's style favored Muay Thai. His ultra-quick and strong hands with a 38-inch reach made the *art of eight limbs* the perfect foundation. Zeus favored Brazilian Jiu-Jitsu. His mighty bulk, natural strength and quick feet developed from years of playing rugby, built a fearsome ground fighter. If Zeus took an opponent down the fight was over.

After watching the twins engage in their relentless sparring for over an hour, Woods called for the twins' attention.

'The reports are correct; your martial arts skills are advanced for your years of training. You two are most certainly dangerous men. Who wants to go first?'

Woods, standing 5'10" with a long athletic build, was inviting the twins to spar with him. Iceman was the first to accept the challenge. Woods held back in the beginning of the engagement, gauging Iceman's skill level. While Woods was well undersized in comparison to the twins, Woods dominated Iceman when fully engaged. Woods repeated the process with Zeus.

'As you can see, we have much work to do before you achieve total freedom. You both have a good foundation for me to work with. In three years, with your continued commitment, I'll get you there.'

* * *

Fingers primary objective on this mission was to train the twins in the art of breaking lie detector tests. He schooled the twins and to no one's surprise Iceman was a natural. He had a unique ability to relive a lie to the point that he made himself believe it was true. Zeus, on the other hand, had to be taught the lessons one step at a time. The fundamentals of controlling and manipulating breathing, pulse rate, blood pressure, using meditation and singular focus were broken down by Fingers and taught by the numbers.

Sufficient time was spent on the art of safe cracking. For the most sophisticated safes, the twins relied on hackers and their technology. For common safes, Fingers taught the three basic tenants: determine the contact points, discover the number of wheels and graph the results. The twins were amazed at their newfound ability to hear the classic click. After six weeks of training with Fingers, the twins were proficient safe crackers.

The lessons with Fingers were always entertaining. Learning expert criminal skills pulled on the twins' diabolical side, especially Iceman. Fingers engaging personality made the intriguing lesson that much more enjoyable. The real test and fun were the late-night card games played on the weekends. With nothing to do at the secluded Barn, the card games became an intense source of entertainment. While Zeus, Conjar and Woods were trained to be exceptional card players, Iceman and Fingers were naturals. They shared that natural gift of feel. They had a sixth sense that could not be taught. They dominated the card matches. While Iceman lost more than he won to Fingers, he closed the gap by the end of training. Both Iceman and Fingers had the skills to seriously compete and would be favored in the World Series of Poker.

* * *

At the end of training Iceman smiled and shook Finger's hand. He pulled him close with his shoulders touching and whispered into Finger's ear. 'See you next year. You might want to bring a bigger bank role. '

Fingers gently pulled away. 'I brought enough. Like your baseball team, the Chicago Cubs used to like to say. *Wait until next year.* Next year took 108 years, that is a good goal for you.'

'I am a White Sox fan. Do you want your wallet back?'

CHAPTER TWENTY-NINE

The twins sat at their usual spot at their favorite JFK airport bar. Their visits to the bar date back to their West Point days. They ordered the usual: Guinness, one Jameson to warm up, a turkey sandwich for Iceman and a ham sandwich for Zeus.

In between sips of Guinness and consumption of Jameson, Zeus commented. 'I thought the training went well. Fucking Woods is amazing.'

'He is. We held our own pretty well and by the end he did not completely dominate us.'

'True. We were competitive, but that little bit more he has is like a canyon to cross.'

'Are you going to finish your chips? We will get there sooner than he thinks. Our sparring during the course of the year will be even better after Woods' training.'

'Yes, I want my chips. I agree we will have a chance next year. Boyo, you sure do like Fingers.'

'Birds of a feather.'

'You two certainly flock together. Do you think you can get him next year?'

'No. Don't get pissed at me, but playing with you is fun, but doesn't make me better. Only playing Fingers makes me better. Know what I am saying?'

'I do and I take no offense. I appreciate how much you help me at cards.'

'Cool.'

'Excited to see Katie?' Zeus asked to begin a delicate conversation.

'Absolutely.'

'You do know, I am all in with your cousin and I call and text her all the time. You also know that Kelly and Katie have become incredibly good friends.'

'I do.' Iceman answered with his attention focused on Zeus' chips.

'Why haven't you contacted Katie since you saw her in Ireland and London? I have reminded you countless times.'

'I know I should, but we were in training, and she would ask where I was and what I was doing. I don't want to go into it.'

'I spoke with the Colonel and it is cool to tell her where we are when not on a mission, as long as we stick to the OWL story. In fact, he said it was good to stay in contact with my mam and Kelly with the OWL cover. Regular contact settles the nerves for the people in our lives.'

'I know. That makes sense. I just focus on one life at a time. When I am with the Elders as Iceman, I am all in. When I am with Katie as Jack, I am all in. Make sense?'

'No, not at all. That might work for you, but it does not work for Katie. Your parents, countless aunts, uncles and cousins might accept that. It's just you being you. Katie and any other rational girl will call bullshit. You cannot act like that; you have to identify yourself as the problem. You cylinder yourself, because you are not committed. You aren't sure if being an agent and having someone that loves you and you love back will work. You are scared to take a chance and step out of your comfort zone. A zone that you have complete control over. Look at the shit you pulled on our first day of the Factory, total control of your life. You must take a chance and release control and replace it with belief. Love is not controllable, man. You are being a dick.'

'What have you been doing when I haven't been looking? Are you watching Oprah again?'

'Sorry to report, but you are not willing to behave in a social norm. You love someone, you put them first. You know that. You do that for me. Rather than be scared, just engage. You'll be good at it.'

'Are you sure you are going to finish those chips?'

* * *

The twins arrived at the Elder's bed and breakfast located in the Back Bay of Boston. Back Bay is an upscale neighborhood centrally located along the Charles River. The neighborhood boasts several of the city's best shops and restaurants. Walking distance to Boston Commons and several other popular Boston sites, Black Bay conveniently reaches other destinations with the subway. Rebecca ran the bed and breakfast and lived in the two-bedroom apartment above the garage located at the rear of the property. The cover story for the B&B was a corporate retreat for OWL.

'What a pleasure to have the twins back. How are you?'

'The pleasure is ours, Rebecca. How you been?'

'I have been well Iceman, thank you for asking. You know where to find your rooms. Why don't you take a few minutes to get settled and we can review your schedule? You will find your room with your wardrobe from last year and all the comforts you like. The Colonel reminded me how much you two like to eat and he wants you to get stronger and be mission ready when you depart. More on that during the briefing.'

Zeus responded. 'That's great news. Thank you.'

'My pleasure. Now off you go.'

The twins returned to Rebecca 15 minutes later, showered with a fresh set of clothes, ready for the briefing.

'My, don't the two of you clean up nicely. Here we go, let's sit down and get started. The briefing won't take long.' They took their seats and the twins were pleased that Rebecca was kind enough to provide a beautiful Italian Charcuterie board filled with Italian meat and cheeses, paired with fruits and vegetables. 'Your schedule is similar to your previous visits with a couple of amendments. Your exercise time has been extended from 0530 to 0830. Rather than running directly to the MIT Recreation and Fitness Center, you will expand the two-mile run to five miles. I have mapped out three routes I think you will enjoy. The early start will alleviate traffic and give you a clear runway. Your time at the fitness center has been extended to 90 minutes. Do not spar at the fitness center. Run back to the B&B and report to the gym in the basement for 60 minutes of sparring and yoga. I will provide you with a special shake, designed by our nutritionist at the Factory, before your 0530 departure, again at 0800 before the basement and another at 0930. With the shake at 0930, I will provide a full breakfast. Your total morning calorie intake will be 4,000 calories. You report for Mandarin lessons at 1100. You have a one-hour break at 1400 for lunch. You will not order or go out for lunch as you did in the past. I will provide lunch designed by the nutritionist. Report back at 1500 hours for your Mandarin lessons and Asian Studies discussion. At 1800 hours, I again will provide your meals. 1900 hours until 2300 is independent assignments in Asian Studies. You are welcome to use the kitchen provided you police after yourself. From Sunday night until Friday night there is no outside food. You are on a strict diet customized by the nutritionist. At 2230, I will provide your nighttime shake designed to help you sleep and continue to inject your body with a healthy power packed diet. Your targeted calorie intake for the day is 12,000. Any questions about your weekday schedule?

The twins shook their heads, good soldiers that they were.

'Good, now on to the weekend.' Both the twins' ears perked up. 'You are free from 1800 hours until 2330 on Fridays. You will drink a shake before leaving and upon return. On Saturdays, you have your exercise routine, meals, and independent study until 1500 hours. You are free after your departure shake until 0100 hours on Sunday morning. Sunday follows the same routine as Saturday except for your return time of 2300 hours. Any questions?'

Iceman spoke and Zeus cringed. 'No questions from me, I am changing the schedule to something reasonable. Friday is fine as is Saturday morning. We are free from Saturday 1500 until Sunday 2300 hours. We are grown men who have trained beyond any reasonable measure and have more than earned this tiny concession.'

Rebecca listened patiently to Iceman before she responded. 'You have your orders.'

Iceman was not in the mood for a debate. 'The orders are dated and made without my input. The orders need to be changed.'

Zeus, anticipating a showdown, intervened as only Zeus could. 'I see both sides of this potential conflict.' Zeus was prepared to offer Saturday 1500 hours until Sunday 0900 until he saw Iceman's eyes. Concessions to Iceman's plan were not in the offering. Iceman was not going to accept anything less than complete acceptance to his schedule. 'I was prepared to offer a compromise, but Iceman's schedule is more than reasonable.'

'Please excuse me for a few moments.'

Once she departed, Iceman turned to Zeus. He was surprised and impressed by Zeus' total support. Ice had expected Zeus to offer concessions to Rebecca. 'Thanks for backing my play, I really appreciate it.'

Zeus simply nodded.

Rebecca returned with her laptop with the Colonel's face filling the screen. 'Gentlemen, I understand we have a problem with the schedule.'

Zeus stared at Iceman for a moment with a look that said *shut the fuck up.* 'No sir, more of a misunderstanding, a slight difference of opinion.'

The Colonel accepted Zeus' response and internally celebrated his consistent problem-solving approach. He loved that Iceman listened to Zeus. 'I see. You can obviously understand our concern. We are concerned about Katie and in all probability, Kelly will fly in to visit.'

Zeus nodded. 'We understand, but the proposed schedule causes more problems than is needed. OWL would never place these demands on a forensic account. Agreed?'

Again, the Colonel was pleased. The use of their OWL cover as forensic auditors was an effective argument, made complete sense and impossible to argue with. Zeus' response was check-mate. 'Well done, Zeus. I agree with your schedule and have all the confidence that the two of you will not abuse the additional privileges.'

Zeus understood the Colonel's concerns. 'There will be no problems.'

The Colonel was comfortable with Zeus' response, but wanted to hear directly from Iceman. He knew without direct confirmation, Iceman would find a grey area to exploit. 'Iceman, are we good?'

'Yes, sir. This is a good mission plan. I will execute the orders and in the spirit in which they are intended. I will stand tall, on time at my post.'

The Colonel, satisfied, turned his attention to Rebecca. 'That is all. Rebecca, thank you for a job well done.'

Rebecca shut down her laptop and turned to the twins. Dinner will be served tonight at 2000 and we start training tomorrow. You have a little over three hours until supper. Go enjoy yourselves.'

Iceman smiled. 'Thanks, you really are quite something.'

* * *

On the walk to Bukowski's Tavern, the local dive bar the twins favored, Zeus asked Iceman. 'Have you contacted Katie yet?'

'Almost.'

'Almost? What the fuck does that mean? Let me help you: there is no almost. You are not getting served at the pub until you contact her.'

'Agreed.'

'Do it now.' Zeus demanded.

Iceman took out his iPhone and sent a text. 'Happy?'

'What did it say?'

'Hi, are you available to chat at 2130 hours?'

'You can't be serious! You are going to get crickets. She won't respond to that.'

'She will.'

'No chance and when you are wrong, you send her a real text in 10 minutes.'

'Agreed.'

10 minutes passed and to the surprise of no one, including Iceman if he was honest with himself, Katie did not respond.

Zeus tackled the issue when time ran out. 'I am serious, handle your shit! You have had 10 minutes to pull your head out of your ass.'

Iceman did not respond. He simply pulled out his iPhone and began typing. *I am sorry for the shitty text and I more than apologize for not staying in touch. I think about you a lot and miss you so much. I am sorry. I shut down to block out the pain of not being with you. I have no experience with missing someone and I suck at it. Please stay with me. I will get better. When you connect with me, you will know immediately that you have always been with me. Talk to me and give me a chance at 2130?*

Satisfied with his text, Iceman ordered. 'Can we get another round please?'

'Coming right up.' The bartender replied.

Zeus asked. 'Let me see what you sent.'

'No.'

'Was it good? Will she contact you?'

'Hope so.'

Iceman received a text. *Hello stranger. I understand you are in town. Forget the call at 2130, I am coming to you. Where are you?*

Iceman was knocked back by the response and texted. *Back Bay, but I have to be back at 2000.*

'Not a problem. Where in Back Bay?'

Jack's head was now spinning. Without the ability to think, he typed. *Bukowski.*

See you soon.

Iceman put his phone back into his pocket and took a breath. *How amazing is Katie and how much do I suck? I don't deserve her.*

Zeus looked at Iceman and turned to the bartender. 'Another round please, but hold the Jameson.' He looked back at Iceman who was lost in his own world. 'Jack, where did you go?'

'What? It's nothing.' Iceman was surprised by Zeus' use of his proper name. He understood and appreciated his friend's subtle nudge to bring Jack out.

'What did she say?'

'She is coming here. I told her about 2000 hours and she didn't care. She is still coming.'

'To kick your ass.'

'No. Well, I don't think so. I think she is excited.'

'That is awesome. I got to take a squirt. I'll be right back.'

While Zeus was away, Iceman was lost in his crazy brain. He was violently processing everything that had transpired. Katie, the Elders, Black Ops, colliding worlds and an uncertain future. He could be dead in a couple of months during his next mission, but he was supposed to be soft and gentle today. He was expected to be an agent of death, yet at the same time, a supportive partner to Katie. There was a reason Batman isolated himself from the world.

'Get out of your head.' Zeus had returned from the restroom.

'What?'

'I know what you are doing and stop. You don't have to figure it all out in the next few minutes. You just have to be present in the moment. You will figure it out soon enough, but for now, can Jack come out and play?'

Iceman drank his beer in solitude and silence, until she walked in. Iceman was so lost he did not notice. He did notice when his head was snapped back and was on the receiving end of Avalon. A magical kiss snapped Jack to the present. He exploded off the bar stool and grabbed Katie with the strongest of hugs. He buried his head into Katie's shoulder and whispered. 'I missed you so much.'

In that moment, Katie knew he was with her every step of the way. Any concerns or fears simply disappeared. She thought. *Kelly was right. He will go dark, but he is always there. He will come back for you.* 'I am here now, so knock it off. Bartender, can we have another round of Guinness and Jameson? We don't have much time.'

Seamus spoke up. 'We have a little more time than you think. I got us to 2300 hours.'

Jack asked. 'How? When did you make that happen?'

'When I went to the bathroom. I called our training supervisor at OWL and explained your situation. I explained that you needed extra time with Katie right now to clear your head, because you are an idiot.' After taking a gulp of Guinness and downing his shot he turned to Katie. 'Our training supervisor really likes Jack. I explained that Jack needed to come out and play. She understood. What she did is amazing. Changing our training schedule is a big deal.'

Katie playfully asked. 'Should I be concerned? Is she after my man?'

Seamus answered. 'She's like 25 years older than us, so I think you are safe.'

'I'll take your word for it, Zeus.'

Jack added. 'But she is still kind of hot.'

Katie knew Jack was goading her, so she changed the subject. 'What training are you here for?'

Jack was excited to be able to answer Katie honestly. 'Mandarin.'

'Seriously?'

Iceman kissed her and answered. 'Yes.'

'Ok then, we are going out for Chinese when Kelly comes. I've got to see it in action. Do you speak any other languages?'

Jack quickly answered. 'Spanish.' He deliberately left out Arabic to avoid suspicion.

Katie knew the twins were not forensic accountants, but did not know the extent of their job description. She thought back to Iceman's injuries when they first slept together, but quickly returned to the moment. 'Our dance card is filling up. Kelly is coming this weekend and two weeks later. She is trying for a third, but she is bumping up into the holiday season and might not be able to shake loose. Sorry, Seamus.'

'It's cool. I'll take what I can get.'

'Speaking of holidays, do you get time off? Kelly didn't know.'

Jack answered. 'I hope so, but I doubt it. We are scheduled for an assignment out of the country, so it doesn't look promising.'

Katie knew not to ask where. If Jack wanted to tell her, he would. She was not going to push it. 'Not to worry, there will be plenty of holidays for us to share in the future.

Strangely Jack was not fazed by the comment. 'Absolutely. We are low men on the totem pole right now, but that will change.

We will be able to better block off time starting next year and even more so in future years.'

Katie was ecstatic with Jack's simple response and the thought of future plans. She was determined to take the next two months slow to build their foundation. Katie could not fully understand her situation. Jack was slowly committing to being a better partner to her. His monkey brain was beginning to take root in their relationship. Once fully engaged, Katie was in for a fabulous journey.

* * *

The twins trained hard during the week, but Friday could not come soon enough. Iceman calculated the twins' calorie intake at 15,000 a day, well above the prescribed 12,000. The food was good and the shakes didn't have much taste which was fine; they expected the healthy shakes to taste like grass.

Dr. Liu was born and raised in Dalian, Liaoning, China. Her parents were professors at the prestigious Dalian University. Dalian is a port city located on the Liaoning Peninsula at the southern tip of China's Liaodong Province. Dalian boasts water on three sides with seven beautiful beaches. The university attracts students from around the world. Dr Liu grew up in a dynamic and diverse environment. She studied economics as an undergraduate and elected to pursue her master's in Asian Studies at Stanford University. She was recruited to OWL while at Stanford. She worked on the Asian desk for five years in analytics and investments. After five years at OWL, she was selected to join the Elders as team leader of the Asian desk. After 10 years as team leader, she was sent to SOAS University of London to earn her doctorate in Chinese and Inner Asian studies. She was a professor at MIT and a statesman with the Elders. As a statesman she was charged with teaching Mandarin and Asian studies.

Dr. Liu was very complimentary of the twins for the work they put in Mandarin while they were away for the year. The twins were closing in on being fluent. In all fairness, the twins' success in Mandarin was partially due to hard work but credit was due to Dr. Liu's excellent teaching. After assessing the twins' impressive work, Dr. Liu sent a report advising she would not require the remaining dedicated time; the twins were ready to start on a new language next year.

Friday came and the twins raced to *Bukowski*. The girls were at the crowded bar with two seats saved. Kelly jumped off her stool, raced to Seamus and leapt into his arms. Her legs straddled his waist. He easily caught the flying Kelly and was rewarded with a pent-up kiss.

Jack casually walked over to Katie, playing it cool and asked. 'Is this seat taken?'

'Why, yes, it is. I am holding it for Jack. Is he here?'

Jack picked up on the not-so-subtle dig referring to Iceman and going dark. He decided to go with it. 'Yes, yes, he is. Just before he left to come here, he had an enema to pull his head out of his ass. He is good to go.'

'If that is the case, sit your clean ass down. Gary, can we get another round, four ways.'

'Coming right up, Katie.'

'Katie? First name basis with the bartender?'

With a devilish grin, Katie teased. 'His cute enough. A girl must keep her options open. What if Iceman hijacked Jack and came in his place? That would simply not do.'

'I got it the first and every time during the week. You can stop celebrating it.'

'Give me a kiss, you sexy boy.'

As Kelly and Seamus approached their stools, Jack got up and gave his cousin a big hug. 'Great to see you. You look great.'

Kelly was surprised by Jack's warmth. She rarely, if ever, felt him so gentle and kind. 'Great to see you too, Jackie.'

'Sit, sit, sit. Tell me what's going on. How are you doing? What's new?'

Kelly's response was delayed and still processing Jack. 'Things are good.'

Zeus interjected. 'Tell him, go on, tell him.'

'Tell me what?'

'It's nothing really.'

Jack was not satisfied. 'Spill it, baby cousin.' Kelly and Jack were born on the same day, five hours apart.

'By five hours. If you must know, I am applying to be a physician assistant.'

'Holy motherfucking shit. That is amazing.'

'Jackie, it's nothing. I only applied and getting accepted is tough. Then, if I am accepted, the course load is a bitch.'

'You'll kill it, no doubt. You killed your BSN.' Jack was referring to Kelly's Bachelor of Science in Nursing. Kelly earned high honors at Loyola of Chicago, while working full-time as a bartender.

'That will definitely help and I overloaded in undergrad and grad school, so I already took some of the required classes.'

'There you go. You got this shit. How are things in the ER?'

Kelly could not stop wondering, *who is this guy? I barely thought he knew I was a nurse.* 'Crazy. The trauma unit I work in is regretfully busy. The west side of Chicago has not let up on gun violence. It's absurd.'

'I was reading up on Loyola Medical Center and you guys are rated high. I was also reading that nurses get evaluated and scored. I am sure you are scoring well.'

'I have, but hold on. I am going to drink my round and you are going to tell me what happened to my cousin?!' She paused, drank her beer and thought for a moment. She turned to Katie and Seamus. 'What did you two do to him?'

Katie and Seamus smiled at each other, conspirators in an Iceman intervention. Katie responded. 'Nothing. I have no idea what you are talking about. My sweet Jack is just a kind soul.'

Seamus and Katie tried to hold in their laugh, but failed. Kelly joined in on the fun.

Jack took a gulp of beer and mumbled. 'They kicked my ass.'

Kelly was still laughing. 'Jackie, they must have done some number. I am a little afraid of this kind, gentle side. Should I expect you to start wearing hair products, get mani-pedis and fully commit to your metrosexual side?'

Jack had had enough of the teasing; Kelly had taken it too far. He set his beer down, turned to the three laughing hyenas and gave them an Iceman stare. They knew Mufasa was done with the hyenas. The joke was instantly over and the four settled back in.

After finishing his beer Jack asked. 'What do you guys want to do for dinner? I was thinking pub food tonight and tomorrow we go our separate ways and have a fancy couples' dinner.'

Katie answered. 'Sounds good.'

'Alright. We grab our last round here then head over to *Solas Irish Pub* for food. Tomorrow afternoon Seamus and I will meet you at the Lenox. I booked us suites for Saturday night. Hope that was alright.'

Katie laughed. She lived at home with her parents, and Kelly was their guest. She was waiting for her older sister, Colleen, to close on a two-bedroom condominium in the financial district. The sisters were set to be roommates. 'Yes, Jack. I speak for the rest of us. A suite at one of the best hotels in Boston somehow meets our approval.'

'Cool. We will follow the same schedule as London. We will go our separate ways on Saturday night and meet for a late lunch/happy hour on Sunday. We will follow the same routine when Kelly is in town. Katie, you and I will make plans when Seamus is flying solo. Sorry old sport, I am kicking you to the curb when Kelly is in Chicago.'

Seamus smiled. He was happy Jack was making the effort with Katie. 'Not a problem, I would be upset if you didn't.'

Katie put her hand on Seamus' shoulder. 'Thank you, Seamus, but we will most certainly look for you to join us on occasion. I enjoy your company and Jack 24/7 can be a bit much.'

Again, the group laughed except for Jack. He ordered the last round and asked for the check. He was hoping a change of scenery would change the topic of conversation, namely him.

* * *

The weekends when Kelly was away settled into a nice routine for Katie and Jack. They went out with Seamus on Friday nights and toured the Boston pub grub circuit. On Saturday nights, Jack dressed properly and the two dined at fine establishments that had no televisions. One weekend without Kelly, Jack asked for and was granted special leave. Katie wanted to go leaf peeping to view the fall foliage in New England where the leaves change colors in autumn. Rebecca passed Jack's request to the Colonel who approved Jack's plan. The Colonel figured allowing Iceman to tour rural New England from 1200 hours on Saturday until 2200 hours on Sunday was better than Ice roaming free in Boston. Jack rented a car and the two started their exploration with the Mohawk Trail. The Trail or Route 2 began in Greenfield, MA and traveled 42 miles ending in Williamstown, MA. After completing the Mohawk Trail, the happy couple drove to Keene, NH. The 47-mile drive celebrated more vibrant colors winding along the I-91 route. Katie reserved a quaint B&B for their stay Saturday night. She made a dinner concession to Jack after the quiet romantic afternoon. She surprised him by taking him out to dinner at the Kilkenny Pub. She figured she had pushed Jack's limit and wanted him recharged for Sunday's drive. After breakfast at the B&B, they explored the Monadnock Region Loop. The 80-mile loop, which began and ended in Keene, had several stops in historical towns. Katie insisted on stopping at each town. Three hours into their loop, Jack surprised Katie. He had asked Rebecca to prepare the same Charcuterie Board she had prepared for the twins. The romantic picnic rocked Katie. She could not believe just how much Jack committed to the tour. She knew he hated everything they were doing, but not only did he not let it show, he kept his happy face. She forever remembered his giving kindness and the romantic picnic he had sprung on her. Returning to Keene, they held hands as they window-shopped the small stores of Main St. The two-hour ride, driving NH-9 and I-93 raced by due to the constant conversation with the leaves turning as the perfect backdrop.

* * *

The Sundays, when Kelly was in Chicago, were a bit dicey. Iceman replaced Jack. When Jack was free from training on those Sundays, he chose to return to South Boston and hang with his favorite Southies. Old Sullivan's was his spot and Billy was his favorite Southie. A police officer, who belonged to a key club just around the corner from the pub, was Iceman's guy. A key club was a private pub with each member holding a key for entrance. Jack was familiar with key clubs, having visited his neighborhood's version on the South Side of Chicago. Jack's South Side club was made up of Irish-American firemen, police-men, union workers and the occasional business and legal professional. The Southie Key Club was more reflective of their neighborhood. The Southie Key Club had the same members as the Chicago Club, but added a rougher, more criminal element as well. Jack loved it.

'Billy, my man.'

'Holy shit, where have you been?'

'Here and there.'

'Well, Old Sully's is better for you gracing us with your visit. How long are you around?'

'Couple weeks.'

'Cool, cool. You want any action?' Billy was excited to see Jack. He enjoyed his energy and outlook. 'You cleaned up last time you were in town. I rode the betting wave with you and did well for myself. What do ya got?'

'My kitty still flush?'

'Yeah, I would say so. $13,500.'

'Give me a G-note this Saturday on Boston College with the points over Notre Dame and another G-note on Wisconsin over Michigan straight up to pull the upset.'

'No pro football games?'

'No, I never bet the pros.'

'Why do you like today's action?' Billy tried to understand Iceman's successful betting scheme so that he could implement it when Iceman was away.

'Every week I bet against Notre Dame and Michigan. Their alumni bet huge with their hearts and not their brains. The lines are always inflated. The professional gamblers bet against the alumni and over the course of the season, the pros clean up. The strategy doesn't work week to week. You have to stay with it for the entire season, especially bowl games. I am going out on a bit of a limb taking Wisconsin straight up, but they are at home and I think the better team. Taking the 2.5 points is tempting and the smarter bet, but I like Wisconsin. You might want to take the points.' Betting Wisconsin straight up paid $1,200 on the $1,000 bet, taking the points paid $1,000.

'Makes sense. Your strategy for the last three years in college basketball sure worked out. Betting on the veteran teams with the spread against programs with young marque players like Duke and Kentucky paid off big.'

Fortunately, the New England Patriots were playing the second game of the day that started at 1630. The Pats were playing at the San Francisco 49ers. Billy and Iceman enjoyed the game, beers, food and each other's company. The following week took a turn.

Before arriving at Old Sullivan's for his Sunday visit, Iceman hired a car service to take him to Logan Airport, wait for him and take him to Old Sullivan's. Iceman entered the airport, found the twins' locker, and retrieved the twins' bag containing $300,000. The bag was filled with the contents from their previous mission. Conjar instructed the twins to keep the cash from Pervert's safe. Iceman stored the bag at the airport until he settled on a permanent location. A location blind to Elders' eyes.

He entered Old Sullivan's and greeted Billy. 'Hello, player.'

'Yes, sir. The fund stands tall at $15,700.'

'Press both. I love Navy with the points against ND. The Irish almost never cover that game. The triple option Navy runs slows down the game and limits the number of possessions. In addition, Purdue over Michigan with the points, putting another $2,000 on the under in the ND game. No way the combined score of both teams reaches 51.'

'Got it.'

Iceman waited for Billy to finish his beer to order another round and ask. 'I want to join the key club; can you make that happen?'

'I was waiting for you to ask me that. There is a problem.'

'What's up?'

'Everything is cool. Everybody remembers your visit last year. Nobody minded the beating you put on Frankie. He pulled a knife and slashed you good. The way you beat him and the way you self-treated the slash with ice, crazy glue and duct tape impressed everyone.'

During his last visit, Iceman accepted Billy's invitation to play cards. Iceman deliberately played down to the level of competition to enjoy the club. Card playing etiquette dictated that card sharks, Iceman clearly qualified, never assaulted a friendly game. Frankie, who was a good player, but certainly no shark, was winning big, not a problem. Frankie won in an aggressively boastful manner which upset Iceman. Big mistake. When the game reached the end with only Frankie remaining, Iceman cleaned him out in deliberate fashion. After the match, rather than shaking Jack's hand as expected, Frankie took out his blade and slashed Jack's arm. Iceman responded, serving Frankie a tremendous beating.

'Then, what's the problem?' Iceman asked.

'They saw you play cards. The only reason you can walk through the door was, because you were cool in the beginning with us average players.'

'Ok.'

'They saw you were a pro. The way you destroyed Frankie, not the physical beating, but the card playing, raised concern. Frankie is a dick, but a very good card player. The best in the neighborhood and you cracked him. You can join the club, but you cannot play cards. You are banned from the table.'

'That's cool. No problem. But I can join, right?'

'Sure, I will sponsor you. It's $500 a year.'

Iceman knew new members required a sponsor to vouch for them. He was grateful for Billy's endorsement and responded. 'No problem. Take it out of my account.'

'There is another thing. Don't worry about gambling, but the club doesn't hold your bets anymore. They place it off to a bigger organization. The club cannot book you and your winnings, it's too much.'

Iceman knew his bets were being laid off to the Irish mob. Having his bets laid off was not a problem unless he could not cover his losses. The key club would be gentlemen and give him time to pay the marker. The mob would not. Covering losses was not a concern to Iceman. He accepted Billy's warning, but dismissed it. He had never gone negative and if he ever did, he never bet more than pocket change. 'I saw there were lockers. How much are those for a year?'

'$200.'

'Get one of those. Another question. I got a guy that might need to access my locker. He is black, but from Ireland. His mother is Irish, is that a problem?'

'Yes.'

Iceman figured as much. 'If an emergency arose, would you be pissed if he went real early in the morning to grab something out of the locker for me?'

'No, that would be fine. Nobody is there.'

Iceman understood Billy knew the locker was not going to be filled with Jameson. Growing up in Southie trumped being a police officer at times. Billy trusted Iceman not to bring trouble to the club. Iceman trusted the club. Nobody was going to break in and steal from the club comprised of police officers, but more importantly the Irish mob.

Iceman found his locker at the club, deposited the bag, and used a combination lock designed by the Elders to secure the locker. He provided Zeus with the address, key to the club and the lock's combination. He returned the following week with a backpack. The backpack contained a small safe, again designed by the Elders, that opened with either Zeus' or Iceman's fingerprint. The money was safe from the Elders. They would never suspect a Southie key club for the twins' *on the run money.*

Navy covered ND, the game totaled 44 points, under 51 and Purdue fell short on a late Michigan touchdown. The kitty hit $17,500 less the club dues. Play money small enough not to draw attention, especially from the Irish mob.

CHAPTER THIRTY

After completing their training with Dr. Liu, the twins departed Boston and headed to Las Vegas. Zeus had made arrangements for the twins to be picked up at the Hard Rock Café rather than at the airport. The twins enjoyed a couple of hours throwing dice and winning a little. Although very tempted to extend their visit in Las Vegas, the twins regretfully secured their ride to their training site.

The Byrne Group, founded in 1992, was a private military company founded by Alec Byrne. Byrne was a former SEAL team six officer who founded the company to provide specialized training to private military contractors. The private military & security (PMSC) market is estimated to reach $475 billion by 2030. The Byrne Group did not have field operators. The company was strictly a training facility located 75 miles northeast of the Nevada Test and Training Range. The facility was close to Tonopah and equidistant from Reno and Las Vegas. The Byrne Group was a small company that had a highly specialized function. The Byrne Group trained advanced predators for large private contract companies. Since its inception, Alec Byrne had worked with the Elders in complete secrecy. Byrne, now deceased, turned over his reign to Barry Little. Little was now the gatekeeper for the Byrne, Elders relationship. The Oasis, the name used by the Elders team, was hidden within the Byrne Group training complex. The statesmen team for the Elders conducted training for agents, senior agents, and fellow statesmen in secrecy. The Byrne trainers and clients operated independently of the Elders with the belief that the agents were training for a different private military company.

Byrne operates a strategic state of the art 10,000-acre training facility. The campus contained specific facilities including an airfield, six tactical ranges over a variety of landscapes, ranges, simulators, armory, driving tracks with fleet, and shoot houses. The shoot houses had a variety of settings designed to mimic take down targets. Offices, hotel rooms, streets, and small buildings were a part of the staging used to train assaults.

The twins trained the previous year with Dale Lawson and Bernie Pettibone. Lawson, called *Wyatt* was a play on Wyatt Earp, or LAW-son. He stood 6'1' with a wiry strong build and Pettibone or *Bone*, as he was called, was 5'11' with a thick athletic build. Both were statesmen and fit the mold of an assassin.

'Well, well, well, the conquering heroes return. Hello Iceman, Zeus.'

Iceman smiled. 'Bone, my man. Hey, Wyatt.'

Wyatt laughed at Iceman as he shook Zeus' hand. 'You were a cocky fuck last year; I hesitate to ask if your head got even fatter after the first mission.'

Zeus jumped in. 'His head had no room for expansion, but I can assure you it hasn't gotten smaller.'

'Funny guys, funny guys.' Iceman enjoyed the banter at his expense. 'You know I am sensitive, yet you insist on picking on me anyways.'

Bone asked. 'How was your pitstop in Loss Wages?'

Zeus laughed. 'Vegas was good. We left with more than we walked in with.'

Wyatt and Bone trained the twins on the prior three annual visits in firearms and tactics training, advanced martial arts training, tactical and off-road driving training, and munitions training.

Bone started the mission brief. 'You are all ours for the next six weeks to keep your skills sharp in the four areas we trained in last year. I am curious to see how much you have improved in martial arts. Have you two kept up with your training regimen? Have you been sparring, challenging each other?'

Iceman, without hesitation, responded. 'I have an idea...'

Wyatt interrupted Iceman. 'You always do.'

'Anyway, as I was saying, how about a tag team match? Me and Zeus verse you two. You can find out firsthand.'

Bone and Wyatt looked at each other, tempted by the offer. They returned their attention to the twins which gave them pause. They didn't like their odds. The twins were extremely advanced when they left them the previous year. If they stayed with their sparring and yoga training schedule, they could be a dangerous challenge. The twins left Bone and Wyatt last year as tough opponents. The twins' size and speed, coupled with another year of sparring with each other, factoring in their advanced training with Woods, the Tiger, made the decision easy.

Wyatt spoke first. 'Regretfully, we must pass; we are restricted by a strict training program.'

Bone added. 'We can look into the match at the end of training.'

Iceman looked to Zeus, nodded and responded. 'That's what we thought.'

After the first day of training that focused on martial arts, the twins chatted on the way to their bunks.

'Nice work.'

'Thanks, Iceman. This year is completely different from the last three years of Black Ops basic training.' Zeus commented.

'Right? Completing basic training and kicking ass on our first mission, it's like we are being welcomed into a bad ass fraternity.'

While the twins made their way to their bunks, Bone and Wyatt headed to their cars. Both live in Tonopah, NV, 20 miles from the Byrne Group campus.

Wyatt turned to Bone and asked. 'Did you see what I saw?'

'Yes, they most certainly spent a lot of time working on their craft.'

'They're scary good.'

Bone nodded in agreement. 'They are still a little rough around the edges but their natural ability, size and speed coupled with advanced technique make them extremely lethal.'

'If they keep up their training, which I am confident they will, they will be the best I have ever seen.'

'That's the thing, the thing that makes them unique. They don't care about you, me, or the world; they just want to beat each other. Having each other pushes them beyond anything we have seen. We didn't witness sparring; we witnessed war.'

Wyatt joked with Bone. 'I'm relieved we postponed that tag team match.'

'A match that will never take place.'

'No shit.'

Bone shifted the conversation. 'They really are good kids.'

'Scary good. They are good people. Glad they are on our team.'

* * *

In addition to their sparring, the twins spent considerable time on the firing range. After the first week, Bone addressed the twins. 'Good work. Your commitment over the last year to your training is obvious.'

Wyatt added. 'Well done. I recognize it is understood but keep up the excellent work. The two of you with Conjar have something special in the making. For the remainder of your stay, you will keep up with your marksmanship, but the training schedule is changing. Because your development is ahead of schedule, we will only be shooting with you in the morning session. We turn you over for the afternoon and evening sessions.'

Zeus asked. 'To whom, doing what?'

Bone replied. 'I let you tell him yourself. Here he comes now.'

A wiry strong 5'9' relaxed man approached the group and introduced himself. 'Greetings. I am Pappy.'

Iceman paused as they all shook hands; he was eyeing Pappy trying to place the name.

Pappy asked. 'You alright, Iceman?'

'Yes, fine. Just give me a minute.' The others shared puzzled looks until Iceman announced. 'Got it. Pappy from *Ba Ba Black Sheep*. Robert Conrad's character.'

Iceman was celebrating himself when Pappy asked. 'No trainee has ever gotten that. How do you know about Pappy?'

'My Dad is a marine, not active, and he and my grandpa loved that show. They had the series on DVD. My aunt got it for them some Christmas. Anyway, my grandpa still had his trusty DVD player, so we watched it together.'

Zeus laughed. 'Unreal. You are so full of useless information. Pappy, we are not trainees. We finished basic.'

Iceman intercepted the response. 'Zeus, you don't get it. We are trainees. Aviation trainees.'

'No shit?' Zeus was shocked with Iceman's revelation.

Pappy smiled. 'No shit, Zeus. That airfield is not just for show. We will spend our afternoons with the aircraft and your evenings are full of homework assignments. The homework is critical and I expect five hours a night, seven days a week.'

Zeus asked. 'Give us five hours, but we will only need three. Besides, we have our Mandarin assignments.'

Pappy, surprised, asked. 'Mandarin? What languages do you speak?'

'Spanish, Arabic and closing in on Mandarin.'

Pappy looked to Bone and Wyatt for an explanation. Wyatt shook his head. 'We told you they were high speed.'

'I would say so. We will make a dent in your training this year and finish next year. In the coming years, we will add more sophisticated aircraft.'

'Give them more than you think. Load them up.'

'Bone, I appreciate your insight, but my program is more than challenging. If they commit three hours, they will be more than challenged.'

Pappy was wrong. The twins' ability to digest his lesson plans baffled him. The more he threw at the twins the quicker they were able to apply the required skill set. The twins left the Oasis having completed Pappy's two-year plan in one. Bone and Wyatt were able to avoid the tag team match.

CHAPTER THIRTY-ONE

After the twins completed advance training at the Oasis, they flew from McCarran Airport to Miami Dade. They took a shuttle to the private airfield and were greeted by Conjar, because of security concerns for the Island, the twins boarded the Elders' Gulfstream G500. The Island was located 45 miles northwest of Barbados. The four-mile-wide and eight-mile-long island served as the Elders' headquarters. The secret facility was originally a naval base used to protect merchant ships from pirates that roamed the Caribbean. With the extinction of pirates in the Caribbean, the base was abandoned and forgotten. The Elders silently purchased the Island from Great Britain.

When the twins and Conjar landed in Barbados on the Elders' private airfield, they were greeted by the four statesmen that were posted on the main island. Blank and Powder manned the airfield. Blank, named so because no one could think of a code-name for him, they drew a complete blank, operated the amphibious helicopter and transport helicopter. Powder, named due to his translucent complexion, piloted the amphibious plane. Every time Iceman saw Powder, he wondered how he survived the tropical sun. When they were not conducting Elders' business, they operated an air charter service for tourists. Standing next to Powder and Blank were Crocket and Tubbs. Like the characters from *Miami Vice,* Crocket was white, and Tubbs was black. Both hail from Miami and had been together since they were agents. They captained two Pursuit SC 365i, luxury fishing boats that were essentially fishing yachts. The boats like the helicopter and amphibious plane could go hot if needed. When the Elders visited, the statesmen were activated and the transports were armed.

Blank was a deliberate man who said little. The twins knew not to joke with or upset him. Powder was the first to greet the twins. He was the talker for the team. 'The conquering heroes have returned from slaying evil. We got your after-action report. Well done.'

Tubbs, who had a nice sense of humor laughed as they all shook hands. 'I suppose you two are under the impression that the mighty twins will be running the training now.'

Zeus laughed with the group. 'Not hardly. Great to see you guys again.'

Tubbs could not resist the low-hanging fruit and commented. 'Let's get into the office before Powder here suffers from self-combustion.'

Once the group settled with their water and bowl of fruit, Conjar started his briefing. 'The first month of training with be spent with Crocket and Tubbs. You will bunk on a Pursuit SC. After your five-mile run and five-mile swim, you will train with them. You will start with a Sea Ray R3 24' and graduate to the Pursuit SC. Every skill set required on the open water will be covered from mornings with Crocket and nights with Tubbs. Once you are finished with the water, you will move to the air with Blank and Powder. Your time spent at the Oasis provides a nice foundation, but you two have much work to do. While training with Blank and Powder, your mornings after PT are dedicated to the classroom. Afternoons will be dedicated to working with the aircraft and your nights reserved for independent study. You both have proven to be exceptional in your independent studies. Just keep up the hard work. Both areas of training are conducted Monday through Thursday. Powder or Blank will transport you to the Island where you will conduct advanced SEAL training on Fridays and Saturdays. On Sundays, you will join the group for deep sea fishing, a well-deserved day off. You will alternate captaining the Pursuit SC docked at the Island's marina during the fishing trip. If there are no questions, I am off to *The Crane*.'

Iceman asked. 'What's *The Crane*?'

Crocket answered. 'Me and Tubbs live in a couple of condominiums at a resort called *The Crane*. It is located on the other side of the Island. We also own a few others that we rent out.'

Iceman nodded his head and asked. 'When do Zeus and I get to go?'

Blank surprised everyone when he finally spoke. 'You'll get an invite if you live to be a senior agent.'

After his comment, the harsh reality of his words hit the twins. The surprise of Blank speaking instantly wore off with his message.

Conjar gazed at the group and wrapped up his part of the meeting. 'No questions? I am off, guys. I'll be back on Fridays to SEAL train and deep-sea fish with you.'

After Conjar departed, Powder addressed the twins. 'Conjar, forgot to mention, there are a couple of bunks in the hanger for your use when you train with us. There is also a gym with free weights and a spar mat. In addition to your scheduled run and swim, we have added an additional 90 minutes to your workout in the gym.'

Zeus responded. 'Great, thanks. We'll see you when we see you.'

* * *

The first month of training with Crocket and Tubbs, Monday through Thursday, was more like summer camp than the other training courses the twins had endured. Their statesmen were hilarious and training on the boats was more fun than work. Beautiful weather, water and honeys set the tone for a holiday-like atmosphere. Fridays and Saturdays were a different story.

Blank flew the twins to the Island on Friday morning after their morning swim and run. He brought them back after morning PT and breakfast on Monday morning 45,000-square-footings.

On their first Friday morning flight, Zeus saw the Island from the air and continued to be amazed with its stealth construction. The 45,000 square foot facility and surrounding compound were invisible from the air. The thick jungle provided natural cover for much of the Island. The roofs on all the facilities were covered with camouflaged solar panels that reflected less light than dirt. The compound was virtually invisible during the day and night. The Elders, through a series of shell companies, purchased the solar company. The panels and advanced storage facilities were revolutionary and provided the primary energy source for the Island. The facility contained three 15,000 sq. foot levels. The upper level was reserved for the Elders and was off limits. The Elders private residence including suites, conference room, private dining room, gym, library, parlor and meeting rooms were for their use and eyes only. The first floor contained permanent residency, kitchen, dining hall, recreation room with a sitting room for cigar and drink consumption, bar, a small meeting room, conference room, medical treatment and rehabilitation and the gym. The basement housed 20 dorm rooms with private baths and an armory. The best comparison for the compound's security was the White House. Bulletproof glass, anti-aircraft weaponry on the roof, sniper's nests and boots on the ground. All the guests were the boots on the ground and when the Elders visited, the statesmen located in Barbados were activated. A five-mile trail that surrounded the property was used for daily runs and transport.

The compound had three areas that spoke from the facility. The first consisted of a large garage that housed two fully armed JLTVs, two Jeep Wranglers and six military Zero MMX motorcycles. In addition to the garage a massive marina on the other end also spoke from the facility. Half of the harbor was a natural cove and the other half was man-made. Like the main building, the roof of the marina was covered in solar panels. The marina docked six SEAL Zodiacs and two Pursuit SC 365i. The Pursuits, the same boats operated by Crocket and Tubbs, were 41 feet long and were motored with twin Yamaha F350 outboard motors that generated 700 horsepower. The main attraction of the marina was the White Palace, named in tribute to the White House and Buckingham Palace. The White Palace was designed by Lockheed Martin with inspiration from a super yacht built by the First Export Association of Dutch Shipbuilders or Feadship. The 212-foot mega yacht had an exterior look and feel courtesy of Feadship, the leader in superyacht design. The production and weaponry were developed and installed by Lockheed Martin, the builder of Freedom class ships for the Navy. The White Palace was equipped with a BAE Mk 49 launcher with eight surface to air missiles, two fifty-inch machine guns and a lightweight torpedo system designed by Penn State University's Applied Research Laboratory, secretly funded by the Elders.

During their three years of Black Ops training, the twins drilled on various methods to assault the yacht. The twins applied that training when they eliminated their first target, Pervert, aboard his yacht with similar design features as the White Palace.

The north side of the first floor of the housing section was a wall of smoked windows. The windows could be set to clear to afford a view of a large outdoor covered kitchen and patio. Beyond the covered patio area was a saltwater pool that was the size of three Olympic-sized pools. The pool was designed with contoured sides and a camouflaged bottom to give the illusion of a lagoon.

Blank landed, quickly dropped off the twins, took off and returned to Barbados. The twins were left standing on a roof that had the feel of a sports stadium. The center, used as a helipad, was the field and the solar panels that surrounded the field were the stands. The twins headed to the elevator, the entrance was built into the stadium's solar panels and rode down to the first floor. They were greeted by Julie McCoy who was the statesman charged with the Island's operation. Her code name was a tribute to *The Love Boat* character.

'Hello, what a pleasure to have you back. From the look of you two, your time with Crocket and Tubbs was not too painful. You both look striking.'

Zeus sheepishly replied. 'Thank you, McCoy.'

'Now off you go to your room for a quick shower. Change into training gear for your time with Tango and Cash. Be quick about it, we're holding the breakfast buffet for you.'

The twins hustled off, driven by the motivation of a big breakfast. They quickly returned and bumped into the Zipprichs, the couple that managed the kitchen for McCoy.

Mrs. Zipprich hugged the twins. 'My beautiful boys are back. I just finished making some of your favorites. I was just so excited to see you.'

Mr. Zipprich shook the twins' hands. 'Good to have you back. Well done.'

When the twins completed the assembly of their mountainous breakfast feast, they were joined by Conjar and Tango. Iceman still laughed every time he saw Tango. He just looked too much like the Sylvester Stallone character in the movie, *Tango and Cash*.

Tango extended his hand to the twins. 'Gentlemen.'

Conjar followed suit and briefed the twins. 'After breakfast, we will have a training briefing to get you up to speed and allow you to digest your breakfast. You may not want to go back for seconds.'

After breakfast, the twins wisely passed on an additional serving, the four sat down and Tango started. 'Similar to your previous visits, you will continue your advanced training in combat diving, maritime operations, and Survival, Evasion, Resistance and Escape, or SERE training. Fridays will follow a set routine. I have you after breakfast until 1400 hours and lunch. You have independent study until 1700 hours when Cash takes you through night training. You bunk in your rooms on Friday nights. At 0500 Saturday, Conjar will take you on a 5-mile run wearing your MK 25.'

Conjar interrupted. 'I will not be wearing the MK 25 on our runs, nor will I be joining you on your swim.'

The twins nodded and Tango continued his briefing. 'Breakfast on Saturdays is your only hot meal until Sunday breakfast. The 24 hours, after the most important meal of the day, will be spent split between the jungle and the ocean. You may be abandoned on a SEAL zodiac or dropped in the jungle. Rather than the SEAL hell week you experienced during basic training, you will have hell day.'

Iceman laughed. 'You guys crack me up. First, we did not enjoy hell week in the Caribbean. We were subjected to hell three weeks in the frigid New York waters. Second, we did not have a singular hell three weeks. We enjoyed the annual tradition for three years.'

Conjar smiled. 'Details.'

Tango looked at the twins. 'Any questions?'

The twins shook their heads.

Tango, Cash and Conjar pushed the twins hard, but Zeus and Iceman had little difficulty tackling the challenge. They were too fit and well trained to be impacted by the demands of hell day. The runs with the MK 25 rebreather, that made running and breathing difficult coupled with the additional weight, were a bit taxing due to the pace set by the twins. Conjar running free of the MK 25, still had difficulty keeping up with them. To their surprise, Sundays proved to be the bigger challenge.

* * *

The twins looked forward to their first Sunday and deep-sea fishing. They expected a leisurely day of fishing, eating, laughing and a bottomless supply of beer. To their disappointment, that was not what the Island had in store for them.

The twins' excitement spiked when they saw the crew of the White Palace preparing to depart. Rather than taking out a Pursuit SC 365i as expected, they were going to travel like rock stars. The White Palace was manned with one of the two rotating teams. Each team had a captain and a crew of five, who lived on the White Palace when stationed at the Island. The two six-man teams rotated three months active followed by three months leave. The captains were retired from the Navy, were read in on the Elders, they were external. After 20 years of service, dissatisfied with bureaucracy while still loving the sea, the captains were identified and recruited. The crew was comprised of former dark operatives. Who's ready for some fun?'

Zeus immediately replied. 'I am.'

Iceman's face exploded into an enormous smile. 'Well let's get started.' After saying hello to the captain and team that the twins had trained against in basic, he offered. 'What can I do to help?'

Conjar, Tango, Cash and the White Palace team all began to laugh.

Iceman asked. 'What's so funny? What did I miss?'

Cash, who looked exactly like Kurt Russell's character in the movie answered. 'I believe we have just the thing to put you to good use.'

Iceman did not like the sound of Cash's response. 'We are going fishing, right?'

Cash smiled. 'Nope.'

'What the fuck are we doing on this ship?' Iceman asked.

'Superstars? What job do superstars perform? That's simple. Whatever we tell you to do.' Cash answered with a dirty smile.

'I see. Like what?' Iceman responded as his temper began to boil.

Tango jumped in. 'Fetch us beers, serve us freshly cut fruit, clean, prepare, cook and present our first catch of the day. Police the White Palace, scrub the latrine, like I said, follow our orders.'

Iceman calmly responded. 'Fuck you.'

Conjar injected. 'Iceman, this is not a joke.'

'I am not laughing. Fuck you. Line up. Zeus and I are bringing you a beating.'

The other members of the trip were not smiling.

Conjar stared at Iceman. 'Don't.'

'Fuck all of you. We are not your bitches anymore. I am fucking serious. I am more than happy to pitch in. I am even happier to do more than my fair share. I'll work kitchen duty, no problem. But fuck you if you think we don't take turns making beer runs or cleaning up after ourselves. One thing I do know, Conjar you know this better than anyone, Zeus and I do not ask for respect, we earn it and demand it. I repeat, fuck all of you. You'll have to kill me if you think this shit is funny. We aren't those other cunts that pass through the Island. Don't even consider treating us this way. You can all blow me.'

Iceman held a calm, frighteningly calm look that expressed no concern for his fate. Conjar knew they had gone too far and now Iceman was digging in. Conjar scanned the trainers and decided he needed to act. 'You will work in the kitchen?'

'Absolutely. I don't care about fishing and besides Zeus is worthless in the kitchen. I don't mind pitching in. As Conjar and Zeus can tell you, I've got culinary skills. You catch 'em and I'll whip something together. With notice, next week will be better. I work for beer and cigars, that is my only requirement.'

Conjar nodded. 'That works for us.'

Zeus jumped in. 'I'll handle the fruit station.'

Iceman added. 'Self-served.'

As the crew guided the White Palace through the marina and out to sea, Iceman and Zeus manned their posts. The captain turned to Conjar and asked. 'If you knew there was no chance the twins would accept the hazing, why would you allow us to bring it up? Iceman looked enraged.'

'He was enraged more than you'll ever know. The twins still need to be presented with all the training rituals just like everyone else. Every now and again, the Colonel and I agree to cut them a little slack.'

'I can see that. I really thought for a moment, Iceman was prepared to follow through with his threat.'

Conjar shook his head. 'Iceman did not issue a threat; he issued a promise.'

* * *

The twins did their duty on the Sunday fishing trips. Iceman worked with the Zipprichs to prepare ceviche, salsa and sides for the catch of the day prior to boarding the White Palace. Most of his work was completed prior to shipping out. As the crew reeled in the main course, Iceman simply needed to prepare the fish to be added to his prepared feast. While he waited for the trainers to fill his galley, Iceman assisted Zeus with the fruit station. The twins were so efficient, they were able to grab a reel in the final three hours of each voyage. The twins' legacy continues to grow in the Elders' community.

CHAPTER THIRTY-TWO

We see in the dark. OWL was the twins' cover story. OWL was a legitimate private equity firm that followed all government laws and restrictions. OWL had offices in New York, London and San Francisco. The work product of the Elders was passed down to OWL when the technology or investment was close to being at market. Market was defined as nearly available to the public and government agencies. Innovative technology and investments in the market were stale to the Elders. The CEO and President of OWL was Paul Stephan. Paul was an agent with the Elders in the investment division. Rather than becoming a senior agent, Paul was transferred to OWL. He was the bridge between the Elders and OWL. Paul was the only person at OWL that knew of the Elders program. OWL received the work product passed down from the Elders group through Paul. All Black Ops personnel were ghost employees of OWL. Black Ops were forensic accountants to document and justify their travels all over the globe. The agents and senior agents in Black Ops were on the grid with their given birth names. The agents and senior agents were classified as OWL employees. They receive their salary, health benefits, 401k, and documented income. OWL managed all financial transactions related to salary. Bills were paid, investments were made, and taxes were filed. The money that was paid off the books was handled by a special Elders team outside the purview of OWL. The special group ensured no transactions were made by an agent in their black account that might draw unwanted attention. The salary was $125,000 a year for agents and $250,000 a year for senior agents. The off the books money was based on performance and was significantly higher.

The Colonel greeted the twins at the breakfast buffet with three days of Island training remaining.

'Gentlemen,' the Colonel began, 'the time has come to build your cover story.'

Zeus asked. 'We are going on our first mission as forensic accountants?'

'Correct. OWL is on the cusp of investing $250 million in a real estate venture. The company insists on privacy, so you need to sign these nondisclosure agreements. Harbor Construction is in Boston, and you are tasked with a deep dive to ensure there are no skeletons in the closet. You will be on site and stay with Rebecca again. You will also continue your lesson plans in Mandarin with Dr. Liu. Harbor has purchased hundreds of strip malls throughout the Northeast and Midwest. Because of the COVID-19 virus, the demand for commercial space has plummeted. No other sector has been hit harder than aged and worn-down strip malls. Many of the malls were purchased out of foreclosure or bankruptcy. Harbor's business model is to purchase dying strip malls in middle to upper middle-class neighborhoods and convert them to six-story residential units. Harbor targets malls located in good school districts and optimal locations to business districts. Older cities are targeted such as the suburbs of Chicago, Indianapolis, and smaller cities such as Hackensack, NJ. When evaluating a location, access to public transportation is a critical factor. Harbor expanded too quickly and is out of funds. Their senior secured lender is demanding more equity to be invested and the bank lines restructured. OWL believes in the business model and believes the core business is solid. Your job is to ensure the core is in fact solid and able to complete the current projects in a reasonable period. The infusion of OWL should not only complete the stalled projects but future projects at a robust growth rate.'

Zeus was excited to put their financial talents to use, he responded. 'That's great. We love Boston and this will be a fun change of pace.'

Iceman added. 'Where are they located in Boston?'

'The Financial District.'

Iceman went silent and waited.

'OWL has already done a deep dive, so this is more for your cover than anything else. The team at the Factory is more than curious to see how you perform in this arena. You have proven to be exciting emerging Black Ops operators but how do you fare as forensic accountants? We have three days to prepare before you take a flight to Boston.'

Zeus smiled. 'I think we will be just fine.'

Iceman remained strangely silent. The Colonel knew he was up to something. Something that required an aspirin.

'Iceman, anything on your mind?' The Colonel asked.

Iceman paused and smirked. 'Before you say no, I have a brilliant idea.'

'Please do tell.'

'I'm thinking from Friday to Sunday night we will stay at Katie's. We earned it and, in all fairness, when Kelly flies in to join Katie, the girls will keep us out of trouble.'

The Colonel was stuck. He should have anticipated Iceman wanting to spend more time with Katie. The fact that she worked and lived in the financial district made his request an exception but also a reasonable request. He agreed with Iceman but having the weekends off was not scheduled. He looked at Zeus who held a pleading look. He turned his attention to Iceman and knew he was powerless. Iceman was digging in. His look, a look the Colonel knew all too well, held resolution. The decision was already made, Iceman was not asking.

'Agreed. 1800 hours on Friday until 2200 hours on Sunday. I trust you will tackle the mission.' The Colonel responded with confidence. He had reflected on his conversations with Dr Monroe and their vow to make more independent and responsible decisions regarding the twins.

Iceman nodded. 'Thank you, we will not disappoint.'

'I know you won't because you both know the consequences. You will be locked down going forward if you come up short. The forensic accounting mission is just as important as the Black Ops mission. Agreed?'

Zeus responded. 'Of course.'

Sitting at the airport bar in Miami, waiting for their flight to Boston, Zeus turned to Iceman and asked. 'What did Katie say when you told her we were coming?'

'About that.'

'You seriously haven't called her? What the fuck? Kelly was off the wall excited. She gets in an hour before us and will be waiting at the bar closest to our gate. Ice, I am sure she has already called Katie. You are in serious trouble my man.'

'Yeah, I know.'

'When is the last time you talked to her?'

'It's been a while.'

'What does that mean? A week.'

'More like a couple.'

'What?'

'You are so fucked.'

'You think?'

'Yes. You are a total idiot. What were you thinking?' Zeus turned to the bartender. 'Please get me another round and hold my friends until he calls his serious girlfriend. A fantastic girl he is on the way to visit, and he hasn't called her in weeks.'

The bartender, shocked, responded. 'What? Is he some kind of idiot?'

'Just get me another round and I will call her after.' Iceman barked.

The bartender and Zeus just laughed. Having been turned away from drink service, Iceman left the bar to find a quiet place to call Katie. She did not answer. Rather than leaving a message he decided to text.

'Hello, how have you been?' Iceman studied his sent text and knew it was lame. As expected, he did not receive a response.

He tried again. 'Hello, hello. Katie are you there?'

'Crickets.' Katie typed back.

'I know, I know, I know. I suck. I am sorry.'

'Continue.' Katie finally responded.

Iceman perked up with Katie's simple response. He had a chance. 'You are great and I suck. I am the luckiest boy in the world that you would even take my call.'

'Continue.'

'I remain in awe that someone as hot, sexy, smart and funny as you would even consider spending time with me.'

'Continue.'

'Knock, knock.'

'Who's there?'

'Orange.'

'Orange who?'

'Orange, you going to give me a break?'

Katie smiled on the receiving end of the text. She remembered Kelly's constant warnings that despite Iceman going dark, he never stopped loving Katie. He would always come back. That didn't mean it wasn't complete bullshit. 'Continue.'

Iceman felt the smile through his phone. 'I love you more.'

'At this moment, I am sure you do.'

'I am sorry.' Iceman continued his pleading text.

Katie was excited to see Jack, but this was bullshit. She started her response. 'Apology accepted.'

'Thank you.'

'I am most certainly not finished.'

'Ok.' Iceman knew the *apology accepted* was too easy.

'This Houdini shit ends. *I am sorry,* cut it last time, not this time.'

'Agreed.'

'And if you want to see me that includes Sundays. You are not sneaking off to a pub on Sundays. You think you are clever, but I know you mister. From Friday 1800 until Sunday 2200, you are mine.'

Jack was surprised at the use of military time and getting busted for his walk about. He was even more frightened than before. 'I wouldn't even consider leaving your side if you are kind enough to forgive me.'

'Will you be charming?' Katie offered as she began to flirt.

'Always, when I am with you.'

'Will you be sexy?'

'I am not boarding a magical plane; a flight of miracles that will transform me, but I will leave that for you to decide.'

'Trust me if you are not as sexy as I remember, I am kicking you to the curb.'

'Fair enough.'

'I know you don't mean it, but it hurts my feelings.' Katie texted to ensure her flirting was prudent.

'I know.'

'Rather than get mad at you, I am going to ask you to do me a favor and I will move past this. But you must take it seriously.'

'Anything.'

'Imagine, just imagine. Imagine, even though your history dictates you disappear for a while and return with everybody else, you elect to stay in contact with me. Imagine how special I would feel.'

'I'm a dick.'

'You are, but you are special enough for me to put up with it. Do I have to?'

'No.'

'No, what?'

'I promise.'

Katie was floored. She thought she had pushed as far as she could. Getting Sunday was the victory she was hoping for. She hadn't even considered Jack would promise to stay connected. She knew he rarely made promises, but when he did, he was completely committed. He never broke his promises.

'Kelly's going with you to your B&B in Back Bay and waiting with the cab. She will bring you straight to me after you check in with NO stops.'

'Perfect.'

'My sister is staying with her boyfriend for all of the weekends you are in town; so, I have my place all set up for the four of us.'

'Perfect.'

'Jack.'

'Yes.'

'I am excited to see you.'

'I think St. Peter has written your name in ink.' Jack texted, finally feeling safe to flirt back.

'How about you?'

'Mine's in pencil.'

The twins landed at Logan as scheduled and didn't have to look hard for the closest bar to find Kelly.

Iceman turned to Zeus and asked. 'Do you think Kelly is more excited to see you or more pissed at me?'

'Not even close, pissed at you. You might have weaseled your way out of trouble with Katie but Kelly's a whole other level of purgatory.'

Iceman hung back as Kelly ran to Seamus and gave him a giant hug and kiss. He was relieved that Kelly's target was Zeus and not him. He tried to loop around them and snake his way to the bar. He didn't get far.

'Where do you think you are going?'

Iceman gave a nod of defeat and smiled. 'Hello, Kelly.'

'Don't, don't you dare even try. You take that awe shucks looks and that smile of yours and shove them right up your ass. I do not have time for you right now. Seamus and I are headed to the left side of the bar. You will leave my sight and plant your ass on the right side until I am ready for you. Take the time to reflect on just how big of an asshole you are.'

Jack humbly shuffled over to his side of the bar. After 20 minutes, Kelly and Seamus approached him.

'Hi, all set. You two ready?' Jack hopefully asked.

Seamus cringed and Kelly started. 'If you mean, am I ready to beat your ass? The answer is yes.' After she punched Jack in the chest, she followed with a verbal assault. 'Katie and Seamus might have accepted and forgiven your behavior; they like you and are good friends to you. I don't and think you suck; I know you better than they do. I can't believe you treated Katie like that you piece of shit.'

Zeus was right. Dante had not found this level of hell. Kelly, without taking a breath unloaded on Iceman, who simply tuned her out. She punished Jack down the corridor to the escalators, down the escalators, and continued at baggage claim. He broke out of his trance when Kelly offered low hanging fruit.

'Blah, Blah, Blah.' Was all Iceman heard until Kelly uttered, 'you could take a lesson from Seamus; he knows how to treat a lady.'

'If he ever finds one, she will be a lucky lady.'

Kelly stared at Jack's big smile and to prevent exploding from rage, she was forced to choose laughter, much to Seamus' relief. 'You are such a dick.'

'I'm excited to see you too.'

'Come give your baby cousin a hug.'

'My baby cousin by five hours.'

As they exited the airport Jack asked Kelly. 'How did it go with your application to become a physician assistant?'

'I thought you forgot. Seamus, you didn't tell him?'

'No. I thought you would want to tell him in person.'

Jack celebrated and gave Kelly a big hug. 'You got it.'

Kelly was beyond surprised by Jack's reaction. 'You almost never hug me. What the fuck? Who are you? Yes, I got in. I'll be busy as hell but without Seamus, I really have nothing to do so it shouldn't be that bad.'

Jack gave her another hug. 'That's amazing. You'll do great. You'll be great as a physician assistant. Incredible. You are incredible.'

Kelly was for the first time in her life was speechless.

* * *

All was forgiven and the first weekend was magical. Each couple picked up right where they left off. The four spent hours together laughing, eating and drinking. Each couple made plenty of time to be alone together to go on long walks, a romantic dinner, and intimate marathons in the bedroom. On Sunday night the twins slept peacefully and full of joy at the B&B. On Monday morning they settled into their routine.

4:55: Wake up.

5:25: Run to MIT exercise facility, workout, run back.

8:00: Report to Harbor Construction.

1700: Depart Harbor Construction.

1800: Dinner.

1900: Lessons with Dr. Liu and homework.

2300: Lights out.

The twins performed well in their role as forensic accountants and even came to enjoy it. Zeus quickly accepted the challenge of performing deep dives into business data, easily manipulating Harbor's software. Nothing was safe from Zeus' assault on their systems. Iceman focused on analyzing the data and business model. He frequently asked for Zeus' assistance to locate and retrieve critical bits of information to bring his vision of Harbor into focus. As much as they enjoyed the work and tolerated their lessons with Dr. Liu, it was the weekend where the twins shined. None shined as bright as Patriot's Day weekend. The twins asked and were granted extended leave on the third Monday of April. Patriots Day celebrates freedom and commemorates the first battle of the American Revolution. Patriot's Day has been celebrated since 1894, the Boston Marathon has been run since 1897, and the Red Sox have played since 1959 on Patriot's Day. On April 15, 2013, Patriot's Day marked the Boston Marathon bombing. Much as September 11, 2001, rallied the best of New York City; Boston stood strong. Boston Strong. The domestic attack did not deter the celebration of freedom Patriot's Day represented. The bombing strengthened Boston's resolve and commitment to the great day.

Katie and her sister, Colleen, lived on the marathon's route and threw a party to celebrate Patriot's Day and cheer on the runners from their sixth-floor balcony.

As the party raged on, Katie cornered Jack and asked. 'Seriously, why are you in Boston?'

Without hesitation, Jack answered. 'Forensic accounting.' He, again, was relieved to be able to tell Katie the truth.

'Bullshit. I know forensic accounting, where?' Katie knew she was crossing a line by asking specifics but was too frustrated to remain completely neutral.

'Harbor Construction.' Jack's response was met with Katie's skeptical gaze. 'For real. I can't say any more, we had to sign NDA's.' Katie looked at him with suspicion, so he continued. 'I might be a dick, but have I ever lied to you?'

'No.' Katie accepted Jack's response. She knew of Harbor Construction and the business reason for being in Boston stood up to the Pepsi challenge.

'There you go. I told you all I could and was honest about it.'

'Fair enough.' Katie's answer was followed with a kind kiss. She took a step back and studied Jack. 'You are up to something.'

'Who me?' He gave Katie his devilish grin and turned to Kelly and Seamus. 'Are you guys ready to get out of here?'

Kelly asked. 'Where would you like to go that is better than here?'

'I donno, maybe Fenway?'

Kelly exploded. She and Jack grew up huge baseball fans. 'Shut the fuck up, you got tickets.'

'You know it. I had to make up for being a dick.'

Kelly turned to Katie, then back to Jack. 'Not enough.'

Jack smiled as he fanned himself with the four tickets. 'Kelly, does that mean you aren't coming?'

Kelly immediately responded. 'No, we are going but you are still a dick.'

Katie added. 'But it's a start.'

***

The group exited Katie's building to find car service waiting to shuttle them to the ballpark.

Katie smiled and kissed Jack. 'You were already out of my doghouse with your promise. This is a nice bonus.'

Jack picked up on the not-so-subtle dig to stay in better contact. 'I am really excited. I love Fenway.'

The car service got as close to Jersey Street as the group jumped out. Jersey Street ran along Fenway Park and hosted a series of outdoor food and beer vendors on game days. The street was closed off and had a country fair-like atmosphere on game days.

So excited, Jack and Kelly ran from the car service to the Jersey Street entrance. 'I love Yawkee Way, named after the famous owner.' Iceman announced.

Seamus asked Jack, 'why is he famous?'

Jack decided to take a shot at his favorite Red Sox fan and looked directly at Katie. 'He wasn't the owner that traded Babe Ruth to the Yankees.'

Katie sneered. 'Not funny and it's not Yawkee Way anymore for your information it is Jersey Street. Come on Seamus.' The two walked to grab the group four beers, adhering to the two beers per customer policy.

Jack yelled out. 'I like Yawkee Way better.'

Kelly, a diehard White Sox fan like Jack, held out her fist, and Jack accepted the gesture with a fist bump. 'Good one on the Babe Ruth comment.' She said to Jack.

After an hour of fun on Jersey Street, the four entered the Cathedral and took their seats. They waited patiently for a randomly picked 12-year-old from Bellows Falls, VT to announce in the microphone behind home plate, *play ball.*

As the crowd settled down from the thunderous roar, the leadoff batter took the plate. Kelly and Jack immediately chanted to the visiting batter. '*Hey, batter, batter, swing batter. Hey, batter, batter, swing batter. He can't hit, he can't hit, saaawing batter.*'

Zeus turned to the cousins and asked. 'What the hell is that?'

Jack laughed. 'No baseball on Mars?'

'Still Ireland, not Mars.'

'Have another beer and by the eighth inning it will make sense and be fun. What movie is our chant from?' Jack asked.

Katie jumped the question. '*Ferris Bueller.*'

Jack gave her a high five. 'Good girl.'

As the Red Sox began to bat in the bottom of the fifth inning with the Sox up 3-1, Jack paused from cracking open his peanuts to comment. 'Man, you can't beat Fenway and Wrigley Field.'

Kelly gagged on her peanut and exploded. 'What are you saying? You a Cubs fan now?'

Chicago supported two baseball teams, the White Sox and the Cubs. The White Sox were located on the South Side and the Cubs on the North Side of the city. Kelly and Jack grew up on the South Side and were raised as White Sox fans. Celebrating the Cubs as a White Sox fan was blasphemy. Jack explained. 'I said Wrigley Field, I never said the Cubs.'

'Same difference.'

'Bullshit. The ballpark and neighborhood are bad ass. Murphy's Bleacher, the Cubby Bear, Yahtzee's for wings? Please, it's awesome on gameday. For fuck-sake, my mom is from the North Side and my cousins on her side are family friends with the owner of a great pub, *Casey Moran's.*'

Kelly relented. 'I see you point.'

Katie asked. 'Which one is older?'

'Fenway Park, 1912 versus 1914 for Wrigley Field.' Jack answered and asked a follow up question. 'Third oldest?' Jack's question was greeted with blank stares. 'Dodger Stadium in 1962. They relocated from Brooklyn with what famous baseball player?'

Kelly yelled, 'Jackie Robinson.' And high fived Jack.

As the game moved on to the top of the seventh, Zeus stood, and Jack asked. 'Where are you going?'

'The restroom.'

'No, you're not.' Iceman demanded.

'Yes, I am.'

'Trust me, hold it.'

Kelly turned to Jack and asked. 'Do they sing, *Take Me Out to the Ballgame*?'

At Wrigley Field, home of the Chicago Cubs, during the seventh inning stretch, the time between teams turn to bat in the seventh inning, a surprise celebrity led a sing-along of the popular baseball song. The celebrities paid tribute to Harry Carey, the hall of fame broadcaster, who brought the tradition to Friendly Confines. Jack shook his head. 'No, this is better.'

Fortunately for Zeus, the Baltimore Orioles went three up, three down. With the Red Sox heading for the dug out to prepare to bat, the crowd rose and sang at the top of their lungs.

Sweet Caroline

Ba ba ba

Good times never felt so good

So good so good

The four lovebirds interlocked their arms and swayed to the music. After singing along with 37,731 of their closest friends, they settled back into their seats, laughing up a storm. Zeus held his bathroom break long enough for the Orioles to bat again. Kelly, Jack, and Katie looked at Seamus and decided to join him.

Hey batter batter, swing batter.

The group exited with the crowd after a 4-2 Red Sox win. Jack suggested they stay in the Fenway-Kenmore neighborhood, and all agreed. The plan was to enjoy Red Sox fever until 1800, jump the car service, return to Katie's to shower, and grab dinner before the twins had to return by 2400. The Colonel graciously extended their curfew an hour for the big day.

On the ride to Katie's, she commented. 'I am not looking forward to walking into the mess from the party. Let's shower quick and get out of there.'

Katie unlocked the door, entered, and screamed. 'O my God.'

Kelly responded quickly; she was concerned that something truly awful had happened. 'What? What happened?'

Over Kelly's shoulder Jack asked. 'Am I still a dick?'

Jack had hired a professional service to come in and clean up after the party. He wasn't done with surprises.

Katie walked into the dining room and shook with excitement.

'How about now, still a dick?'

After the cleaning crew was finished, Jack also hired a personal chef to prepare a proper New England clambake.

'You, you. You are just too much.' Katie had trouble uttering her thoughts, still dazed from the surprise.

'Katie, I love you more.' Jack whispered, not waiting for Katie to express the sentiment.

From the kitchen Kelly could be heard. 'Still a dick.'

The next day, the twins left their audit at lunch to join the girls to say goodbye to Kelly. The four sat at the bar in the dive Irish pub, Biddy's Early, waiting for Kelly's car service to take her to the airport.

Seamus broke the silence. 'That was some weekend. Sucks we only have two weeks left in Boston.'

'I am sorry, Seamus. I really wanted to make a third visit, but I just can't. My job and my schoolwork are just too demanding. You know I want to come.'

'I understand.'

After Kelly took her drink of sadness, she turned her attention to Jack. 'What are you smirking at?'

'Who me? Nothing.'

Katie now noticed Jack's expression. 'Bullshit, what are you scheming?'

'Nothing, it's nothing really. Nothing Kelly would be interested in anyway.'

Seamus knew Iceman and not Jack had a plan that would hook Kelly to come back for a third visit. He was excited to watch Iceman work his magic. Kelly stood no chance with Seamus the beneficiary of one of Iceman's irresistible master plans.

The group remained silent not wanting to be the first to fall for Iceman's temptations. To his credit, Jack celebrated the silence, drank his beer in silence, and waited. Then he continued to wait. The air of anticipation and curiosity grew.

Katie unable to wait any longer was the first to break. 'Spill it.'

Jack looked at her with a confused face. 'Spill what? I thought you three weren't interested in my silly plan, not really a plan, more of an idea really. Forget about it.'

Katie was getting playfully pissed at Jack. 'Enough. Give it up.'

'If you insist.' Jack extended the dramatic suspense by drinking his beer before he started. 'Kelly, I was trying to figure out something to lure you back for another weekend, but I only came up with dumb ass ideas. Sorry, Seamus.'

Jack looked at Kelly and knew he had her on the hook. He just had to reel her in. She demanded. 'What is your best dumb idea?'

'The Blackhawks are playing the Bruins in two weeks in one of the last regular season games before the playoffs. Lame, I know, but it was the best I could produce.' Jack knew he had her.

'Fuck you, Jackie. You are such a dick.' Kelly exploded with frustrated delight.

Kelly's and Jack's family had season tickets to the Chicago Bears, White Sox, Blackhawks, and Bulls. Jack's parents, Kelly's mom, and their three uncles split the cost of season tickets and each family unit had a draft to choose an equal amount of games. After the NHL lockout in 2005, the Blackhawks hit rock bottom. The Hawks were rated the worst franchise in all of sports. Jack saw a tremendous opportunity for the next generation, his cousins, to secure fabulous seats. The family had first row of the 300 level, the highest, rowdiest section. He sold his cousins on purchasing seats in the 200 level or club level. The Blackhawks were stacked with young talent that once matured would be a force in the NHL. The club level was a small section of seats with better bars, bathrooms, full private dining area, waitstaff, perfect viewing, and most important, reserved seats for concerts and shows at the United Center. The United Center was not only the arena for Bulls and Hawks games but was also the main venue for the biggest acts that visited Chicago.

Jack's family was rewarded for their gamble with the Black-hawks winning the Stanley Cup, the NHL championship in 2010, 2012, and 2015. The Blackhawks were the hottest ticket in Chicago with their club seats worth three growing to six times face value during the playoffs. In addition to the magical run of the Blackhawks, Kelly and Jack saw the Rolling Stones, Cold-play, U2, The Who, Prince, Rihanna, and several other amazing concerts.

Being a rabid Blackhawks fan, Kelly was quickly calculating how she could make the third visit happen. Jack watched her struggle and went for the jugular. 'I don't know if it makes a difference, but it is a battle of the Original Six.'

The six teams that founded the NHL and competed from 1942-1967 were referred to as the Original Six. The NHL had grown from 6 teams in 1967 to 32 teams. When the Original Six teams played, the atmosphere and intensity was like no other regular season game. The games between the Six were a tribute to the history and memories of previous generations.

Kelly stood from the bar and announced. 'My ride is here.' She gave Katie and Jack a hug goodbye; Seamus waited patiently to escort her and say goodbye. As she approached the pub's exit, she looked back and celebrated. 'See you in two weeks.'

As Seamus and Kelly said their goodbyes outside in front of the car, Katie turned to Jack. 'You are too much. Being with you is like a carnival ride.'

'Thank you.' Jack responded with genuine pride.

'What a great plan for two weeks from now. About next weekend you are not the only strategist in this relationship.'

'No?'

'No, you know I have loved everything you have mapped out for us. Our weekends are unbelievable. My sister goes nuts when we grab a glass of wine in our flannel pajamas on Monday nights and I tell her about our adventures.'

Jack knew where Katie was headed. He was well overdue for a chick weekend. He waited for his sentence to be administered. 'What are you thinking?'

'I would like to take the train to New York City, visit museums, and catch a fancy dinner and Broadway show.'

Jack nodded to Katie's surprise; she was expecting some form of protest from Jack. 'I'm cool with that, totally fair. A couple of conditions. No musicals, I hate musicals. Second, we dedicate a significant amount of time to The Metropolitan Museum of Art. I really like art. I told you that.'

Katie was beyond shocked by Jack's revelation. 'No, you didn't. I am pretty sure I would have remembered that. How in the world did you come to appreciate and enjoy art?'

'Pretty sure I told you this. My dad hooked me up with a job on Sundays. In Chicago, Catholic High Schools cannot play or practice on Sundays. The Sunday after my 16th birthday, I started working as a security guard at The Art Institute of Chicago. My job was to guard an area to make sure visitors did touch the paintings or break any of the rules about food, drink, behavior, etc. I was usually assigned to the Impressionist gallery, so that is my expertise. I listened to the tour pass every Sunday for eight hours all year round. A little after my 17th birthday, I asked to be assigned to security in different galleries, so I wouldn't have to listen to the same tour Sunday after Sunday.'

As Katie was processing Jack's surprise, Seamus returned. She asked him. 'Did you know Jack was an art aficionado?'

'Sure. He worked at The Art Institute. His specialty is impressionist art.'

She looked back at Jack with wonder. 'You certainly are *a riddle, wrapped in a mystery, inside an enigma.*'

'Churchill's quote about Moscow, good one.' Jack answered impressed with Katie's knowledge. Zeus laughed with responsible concern at their exchange. *Those two are nuclear; brilliant energy and a force of nature but what if?* Seamus elected to defuse his concerns and offered a nervous laugh at his friend. 'Ladies and gentlemen, meet Mr. Google. From the absurd to the trivial to the historic, Jack is a one-man app.'

* * *

Katie and Jack debated taking the train from Boston to Manhattan, but elected to take the one-hour flight instead. The idea was romantic, but they just did not have enough time. They landed at LaGuardia and caught a cab to The Trump International Hotel and Tower. Jack favored the Central Park location over Midtown because of the noise of Midtown and the great walks provided by Central Park. Central Park in the spring hosted the loving couple for hours. As promised, they visited The Metropolitan Museum of Art, caught a Broadway show, and enjoyed Sunday southern-styled brunch at Jacob's Pickles. The weekend was a smashing success and set the table for quite a unique experience during the coming weekend.

* * *

'Did you bring it? How about the hat? Did you find my hat?'

Kelly arrived late Friday night because she had to switch shifts to get the weekend off. She arrived at Bukowski only to get peppered by Jack and his wardrobe concerns. He asked Kelly to go to his parents to grab his Bobby Hull jersey and his St. Patrick's Day green Hawk's hat.

'Yes, Jackie I filled your order. Nice to see you too. Now can I say hello to Seamus?'

'Yeah, sure. But you're sure you got it?'

Katie was amazed at Jack's excitement level. 'Settle down Sparky, the game is not until tomorrow.'

'You're right. Kelly did you bring your Kaner sweater?' Jack tried to settle down but without success.

'Yes, Jackie, and I brought my hat too.' She turned to Seamus. 'I grabbed you a hat. You are a Hawks fan now. There is nothing we can do about Katie. Sorry Katie, no gifts for Bruins fans. Our friendship is suspended starting tomorrow at lunch.'

Katie smiled. 'I understand and agree.'

Zeus jumped in. 'Thanks for the hat. What is a Kaner sweater?'

Kelly explained. 'A hockey jersey is also called a sweater. Sweater is the proper term because jerseys were originally made of wool like a sweater. Real hockey fans use the term sweater. I got a Kaner sweater right when the Hawks were getting good. He was 18 years old when I bought his jersey. I grew out of my first sweater and have had this one for over 10 years. Patrick Kane, Kaner, is a star and was beyond yummy as an 18-year-old heart throb.' Kelly paused to take a drink from her beer. 'He's still a fox.'

Seamus understood Kelly's crush without any offense taken. He asked Jack about Bobby Hull. 'The Golden Jet?' Jack responded. 'He played during the Original Six for much of his career. The same six teams played each other over and over again. They hated each other and fights broke out several times in a game. He was not only a great hockey player but a bad ass. My grandpa loved him. Tomorrow is going to be great.'

* * *

Saturday afternoon brought a late lunch and a tailgate to get ready for the game. The group headed straight to the West End to be close to TD Garden, home of the Boston Bruins.

Jack and Kelly consistently raced ahead from one bar to another. The cousins prepared for the big game with a bar sprint not a bar crawl. The group ate at the Harp, popped into West End Johnnie's, and left Johnnie's because, while the sports memorabilia was cool, it was a little young and touristy for the group's taste. On to Sullivan's Tap, a true dive bar favored by the four.

On the walk that took them past the Garden, Jack turned to Kelly and shouted. 'How great is this? Seamus and I caught a Celtics game a month ago at the Garden, which was cool, but the Hawks? This is the shit.'

Kelly smiled. 'I'm ready. Are you ready?'

'You know I am.' Jack added a high five to his response.

Kelly and Jack entered Sullivan's Tap well ahead of their better halves. The bar was loaded with Bruins fans that were not too pleased to see the mission ready Blackhawks fans. Some at the bar wanted to give the Chicagoans a hard time, but Iceman immediately replaced Jack when they entered the bar. Iceman gave them pause and when Zeus appeared several moments later all thoughts of trouble disappeared. As they settled down at the bar, good-natured shit talking started. The group was welcomed to the neighborhood.

One of the Bruins fans, that were in full pregame tailgate mode, asked. 'Hate the Hawks, but love the Hull jersey. What did he sign on his number?'

The back of Jack's red sweater had a big white 9, Hull's number. He signed the back. *To Jack, keep your blood off my sweater when you drop gloves. Bobby Hull. The Golden Jet. #9 HOF.*

Seamus asked. 'What does that mean?'

Even the Boston fans listened attentively to Jack's response. 'See the blood stain on the front and on the right sleeve? Bobby asked me, *who's blood?* I responded. *Not mine.* He laughed and signed it. Great guy.'

One of the Boston fans asked. 'Do you know him?'

'Sure, one of my uncles and Bobby go to the same pub. Well, it's more like a 70's lounge with a piano player and a supper club. I'd go there once and a while as a senior in high school after work on Sundays to drink with them for a couple of hours.'

The Bostonians were impressed, as was Katie. Kelly was annoyed with the mighty Jack and his stories but secretly was proud of him. Seamus was still a little confused. 'Drop gloves? What's that?'

Jack cooled the Bruins' fans and explained. 'He's from Ireland, he's legit.' The largely Irish American crowd accepted Iceman's explanation noting Zeus' accent. Jack continued. 'In hockey when you are ready to fight, you drop your gloves to the ice and fight bare knuckles. Drop gloves is hockey speak for fighting. It's elegant.'

'Bare knuckle fighting is elegant?'

'Seamus, chivalrous is a better word. You'll see. Fighting is way down in hockey but with the Original Six teams all bets are off.'

Half of the bar departed for the Garden and the other half remained to watch the game. The game was as advertised. Seamus was amazed at the speed and veracity of hockey. As Jack had predicted, there were two fights, and the crowd grew rabid. The Hawks won 4-3 on a late minute goal.

* * *

At the end of their final week, the twins said their goodbyes to Rebecca and Dr. Liu, and headed to Logan Airport. As they settled in at their usual spot at the airport bar, Zeus ordered a round and sandwiches. After placing the order he turned to Iceman. 'What a trip.'

'Absolutely. We had a great time, and the girls are amazing. I am a little surprised by the quality of our work product. We got our Mandarin about down and I think our forensic accountant report rocks.'

'Agreed. Sucks, we won't see the girls for a while.'

'It's not too long. I am going to push the Colonel for more leave next year. Four weeks is fair and throw in Thanksgiving and Christmas.'

'I like it.' Zeus paused to catch up with Iceman and finished his beer. With the beer emptied, he asked for another round, then turned serious. 'Iceman, you cannot…'

'I know. I know. Zeus, I won't fuck it up. I'll stay in regular contact with Katie. I get it.'

'You had better.'

'Roger that.'

CHAPTER THIRTY-THREE

Zera was the last to enter the conference room. He scanned the room and saw Dr. Monroe, Sullivan, Duke, Conjar and Segal all present and accounted for. 'Thank you for coming. As you are aware, we have a meeting with the twins set for Monday. I wanted to take a moment to share our thoughts and observations so that we are all on the same page. I would like to go around the room without interruption and give each of you a chance to speak. After we have all said our peace, I will open it up for free discussion. I would like to shelve the twins' report on the COVID project for Monday. Please direct your comments on their training. We will address the COVID report and subsequent mission on Monday. Lori, why don't you start us off?'

'Thank you. My experience with the twins has been their work at the Factory with my team and their forensic audit report. Their time at the Factory was exceptional. Both are incredibly bright, hardworking, and work well with others. Both are down to earth and humble. Rather than look down at the support team housed at the Factory, as some Black Ops agents have, they celebrate the team's importance and show sincere gratitude. They emit no macho persona, again, as other Black Ops agents have.'

Lori continued. 'I was blown away with their forensic audit report. As all of you have read and studied their report, I will be brief. The twins' mission was designated as a follow-up exam. We had already conducted the final review and used the audit as a final test for the twins. They were provided with no work product from the previous exam. They walked in blind. Not only did the twins uncover every exception found in the previous exam but several other critical exceptions that were not identified. The best example of their work is Iceman's due diligence with contractors. Harbor's business model is the purchase of defunct commercial real estate in markets that show promise to convert the targeted space into residential. Harbor does most of the construction but outsources some, and all the sales and marketing. Iceman identified a valuation that he felt curious. Steering Zeus to perform deep dives, Iceman gathered information. He used that information to challenge the subcontractors for the real story. Quite frankly, I was amazed. The first diligence team did a very respectable job contacting the subcontractors, but did not unveil what the twins reported. Iceman unveiled that several of the projects were behind the represented schedule. He also discovered that invoices were held back by the contractors to inflate Harbor's cash on hand. Second, Iceman remembered an OWL/Elders transaction in a solar company. He offered the idea of requiring new construction projects to use the solar company. If OWL hadn't sold the company, which they have not, not only would that increase the valuation of the solar company, but also provide tax breaks for Harbor. The final aspect of the report I would like to highlight is his vision for the finished projects. He outlined in detail reaching out to local governments to create a homeownership program for firemen, policemen, teachers, and civil servants. Iceman recognized the projects targeted run-down properties within a promising community. His special program proposal offered down payment assistance for community workers. Workers cannot afford to live in the affluent areas and are forced to live outside the community they serve. What better way to breathe life into a depressed area than rewarding your workers? The community benefits from keeping their employees as residents and the workers benefit from home ownership in their community. He went so far as to recommend Harbor match the community government's down payment up to $5,000 with the caveat that the list price is set, no negotiations. Harbor will maintain the same forecasted gross profit per unit with the one-price strategy even with the $5,000 down payment match.'

Zera nodded. 'Thank you. Grace, you are up.'

'Thank you, Bill. The twins, after brief resistance have been open in therapy and willing participants. Zeus has embraced the experience and has demonstrated healthy mental health. Our sessions are very productive, and he is an open book. In terms of Iceman, I followed the agreed-upon plan to monitor his bipolar tendencies. He has been able to control his cosmic highs in part due to Zeus. Zeus balances Iceman manic moods by being a stabilizing force that Iceman respects. The nature of being an agent is a perfect fit for Iceman. Constant challenges allow Iceman to achieve his way out of depression. The bigger the challenge, the frequency of new challenges, new stimuli occupy his powerful brain. He does not require medication at this time, and I will hold off on medication for now. The medication will regulate Iceman's moods and dull the cosmic highs. Conjar, Tom, you two are critical. The two of you are our front line of protection for Iceman. Continue to monitor his mood cycles. Always remember, manic highs are important but dangerous, more dangerous than depression. You both have done an excellent job identifying his mental health and have provided accurate reports to me. Thank you.'

'Tom raised a crucial element to the twins' continued success. Some, if not most of our agents isolate themselves from society. Those agents who joined us were programmed to be isolated. Being an island unto yourself is a successful method of managing the demands of being a Black Ops agent. The twins are not built to be isolated. Tom identified the importance of society to them, specifically the twins need to have a connection with loved ones. As the twins call it, *their tribe* is a source of strength and stability for the twins. Their close knit family and friends provide a foundation for the twins.'

Duke asked. 'Security concerns? Are they too close to their *tribe?*'

'None. Their loved ones know they are not forensic accountants. While the twins have not broken cover, their loved ones know them too well to accept the cover story. They believe the twins are involved in a special forces, dark Ops, like operation for the US government. Tom's observations were validated by his mission plan to send the twins to Ireland and surround them with trusted loved ones. The twins returned mentally rested, more trusting, and more open in therapy. Going forward, my mental health program will include scheduling more leave time for the twins to maintain contact with their support group.'

'Thank you, Grace. Tom, as you were just referenced, why don't you go next?'

'Thanks, Bill.' The Colonel paused a moment to gather his thoughts about Lori's and Grace's report. 'I don't have much to add. I have reported on the twins' work at West Point, Black Ops training, and their first mission. I joined as an advisor to their chain of command and have nothing new to report. They are good, incredibly special. I am comfortable with the twins' development program with one caveat. Yes, all the areas identified are important, but I must add two concerns. One, do not mislead the twins in any way. They trust us but trust is something that is earned with them and easily lost by betrayal. Iceman continues to reference the camps that conduct the kidnapping of young college students that are given as gifts to the former target's clients. We promised the twins we would terminate those camps with prejudice. To date, we have not, but trust me, Iceman will never let the subject go. He will hold us to that promise.'

The group turned to Duke, who replied. 'We have most of the data recovered from their first mission. The clients involved and the location of the camps are almost complete. Once all the data is secure, a mission plan and target list will be submitted to the Elders for approval. Iceman needs to stand down; the issue is being worked on within the construct of Elders' operating procedures. He needs to show more respect for how we do things here. The mission brought a wealth of information and identified characters of concern that we had yet to identify. We are not in the vendetta business. The process is not flexible, nor am I.'

Sullivan nodded. 'Understood. I will address the subject with the twins and relay our concerns regarding valuing our operating principles.' While he supported Duke's message for now, Sullivan remained silently concerned about Duke's reception of his warning. The twins would never stop their pursuit of the student slavery camps. He turned his attention back to the group. 'My second discussion point is that the twins need to be thoroughly involved in their mission planning.'

Before Sullivan could continue his report, Duke interjected. 'Absolutely not.' Grace, Sullivan, and Conjar bit their tongues to allow Duke to continue. Duke realized his aggressive interruption was a mistake. He betrayed his commitment to hide his true opinion of the twins until the right moment presented itself. He needed to recover quickly. 'I agree that the twins are impressive. I was surprised at their commitment to the forensic audit report. They exceeded my expectations. As I have stated before, their field training reports are to be commended. Finally, Iceman's analytical skills in identifying Mexico as a potential source for the Chinese to exploit were on target and impressive. Having said that, we must continue to proceed with caution. As fine a performance as they have delivered, the twins are still young.' Duke was feeling confident in his recovery. 'We have sound operating principles that have proven successful. I agree, the operating procedures need to be accelerated for the twins, but we must do so guardedly.'

The room fell dead silent, as they processed Duke and his message. Zera felt the deafening silence and turned to Conjar. 'You have not had a chance to brief us on the twins. Why don't you go?'

'I have nothing new to report.' Conjar was curt. He wanted to use his time to attack Duke's arrogance and the perceived insult lobbed his way but showed restraint. 'I know we have already addressed the twins' abilities and status within the Elders. You refer to our operating principles. The twins have followed every single step, just at an accelerated timeframe. We have and continue to build a better team. I would like to address mission planning. We have moved past the discussion. My team will be involved in mission planning.' Conjar stopped communicating with the room and focused solely on Duke. 'Period.' He paused to allow Duke to absorb his violent stare. 'The more my team is involved in the planning process, the less chances the plan will change in the field. You want more control of the twins? Let's build a better plan.'

Sullivan and Monroe were ready to forcefully vocalize their support for Conjar but took note of Zera's reaction. 'Conjar, you are correct. We have moved past this discussion, but Duke's point is valid. We move forward with caution.' Zera's last comment served to appease Duke. Zera, like the rest of the room, recognized Duke's initial outburst as a reflection of his true feelings about the twins. Rather than sanction Duke for his initial outburst, Zera elected to reinforce Duke's positive recovery.

Zera's comments were not lost on Grace. She recognized that Zera was not at all pleased with Duke's interruption. Duke's outburst had said it all. His anger and frustration regarding the twins was on full display. Duke's attempt to recover with positive remarks about the twins was nothing more than an attempt to masquerade his true feelings. Duke hadn't fooled anyone at the table, least of all Zera. Grace could feel the tension in Zera's body when he responded to Duke. Zera was a patient man, but as the quote goes: *beware the fury of a patient man.*

Duke took a moment to gather his composure and prepare his response. Duke knew he had made a significant mistake. If possible, his disdain for Iceman grew. Duke was savvy enough to push his emotions aside and rather than remain silent to mitigate the damage, he responded. 'My concerns were directed at protecting the Elders; I intended no disrespect. My voice was heard and for that I am grateful. I fully accept the decision made here today and look forward to working with team Conjar.'

While the group was relieved, and the tension left the room with Duke's humble response, no one believed the issue was resolved.

CHAPTER THIRTY-FOUR

The twins boarded their flight to Austin and celebrated their time in Boston. They were ticketed in coach, but Iceman managed to talk the flight attendant into giving the twins two open first class seats. They both ate, drank, and caught some sleep after a sensational time with Kelly and Katie.

As they rode down to exit the airport, Zeus asked Iceman. 'Where do you want to stop on the way to the Factory?'

'I am thinking The Liberty?'

'I like it. I like it a lot. I could use some food truck love. Who do you think is going to pick us up?' Zeus asked wondering if the Factory would send a duty driver or if Trinity would make the trip.

'Hopefully, no one, so we can make our own way back at our own pace.' Just as Iceman finished his comment, he saw the two of them and offered Zeus. 'This is either a great or a shitty development.'

'What?'

'Look over there.' Iceman pointed to Zeus' right.

Zeus saw them immediately. Atalanta and Trinity had come for the twins. 'Great development, definitely great.'

'Ok, Rain Man.' Iceman laughed and reached out to Trinity to accept her hug. 'To what do we owe the honor to have the talent here to receive us?'

Atalanta responded. 'Trinity is responsible for dispatch, so she just made it happen.'

Zeus smiled and hugged Trinity. 'That's great, just great.'

Trinity asked. 'Where do you want to stop?'

'What, no banter? No refusal to take us? Takes the fun out of it.' Iceman responded, teasing Trinity.

Trinity pushed back on Iceman's taunts. 'Does that mean you don't want to go?'

Iceman laughed and simply responded. 'The Liberty.'

After pushing Iceman in the shoulder, Trinity snapped back. 'That's what I thought. You better watch it, Buster.'

'Yeah? What is there a new sheriff in town?' Iceman asked Trinity.

'You betcha.'

Iceman laughed and asked. 'Is his name Reggie Hammond?'

Trinity was confused, but Atalanta understood Iceman's reference. '*48 Hours,* I got it.'

'Nice catch.' After Iceman high fived Atalanta, he turned to Zeus and explained. '*48 Hours* is a movie starring Eddie Murphy and…'

Zeus was more than tired of Iceman's constant jabs during moments like this and offered his canned response. 'Still born in Ireland and not Mars.' Zeus didn't recognize the movie reference.

After the group settled into Trinity's Grand Cherokee, Iceman asked. 'How much did you miss us? You can be honest, you really missed us, right?'

'We certainly missed Zeus.' Atalanta answered with a dark stare at Iceman then turned to smile at Zeus.

Iceman was playfully confused and asked. 'What? Just Zeus? You know we are a team, right?'

'That may be, but Zeus had the decency to stay in contact with us.' Atalanta smiled at Zeus again, then continued. 'You, you Iceman, you just suck.'

Iceman turned to Zeus and asked. 'You stayed in contact with them? Why didn't you tell me?'

'Don't, just don't. I told you they were texting. I showed you when they did a group chat with us, and you were included. I responded for us, and again you were copied.' Zeus plowed through his text messages and stopped at the conversation he wanted. 'Here, right here dickhead, is the texting I am talking about. Piss off.'

Trinity, feeling the temporary tension in her car, announced with enthusiasm, 'We are here.' As she pulled up to The Liberty.

'There you have it. We're here and Zeus stays in contact for the both of us. As I mentioned earlier, we are a team.' Iceman paused to look at the annoyed passengers. 'All that matters is that we are here now. Snap out of your silliness and let's go make a memory.'

Iceman exited the driver's side with Trinity and headed for The Liberty. Zeus exited the passenger side with Atalanta, who pulled him aside. 'How do you deal with him all the time?'

'I get that a lot.' Always Iceman's guardian, Zeus continued. 'Look, it's best to not think, better to just enjoy. He obviously cares about the two of you, he just goes about showing it in his own way. Let's go have fun.'

While enjoying the food and drink, the finest offered by a dive bar, the girls peppered the twins with questions about their time away from the Factory. They had little interest in the training portion, they were only interested in juicy details. To the girls, Black Ops agents led a romantic existence. While Atalanta and Trinity were stuck in the same town, in the same cubicle, reporting to the same people, regarding the same work, the twins were on the go. Doing things, seeing places, meeting people; two good looking guys on the move must have wonderfully glamorous stories. James Bond type adventures that included working hard, playing hard, and bedding the girl. Atalanta and Trinity would never accept the twins' life was packed with intense training that was all-consuming. Training and the mission took all their time and energy. They had to be granted controlled leave with curfews to sneak off to have some fun. The thought that a great portion of that fun was invested in a meaningful relationship would have crushed the girls' perception of the secret agent world that held their fantasy.

After the twins successfully deflected the girls' exploration, Zeus turned the conversation. 'Enough about us, let's talk about you two. You didn't really give me much info in your texts. Any men in the picture?'

Before Trinity could protest the inequity of the question, the girls had probed the subject of romance in depth with the twins with no success, Atalanta answered. 'I met a guy.'

Zeus raised his bottle in salute and offered. 'Nice, very nice. Solid guy?'

'We'll see.' Atalanta answered, twirling a fry in her ketchup. 'We only met a few weeks ago.'

Iceman, who had been ignoring the conversation to this point, asked. 'When do we get to meet him?'

Atalanta was horrified. How could she begin to explain the twins to her new guy? She thought, *look at the two of them, gorgeous studs with an air of danger. Any guy would shit himself meeting these two.* She took a break from worrying to drink her beer. As she sat her beer down, she made eye contact with Iceman, who had been intensely staring at her awaiting her answer. Then she saw it. 'Fuck you, Iceman.' Atalanta realized Iceman had been teasing her. 'You are such an asshole.'

'Guilty as charged.' Iceman laughed and saw his opportunity. He had one item on his agenda that was important enough to suspend the fun for a moment. 'How was the Factory without us? Dull right?'

'Yep.' Trinity knew Iceman well enough now to know he was not asking an innocent question.

'With the exception of Atalanta's new guy friend, of course.' Zeus added.

'Of course.' Trinity wanted Iceman to know that she knew he was up to something. 'Iceman, we all know you don't give a shit about how things were without you, given you ghosted us after you left us. Yes, it was dull. We can skip the rest and get to your real question.' Trinity was instantly concerned that she was too harsh on Iceman.

His response alleviated her concerns. 'You're right. I don't give a shit about this personal life bullshit. If you had something interesting to say, you would have said it. I don't give a shit because I know you two are bad asses. If you need something, ever, or if you want to share something, I am your guy. Texting about the weather does not interest me.' Iceman stopped to drench his dry throat and then continued. 'I am interested in your work while we were gone.'

Trinity was relieved for a moment, then felt defensive. 'What about our work?'

'The C-Files of course. When Zeus and I left, you were put in charge of the C-Files. What happened?'

'We were put in charge in the beginning, but we were replaced after two months.' Trinity explained still stinging from the decision.

Zeus asked. 'Why? There is no chance you two didn't do an excellent job. Why did you get pulled?'

Iceman answered for the girls. 'They did too good a job. The C-Files are very real.'

Trinity dropped her head in embarrassment and answered. 'Yes, the C-Files are real.'

Iceman regretted having to ask. 'Duke?'

Trinity lifted her head, replacing embarrassment with anger. 'Yes. Duke took the project from us.'

The table fell silent until Zeus mumbled. 'Prick.'

* * *

The next morning, the twins woke up early for an extended workout session including their improved sparring sessions. The twins' hand-to-hand battles became a bit of a legend in Factory circles and drew a small audience from the windows. After a shower and breakfast, the twins headed to medical as instructed. After a couple of hours, the twins exited medical with a clean bill of health and made their way to visit Dr. Monroe.

'Pretty much a waste of time.'

Zeus turned to Iceman and asked. 'The physical exam? They were just checking that we didn't re-injure anything during training. They want to ensure we are in top form before they send us out to hunt.'

'You're right, but I could have told them I was fine.' Zeus stared blankly at Iceman. 'Alright, I see your point. I would have lied if I were injured and said I was good to go.' As Iceman finished, Grace waved at the twins from her doorway. Iceman turned to Zeus and smiled. 'Showtime. Remember don't bring up…'

'I know, I know. I got it. Keep quiet about the girls. We cleared our physical evaluation, now off to our mental health evaluation. Don't do anything stupid.'

Iceman's dismissive look was interrupted by Dr. Monroe. 'Hello gentlemen, do come in. Can I get you anything?'

'No, we are good.' Iceman replied.

'Very well. I have read your first forensic accounting report. Lori distributed it to Zera and a few others.'

'Who?'

'Iceman, relax. You did fine work and she wanted to share it. Duke, Conjar, myself, and the Colonel were all copied. We had a meeting earlier in the week to discuss your report, review your time at the Factory, and discuss your training program for the next four weeks.'

'Who will be in attendance at this meeting?'

Grace knew Iceman was not interested in Duke's involvement in anything having to do with the twins. He reluctantly agreed to work with Duke when mission critical, but Iceman wanted to create as much distance from Duke as possible. 'Iceman, it will be a very productive meeting. Give it a chance and then judge. The meeting will include all those copied on your report.'

Iceman considered Grace's response and request. Conjar, Grace, and the Colonel all being present bodes well for the twins. 'You are right, I should give it a fair shake, thanks.'

'Bring me up to speed, how was training? How are you feeling?'

Unlike their introductory meeting, Iceman rather than Zeus answered for the twins. 'Good. We feel good. The audit went well, the training went well. We are zeroing in on being damn good with Mandarin and our bodies healed nicely. We were able to do some considerable damage in our martial arts training.'

Grace smiled. 'From what I gathered from the post-training reports, Woods did most of the damage.'

Iceman smiled. 'He did, true, true, but we closed the gap by the end of training. We were good enough for Wyatt and Bone to chicken out of fighting us. Zeus and I have a training regime to be ready for our rematch with Woods next year. We'll see who's talking shit then.'

'So that's it? Nothing else on your mind?' Grace began her probe.

Zeus answered. 'Pretty much.'

'I see.' Grace had waited patiently during their previous visits for the twins to bring up the subject of Katie and Kelly. The Colonel and Conjar had both briefed Grace regarding the twins' love interests. She was growing impatient and recognized the subject needed to be addressed. She preferred the twins to volunteer to discuss the subject but was coming to the realization that she may need to force the issue. Grace needed to brief Zera on the development and wanted to be able to report that she had discussed the subject with the twins in treatment. The last thing she needed was Duke to catch word of the relationship and run to Zera with a concerning report. She elected to hold her tongue for the moment, but time was running out. 'If there is nothing else, tomorrow you are to report to your same duty station. After morning PT, Zeus report to Comer and the hackers. Iceman, report to Lori and analytics. We will meet with Zera on Monday. Enjoy your Friday and the weekend. Monday will bring serious business.'

CHAPTER THIRTY-FIVE

After completing Friday morning PT and eating breakfast, the twins reported to their duty stations. Just after lunch, Zeus was pulled from his work with the hackers to meet with Dr. Monroe. Grace elected to meet with Zeus first. She believed he would be more open and provide her with much needed information to build a base with her meetings with Iceman.

Zeus entered Grace's office and announced. 'Reporting as ordered.'

Grace smiled. 'Hello, Zeus. At ease, we are not in a military setting; we are just going to have a nice chat.'

'Yes, ma'am.'

'Zeus, I am too young to be called ma'am. You know to call me Grace. Take a seat.' Grace knew Zeus was being overly formal because he was nervous about the session.

Zeus took his seat and asked. 'What do you want to talk about?'

Grace gave him a look to convey that they both knew why Zeus was in her office. 'Tell me about the ladies in your life.'

'Nothing much to tell.'

'Indulge me.'

'Kelly, that is Jack's cousin. Well, she and I have grown close.'

Grace immediately noticed Zeus' use of Jack and not Iceman in a personal setting. 'How did it all begin? Take me through how you connected.'

'Jack and I met a girl, Katie, at the airport. She was traveling with her sister to London, and we were heading to Austin.'

'To report for your first day at the Dungeon?

'Correct.'

'Well, it goes like this. I contacted Katie to let her know we were headed to Ireland.'

'To Ms. Boyle for controlled leave after your first mission and your brief visit here at the Factory.'

'Correct.'

'Continue.'

'Katie elected to accept the invitation. Her sister's meeting got cut short, so she surprised us a week early, which was hilarious. Jack was so uncomfortable at first.'

'The surprise of your parents coupled with Katie had to make for good theatre.'

'It did. Jack and Katie really hit it off.' Zeus dived into the details of their first encounter with Katie at the airport. 'Jack was prepared to walk away when I intervened. I gave her our numbers and my mother's number.'

'You intervened on Jack's behalf, why?'

'He was being an idiot.'

'How so?'

'You'll have to ask him.'

Grace nodded; she understood Zeus would not speak for Iceman. 'Colonel Sullivan set up a family reunion and Katie showed up?'

'Yes, I invited her to Ireland not knowing the Colonel's plans. Kelly, Jack's cousin, joined his parents on the trip. I met her for the first time and the four of us hit it off right away. Kelly and I, and well, the four of us became close. The rest is history.'

'Let us talk a little bit about the history you were referring to. How are you managing being with Kelly and the Elders?'

'It's a little challenging but things are good. She is busy, I am busy, but it's working.'

'Do you stay in contact when you are apart?'

'Yes, our lines of communication are good.'

'How about your cover story? Obviously, we are concerned about the girls and how much they are read in.'

'Iceman and I have maintained our cover story, but the girls and our families are not stupid. We don't exactly fit the forensic auditor profile to people who know us well. Especially when it comes to Iceman. I could pull it off but there is no chance they believe Iceman sits in a cubicle all the time.'

'What do they think?'

'They have no idea about the Elders. Iceman and I are certain they believe we work for the military in a sanctioned special, dark unit.'

'They are comfortable with that?'

'Yes, in fact they are proud of us.'

Zeus and Grace spoke for another hour about family and the girls. She probed Zeus to find out how the twins were holding up. No other agents had gone through as intensive training as the twins. They were so talented and committed, she was concerned about their mental stability. The twins worked nonstop for seven years with little time off. Their time with family was almost nonexistent and they had only small snapshots of a personal life. Grace never lost sight that they entered the program little more than boys and now were men without a foundation of a life outside of the Elders. Grace had decided the focus of her future meetings with the twins was to create a balance in their lives. Grace believed the twins needed to be surrounded with unconditional emotional support to maintain their moral compass. Other than Colonel Sullivan and Conjar, the other members of the Elders viewed the twins as blunt instruments of death. Grace recognized a healthy person, both physically and mentally, was critical to building the best agents of death.

As they concluded the meeting, Grace asked. 'Any last thoughts until we meet again? Anything you want to get off your mind?'

Zeus paused and Grace gave him time to gather his thoughts. Zeus was torn between protecting Iceman's privacy. The twins maintained a vow of silence regarding each other, and helping Iceman. The last time he intervened, he saved Iceman from walking away from Katie. He decided to take a chance on Grace. 'I am considering talking to you about something, but it has to be off the record, can never be in a report and must stay between us.'

'I have made it perfectly clear to Zera that our sessions require the use of confidential, off-the-record conversations.'

'Yeah, OK, sure.' Zeus didn't believe the meetings were completely confidential. 'This is different. I cannot stress that enough.'

'I understand.'

'Iceman is being an idiot; he is sabotaging his relationship with Katie. Don't get me wrong, when he is with her, he is amazing. The second he is away from her she is shut out of his life. When he is with the Elders, he is with the Elders. When he is with Katie, he is with Katie. He breaks all contact with her, then weasels his way back in when we can see the girls. He has promised to change, but if he doesn't, he will lose her.'

Grace understood immediately. She had briefed Zera, that Iceman had not been experiencing his dark episodes during his time as an agent. She was wrong. He was going dark, but his depression was cylindered. He does control his depression triggered by his bipolar tendencies by blocking, shutting down. He is unable to talk to Katie when they are apart because it hurts. 'Thank you, Zeus, I know that was difficult. You can trust me.'

Zeus stood to leave and left Grace with one last thought. 'For both our sakes, if Iceman gets betrayed on this, good luck.'

* * *

Iceman sat in his tiny cubicle. He felt like a caged animal. As he plotted his escape from the torturous monotony of reviewing old cases, he was interrupted by Trinity. 'Grace would like to see you.'

He laughed to himself; *never thought I would be excited to get my head shrunk.* 'Thanks, Trinity.'

On the way to Dr. Monroe's office, Iceman stopped at the cafeteria to grab a snack. He arrived 15 minutes later and greeted Dr. Monroe. 'Hola, let's light this candle.'

'Hello, Iceman, I would offer you a refreshment, but you already addressed that.'

'I did, but thank you for asking. What's up? What do you want to talk about?'

Grace sat silently and waited.

After four minutes passed, Iceman broke the uncomfortable silence. 'So, you are waiting for me to break the ice and make the first move. You can have your moment of control but please keep in mind, I am only blinking first because I made you a promise to give you a chance.'

Grace sat silent again. Iceman made the first move; he was determined not to make the second. After three minutes Grace finally responded. 'Thank you, Iceman, please proceed.'

'I know what you want. I really like Katie a lot. Are you ready?'

'Yes.'

'When I am with Katie, things are amazing. When I am with the Elders, I enjoy the work and mission.'

Grace was surprised by Iceman's direct response. 'What's the problem?'

'We do not need much time; I know the problem. A couple of things. First, I do not like mixing worlds. I don't like having her invade my work with the Elders. I most certainly will not allow the Elders to invade my time with Katie.'

'Before you continue, let's talk about problem one.'

'It's not really a problem.'

'Fine, call it situation one. If your cylindered approach to your two vastly different worlds is effective, why did you raise it?' Grace asked with the hope of peeling away one layer of Iceman's defenses.

'It works for me and the Elders.'

'And Katie?'

'Nope, not at all. She has given me two strikes and as the expression goes, three strikes and I am out.' Iceman responded with a clinical tone.

'Why did you push your relationship with her to the breaking point?'

'I'm not good at it.'

'I see. In what other areas of your life have you failed when you have made the effort?'

'Singing.'

'I'll accept the joke, but you promised not to deflect. Are you scared?' Grace asked, bringing Iceman back into focus.

'Of what?'

Grace returned to silence.

'Fine. Yes, I am testing her. It is easy to love me on the surface. Tall, good looking, former stud basketball player, funny, smart, loyal, blah blah.'

Iceman took his turn at silence and Grace waited to speak. 'Iceman, you are on to something. Stay with it.'

'What if, after she sees the other guy -' Iceman interrupted himself to change the narrative. 'What if she sees the complete picture of Jack and gets scared?'

Grace zeroed in on Iceman's slip. She caught *the other guy,* and elected to hold that thought for the moment. 'I thought you liked, and if we are being honest, you loved Katie.'

'Ok.'

'Have you ever been in love?'

'No.'

'Do you think you could fall in love with a stupid person who wasn't strong? What about a person both intelligent and strong enough to offer you a challenge? Does she bore you?'

'No.'

'Does Zeus bore you?'

'No, I get it. She repeatedly tells me she loves Jack and digs Iceman. Fine, I'll try. Good session. Heads up, I am blowing off my cubicle from hell, and heading to the pub. I have had my fill of the Factory.'

'Ok, once we are finished, I'll sign a pass for you and Zeus.'

'We are finished and just a pass for me.'

Grace understood. Iceman wanted to isolate himself after being vulnerable. She was not ready to allow him to close the door and shut down just yet. 'Almost. Tell me about situation two.'

'You mean problem two? Fine, but then I am out of here. I don't like living a lie. She doesn't know what she is signing up for. It's not fair to her to live with an assassin and not know it.'

'Zeus believes the girls know your life goes beyond forensic accounting.'

'They do, some secret military group, special Ops kind of thing.'

'Is she alright with that?'

'Yes, again, she kind of digs it. I never broke cover, but she's not a fool.'

'Let me ask you Iceman, do you have a problem being an agent of death?'

'No.'

'Then, what are your concerns? Katie knows what you do is dangerous and she *digs it*. You are proud of your work as an agent. Why not make a commitment to her?'

'What if I die?'

'Are you afraid of dying?'

'Afraid of failing. If I die, I failed Zeus and the mission. I have tremendous fear and hate of failure.'

'Jack, that has been more than obvious to me since I picked up your file come 10 years ago.'

'Dying doesn't bother me, I mean taking the failure part out.'

'But?'

'She wasn't part of the plan. The lone assassin, that's in the job description. Every book I have read the assassin can't have a relationship. The demands of the job prevent any normal relationships. When I signed up, my plan was to isolate myself and focus on the mission. I accepted isolation because I have no interest in being with someone. I'm good with my plan. I am good with being alone.'

'Are you?'

'No, and it is because of her. The odds of me meeting her were one in a million. In all the books when the assassin falls for a girl, despite their efforts to build a normal relationship, the relationship is doomed. The thing is the girl dies or leaves in several of the books. Ted Bell's character, Alex Hawke, his wife was assassinated on their wedding day; same with James Bond.'

'Those books are works of fiction; we are talking about you and Katie.'

'There is truth in fiction.'

'Agreed, but *truth is stranger than fiction*. You are using fiction to redirect our conversation. Kindly stop. Are you using fiction to mask your feelings? Let's stay with you and leave James Bond out of it. What are you afraid of?'

'Nice use of the famous Mark Twain quote.' Iceman tried to redirect and lighten the conversation, but Grace was having none of it. Iceman was forced to continue. 'She'll get hurt being with me. I don't want the responsibility of a relationship. She deserves a great partner, who has a great normal life, and raises great kids, in a safe environment.'

Grace sensed Iceman was coming around to address the concept of *the other guy*. '*You* don't think you are hurting her now?'

'Yeah, but it will go away, and she will thank me later.'

Grace felt Iceman's defenses were breaking, she asked. 'Katie doesn't have a say in the matter?'

Iceman smiled. 'Well played. I know what you are doing.'

'Look, I am not invested in you and Katie. That is a decision for the two of you. What I am invested in is you maintaining contact with humanity. You treasure your relationships with your parents and big extended family, but you have built a wall. The respect and admiration for Zeus' mother; those relationships and others are mission critical. You need to be vested in others to maintain your moral compass. Your life cannot be solely your missions. You are not an agent. Being an agent is what you do, it is not who you are. You are Jack and not Iceman. I am concerned that you might risk Jack in the theatre that is Iceman.'

'I get it. Our session is over.'

'Almost.' Grace really wanted to strike on *the other guy*, while Iceman was still open for business. 'Are you sure you want to stop our session?'

Iceman took a long pause. The silence was deafening. Iceman was processing his thoughts and struggled to remain silent. He thought to himself, *I can't believe I am thinking about doing this. Where is Freud when you need him? The Irish, we're the only people who are impervious to psychoanalysis. Grace better be all that and a bag of chips.* Without concern, inexplicably Iceman found himself talking. 'We have spoken about the concept of Jack and Iceman. Iceman, the character that excels with the Elders, and Jack, the guy that is warm and fuzzy and all that.'

Grace knew the moment had come to seize *the other guy*. 'Jack, we never identified Jack as warm and fuzzy. You have an enormous heart but there is more to Jack than the one-dimensional characterization than warm and fuzzy, but I understand what you are describing.'

'Whatever you want to assign it, the reality is, I am both Iceman and Jack. I have played along with the concept that Iceman is what I do, and Jack is who I am, so I could get out of these sessions faster. There is something scary housed in Jack that allows him to be Iceman.'

'What is that?'

'A monster.'

A monster, the other guy, Grace, found the answer she was searching for. 'Yes. Yes, there is, and the Elders have tapped into the monster to build a very deadly agent. That is why it is so important for us to have these sessions. That is why it is so important for you to maintain intimate human contact. Is there a scenario that you can imagine being a monster to your cousin Kelly?' Grace chose Kelly because Jack's early files reported a very violent confrontation he had with Kelly's abusive boyfriend. Jack used violence, his inner monster, to protect his cousin. The boyfriend suffered a mighty beating for his behavior and never hurt or saw Kelly again.

'No.'

'Have you ever been a monster to a loved one?'

'No.'

'No, you have a history of being a protector. I wrote in my first evaluation, and have continued to report, you have a special moral code that drives you. You use your monster to protect that which you believe in. The innocent that cannot defend themselves is very high on that list. We did not select a monster; we chose Jack because he is a protector.'

'Like Batman.'

'I suppose.'

'He isolated.'

Grace laughed at Jack's turning the tables. 'Nice try Jack. Yes, you could go the path of Batman and the Elders would be thrilled.'

'There you go.'

'How happy was Batman?'

Jack smiled. 'Nicely done. I get it.'

* * *

Iceman walked out and headed straight for Dirty Bill's. He needed his local refuge and elected to walk the almost two-mile route. He decided to use the 30-minute walk to be productive. He pulled out his phone and made the call. On the third ring, Katie picked up. 'Headed to or from a bar?'

'To the pub.'

'So, this is not a drunk dial.'

'No, but I would like to reserve the right for the walk home. I miss you. How you been?'

* * *

Sitting at Dirty Bill's, blankly staring at the sports highlights provided by ESPN, picking at the label of his Budweiser, Iceman processed his meeting with Grace. As he was lost in his mind, he suddenly wondered why he still watched ESPN. After Disney purchased the leader in sports television, ESPN turned into a horrible sports version of talk shows like *The View*. Iceman hated *The View*, which was unfair because he had never watched it, and resented Disney for ruining ESPN. Iceman's silent rant was interrupted by a text from Zeus.

'I am looking to get out of here. Want company?'

Iceman immediately texted back. 'No.' He set his phone down, finished his beer, and ordered another. He took a healthy pull from his beer upon delivery. Unable to endure the Disney travesty any longer, he elected to replace ESPN with a spy novel stored on his iPad. As he scrolled through his library, he changed gears and chose a book from the Amos Decker series, *Memory Man.* Iceman identified with the detective and his twisted brain. After a little reading, his attention returned to his phone and Zeus. Disappointed with himself at his response, he texted Zeus again. 'Yeah, I do want company. Can you give me an hour?'

His iPhone immediately chimed Zeus' response. 'You got it. Where?'

Iceman knew Zeus was really asking permission to join him at his fortress of solitude. Iceman texted back. 'My place.'

Zeus arrived a little early to find Iceman engaged in friendly flirtatious banter with the bartender. He took note that the bartender was a cutie. He carefully approached Iceman, not sure of his mood, and asked. 'What's up?'

'Seamus meet Shirley, Shirley meet my lad, Seamus.'

Zeus was relieved to find Iceman in good spirits. He knew the sessions with Dr. Monroe took a lot out of his friend. 'Nice to meet you, Shirley.'

'The pleasure is mine.' Shirley gave Zeus her best smile, clearly impressed with him. 'Irish?'

'Guilty as charged.'

'Nice. I didn't think Jack had friends and certainly not any like you.' Shirley continued her frisky behavior, clearly smitten with Seamus.

Iceman interrupted. While he was more than familiar with the reaction Zeus stirred just by being Zeus, he never tired of being annoyed by it. 'Yeah, yeah, we get it. He is good looking. Can we just get another round please?'

The twins and Shirley shared friendly exchanges until the bar began to fill up. As Shirley was busy with other customers, Zeus asked Iceman. 'What do you want to do this weekend?'

'I don't give a shit.'

Zeus knew Iceman was full of crap. He always had a plan. 'Seriously, what's up for the weekend?'

'I donno. Maybe we just chill tonight and do this. We should connect with Trinity and Atalanta at some point.'

'What are you thinking?' Zeus asked again for Iceman's plan.

Iceman feigned interest in the disappointing ESPN talk show and responded. 'Nothing. I am thinking of nothing right now and would like to keep it that way.'

Zeus got the message. The twins would just kill some time, a million miles from the Elders, and enjoyed the moment. Shirley found every opportunity to join the twins in their day drinking retreat. Laughter and stories were shared, and the day turned to night, not that the twins noticed. At one point, a plan was made for the weekend. The twins planned to exercise in the mornings. Iceman would then go on one of his walk-abouts. On Saturday they would meet the girls at 1500, and on Sunday Zeus would catch up with Iceman at some point for dinner. Eventually, Zeus turned to Iceman and asked. 'What are you thinking about for food?'

'I'm not.'

'Got it. Let's move our fog down to The Liberty and keep it rolling fueled with food truck platters.'

'Sounds good.'

Before the night was lost, while Zeus still had Iceman's attention, he asked. 'What do you think about Monday?'

'I'm not.'

Zeus knew the Monday meeting with their leadership council was important. Grace had said the meeting was to discuss the next four weeks for the twins. Zeus figured the meeting was to discuss the twins' next mission. The twins had completed their training cycle and were due for a Black Ops mission. He was anxious and wanted to tap into Iceman's sixth sense to shine some light on the subject. He turned to Iceman with the expectation of asking again, but when he saw him, he gave up hope. Dirty Bill's was a no-fly zone. Iceman was in another place and had deliberately made every effort to block out the Elders. Zeus decided to leave the subject alone for the weekend and join Iceman in his Elders free zone. Monday would come soon enough.

* * *

While the twins were engaged in their Saturday morning routine of extended exercise followed by breakfast, Duke was seated at a local diner waiting for his host. After Thursday's leadership meeting, Zera pulled Duke aside and invited him to breakfast. Duke initially declined, but quickly accepted the invitation given the look of Zera's expression. Duke was being ordered to breakfast.

Anxious for the meeting, Duke arrived 15 minutes early to the diner. He knew the reason Zera had ordered the breakfast meeting and Duke spent the evening preparing his case. Duke was ready and excited to spell out his case regarding the twins in a private meeting with Zera. Without the stream of interruptions, and looks that ranged from disappointed to angry, leveled at him by Monroe, Sullivan, Segal, and Conjar, it was no wonder Duke couldn't effectively communicate his accurate assessment of the twins.

Duke sat facing the door, saw Zera enter, and began to stand to welcome him. Zera held up his hand, and Duke remained seated. The waitress walked over as Zera took his seat to pour coffee. Zera without a word, raised his hand again and sent her on her way. Duke began his greeting, now uncomfortable with the tension that had arrived with Zera, but the only greeting offered was another hand of rejection. Duke began to understand the gravity of his situation. Zera had not invited him to breakfast, Zera had invited him to a public place. Zera did not want the privacy of his office to allow Duke the opportunity to engage Zera in one of his outbursts. He chose the public setting deliberately.

'Duke, I have no interest in being here, no time for pleasantries, and less time for any thoughts you have to offer. Your behavior towards the twins started with an evaluation I considered at best questionable, but because it was you, I gave it thoughtful consideration. As the twins consistently provided exceptional results, your evaluations deteriorated from questionable, to bitter, then embarrassing to you, culminating with your last report that I found disturbing. While the intended purpose of the meetings was to provide a clinical assessment of the twins, I have come to a better understanding of you, and it is not good. I examined all the potential motivations behind your erratic behavior towards the twins and I walked away with one conclusion. I don't give a shit; it is your problem and yours to solve. Good luck, I will see you on Monday.' Zera stood, left a stunned Duke, and threw a $20 bill on the table. 'Enjoy your breakfast.'

Duke watched Zera leave the diner and turned his attention to his coffee. He waved the waitress over to refill his cup and gave her his breakfast order. He enjoyed the hot coffee and whispered to himself that *the twins got to Zera.* Duke was never more confident in his conviction that the twins posed a tremendous risk to the Elders. With the arrival of pancakes, biscuits and gravy, Duke chastised himself for his behavior. He should have seen that Zera was also fooled. He understood the others, but Zera should have agreed with Duke. All he had done for the Elders, how could Zera question his dire concerns? He nodded for another refill with the determination to change his behavior. He was already on the record with his concerns about the twins, so his next move was to better placate the others. He vowed to play even nicer, give the twins enough rope to hang themselves, and then pounce. Duke was so satisfied with himself; he threw another $20 bill on the table for the waitress in her role in his moment of eventual triumph.

CHAPTER THIRTY-SIX

The twins arrived at the Monday morning meeting to find Zera, Grace, Sullivan and Conjar already present. As the small group prepared their coffee and made small talk, Zera asked Iceman and Zeus. 'No coffee for you two?'

Iceman responded. 'No sir, never touch the stuff. We are high on life.'

The group laughed and were joined by the Colonel and Lori Segal. After waiting for Duke's arrival, the meeting began.

Zera welcomed the group and gave a summary of the twins' performance to date. Iceman casually listened to Zera's comments. While he appreciated the kind words, he was more interested in Zera. As Iceman reflected, he realized he didn't really know Zera. The twins had spent little time with the leader of the Elders. He understood and accepted the chain of command that began with the twins, moved through layers of leadership and ended with Zera. Iceman studied the leader. With his black suit coat, starched blue shirt, and overlooking the short salt and peppered hair, Zera certainly looked like a man who could still play in the NFL. As a decorated college athlete himself, Iceman was tremendously impressed with Zera's time playing professional football with the Rams. Iceman knew the dedication required to push talent to that elite level was something to be respected. He found Zera naturally likeable and trustworthy. Iceman looked forward to working more closely in the coming years.

Iceman's reflection was broken by Zera's comment about the C-Files. Iceman rejoined the moment with his total attention. 'After your last visit, you left us with a unique gift. Your leadership team has offered high praise for your fieldwork and exceptional marks in training, but the C-Files were certainly a surprise. A delightful surprise that, quite frankly, I was a bit skeptical of at first. My expectations for your analytics training were not high enough. Black Ops agents are not provided the training, not given the incentive, and not motivated by leadership to produce this level of work product.'

The twins accepted the compliment in silence while Zera refilled his water glass. He took a drink, surveyed the room, before he continued. 'Please open your copies of the report. Duke and I had the chance to take a rather good look at it and found it remarkably interesting. Lori, you took the C-Files that the twins produced, and after several months of intense work, produced the file before us. Would you please take us through the power point presentation you have prepared to summarize the last version of the C-Files?'

Before Lori could respond, Iceman interrupted. 'Sir.' Iceman focused his attention on Zera. 'I think Trinity and Atalanta should be included in this meeting. Zeus and I worked very closely with them to create the C-Files and found them to be an invaluable resource.' Iceman was upset that Duke had deliberately excluded Trinity and Atalanta. Rather than wasting effort confronting Duke, Iceman took the patient, subtler, more effective path.

Zera paused to assess Iceman and his comment then turned his attention to Lori. 'It's your presentation, what do you think?'

From his seat at the head of the table Zera stared directly at Duke while Lori spoke. 'If we plan to use Trinity and Atalanta going forward, I agree with Iceman, they should be included.'

Duke wanted to voice his objection. Why would Atalanta and Trinity be included? They were nothing, just fact finders that fed Duke. With Duke in the room why would they be needed? Duke struggled to mask his anger, grappling with the plan he had made for himself after meeting with Zera at breakfast. *Play along, just play nice until the shit storm hits*. Duke relaxed in the comfort of his internal warnings. Zera, sitting across from Duke at the head of the table, dissected Duke's every micro expression with disappointment.

Zera held his stare at the silent Duke when he ordered. 'Lori, please find Trinity and Atalanta and have them join us.'

Minutes later, Lori escorted them into the conference room. Both were nervous and confused. Iceman smiled to himself, guilty of pushing the invitation. *They will settle down once the meeting gets started,* he thought. *They will be amazing.*

'I am sorry. I do not have extra copies.' Lori apologized to the new guests.

Iceman slid his copy of the report across the table to Trinity. 'Take my copy. I already read it.'

Zera paused in confusion, but accepted Iceman's gesture when no one at the table including Duke showed concern. *If they are confident Iceman doesn't need the report, who am I to question?* Zera's already heightened interest in Iceman grew.

With the group settled, Lori began. 'The series of COVID variants has been simplified in this report as C-Files. The C-Files were in fact a result of an accident, however the C-Files document the creation and expected deployment of the virus was no accident. The virus was created in a laboratory and that lab was the Wuhan Institute of Virology. The virus leaked from the WIV lab via infected scientists and hit the wet market and the rest is history, or so we thought. The leak was an accident, but the C-Files uncovered the true purpose of the virus, a WMD. The full report documents the minute details of the operation, but a simple summary, China manufactured the virus with the intent of attacking the United States. The accident forced the CCP to amend their mission statement. Rather than launch an attack to add tremendous additional pressure on the United States government and economic markets, the accident forced the CCP to play catch up. As detailed in the report, no country was impacted by the virus more than China. The CCP attempted, with success, to cover up the accident and the subsequent impact, but the C-Files discovered the truth. China developed the virus to create a significant competitive advantage on the world stage. After the accident, the CCP deployed the virus through silence and a series of cover-ups to maintain a level playing field. The CCP kept the accident a secret to have it spread into the global theatre. America, while not perfect, was far superior to China in managing the outbreak. The virus had the opposite effect the CCP had intended. America, due to better virus protocols including superior vaccines, has the competitive global advantage against China. Due do their poor handling of the virus, the CCP has been forced to continue to actively spread the virus to limit America's advantage.' Lori took a sip of her water and asked. 'Any questions at this point?'

The room remained silent and waited for Segal to continue. Zera broke the silence. 'I have to ask before we continue, Iceman what made you want to explore and create the C-Files?'

Iceman shrugged his shoulders and answered. 'Don't know really. I was bored after completing my training and the COVID phenomenon intrigued me. The reports I read online seemed like BS. I was curious what work was done here. Once I saw the files, I became engaged. I was amazed by the quality and volume of data the Factory assembled. I just came at it with a fresh angle.'

Zera shook his head, clearly impressed. 'Glad you did. Lori, please continue.'

'The critical point in our research was identifying the original CCP attack plan. A hypothesis was formulated on the driving question, *what would China do?* After extensive digging, the answer emerged as Mexico. Mexico has long been viewed as America's weak underbelly. Efforts have been made in the past to solicit Mexico's help in attacking the United States. The most famous attempt is the *Zimmerman Letter.* During WWI, the Germans sent a letter soliciting Mexico to join the fight. Mexico declined, the letter was intercepted, and became a rallying cry for America to enter the war. The question, *WWCD?* is the governing theme of the C-Files. The investigation easily dismissed the Mexican government and moved on to the cartels. The cartels were nearly dismissed as well, and the C-Files were on the verge of being closed. The critical moment for the C-Files was identifying Juan Garcia Abrego, or GA. The infamous drug lord is a pillar of the C-Files. The question was posed, *what happened to the money and the business model?* The money was important, but the business model was invaluable. GA was a certified genius. He had a brilliant military and business mind that built revolutionary operating systems. GA, his money, and his operating model did not simply vanish. He is still alive, in prison, age 77, with lieutenants that continue to operate.

'The Gulf cartel is viewed as an afterthought in the Mexican cartel arena. The region's dominant cartel is Los Zetas. The Gulf cartel is fractioned, a small player with no leadership, so the world was led to believe. The current perception of the Gulf cartel was cleverly crafted by Garcia. GA has moved the focus of the Gulf cartel from criminal to more legitimate. One area the Gulf cartel shifted their resources and deployed the logistical operating methods developed by GA was in maquiladoras. A maquiladora, as we all know, is a company that allows delivery from Mexico to the United States, tax and duty free. A full detailed account of the maquiladora industry is included in your report. The C-Files were presented to me with a good working outline and support for the thesis that Juan Garcia Abrego controlled the targeted maquiladoras, and those maquiladoras were working with China to infect the United States with undocumented immigrants. My team went to work to prove or disprove this working thesis. Any questions?'

The room moved their attention from Segal to Zera, who instructed. 'I have nothing, please continue.'

'The basic summary begins with my team going back into US and Mexican authority records, DEA, FBI, all American and Mexican agencies. Once GA was convicted both governments took the win. We found the system of shell companies used to hide and deploy enormous amounts of capital, then we discovered similarly structured shell companies with restructured banking systems, and updated operating systems being deployed by the maquiladoras. We unearthed drug and mule routes that found the same destinations as GA's system, only utilizing better methods. A key component to GA's operating tree is the maquiladoras. We confirmed that Garcia and the Gulf cartel are far more active in illegal border activity hidden within the constructs of their *legal* maquiladoras' fronts.

'The C-Files presented Fernando and Eve Chavez, who are twins, as critical operators within Garcia's operation. On the surface, the Chavez siblings are the model of maquiladora success. Raised on a modest farm by a single mother, the siblings traveled to the University of Michigan for undergraduate and graduate work, and returned to Mexico to operate, with a significant ownership stake, extraordinarily successful maquiladoras. This is where it gets interesting, or I suppose more interesting. The C-Files identify Fernando and Eve as Garcia's children born to one of Garcia's favorite mistresses. While not on any legal documents, Garcia is linked to the children. As a part of his terms for surrender it was rumored and denied that Garcia was allowed conjugal visits from three of his favorite mistresses. The rumors are true and Gloria Chavez, the mother and mistress, made several visits to GA while in prison. In addition, Gloria has enjoyed a good, modest life that could not be supported without Garcia. Fernando and Eve are his children, and it is clear he cares for them and their mother. We have established Garcia is still active, has improved his methods of operations to include maquiladoras, and is the father of two of the most successful maquiladoras principles. Any questions?'

Zera shook his head and Segal continued. 'We have established an impressive operation; our ultimate step was to verify or refute the CCP's involvement. Let me talk about Garcia's specific utilization of maquiladoras in his operation. The identified maquiladoras offer faster delivery, better containers that include air conditioning. Using Garcia's network in Texas, Chicago, Denver, and to a lesser extent, New York, Philadelphia, and Charlotte, deliveries are hidden within maquiladora shipments and delivered in one to three days. My team verified, in general, that only 4% of the containers imported into America are inspected. Maquiladora's container inspection rate is much lower. Garcia made the brilliant decision to limit the number of illegal drug shipments made to the United States. By reducing exposure to border activity, Garcia's team, now led by the Chavez twins, can focus their attention on their most profitable enterprise, money laundering. Garcia realized that he could virtually eliminate risk, by deploying his network of shell companies to launder money rather than smuggle drugs. He no longer wanted the risk that comes with vast drug trafficking. He focused on the single biggest problem cartels face. What to do with the money?'

Duke interjected for the first time. 'That's where China comes in.'

Lori responded. 'Exactly. The CCP directs legal, legitimate business ventures to the maquiladora controlled by Garcia to provide a legitimate business reason for the relationship. The business relationships with the Chinese are the reason the maquiladoras are so successful.'

Duke continued the thought. 'In return, the CCP gets cargo containers filled with infected Mexicans across the border.'

'Yes, what makes the maquiladora system unique is that only Mexicans are included. Migrants are not limited to Mexicans. We estimate that 40% of illegal crossings come from other countries most notably the Northern Triangle, El Salvador, Guatemala, and Honduras. The Northern Triangle has a much higher detention rate because of inferior delivery systems.'

'How big are we talking?' Conjar asked.

'We do not know for certain, but a conservative number, GA's operation accounts for between 15,000-25,000 a month. Record numbers of immigration apprehensions, estimated at 2.5 million, keep Homeland Security busy. The record number of apprehensions coincides with a record number of illegal crossings because the estimated apprehension rate has fallen to 38%. The total number of illegal or undocumented immigrants residing in the United States has exceeded 12 million. The dramatic increase stems from repeat offenders and the dramatic increase in migrants from other countries, mainly Guatemala and Honduras. The Chavez maquiladoras are so dangerous because the travel time is so short. The infected immigrants arrive at their communities at a very contagious period. They arrive at communities composed of undocumented immigrants. Communities with little access to health care, who work in very public businesses: movie theatres, hotels, restaurants, etc. These workers cannot afford to take time off work and are very unlikely to report symptoms. They need their job. What do Garcia's hubs of operation have in common besides large Mexican populations?'

Duke answered. 'Busy airports. Houston, Chicago, Denver.'

'Pretty incredible stuff.' Lori commented and continued. 'My team thought we had the package ready for presentation when

Trinity confirmed the most crucial operational link. Trinity, why don't you explain what you found?'

Trinity was surprised by the request. She was instantly stunned but was not afforded the time to worry about her presentation. She quickly gathered herself and started. 'The C-Files, as an afterthought, made a note to investigate the maquiladora located in the Baja region, along the west coast of Mexico. The pandemic has been a well-documented massive disruption to the shipping industry. A significant business industry has emerged from purchasing empty containers and shipping them back to China. The purchase price of a container is next to nothing, the cost is shipping. By assembling a significant block of containers, the west coast maquiladora has produced a rapidly growing business. In studying the operation, I was struck by the number of containers that originated from the east coast. These containers are placed on rail and shipped cross-country. The rail delivery significantly cuts into the profit margin.'

Duke commented. 'Unless the containers contain drug money to be laundered.'

Trinity felt a moment of satisfaction. She had arrived in the big leagues and knew her presentation was an important moment for her to establish herself as more than a glorified office manager. She found the Holy Grail of evidence and watched Duke stomach the moment. Her satisfaction was replaced with disdain for Duke. He had held her back. She managed to swallow her emotions and remain professional. 'Yes, the money train as we call it, is the next generation of genius for Garcia. Through his series of shell companies not only does he ship his cash but the Los Zeta's as well.'

Conjar, amazed by Trinity's revelation, asked for clarification. 'Let me understand this. The Zetas are paying the Gulf Cartel to launder their money?'

'Without their knowledge.' Trinity responded, managing not to sound boastful.

'Amazing, revenue without operational expenses, and front-line risk of seizures, murders and turf wars.' Conjar simply replied. 'Amazing, that certainly ties in China.'

'China receives the shipment of cash, washes it, and takes a well below market fee. The Gulf Cartel, through their network of shell companies, charges a 25% fee to the Los Zetas and The Zetas receive 65% of their deposit in return, all cleaned.'

Conjar suddenly laughed and observed. 'Los Zetas, thinking they have a great deal, is paying over 35% of all their hard-earned revenue to the Gulf Cartel, who the world believes is irrelevant in the grand scheme of the drug business. The reality is, without all the work and risk that comes with being a drug lord, Garcia controls the market.'

'Yes.' Lori replied.

Zera injected himself into the meeting. 'We have our targets. I think we have done enough for today. Duke, you have been busy building our Black Ops mission.'

Duke answered. 'Correct. We have targeted Fernando and Eve Chavez.'

Zera turned his attention back to Lori. 'Before we stop for the day, where do we stand with the C-Files in terms of leaking information to the proper authorities after the mission?

Lori looked to Atalanta and asked. 'You are heading that phase of the project, why don't you respond?'

Atalanta, unphased by the moment and audience, answered clinically. 'The data quality is high. A noisy and big project, but the data is there. More than enough.'

Lori added. 'We have enough data to take down major operations. The issue will be just how far the respective governments will take it.'

Zera replied. 'That is not our problem. I am interested in knowing the cover story used by Black Ops.'

Duke answered. 'I have plenty to work with. Lori did a fine job.'

Trinity made eye contact with Atalanta with a look of resignation in response to Duke complimenting Lori and not her team.

Lori added. 'The data leak, at a minimum, will provide large drug busts. If government agencies dedicate the financial resources required, high level arrests will follow.'

Zera stood and addressed the team. 'Let's meet tomorrow to discuss the mission plan. Trinity and Atalanta, nice work today, please join us tomorrow.'

Iceman could not hold his grin while the girls accepted Zera's invitation. He quickly made for the exit to hide his face from the room. His enjoyment was only exceeded by Duke's anger over the invitation.

* * *

After the meeting, Trinity tried to find Iceman to discuss the turn of events that led her to be in the meeting. Not surprisingly, Iceman was nowhere to be found. Frustrated, she stomped off in search of Zeus. She went to his cubicle only to find it empty. She continued her search and was finally rewarded in the cafeteria; Zeus was eating a late lunch.

Zeus saw Trinity marching towards his table and offered. 'I am guessing I am your second choice.'

Trinity took a seat next to him and snatched a fry off his plate. 'Where is he?'

Zeus wiped his bacon double burger face with his napkin and smiled at Trinity. 'There is no way you went searching for me to ask that silly of a question. You know him, you know what he is like. After those meetings, he's gone.'

'Find him.'

'Yeah, okay Trinity, that's exactly what's not going to happen. Leave him alone, he'll catch up with us.'

Trinity took her frustration out on a couple more of Zeus' fries, chewing aggressively. 'Fine, but the four of us are meeting at The Liberty at 1900, got it.'

As Trinity stood to march off, Zeus returned to the last of his fries, and mumbled, 'got it.'

* * *

Iceman arrived at The Liberty promptly at 1900 to find his three amigos sitting at their usual table. 'Cadet Collins reporting as ordered, ma'am.' He had considered blowing off the meeting or arriving late to get a reaction from Trinity but decided against it.

Atalanta smiled and welcomed Iceman. Zeus gave a modest head nod, anxious to move past Trinity's drama. Trinity greeted Iceman. 'We took the liberty.'

Iceman looked down at his usual drink order and took a swig of his beer. 'No pun intended.'

Atalanta laughed and Trinity asked. 'What's so funny?'

Atalanta explained. 'No pun intended? You took the liberty; we are at The Liberty.'

'Right, ha, ha.' Trinity returned her attention to Iceman. 'What was that? What happened today?'

Iceman held up his index finger to ask for a moment. He was drinking his whiskey. 'Sorry about that, what has you all worked up? Today? That was brilliant. You got a well-deserved seat at the table, performed admirably, and were invited back. Take the win and enjoy it. The two of you very much deserve it.'

Iceman retreated to his beer, Trinity went to protest, and Zeus intervened. 'Let it go Trinity, good job.'

With a bit of frustration still simmering, Trinity complained. 'I, we, should have known beforehand and not at the last second. I would have worn something different and been better prepared.'

Iceman set down his empty beer, made eye contact with the waitress to summon another round of beers, and smirked at Trinity. 'You weren't advised ahead of time, but you are now. Looking forward to seeing you tomorrow in your fetching outfit.' The drinks were served, and Iceman toasted. 'To sensible, well-deliberated fashion.'

The table laughed and after a moment Trinity jumped in on the fun. After an hour of light banter and polite teasing, the subject returned to the Factory. Trinity asked with concern in her voice. 'What did you think of Duke's reaction to today?'

Zeus answered. 'I thought it went well. He seemed on board with everything that was discussed.'

Atalanta responded. 'I agree. Trinity, I did catch your look when he left us out of complimenting Lori, but that is just his thing. Overall, like Iceman said, a good win.'

'I suppose so.' Trinity paused. 'It was good to be included. Yeah, I thought Duke treated us fair, given the circumstances.'

The table went silent for a moment, then realized Iceman was strangely silent. Atalanta asked him. 'You haven't said anything. What do you think about Duke and his reaction to me, and Trinity being included?'

Iceman, who was focused on the television, watching a baseball game, half turned. With one eye on the game and one eye on Trinity he answered. 'I thought I said let it go. You both did well today, be great tomorrow and continue to be great going forward. The rest will take care of itself. Don't focus on Duke, fuck the Duck, focus on you.'

* * *

The next morning Iceman was one of the last to enter the conference room. He took his seat and smiled at Trinity. 'You look especially smashing today. Sensible yet fashionable.'

Dr. Monroe noticed the exchange and understood an inside joke was at play. Grace also laughed quietly when she observed Trinity reaching for her water with her middle finger extended towards Iceman.

Once all the invitees were assembled, Duke looked to Zera and received his consent to begin the meeting. 'As discussed yesterday, our targets are Fernando and Eve Chavez.' Duke handed out a copy of his power point presentation and supporting documentation file. 'We did the usual deep dive into their routines and habits, searching for our best opportunity. For the most part both subjects lead conservative lives. Both drink but not to excess, neither use drugs. Neither are married, which is a bit unique considering their age, and neither are in a committed relationship.'

The Colonel interrupted. 'Married to their work.'

'Exactly.' Duke confirmed, and the group agreed, except for Grace. Duke continued. 'Both live on separate estates in the upscale area of San Francisco, Tamaulipas. The estates are large but in concert with their income generated by their maquiladoras. They both have drivers and mild security services provided to any executive operating in the region. While they work together, their positions in the company are quite different. Eve runs the corporate side of the organization; Fernando is the brains behind operations. They rarely work at the same location. Eve spends much of her time in their corporate office in Matamoros.

369

Fernando spends most of his time at their maquiladora factories. He pilots the company jet to visit the factories in person to gauge the operation. There is some overlap when both are in the corporate office. Eve joins Fernando on his flight when she attends the maquiladora's quarterly meeting. The heads of all the maquiladoras meet at an offsite location to present their quarterly results and forecast plans.

'They dine together when Fernando is in town, usually at dinner but also some lunches. They dine in private rooms at one of three restaurants. The lunches and dinners are their opportunity to discuss business in private without interruptions. Fernando frequently visits Eve's home on the weekends. The two of them are machines. Nothing about them indicates a criminal element. They have done well with their cover.'

Zera paused the presentation. 'Any questions or comments?' He took inventory of the room and settled on Dr. Monroe. 'Grace, you appear to be lost in thought. Anything you wish to share?'

'I suppose I have.' She continued to gather her thoughts while she drank from her water. 'You mentioned Eve and Fernando were married to their work.'

Duke answered a bit defensively. 'That is correct. Not much of any social life, as I just said the two are machines.'

'Agreed. The meals they share together, the private dining rooms are dark and intimate?'

'I suppose so.' Duke replied wondering where Grace was headed.

'On the frequent weekend visits, Fernando stays the night? Has his own room at Eve's estate?'

'That's correct. Why is this important?' Duke asked. He did not like to be questioned.

'The two are married to each other and not simply to work. I am not suggesting something sexual, but certainly a strong intimacy is shared. Growing up as bastard twins with rumors swirling about who their father is certainly brought them together. Typically, twins share a unique bond given the nature of their birth. Add the isolating factors of being bastards, and the twins grow even closer. Eve's estate is the nest. Fernando stays on his estate but in fact lives with Eve on her estate. The meals shared at the restaurants are more than reviewing business plans and results. The lunch and dinner meetings are a form of a date. Fernando and Eve do not date others seriously because they are in a committed relationship to each other, no room for anyone else.'

Zera commented. 'I see your point. How should we use this information?'

'The Chavez twins' tragic flaw is their relationship with each other. They draw strength from their powerful emotional connection, but that is also their greatest weakness, where they are most vulnerable. I offer my insight to be used in consideration with your Black Ops mission.'

'Thank you, Grace.' Duke acknowledged Dr. Monroe's words in a rare moment of acceptance of outside input to his mission plans. He quickly reverted to his true self. 'While I had not directly come to that specific observation, the mission plan does factor in the relationship you described so well.'

Iceman and Trinity shared the same silent thought. *Of course, it did. Somehow, Duke had already included valuable information that was unknown to him in his plan. Must be a divine power guiding him.*

Zera took a moment to observe Duke after his comment and reflect on its validity. He decided to reserve judgement until Duke presented his plan. 'Good, we all agree on Grace's insight. Let's move on to the plan.'

Duke had already dismissed Grace's words as trivial, a brain shrinker's babble when he continued his presentation. 'I have elected to attack Fernando and Eve when they are aboard their corporate jet. We will execute the plan during their next scheduled quarterly visit to meet with the maquiladora's leadership. I considered Eve's home as a potential target but dismissed it in favor of the plane. Small aircraft have a history of deadly accidents due to pilot or mechanical failure. The Black Ops team will gain access to the plane, tamper with the controls, and send the plane to a fiery crash. The headlines will read, another small aircraft tragedy, and the Chavez twins will be eliminated.'

Zera responded. 'Team Conjar has been selected for this mission. What are their next steps?'

Duke answered with his usual arrogant tone. He wanted to send a message of control to Conjar. 'We have 60 days to prepare and execute the mission. I have identified the flight and will work with Conjar on the insurgence plan. He and I will develop the steps needed to grant his team access to the plane. The hanger where the plane is housed is not under tight security, accessing the plane is manageable for an inexperienced team. My current training plan for the team is to fly to Barbados, study plane mechanics, and rehearse the sabotage required. In addition to the sabotage training, Conjar can use the time to get his agents in peak physical condition and any other items that he sees fit with my approval of course.'

Iceman and Trinity shared the same silent thought again, but this time they made eye contact and a small smile. *Of course. Of course, with my approval.*

Satisfied with Duke's presentation, Zera asked the group. 'Any questions? Comments? Feedback?'

The room remained silent, with eyes that slowly and subtly turned towards Iceman. Iceman did not accept the attention. He continued to stare blankly at his closed report. He was not reading the report, he was beginning to get lost in his monkey brain. His vision was interrupted by the Colonel. 'Iceman, do you have anything to add?'

Iceman did not immediately respond to the Colonel's question. He had to be asked a second time. 'I am sorry, what was the question? Do I have anything to add? No, I do not. At first look, the plan looks solid, and I am confident Duke and Conjar will work out the details.'

Duke was pleasantly surprised by Iceman's humble response. He accepted Iceman's consent, yet another notch on his belt. *Damn right, the plan is solid, I built it, of course it is solid. Shit, solid does not begin to describe the simple brilliance of my plan.*

Duke's brief celebration ended when Iceman continued. 'When are we meeting again to finalize the plan?'

Zera was a bit confused when he asked. 'Iceman, I thought you were satisfied? You just said the plan looked solid.'

'And it does.' Iceman continued. 'At first glance, Duke has given us a wealth of supporting information to consider. After reading it, the plan looks solid. I would like to digest the plan presented, study and critique the wealth of data with fresh eyes, factor Grace's insightful diagnosis of the Chavez twins, and discuss a few of the details Duke and Conjar will iron out.'

Duke was an internal volcano after Iceman's comments. *Who does that little worm think he is? Critique me, my data, my plan? He needs to drink the cup of shut the fuck up I am serving and follow orders.* Duke found it difficult to retain his fake persona. His face slightly betrayed him but to his credit he remained silent. He chanted to himself, *Now is not the time Duke.*

Zera felt the sudden tension in the room and decided to take immediate action. 'Yes, Duke has provided us with a great deal of information and the plan is well done. Duke, get with Conjar and sort out the details. We will meet back here in three days. That gives us all plenty of time.'

As the room stood to leave, the Colonel whispered to Grace. 'Where do you think he is going?'

Grace knew the, *he* in question was Iceman. 'Meet with me in my office is 30 minutes?'

As Grace and Sullivan reacted to Iceman's comments, Trinity approached Zeus. 'What's he up to?'

'Donno, but he'll tell me soon enough.'

'Tell him to meet us at The Liberty at 1900.'

Zeus looked at Trinity like she was crazy. 'When are you going to learn? No chance am I doing that. He will contact me when he is ready.'

Once a frustrated Trinity walked far enough away, Zeus took out his cell phone and texted Iceman. 'Ready, don't wait too long to contact me. You promised.' Zeus reflected on his text before he hit send. Iceman had promised Zeus to include him as early as possible in Iceman's laboratory of solitude. Feeling the message was fair, Zeus hit send.

He was immediately rewarded with Iceman's response. 'Roger that.'

CHAPTER THIRTY-SEVEN

After the meeting, Iceman headed straight for his room. He removed his hidden bottle of whiskey, a bottle known to all, but he still considered it hidden, took a drink, no glass required and studied Duke's data packet. His second read of the documents confirmed his initial conclusions. Duke's packet was nothing more than the compilation of information generated by the C-Files. Some minor details of note such as the Chavez twins' routine including the company plane were important and Iceman made a mental note of the pockets of that sort of useful current information. After a quick third review, Iceman was satisfied that he had fully digested all information presented regarding the Chavez twins. He donned his 1959 Chicago White Sox baseball hat, his thinking cap and headed to Dirty Bill's to build a better mouse trap.

He skipped the Uber, electing to make the walk with a cigar to his dive bar oasis. On his walk, that extended to his bar stool, he imagined a blank whiteboard in his mind. He began to populate the imaginary board with the key players, the purpose of the mission, the impact of the mission and all the targets. Iceman believed that the target list was too focused on the Chavez twins. They were certainly important, but the mission required more than their elimination. The mission parameters needed to be extended to terminate the entire operation and not just the Chavez twins. Yes, terminating them would be a serious wrench, that was granted, but the mission could take down more than just the Chavez twins, if done correctly. He created a second blank whiteboard in his mind, and set to work the problem, *if done correctly.*

He entrenched himself on his barstool, accompanied only by his Budweiser, and got lost in his white board universe. He moved characters from one board to another and orchestrated a ballet of movement between entities and individuals. He calibrated a series of if then scenarios, plotting his course to conquer, *if done correctly.* After three or four hours, Iceman was not sure, he had lost the concept of time. He rose from his stool, told Tim the bartender to hold his spot, and went for a walk. The air and movement helped Iceman visualize the final, most intriguing part of his solution, *if done correctly.* With only the conclusion of the enjoyment of his cigar to mark the time, Iceman returned to his bar stool a changed man.

'Tim, I have returned. Grab me another and throw in a shorty.' Iceman waited for his whiskey, the shorty, to arrive. After making quick work of the shorty and a healthy pull from his Bud, he texted Zeus. 'Where you at?'

Zeus immediately texted back. 'On my way to see you.' Zeus needn't bother to ask Iceman's location, he simply logged off his computer and headed to Dirty Bills.

Zeus arrived 15 minutes later to find Iceman's barstool empty. Tim walked over and served him a round with a shorty. Zeus asked. 'Is he in the bathroom?'

'No, he went for another one of those walks of his.'

'Did he take a cigar with him?' Zeus knew the length of Iceman's walks. No cigar meant short walk; con cigar was a long walk. Zeus settled in, watched ESPN, and waited patiently for his friend.

Iceman strolled into the bar 40 minutes later with a big smile on his face. The smile told Zeus that Iceman had solved some riddle. Like a cat that ate the canary, Iceman's combination of smile and smirk radiated that he was on to something. Zeus properly assumed Iceman had built a better mission and was going to upstage Duke again. Zeus was not anxious to engage in another confrontation with Duke, but he was very anxious to hear Iceman's plan. Zeus initially attempted to talk about the mission upon Iceman's return but was met without success. Iceman was in the recovery phase of his white board exercise. Mentally fried from the attack on his white board, Iceman was in the process of rebooting his system. He was shut down for the time being.

While Zeus waited for Iceman to reboot, he patiently engaged Ice in light banter. The subjects were all over the board. Iceman transitioned from his beloved White Sox relief pitching needs, to the origins of clichés.

'Do you know this one?' Iceman had already explained the origin of, *wet your whistle,* and *on the wagon. 'Mind your P's and Q's?'*

Tim laughed. 'All your clichés have alcohol as a theme.'

Zeus interjected. 'You already told me about P's and Q's countless times.'

'True, true. Given our environment, I felt it appropriate.' Ice took a nice serving of his Budweiser and went back for seconds before continuing. 'Where was I? Right, since the audience is always right, I will prove to Tim that my clichés are not limited to bar experiences. My range of knowledge has no boundaries. I will also placate Seamus with a new riddle. Let us talk a little bit about, *raining cats and dogs*, any clue?'

Tim was pulled with interest into asking. 'Don't know, but I am still curious about *P's and Q's.*' Zeus had become quite familiar with Iceman's various techniques to lure his audience in. *Please can I have one volunteer from the audience?*

Iceman dragged Tim further into his story telling world when he responded. 'I'll tell you about *P's and Q's* later. Seamus demands and deserves fresh material.'

Zeus smiled as he reached for his beer, there *he goes again sucking Tim further in using suspense. The old ploy, I'll tell you later.*

Iceman continued. 'Imagine yourself in the days of *Braveheart.'*

Tim asked. 'The movie?'

'Yes, you are in his Scottish village with thatched roof homes. The weather is cold and damp and on one spectacular night the rainstorms turn fierce. Cold and wet, so very cold, so very wet, that your pets seek shelter. The pets are not permitted into your small home, per your mother or wife, depending on your age, so they climb up into the relative comfort of your thatched roof. Makes sense, right?'

Iceman waited for Tim's answer to further engage him into the story. 'Sure, makes sense.'

'The storm is so fierce, raining like crazy, that'- Iceman took a drink to promote his dramatic pause. 'The storm is so fierce that the roof is weakened, and the pets start falling into your home. The cats and dogs that sought shelter from the rain, rain into your home. My goodness, *it is raining cats and dogs.*'

After polite applause and the serving of another round of beers, Iceman switched gears again. 'Did you know James Joyce and Earnest Hemmingway, both brilliant writers, were lads? Seamus, you are from Ireland, did you know that?'

Zeus had to laugh. *There he goes again, bringing another member of the audience into his show, like a magician on stage.* 'Yes, I did know that.'

'But did you know, Joyce, when properly served…'

'Drunk.' Tim interrupted. Zeus again laughed. *Another audience member joins the great show.*

'Properly served, I says. Joyce would pick a fight during this beautiful state of mind, then hide behind his mighty friend Hemmingway for protection.'

The conversation continually moved like a mouse through a maze from movies, back to sports, to history, and raged on with the inclusion of other story tellers from the bar audience. Iceman drew Tim, Zeus, and other patrons as they entered the bar into the conversation. Now the audience became the new story tellers. Consumption marked the time, as all were lost in thought for the evening. Iceman had found his pressure release. Recognizing Iceman had successfully rebooted, Zeus raised the question of the mission, only to be rejected in favor of the more pressing issue of pizza ordering. After the great debate on pizza, what city had the best, what toppings were the best, what style of pizza was the best, Iceman ordered enough pizza to be delivered to serve the entire bar. Only when the pizza arrived, and was consumed, did Zeus grow closer to successfully asking his question.

'I don't see any cocktail napkins.' Zeus commented.

Iceman, engaged in a debate regarding the greatest college running back of all time, offered Zeus. 'Herschel Walker is way better than Archie. I will give you Bo Jackson and because we are in Texas and I do not want to be shot, Earl Campbell, but Archie Griffin is the most overrated running back of all time.' Zeus waited and was rewarded with a curt response. 'The napkins are right across from you in the holder, same as usual.'

Iceman returned to the debate and Zeus tried again. 'Iceman, you know what I mean.'

'This conversation is beneath me. How you people could be so wrong is amazing.' Having excused himself with the life-changing debate on college running backs, Iceman returned his focus on Zeus. Zeus recognized Iceman's intense stare and knew something big was coming. 'I am not yet at the cocktail napkin stage but will be tomorrow afternoon. Have the girls meet us at The Liberty tomorrow at 1600 hours.'

'Got it.' Zeus' blood was now flowing with anticipation. His curiosity was not satisfied; Zeus took another run at Iceman. 'Give me something.'

Iceman held up his hand, his signal to give him a minute. He ordered another round for the two of them and the guy that promoted Archie Griffin as the best college running back of all time. While a valid argument given Archie won two Heisman trophies, Iceman had shot him down pretty good and bought him a beer to show there were no hard feelings. Zeus patiently waited. The round came and Iceman spoke, 'We are taking out the Chavez twins, Garcia and his system, the Chinese attack and the Los Zetas are going to help us do it. You and I with Conjar will cut off the head, The Zetas will eat the body.'

* * *

Iceman snapped alert from his sleep at 0445. He brushed his teeth, rinsed with his whiskey-flavored mouthwash to lift the fog created by yesterday's exploits. Not satisfied, he took a second dose of the magical elixir. He went to the pool and swam three miles and headed to the cafeteria with a clear head. Preparing for the mission, he had a tremendous breakfast, even for his standards, and went for a walk. During the walk he focused on his training, leaving the mission plan for later in the day. Satisfied he had digested his meal, Iceman returned to the gym for a full workout. After the workout he returned to his room, showered, got dressed for the day, and meditated for 30 minutes. He blocked out all the noise that filled his mind to be able to channel his energy for the rest of the day. At 1000 hours, he headed to Dirty Bills.

He arrived at Dirty Bills, and pleasantly knocked on the door for an early entrance. Tim, as usual, was there doing inventory, and opened the door for Iceman. 'You know where to find everything.' Remembering the conversation from last night, Tim added. 'And you owe me the story of *mind your Ps and Q's.*'

Iceman laughed, grabbed a Budweiser from the cooler under the bar, took his usual seat, and reached for the cocktail napkins. At 1300, Iceman reviewed his work product.

C-FILES: FINAL REPORT

PRISON HE IS HELD, GA'S HEALTH, MEDICAL ROUTINE (DIABETES LIKE HIS BROTHER?) HOW CAN WE KILL HIM?

WHERE WILL HE BE BURIED, WILL TWINS SHOW? (ASK GRACE), THE AREA THAT SURROUND IT, WHERE CAN WE SET UP A SNIPER NEST

ZETAS TO BLAME FOR SNIPER ATTACK, WEAPON OF CHOICE?

USE ZETAS AND NOT THE GOVERNMENTS FOR CLEAN UP.

HEADLINES READ: DRUG WAR ERRUPTION.

Satisfied with his napkin, Iceman folded it into his back pocket, and went for a walk with a cigar. He returned an hour later and relaxed in Dirty Bill's until his meeting at The Liberty at 1600.

He arrived 30 minutes early because he was hungry, expecting to wait on the others. To his surprise, they were already seated at their usual table.

'I take it, you are excited to see me.' Iceman started. 'I am excited to see you as well, but before we start, I need to eat something.'

Zeus took this as a good sign. Iceman had his appetite which meant he was mission ready. 'That sounds more than reasonable.'

After a full serving of the right side of the menu, the girls were almost sick from watching, until Iceman cleared the girls' uneaten portions. Trinity had to speak before she became ill. 'Alright, that is more than enough food, let's hear it, Iceman.'

Iceman raised his hand, calling for patience, waited for the table to be cleared and cleaned, and ordered a bucket of beers, before he reached into his back pocket. 'Here is what you have been waiting for. Now let's talk about what I need from you.'

Iceman gave an overview of his plan, so the team understood how their research was critical to the mission. After everyone had their assignments, the group relaxed and basked in the camaraderie they had built.

* * *

After their relentless work, the exhausted team was ready for the third C-Files meeting of the week. When everyone was seated, Zera took control of the room. 'Welcome back everyone, let us begin. We were set on the basic mission to terminate the Chavez twins using an airplane crash. The purpose of the meeting today is to review the detailed mission plan, giving Duke and Conjar some time to give us a draft of their thoughts.'

Iceman raised his hand. Zera asked him. 'Do you have something for us?'

'I do.' Iceman began, confident in his team's work. 'My last comments in our previous meeting centered around Duke's plan being solid and my request to review the wealth of supporting documentation he provided us. I stand behind my position that Duke's plan is solid. After having time to review the supporting documentation and reflect on the mission, I am more committed to the plan's validity. I am more than confident in the mission details, Conjar and Duke will present to us today, will be thorough and excellent.'

Duke nodded his head appreciably. 'Thank you, Iceman.' He was genuinely surprised by Iceman's calm confidence in his work.

'If the mission is to simply eliminate the Chavez twins, this is the right plan for the job. However, if the mission is to eliminate not only the twins, but also Garcia's business model and logistical network to include financial schemes that implement shell companies and close our southern border to China; then the C-Files team has a mission plan for your consideration.' Iceman paused to allow Trinity to distribute the C-Files team presentation book. While he waited, he gauged Duke's reaction and recognized his need to throw more compliments the Duck's way to allow a clean presentation, free of Duke's constant interruptions. 'As Trinity hands out the books, I would like to reiterate that the wealth of information and clarity in presentation in Duke's plan was critical in the development of this plan.'

The group opened the presentation to find an inexplicable summary page; an imaged copy of a cocktail napkin with chicken scratch. Dr. Monroe and the Colonel had grown to appreciate Iceman's methods, but they were not certain the others would appreciate it.

PRISON HE IS HELD, GA'S HEALTH, MEDICAL ROUTINE (DIABETES LIKE HIS BROTHER?) HOW CAN WE KILL HIM?

WHERE WILL HE BE BURIED, WILL TWINS SHOW? (ASK GRACE), THE AREA THAT SURROUND IT, WHERE CAN WE SET UP A SNIPER NEST

ZETAS TO BLAME FOR SNIPER ATTACK, WEAPON OF CHOICE?

USE ZETAS AND NOT THE GOVERNMENTS FOR CLEAN UP.

HEADLINES READ: DRUG WAR ERRUPTION.

Trinity quickly advised the group to turn to page two and started her presentation. 'Our team has come to appreciate that Iceman has a process that he calls whiteboarding. He puts all the players, strategies, impacts, and outcomes on a series of whiteboards. He works to minimize the number of whiteboards until he arrives at a common cocktail napkin. He believes all plans should be simple and well defined enough to fit on a cocktail napkin. Bullet one: PRISON HE IS HELD, GA'S HEALTH, MEDICAL ROUTINE (DIABETES LIKE HIS BROTHER?) HOW CAN WE KILL HIM? The C-Files team went to work in the operating theatre with the critical character being Juan Garcia Abrego, the architect of this grand scheme. Garcia is imprisoned at USP Hazelton, a high security prison in Preston County, West Virginia. Eliminating him will set off a chain of events vital to the mission. His brother died of diabetes, but we show no evidence Garcia has the disease. He is 77 years old and remains in elderly good health.' Trinity turned to Duke at this point, per Iceman's instruction, to include him in the plan. 'Duke, this is one of several points where we need your expertise. We need you to target Garcia however you deem best.'

Duke paused, very guarded and cautious with his next words. He stubbornly acknowledged to himself that he was interested in the plan, and a bit surprised to be included at a prominent level. He decided to reserve judgement and hear the presentation. 'I can handle that, getting to a prisoner in the US federal prison system is not a problem. At 77 years of age, Garcia will most certainly be on an aggressive medication plan. We can tamper with his medication, so that he unknowingly takes a deadly, untraceable toxin.'

Trinity continued, privately relishing assigning tasks to Duke. 'Thank you. I'll turn the presentation over to Atalanta for the second bullet point.'

'Good morning.' Atalanta began. 'Bullet point two: WHERE WILL HE BE BURIED, WILL TWINS SHOW? (ASK GRACE), THE AREA THAT SURROUND IT, WHERE CAN WE SET UP A SNIPER NEST? I was able to find the land prepared for Garcia's death. In an area west of the Presa Vicente Guerrero, near a large body of water, south of the town of Padilla. Garcia, through a series of shell companies owns are large area of land, several hundred acres. The Chavez family's agave farm is located on the northern most point of the property. The area features warm plains with robust vegetation and high rolling sierras. He will be buried here.' Following Iceman's script, Atalanta paused to include the Duck. 'Duke, the plan requires your expertise to identify a sniper nest location and extraction plan.'

The presentation continued to grip Duke's attention. 'Got it.'

'I turn the presentation over to Zeus to discuss. WILL TWINS SHOW?'

'Thanks Atalanta. I posed the question to Dr. Monroe, and she believed the Chavez twins would attend the funeral with high probability. The desire to be recognized as the children of Garcia, coupled with their need to validate themselves as the most successful of Garcia's unique family structure will create a burning desire to attend. Grace is willing to answer any questions regarding this point.'

'My question is not directed toward Grace.' Duke began. 'I am wondering what the plan is if they don't attend the ceremony?'

Iceman had prepared Zeus for the question, he quickly replied. 'We revert back to the first plan.' Iceman had deliberately instructed Zeus to refer to the plan as first rather than Duke's plan. Iceman wanted the names removed from identifying the plans to prevent the discussion from being personal. 'If there is nothing else, I will turn the presentation over to Iceman to bring us home.'

'Thanks Zeus. The next bullet point works to achieve the mission statement I described earlier. *To eliminate not only the twins, but also Garcia's business model and logistical network including financial schemes that implement shell companies and close our southern border to China.* The referred bullet point: ZETAS TO BLAME FOR SNIPER ATTACK, WEAPON OF CHOICE? Duke, again the plan calls for your expertise. The Zetas have recently recruited snipers to add to their arsenal of sicarios as a method of terror. The snipers not only eliminate human targets but light helicopters and planes as well. We are framing The Zetas; the plan relies on you to sell it.'

Duke, to his surprise, continued to believe in the plan. 'Not a problem.'

'Great, next bullet. USE ZETAS AND NOT THE GOVERN-MENTS FOR CLEAN UP. After the mission is successful, we will leak the details of the Chavez twins' secret money laundering scheme. As we discussed in approving the Chavez twins as targets, The Zetas are unknowingly paying the Chavez twins and by extension the Gulf Cartel to launder their money. After the Battle for Juarez Plaza in 2009, The Zetas believed they were the king of the region. The reality is The Zetas are funding their perceived weak rival. Their money laundering and relationship with China, have made the Gulf Cartel secretly stronger than The Zetas. The Zetas may not understand why they are being blamed for the assassination, but when they discover the laundering scheme, they will take violent action. The plan will leave a mountain of data for the affected governments to pursue high level prosecution, but the plan is not dependent on the governments. We have witnessed governments' willingness to stop the hunt once a couple of high-value targets are taken off the board. A couple of pieces are missing, but the game continues to be played. The Zetas, on the other hand, will scorch the earth. The Zetas will destroy the Garcia business model, but do not have the sophistication to replace it. That is where China fits into the puzzle. With the Chavez twins AND their operation burning to the ground, China will no longer have a partner to execute their C-Files attack. Last point: HEADLINES READ: DRUG WAR ERRUPTION. The world will view our mission success as just another day in Mexico.'

The room was silenced by the simple genius of the plan. Zera was the first to speak. 'That is some plan. Anyone have any thoughts?'

Duke was the first to speak. 'I'll take Iceman's approach and ask for a day to digest all the information provided. On the surface, the plan has nice upside with minimal downside. I also like that there is a backup plan in place.' Duke was obviously referring to his plan, using it as the foundation of the C-Files team plan. 'As I prepare my thoughts regarding my building of the mission plan, at the center of the plan will be to call abort at any moment the mission faces a challenge. We have a sound plan with the airplane accident and cannot risk exposure and spook the target.'

* * *

The meeting broke, groups formed, and went their separate ways. Zera returned to his office. Duke and Conjar moved to the smaller conference room to discuss the Ops plan. The Colonel and Dr. Monroe adjourned to her office.

Once settled, Grace asked. 'What do you think?'

'Impressive, that is an unfair assessment, call it speechless. Both the mission and presentation left me humbled. I cannot express why I continue to be amazed by the twins, but that mission plan was something. So complex on the surface with all the moving parts, but the plan is brilliant in its simplicity. Father dies, kids go to funeral, kids terminated, villain is blamed. Amazing.'

'I agree, the plan is pure genius, but I was more humbled by the presentation. Iceman's plan, and we can call it for what it is, was a symphony of moving parts that played beautifully. I was more amazed at how he just flowed through the room seamlessly. He deliberately distanced himself from the labeling, using names, to avoid a showdown with Duke. The expected violent confrontation between Duke's plan versus Iceman's plan, let the battle begin and may the best man win, never materialized. He incorporated Duke's direct involvement into his plan. He recruited Duke to build the Ops plan, and used Atalanta, Zeus, Trinity, and me to do it. Iceman did not speak until the room was already sold on the plan. Rather than fight Duke's mighty ego, he used it against Duke to gain his support. Brilliant.'

'Duke is responsible for minor projects but feels as if the plan is his because Iceman sold the first plan as the core of the second plan, which is bullshit. The plans have absolutely nothing in common. Plan one is good, plan two is spectacular.' The Colonel observed dazed in thought.

'Exactly.'

* * *

Iceman desperately attacked his escape plan, but the C-Files team provided a counter-assault. They had no interest in spending any more time at the Factory and were determined to corner Iceman. Just as Iceman thought he was free, Trinity intercepted him and offered. 'I know what you have planned, mister. You have a job to do but that job includes us. We go to Dirty Bill's; it is so much closer than The Liberty.' Feeling overly confident in herself, Trinity elected to tread on sacred ground. She had a burning desire to be included in Iceman's bat cave.

Iceman summoned his belief in individual freedom inspired by Luke Jackson, and responded, *'I never planned anything in my life.'*

Zeus and Trinity were silent, only Atalanta understood the quote. The computer genius. Barbie doll, reclus, understood the *Cool Hand Luke,* reference. She also understood that she did not fancy her boyfriend. She fancied Iceman, time to play along. '*Nah - Calling it a job don't make it right, boss.'*

Iceman locked eyes with Atalanta and in that moment he understood the message. He regretfully was forced to accept that he was more than flattered. Iceman was extremely drawn to Atalanta; she was attractive, loved his jokes and caught all his movie references. She also represents freedom. Freedom from the responsibility of being Jack. Freedom to walk away from Katie and fully identify himself as Iceman. His world would certainly be simpler, but would it be better? With a bit of regret, Iceman understood he needed to walk away. Atalanta was amazing and deserved more than Iceman. She deserves Jack. The problem was that Jack was in love with Katie.

'We are going to The Liberty.' Iceman replied with a cold tone.

Trinity was not satisfied. 'Why can't we go to Dirty Bill's?'

'Too soon.'

Before Trinity could respond, she caught Zeus' look that told her to stop. She ignored him, still riding her high from the meeting. 'Why does Zeus get to go and not us?' Trinity looked at Atalanta to draw her into the debate. Neither Atalanta nor Zeus wanted any part of Trinity's effort.

'Now, you are comparing yourself to Zeus?' Iceman asked in a gruff tone.

Ouch, Trinity thought to herself. She knew she had pushed too far. With Iceman's blunt response, she recognized the success of the meeting and the high she felt had made her feel limitless. Returning to a world with limits, she accepted. 'The Liberty it is.'

The four arrived at their usual table and took their usual seats and were immediately served their usual drinks. While they waited for food, Trinity nervously asked. 'Well, what did you think? How did we do?'

The question was directed to Iceman, but he had already tuned out the table. Zeus fielded the question. 'You two knocked it out of the park. The room was floored.'

'Really?' Trinity asked knowing she was great but like an insecure movie star, she searched for more compliments.

Zeus answered. 'Yes, really.'

Atalanta joined the conversation when she asked. 'What do you think Duke will have to say tomorrow?'

Zeus remained silent and waited for Iceman to answer. Atalanta had to ask her question a second time before Iceman responded. 'Duke has nothing to say. He'll spend 15 minutes tomorrow inflating his importance to the mission and to the universe but in the end, we are a go.'

Bored with the conversation, not interested in food, still upset having been forced to avoid Dirty Bill's, and frustrated about Atalanta; Iceman walked over to the bar to chat with one of his favorite bartenders. Kimmy was a single mom with three kids. Her ex was your typical deadbeat dad. Kimmy worked the day shift while the kids were at school. Her mother provided the rides to the various sports the kids played. Iceman enjoyed Kimmy's company, and for some reason she reminded him of being back in Chicago. Iceman stayed current with Kimmy's kids, especially their accolades in sports that sparked flashbacks to his childhood. He was always overly generous in tipping Kimmy.

With Iceman away, Zeus was now the center of attention. Trinity asked him. 'Do you really think Duke will just go through his usual blow hard routine then return back to our mission?'

'Yes, I do.'

Atalanta asked. 'It seems to me, Iceman put a lot of confidence in Duke to develop the Ops plan.'

Zeus laughed. 'You think so?' The girls nodded their heads, so Zeus continued. 'No, he didn't. The two of you know exactly what the plan entails, and he even managed to fool you. Let's build the Ops plan right now. Iceman already laid out the bread-crumbs for us and Duke to follow. Take care of Garcia, check. Find a base to operate from, check. Find a sniper nest, check. Develop an exit strategy, check. There you go, you already have your mission plan. Iceman made his list; Duke must merely shop for the groceries.'

'Do you really think it is that simple?'

'Yes, Atalanta. I do. Besides Iceman will sign off on Duke's Ops plan just to get a go for the mission. If he doesn't like any part of the plan, or if conditions on the ground change, he will just implement his new plan. Duke can debate all he wants now in the conference room; Iceman has no interest in that. Duke's hands are tied once Iceman is in the field. Ice will wait until we have boots on the ground intelligence to author the Ops plan that we will ultimately execute.'

CHAPTER THIRTY-EIGHT

The mission plan was approved without debate. Conjar and Duke took over the small conference room to continue to critique the final Ops plan down to the smallest detail. Trinity and Atalanta returned to their workstations to assist Conjar and Duke with the Ops plan. Iceman and Zeus were shipped to Nevada to train on the M107 Barrett .50 caliber sniper rifle. Before their arrival at the Elders training facility, the Oasis, located on the Byrne Group campus, and their reunion with their pals, Wyatt and Bone, the twins took a brief detour. Iceman had vowed to never visit the Oasis again without a stop in America's playground. Immediately after assignments were issued, Zeus and Iceman raced to their rooms at the Factory, showered, changed, packed an overnight bag, and caught an Uber to Austin-Bergstrom International Airport. They were gone before anyone at the Factory had noticed.

They booked themselves first class tickets on the first flight to Las Vegas. They had two hours to kill, so they sat in their usual airport bar.

Zeus, concerned with their stealth departure and plan, asked Iceman. 'Do you think they are going to be pissed at us?'

'No, we are past all that bullshit. When we land in Vegas, I'll shoot Wyatt and Conjar a text to pick us up Monday morning.'

Zeus took comfort in Iceman's reply. Two nights and one day was more than reasonable. Zeus' anxiety returned; he needed confirmation. 'Look Ice, no bullshit, set the time for departure, and stick to it.'

'Agreed. Stop with the worry, you are annoying me. We go mission ready on Monday.'

Zeus knew Iceman never fucked around when it came time to be serious, he was able to relax again. 'So, what's the plan?'

'We don't have much time, and we really only have Sunday to attack Vegas, so I figure we can pitch our tent at the Hard Rock.'

Zeus was a huge fan of the idea. The twins always enjoyed their Sundays at the Hard Rock with the Mexican restaurant, Pink Taco, on site, and of course rehab. Rehab was the slang used by the Vegas industry professionals who worked in the casinos. The pros worked hard and played harder. The pros used Sunday by the Hard Rock pool as a form of rehab. Rehab was not used in the traditional sense. Rehab was a rocking pool party filled with beautiful people day drinking. The twins fit right in. 'I like it.'

'I like the dice tables there.'

Yeah right, Zeus thought, *the dice tables.* While the casino, specifically the dice tables were fun and not stuffy like some of their other choices, Zeus knew better. Iceman loved Rehab. 'Even though we only have 36 hours, we have to make time for sleep.'

'We'll take a nap.'

'I am serious. We need our sleep.'

'We aren't sleeping tonight; I'll tell you that much. We are pushing straight through to Rehab. We'll grab a nap Sunday night.'

Wyatt, to the twins' surprise, arrived promptly at 1100 on Monday to drive the twins to the Oasis. 'How ya doing fellas?'

'Good, good.' Zeus answered. 'Surprised to see you driving us.'

'When I got Iceman's text, I had to laugh. I wanted to see for myself the damage you did to yourselves in 36 hours. I have to admit, you don't look much worse for wear. I grabbed you a bunch of In-N-Out burgers there next to Zeus in the backseat, figured you could use some grease.'

'Thanks.' Zeus replied and handed Iceman a Double-Double.

'Zeus, behind you, there is a cooler.' Zeus looked in the cargo section of Duke's Durango and opened the lid to find a cooler of beer. 'Thought you might be thirsty too, a little *hair of the dog.*'

Iceman replied. 'No, we feel good. We are ready to go.'

'We ain't shooting today, just a couple of hours of classroom work. Real training starts tomorrow.'

Iceman did not hesitate. 'Pass one up, Zeus.'

The twins entered the Oasis classroom after the 75-mile drive, three Double-Doubles with beer chasers, and were greeted by Bone. 'There they are.'

Handshakes and pleasantries were exchanged, and a new member of the team arrived. 'Fellas, this here is Wilson, he will be giving us a hand the next two weeks.

'The mighty twins, we meet at last.' Wilson introduced himself.

'Wilson?' Zeus asked referring to his common code name.

'As in Wade Wilson.' Iceman recognized the use in reference to the potent assassin in the Marvel Universe. 'Zeus, you know him better as Deadpool.'

Wilson was impressed. 'Very good Iceman, you nailed it.'

Zeus mumbled. 'Should have known, fucking Iceman.'

Wyatt explained. 'Bone, Conjar and me are pretty damn good instructors in sniping, but Wilson here, he is the best shot we got.'

'Thank you, Wyatt.' Wilson got right down to business. 'We are going to be training on the M107A1 Barrett .50 caliber sniper rifle. The Zetas sicarios made a curious choice. She is one powerful beast. You have been working with the Mawhinney's M40 sniper rifle. The two weapons have their similarities but their differences too. But let's face it, if you can shoot, you can shoot, and I understand the two of you have some talent when it comes to shooting.'

The group moved to the front of the classroom and gathered around a tall display table to view the M40. 'You boys have been trained on the M40; understand you have some talent with her. To be honest, the M40 is a bit dated. A fine weapon, does the job, but she would not be my weapon of choice for your mission. I told Conjar as much.' Wilson took the M40 off the table and replaced it with the Barrett M107A1, the weapon of choice for the mission. 'The Barrett is a little newer in design, and like I said has more power. You two have been firing .308 caliber rounds, the M107A1 fires .50 caliber. The Barrett is not the ideal weapon of choice either. She is designed to be an anti-material rifle, can blow through helicopters and even concrete walls. I suppose The Zetas were drawn to the firepower to feed their egos; little man, big gun kind of thing. Any questions?'

'Will there be much more kickback?'

'Some but take a little closer look at the design. You can see the cushioned and stable front tripod design, highly effective. She has a fine shoulder harness in the rear to absorb the punch back I was describing earlier.' Wilson guided his tour from the rear of the rifle to the top center. 'What you see there is the Picatinny rail that covers just about the front half of the weapon, that will take your scope. A useful design that will accept my modified scope. I got my own scope made special for me by the Elders, and had it modified to fit the M107A1. The rifle accepts a suppressor that you will be using on this mission. The suppressor will limit the range some, but not much.' Wilson did not need to explain barrel harmonies. The slightest change to the rifle, naked to the human eye impacts performance, to the experienced group. 'Barrett makes the claim that the weapon is accurate up to 2,000 meters. I got here yesterday, tested the weapon and 2,000 meters is a stretch. Granted, I wasn't using my modified scope, she is not ready for another couple of days, but 1800 meters is a more accurate figure. I was impressed with the suppressor provided by our weapons team, only cut accuracy to 1600 meters. For this mission, I recommended Duke and Conjar to build their nest in the 1200 meters range.'

For the next four hours, Wilson guided the twins through the intricacies of the M107A1. The twins broke down and cleaned the weapon several times, and left the classroom prepared for the range. For the next two weeks the twins trained on the weapon and got a significant boost in performance once Wilson's scope arrived. The mission called for the nest to rest with a slope of 300 feet. Wilson built an exact replica of the sniper nest in the mountains of Nevada inside the Byrne campus. The intense training on the M107A1, coupled with the twins' elevated physical training, allowed Wilson to extend his recommended target range to 1400 meters. The twins were ready and shipped off to South Padre Island, TX. The mission was a go.

CHAPTER THIRTY-NINE

The twins arrived at South Padre Island, TX and awaited further instructions. The Chavez twins' portion of the mission was in Conjar's charge now, and he wanted the twins close to the border. Prior to every mission a safety deposit box was opened for emergency contingencies. After Conjar opened the box in Houston with $250,000 in cash and three sets of alternative identifications, he set out to establish base camp. Duke was charged with kicking off the mission with the timely death of Juan Garcia Abrego. The twins reported to the Pearle South Padre Island Beachfront Resort Hotel. The twins called it the Pearle. While they waited for Duke, the twins used the time at the Pearle to establish their cover as a couple of forensic accountants on holiday from Austin. On the day of their arrival, the twins quickly made friends around the pool, were a hit with the staff, and ingratiated themselves with the bartenders with their charm and generous tips.

After an enjoyable first night, Iceman got an early start at the bar the next morning. After his morning run and swim with Zeus, Iceman relaxed by the pool until the bar opened at 1000 hours. He had met and liked a lovely bartender named Molly. Iceman had come to learn that Ms. Molly was from Houston, the youngest of three children, father a neurosurgeon, and mother a homemaker. Molly had recently graduated from the University of Texas, hook 'em horns, and was taking a couple of years off to just chill before entering the job market. Iceman was not so cliché as to ask, *what do you want to do for work when you finally grow up?* If Ms. Molly wanted to chill, who was Iceman to question her? Over the course of the night, Molly and Iceman stumbled upon a connection. Between Molly serving drinks, and Iceman making himself popular, the two enjoyed each other's company. Iceman's early arrival at the poolside bar was in part to establish his cover, but he also wanted to get to know Molly a bit better. Iceman became fascinated with the concept of a gap year or two. Iceman had worked since he was nine years old, busy cutting neighbors' yards and doing chores. He went to West Point, graduated early, went straight to Black Ops, and enjoyed extremely limited leave all those years. Taking time for yourself was fascinating to Iceman. It had never occurred to him.

'Well, hellooooo stranger.' Molly thickened her Texas accent; she picked up right where they had left off.

'Howdy, ma'am. How'd you sleep?'

'Just fine thank you.' She popped open a Budweiser using the bottle opener attached to the bar. 'Here you go.'

'I'll take a whiskey as well. Irish, if you have it.'

'Whiskey?' Iceman and Zeus had agreed to stick to beer in moderation with no whiskey to be mission ready. Iceman explained his whole Churchill's mouthwash philosophy while Molly poured. Mouthwash did not break his covenant with Zeus.

The two enjoyed each other's company for about an hour. The poolside bar began to get busy with the lunch crowd, so Iceman excused himself. As he walked back to the room to shower, he reflected on the gap year phenomenon. Take a year or two to be just you? Amazing. Iceman wondered what he would do if he took a gap year or two. He then wondered if he would ever come back from his gap year, or would he be tempted to extend the gap indefinitely? Just disappear and walk the earth like Caine from *Kung Fu. I could do that,* he thought.

Iceman walked out of the shower to hear his phone ring. 'What's up?'

'There you are. I have been calling, we are up.' Zeus responded with urgency.

Iceman knew Zeus' urgency meant Duke had been successful and Garcia was dead. The mission planned for the funeral to be three days after Garcia's death. A brief autopsy would be performed. He was 77, nothing much to raise suspicion. 'Right. Up for some lunch? I'm hungry.'

For the next two days, the twins continued to build their back-story. Their arrivals at the bar became later, the departures earlier, and the break in between was longer. They intensified their workouts. Walking back to their room on the third day, the twins were stopped by the front desk clerk. 'I have a package for both of you.'

Zeus thanked the clerk, followed Iceman to his room, and opened the package. Two wristwatch-looking GPS devices were in the package with a simple note. *2100.* The twins understood. They were to take a sunset swim to the GPS coordinates prepro-grammed in the device and arrive at 2100. Iceman looked at Zeus without a care in the world and shrugged. 'Game on.'

* * *

The twins left themselves plenty of time to make the 3-mile swim. Because the twins swam so frequently, their departure went unnoticed. They kept a strong steady pace with the water cooperating. A calm sea made the swim routine. They arrived at their coordinates to find a Pursuit SC 365i, the same model they trained with in Barbados, waiting.

Iceman asked. 'Permission to come aboard, captain?'

'Permission granted.'

Zeus assessed the captain as they boarded. He was roughly 50 years old, in great shape, with a hard, weather-beaten face that he wore well. He extended his hand. 'Zeus.'

The captain shook the hand, as he commented. 'Yes, right.' He turned his attention to Iceman and shook his hand. 'Iceman.' The captain smiled and took a step back to inspect his new passengers. 'The mighty twins.'

Iceman became curious about the term *mighty twins*. He hadn't thought much of it when he first heard the reference but now it has become common place. He wondered when the twins became the mighty twins and who coined the phrase.

Iceman's attention was returned to the captain when he introduced himself. 'Coco, nice to meet the two of you.'

The twins were surprised by the call sign. Coco had expected the reaction. 'I am from Hersey, PA.'

Zeus responded. 'Hersey, chocolate, Coco.'

Iceman laughed. 'Would ya look at Zeus now? So handy with deciphering the call signs. Well done.'

'Fuck you, Iceman.'

Coco laughed, recognizing the reported camaraderie the twins shared. 'Didn't like being called Coco in the beginning. It started as a joke, and then just stuck with me. I have grown to like it over the years.'

'As well you should.' Iceman smiled.

Coco steered the Pursuit south towards the next set of GPS coordinates. After several hours, he stopped five miles off the Mexican shore, 20 miles north of La Pesca. As he lifted the storage compartment lid, Coco pointed to two LAR V Draeger

Rebreathers, designated as MK 25. 'I understand you are pretty handy with these.'

Zeus responded. 'Plenty of hours logged.'

Coco gave the twins new coordinates to enter in their GPS wrist units. 'We are five miles from shore. We traveled outside the international border for our trip. I snuck in to reduce your swim, but this is as close as I should get. Conjar is waiting for you on shore.' Coco waited for the twins to finish donning the MK 25s before he continued. 'It was a pleasure to meet the mighty twins.'

They exchanged firm handshakes while Iceman's attention returned to *the mighty twins. There it is again,* he thought. The twins fell back into the water and were off. Coco, ensuring the twins were clear, gunned the boat back to international waters, and his return trip.

The twins reached their destination. Conjar was there to greet them. 'Store your gear in these bags and dump them into the back of the truck. You will need the gear for your extraction.'

The twins stowed their gear in the beat-up Toyota cab pickup truck, and changed into dry shorts, t-shirts, and flip flops. Once settled Conjar explained. 'We have a 90-minute ride to base. We are mission hot.'

The team arrived at Conjar's base, and he began his brief. 'We catch a little sleep here with one of us standing guard. Here are a couple of MREs to chow on. You leave for the nest at 0500.'

Conjar broke out his Toughbook tablet and walked the twins through a map of the area. The twins studied the assigned route to the nest while they ate their MRE's. The two-mile route was covered by a series of rolling hills that ended on the targeted Sierra. The nest rested 300 feet on the apex of the Sierra, giving the twins cover for both approach and extraction.

Conjar began his description of the area. 'As you can see from your ariel photos, the region between the base camp and the snipers nest affords good cover. The thick desert vegetation coupled with the small rolling hills and the tall Sierra are conducive to a successful mission. Your route takes you around and not over the rolling hills, affording you good cover.'

The twins nodded their consent, and Conjar continued. 'During extraction, you are called to haul ass on foot back to base. The area between the base and the nest does not provide cover for a vehicle. Given the terrain and your running pace, I expect a 12-minute dash back to base. The extraction route leaves you exposed for 200 meters of open land between the sniper hill and the 90-degree turn near the end of your escape, as you see here.'

Conjar pointed using the images from his Toughbook to identify the open land and the 45-foot hill that covered the 90-degree turn. The hill was lush, and the opposite side of the path was relatively flat, covered with agave plants.

'Once you make the turn.' Conjar abandoned his Toughbook and pointed to the 90-degree hill. 'You have a straight covered 50-yard dash to base. If you are coming in hot, the 50-yards will be our kill zone. Any questions?'

Zeus asked. 'On our extraction, where are we most vulnerable? I understand the exposed area is a hot zone, where should we expect fire?'

'Good question. If your pursuit reaches one of these three hills, we have an issue.' Conjar reverted to his Toughbook and pointed to the hills that surrounded the exposed area. 'You will not be traveling with your HK 45's, speed is your weapon of choice. Having a Mexican stand-off, no pun intended, would not work in our favor.'

After chow, Conjar released a drone to give the twins a live view of the target area. The drone was equipped with night vision generating a green tinted view. The mission was straightforward and three contingency plans were made in the event of a hot evac.

At 0500 hours, the twins affixed fake silicon fingerprints. To Duke's credit, he had a set of prints manufactured to match two known Zeta's assassins. The mission called for the twins to retreat, leaving their weapons in the sniper's nest to allow for rapid retreat. Duke's idea of leaving further evidence and leaking evidence to The Zetas was ingenious. Even Iceman was impressed. Once fully prepared, the twins made their way running in sand hiking pants and desert camouflaged tops to the nest Conjar had set up for them. Conjar had conducted a dry run 24 hours earlier to prepare the nest for the twins. When the twins arrived at the nest less than 10 minutes later, they almost stumbled over it. In addition to the camouflaged netting that covered the nest, Conjar added dirt to offer additional concealment. The twins snaked under the net, doing their best not to disrupt the dirt that shielded the net. The camouflaged netting and dirt hid two M107A1 rifles. The rifles were the exact rifles they had used in training. The twins identified their specific rifle and settled into the nest and waited. They moderated their water and power bar intake, to stay fit but limit their bathroom needs. When required, they dug a small hole in the nest, then covered the hole when their business was completed.

At 1100 hours the funeral procession arrived as expected. The sun was slightly in the twins' faces but not low enough to present a problem. As reported, 92 degrees with a slight breeze, a little warm but still a perfect day to be a sniper. The audience was to assemble on the east side of the burial, facing west directly into the twins' field of vision. The 2500-foot Sierra further east in the distance provided a nice backdrop for the mission. In a need to establish themselves in the hierarchy of the family dynamic, Dr. Monroe had anticipated the Chavez twins to be in the front row of the small congregation. The mission called for the twins to make a simultaneous shot. Communication between Iceman and Zeus was vital.

Iceman's mic cracked. 'Conjar, we have a wee bit of an issue. The security force is a little beefier than expected.'

Conjar studied the target zone provided by the drone, and calmly replied. 'Report.'

'In addition to the bodyguards we expected, we have four tangos on dual sport motorcycles.'

'Roger. Mission status?'

Iceman took a moment to review the clear and present danger they faced. He considered Duke's mission parameters that demanded the mission be aborted and Duke's original plan be implemented in the event of any threat. Iceman understood Duke's practical plan to sabotage the Chavez jet served to delay more than address the problem. Iceman was resolute. He wanted the network not just the Chavez twins. Using his scope, he identified the bikes as Honda KRLs. He knew the quality motorcycles had exceptional off-road handling. He studied the riders, who appeared very capable. The savage motorcycles reaching the most dangerous three hills that provided fields of fire during the twins' retreat through the 200 meters of open space was very real. Iceman understood that wins rarely are achieved when faced with an unexpected and overwhelming challenge; the CCP and Gulf Cartel had won this round. Satisfied, Iceman deferred to his most spectacular internal rage. 'We are a go.'

After Iceman's report, Zeus thought to himself, *this should be interesting.*

Cars emptied with the Chavez twins exiting a black Escalade in the front of the procession. At that moment, the twins had clear sight lines and could have engaged the targets but elected to wait for the targets to be stationary per the mission plan. If the Chavez twins were hidden within the small assembly and not in the front row, the twins were confident a shot would present itself when they returned to the Escalade.

The Chavez twins did make their way to the front as Grace had anticipated. Zeus studied the Chavez twins closely; they were pushing their way to the front rather than being invited. Dr. Monroe was again correct; the Chavez twins wanted to establish their position of power within the unique family and business hierarchy. As the crowd was settling in, Iceman took a moment to check the status of the unexpected motorcycle security force. Comfortable with his assessment, Iceman regained target acquisition. With the small crowd assembled, Iceman recognized what was happening when the audience began to bow their heads. The mission called for the twins to strike when the priest asked the assembled to bow their heads in a moment of silence.

Iceman triggered the mission. 'On my count, 3, 2, 1.'

In the blink of an eye, Iceman coolly reported. 'Contact.' Eve was eliminated.

Zeus, already beginning to slide out of the sniper's nest in retreat repeated. 'Contact.' Fernando was eliminated.

Before Iceman cleared the sniper's nest, three explosions rocked the area. As part of the mission plan, before Conjar built the sniper nest, he used the drone to drop three C-4 remote explosives in an area away from the extraction route as a distraction. As the dust just began to settle from the explosions, the twins were already on their feet, sprinting downhill back to base.

The explosions created chaos. Most of the sympathizers had not realized the Chavez twins had been eliminated, they were focused on the explosions. Those standing close to the targets were stunned by the destruction of the targets' faces courtesy of the .50 caliber bullets. Little of their faces remained. Eve and Fernando were unrecognizable. Because the weapon was designed to go through material and not personnel, both silent and powerful bullets raced through the targets. Iceman's shot had blown through Eve's right eye and struck a man standing behind her in the shoulder. Zeus' bullet raced through Fernando's nose, demolishing his face, and impacted into open ground with no further injuries.

While the crowd and their bodyguards were slow to process and react to the brutal events, the four-man security team on motorcycles was not. The security team leader only needed a few moments to decipher the events. Due to the damage inflicted, the targets left no clues. The man injured by Iceman's shot provided a vector to the sniper's general location. Zeus' bullet struck open land, leaving no immediate evidence. Iceman's bullet did. Seeing the wounded man in relation to Eve, the leader was able to follow the flight path of the bullet. The leader had a fix on the general location where the shots had been fired. Perfect plans rarely produce perfect results. A perfect example was Iceman's bullet. Because the leader was only able to pinpoint the general location of shots fired, he ordered his team to attack in a vector. The four-man team fanned out to maximize the controlled search.

Conjar, using the drone, carefully studied the security team. When the team began their hunt, Conjar reported to the twins. 'We have a situation. Security was not much distracted by the explosions; trouble is coming your way. I have you six minutes ahead of them. How far from the turn?'

'Four minutes.' Iceman responded.

Conjar did the calculations in his head. The plan called for the twins to cover the two-mile retreat over uneven terrain in 12 minutes, an aggressive forecast. Iceman was reporting 10 minutes. He calculated the security team had a high probability of being on high ground at the time the twins would be running through the open space, the area without cover. Conjar continued to monitor the drone and readied himself to give the twins support.

Iceman reported in. 'I can hear the bikes; we are entering the open area.' Iceman expected Conjar to order the twins to take evasive action.

Conjar reported. 'Roger.'

Iceman and Zeus were a bit confused by the simple report, but they trusted Conjar, and responded by digging a bit deeper to find extra speed fueled by adrenaline. The prospect of death chasing you had a way of doing that.

One of the team members spotted the twins crossing the open space. Rather than setting up for a long-distance shot, the team member elected to increase speed to close the distance. In a matter of seconds, he found satisfaction and raised his weapon.

Iceman reported. 'We have a tango on top of us.'

Conjar replied. 'Roger.'

The twins continued with the mission at a furious pace. The shooter locked on Zeus and fired. The shot was high and wide but registered with the twins. The bumpy terrain and the speed of the motorcycle made shooting with accuracy difficult. The shooter decided to close the gap even further and come to a stop before he fired again.

The twins had no choice but to trust their feet. They were not weapons ready; the mission chose speed over fire power. Zeus could not match Iceman's pace or desire; in desperation Ice considered taking a stand. His panic led to desperation; Iceman could not be the reason for Zeus' death. In that moment, Iceman remembered Conjar's briefing. *Having a Mexican stand-off, no pun intended, would not work in our favor.* Without hesitation or need for explanation, Iceman stopped, turned and assumed a shooting stance. Before Zeus could protest, Iceman screamed, *'YOU GO, WE GO!'* The hired assassin and Iceman's refusal to allow him to die, pushed Zeus to run faster than Forrest Gump. Zeus was rewarded with a moment. In that moment, he found peace. The Collins twins were real, Iceman was real, Kelly was his, and he deserved her. Seamus was no longer alone, he was Zeus.

The shooter, unaware that Iceman was unarmed, took immediate evasive maneuvers buying the twins precious seconds. Once Zeus had passed him, Iceman rejoined their sprint to safety. Another shot rang out.

CHAPTER FORTY

The shooter had quickly realized his error by falling for Iceman's ruse; he charged forward, came to a stop and was pleased with his positioning on the stationary motorcycle. He was well in range and had Iceman dead center. After he fired, the gunman was confident the shot would find its mark. Then the unexpected happened. The twins had suddenly disappeared from the gunman's crosshairs. Iceman was alive, because the twins had reached the 90-degree turn just as the shot was fired. They disappeared under the cover of the extraction route. If not for the timeliness of the turn, Iceman would have been killed. The shooter, frustrated and angry with himself, returned to the chase. He quickly found his adversary, the 90-degree turn, and headed straight for it. Another shot was fired.

The twins heard the shot, but nothing registered in their area. The twins heard Conjar report. 'Tango down. Head for base, execute extraction plan bravo. I am one minute from position three plan bravo.'

As soon as he saw the security force engage, Conjar knew the chances of the twins clearing the open space were tight but acceptable. He was more concerned with the twins making base before the shooter closed the 200 yards of open space. Conjar grabbed his MP7 and made for high ground with a view of the open space. He monitored the security forces' activity using his iPhone that was linked to the drone.

Prior to the first shot being fired, the other members of the security force continued to monitor their vectors. If the security force had been equipped with radio contact, the moment the twins were identified, the entire team, and not just the lone biker, would have locked on the twins. The radio silence was the only advantage the twins held until the first shot rang out. Following the sound of gunfire, the three other shooters had a better sense of where to attack. If the shooters did not locate the twins in the next two minutes, the hunter would become the hunted.

The twins were a minute from base and heard two motorcycles in the area. As they grew closer to base so did the sound of one of the motorcycles. The twins arrived at base, immediately secured their HK45 handguns and MP7 assault rifles from the truck. Both weapons were common, neither jeopardized the mission cover story linking the killings to The Zetas. Iceman smiled at Zeus and ran for position two plan Bravo. Zeus held position one plan bravo, a fortified position near base. Zeus had Conjar to the northeast and Iceman to the southeast of his position. Plan Bravo, one of the action plans in the event of a hot evac, called for team Conjar to form a triangle to lure the attackers into their kill zone.

Conjar reported. 'I have one tango entering the zone, guardedly. I have another tango a minute behind him, coming hot. After consulting his iPhone for confirmation, Conjar reported. 'The third tango is a little miss peep.'

The third remaining security force member was a lost sheep, nowhere near the action. Conjar instructed the team to allow the first tango to move further into the kill zone to allow the second to enter without being chased off by gun fire.

Conjar reported. 'Zeus, you have tango one. I have tango two. Iceman, you are security. Rotate behind the tangos to cover their retreat.'

The twins prepared themselves per Conjar's orders. Seconds later, Iceman reported. 'In position.'

Conjar asked. 'Zeus?'

Zeus reported. 'Have target lock.'

Conjar reported. 'On my command, execute.' Conjar acquired his target and reported. 'Execute.'

Both targets went down. Iceman quickly swept the area and put two bullets into each of the tangos' heads.

Conjar reported. 'Tango four is no threat, he has retreated. Time to evac.'

CHAPTER FORTY-ONE

Conjar studied the drone to monitor their evac while Iceman drove. Following the course Conjar had mapped, Iceman worked the small, deserted roads until he reached Carretera Matamoros-Ciudad Victoria, Mexico 101. As he entered MX 101, he was able to gun the engine and head east to the coast. With the team secure on MX 101, Conjar flew the drone over water to sink the fourth member of the team. Conjar, Iceman and Zeus discarded their camouflaged tops, wearing only tee shirts over their sand hiking pants to offer the appearance of innocent hikers.

'Drone is gone.' Conjar reported. 'We are clear.'

The team road in silence, decompressing, while Iceman navigated the route. Iceman continued on MX 101 for 22 miles, took another couple of highways that eventually linked to MX 52 and the final extraction point. The team arrived without incident at the extraction point, the same location as their landing point.

Conjar instructed the twins. 'Gear up in your MK 25s, and head to your extraction pick up.' Conjar gave the coordinates to the twins, who loaded them into their GPS. 'Coco is linked into your GPS device; he will be able to track you. Depending on conditions, you should expect to be picked up five miles out, the same swim as before. If conditions get hot, he will approach closer to shore to get you out.'

Without a word or acknowledgement, the twins set out to sea. Though both physically and mentally exhausted from the mission, the twins swam the five miles briskly. They removed their silicon fingerprints as a gift to the sea. Two miles into their swim, Iceman felt a calm that came with being underwater. He relaxed and let the water serve as a release. From his first experience in the subaquatic world, as a cadet at West Point, snorkeling in Key West on holiday, Iceman found a peaceful retreat. When the twins approached the pursuit, Iceman felt strangely calm. The solitude and refuge of the water had worked its magic. Coco had no difficulties locating the twins, once quickly settled, he gunned 700-horsepower courtesy of the dual engines and headed north.

Coco instructed the twins. 'Keep the MK 25s handy in case of problems. When I drop you off, leave the gear, and swim to shore.'

With his eyes closed, Iceman sat lazily on one of the ship's captains' chairs and absorbed the sunlight on his face. He opened his eyes, looked around the boat and his eyes settled on a point of interest. He walked over to the large fisherman cooler that he had just discovered and opened the lid expecting the treasure chest to be empty. To his delightful surprise, he found the cooler stocked with ice, bottled water and Budweiser.

Coco watched Iceman make his discovery and commented. 'I believe that is your brand.'

Iceman threw a beer to Zeus, opened his, finished the ice-cold beer in one mighty pull, and replied. 'It is.'

The twins arrived at their drop off point without incident and said their goodbyes to Coco. Pleasantries were exchanged with a knowing look, a look shared by men who cheat death.

During their swim, Iceman again found refuge in the ocean. His thoughts drifted lazily until he stumbled across the concept of *the mighty twins. Who coined that phrase?* He directed his thoughts to rewind the twins' journey, stopping on the first time the term had been used to greet them. He struggled through his memory bank, stumped for a bit. He knew the *mighty* was added to the twins after their first mission, but by who?

They arrived at Pearle's beach at sunset and made their way to the poolside bar. On the walk to the bar, the answer hit Iceman out of nowhere, Grace. Grace was the first to use the phrase when they first met her after their first mission. She was the one to coin the phrase, *the mighty twins.* Iceman smiled with his discovery, but more importantly at the source. *Grace is the best.*

Walking to the bar both shirtless and shoeless, the concept, *no shoes, no shirt, no service,* did not apply. Iceman saw Molly working behind the bar and smiled.

'Back from your afternoon swim?' Molly asked casually.

'Yep.' Iceman answered. As Molly served the twins their beer, Iceman asked. 'Please add double whiskey to our order.'

Molly smiled and replied. 'Good day, huh?'

'Just another day in paradise.'

AVENGING ASSASSINS
THE COLLINS TWINS SERIES, BOOK THREE

After their successful second mission, the twins return to Austin, TX. Upon completing their physical exams and mental health evaluations with Dr. Monroe, the twins are surprised to report to the main conference room. The Elders have approved the termination of eight human trafficking camps scattered throughout the United States. The camps are identified in, *Raising of Assassin,* and have caused Iceman tremendous concern. The camps kidnap college students to be used as gifts for the terrorists. The twins are dispatched to Yuma, AZ to eliminate one of the camps. Throughout the year, *Guardian Assassins* chronicles the twins' blossoming relationship with Katie and Kelly. In the dark universe of the Elders, the twins successfully manage to celebrate fun adventures in their serious relationships.

After the successful mission the twins return to the Factory for training. Iceman quickly becomes bored with the project and assigns himself to the dismissed targets. During his careful study of the targets that did not qualify for termination, Zuhair Zain catches Iceman's attention. With Trinity's assistance, Iceman reconstructs the file to better examine Zain. Zuhair Zain started Wahid, a $25 billion investment fund based in London in 2018. Zain pulled himself from poverty in Saudi Arabia to excel at top universities and worked for a prestigious financial firm prior to launching his own firm. Wahid boasts profitable investments in Arab communities in need of infrastructure. Zain captured the attention of the Elders due to the location of the investments. The Elders' investigation raised some concerns that were dismissed. Iceman was not satisfied with the investigation; he held concerns with Wahid's rapid growth since being formed in 2018. In 2017, Saudi Crown Prince Mohammed bin Salman, officially next in line to the Saudi throne to his father, began his two-year purge of his rivals. A reasonable estimate, 100 royal family members, government officials, and leading business executives were rounded up and imprisoned in the Riyadh Ritz Carlton beginning in 2017. Prince Mohammed cited corruption and a cleansing campaign that brought the imprisonment without legal proceedings. The wealthy prisoners were blocked from all outside contact, securing their relief by paying massive fines. Saudi officials had questioned over 200 people in the anti-corruption campaign resulting in the theft of at least $100 billion by Prince Mohammed. Iceman was convinced the victims, if they can be called victims, of the prince's scheme would respond to the assault. Iceman is convinced the timing of Wahid and the purge are related. Trinity and Iceman require Atalanta and Zeus to join them, and the C-Files team is united. The title of the team is amended from COVID- Files to Conspiracy- Files.

After leave and Black Ops training, the twins return to Austin to discover Trinity and Atalanta had made tremendous progress on the new C-File. The team works at a frantic pace, set by Iceman, to submit a report worthy of Elders final investigation. The team documents the troubling investments made by Wahid to companies and foundations linked to Wahhabi Islam. For over two centuries, Wahhabism has been the dominant religion in Saudi Arabia and the greatest threat to the House of Saud. Prince Mohammed's purge was a proactive attack to eliminate and control his rivals for succession from the radical Wahhabi. The fund avoided Saudi Arabia and Prince Mohammed by investing in neighboring countries. Wahid made investments in Egypt, Libya, Algeria, Iraq, and Afghanistan to expand the Wahhabi faith in the region. The C-Files team argues Wahhabism is the greatest threat in the Middle East to democracy and the West. The use of financial investments made through regional Wahhabi leadership, built support for the growing radical faith, and applied pressure on the House of Saud. The investments made by Wahid threaten oil fields, shipping in the Mediterranean and Red Sea, government stability, and terrorism. After careful study of the C-File report, the Elders are not satisfied. The twins are deployed to London, using their cover as forensic accountants, to investigate Wahid, submit their findings, and if approved, terminate Zuhair Zain.